CREEK COUNTRY SAGA
Book 2

The Sacred Writings

Beneath the Blackberry Moon

APRIL W GARDNER

Big Spring Press

Beneath the Blackberry Moon Part 2: the Sacred Writings
©2016 by April W Gardner
SECOND EDITION, 2017

Cover design by Roseanna M. White.
Big Spring Press logo: Karen Gardner

Scripture quotations taken from the King James Version.

Library of Congress Control Number: 2017906376
ISBN-13: 978-1-945831-06-5
ISBN-10: 1-945831-06-5

Published by Big Spring Press
San Antonio, Texas

Printed in the United States of America.

To my sweet boy, who asks me every
day how my writing is going.

MISSISSIPPI
TERRITORY
1811-1817

Coosa
River

Tallapoosa
River

Kossati

Horseshoe
Bend

Tombigbee
River

Alabama
River

Fort
Claiborne

Burnt Corn
Creek

Camp
Crawford/
Ft. Scott

Fort Mims

Mobile

San
Marcos
Negro
Fort

Pensacola

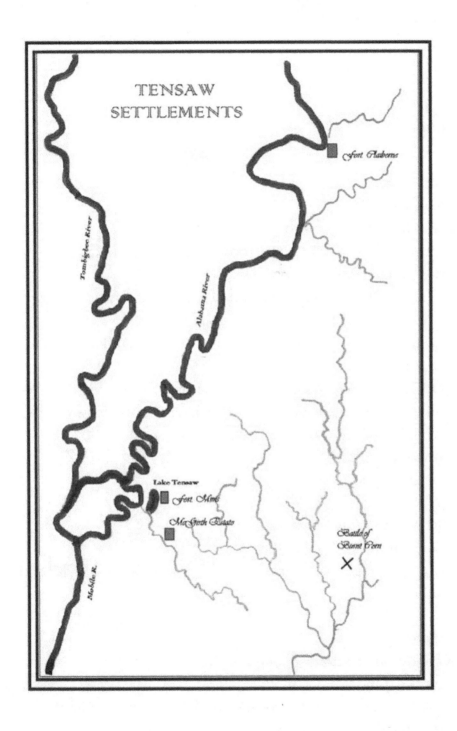

TENSAW
SETTLEMENTS

Tombigbee River

Alabama River

Fort Claiborne

Lake Tensaw

Fort Mims

McGirth Estate

Mobile R.

Battle of
Burnt Corn

✗

Cast of Characters

Wolf Clan

Leaning Bow, clan headman

Cetto Imala, head of family, uncle ("pawa") to Totka (and siblings) and Tall Bull

Totka Hadjo (Mad Fire), also known as Totka Lawe (Hungry Fire)

White Stone, elder sister to Singing Grass and Totka

Singing Grass, wife of Nokose Fixico
Children: Fire Maker, Rain Child, Speaks Sweetly

Little Warrior, also known as Fire Maker, son of Singing Grass

Lance/Tall Bull, cousin to Totka (and siblings)

Amadayh, widow

Zachariah McGirth, adopted Wolf

Off-screen Wolf Characters

Rain Falling, Totka's mother

Singing Voice, Totka's grandmother, wife to Grandfather Wild Edge

Beaver Clan

Grandmother Kit Fox, Nokose's grandmother

Ayo, Leaping Waters' mother

Nokose Fixico (Heartless Bear), husband to Singing Grass, pawa to Leaping Waters and Long Arrow

Leaping Waters, wife to Tall Bull
Long Arrow, brother to Leaping Waters
Adela McGirth (Copper Woman), adopted Beaver Clan
Lillian McGirth (Bitter Eyes), adopted Beaver Clan

Off-screen Beaver Character
Strong Deer, Leaping Waters' aunt

McGirth Family
Zachariah McGirth
    Daughters: Adela, Lillian

Other Notable Characters
Gray Hawk, Totka's father, Deer Clan
Lachlan Gibb, Scottish blacksmith
Old Grandfather, Kossati's Beloved Man
Bird Creek Fekseko, Kossati's peace chief
Slim Face, stickball player from Tuskegee
Minko Yellow Tree, Choctaw chief
Rainmaker, Choctaw warrior
Hilaho, Choctaw warrior

Dear Reader:

I've provided a **boldfaced** glossary throughout for a deeper experience.

Enjoy!

April W Gardner

www.aprilgardner.com

Chapter I

Big Warrior Totka Hadjo, reluctant to take the familiar path, came to a slow halt, stopping when his feet touched the grasses that butted up to the forest's edge. The tread of those who followed went silent.

Dawn was moments away.

To his left, Wind Chaser stomped a hoof and tossed her head, ears twitching. The gnats were out in such maddening swarms they put the mosquitoes to shame. Picking one from the corner of his eye, Totka peered across the open field.

At his right, Copper Woman did the same, her forlorn sigh becoming pitch paste to his soles and floodwaters to his resolve. Twelve moons past, they'd stood as strangers in the same meadow, each wary of the other, of their motives, their intentions, their skin tone. His heart had beat with the nervous energy of a war drum, and hers—bold, brave, beautiful—had begun to gently transform him.

They would have parted company in Mobile three **sleeps** past except for her request to accompany him as far as Tensaw. He'd been glad for the additional days with her, but now, he wished the painful farewell were over.

Bit clacking against her teeth, Wind Chaser lipped his ear, her breath grassy and sweet. She was a good animal, if a bit untamed, and over the long seasons ahead, she would quell his loneliness. He stroked her velvet nose and released her tether to let her forage.

9

Amadayh, leading the packhorse burdened with sacks of maize, bypassed him with a poorly disguised teary sniffle and a hasty kiss to Copper Woman's cheek. For all her bravado, she was still a woman with a heart wounded by war and loss. She plunged into the meadow, burying herself to the knees in thick pasture.

His mind filling with the dangers of the trail ahead, Totka faced north. In that moment, the **Fire Spirit**, Grandmother Sun, broke free of the horizon and pierced his right eye. He winked and turned, but it was too late. It was shameful enough he'd not **gone to water**. Now he'd missed the breaking dawn.

The grasses, colored now in hues of green and gold, received the spirit's full blessing. The Fire Spirit dwelt in the **east**, the sacred cardinal direction that was connected with purity and success. Life.

North, on the other hand, symbolized cold and trouble. Defeat. Today, the north also represented **Kossati** — home.

Was it an omen that he'd been facing north when the Fire Spirit greeted him? If so, it was not a good one. To add to his unease, not a whisper from the **Wind Spirit** influenced the morning. Only sticky heat.

The grasses stood unmoving, tall, and regal, except for their heads, which bowed heavy with moist grain. A colony of red-winged blackbirds, roosting in the pines on the opposite side of the meadow, chattered and fussed, then took flight as one and let calm reign over the field.

Only Totka's wrenching heart defied the peace that settled around them.

He doused his face in Grandmother Sun's beautiful brilliance, looking straight into her mighty eye. *I beg your blessings on my homeward journey, on my return. Bless me. Give me a vision, a sign of good to come.*

It wasn't often Totka asked for a blessing or a sign, but on this day as his life veered off course, they were vital. He could use some reassurance that Copper Woman would do well without him, that he would see her again.

10

Staring into the sun, he repeated his prayer **four** times. His eyes burned and watered until wetness trickled over his cheek, and he saw nothing but white. A small sacrifice.

A warm hand joined with his and squeezed. "Totka, where have you gone?"

He blinked hard to regain his vision, and when he looked down, he encountered a sun of a different sort.

Copper Woman—amber hair alight with the sun's own glory, eyes big and green and wise—gazed up at him, and he wasn't sure which sight was more stunning. While the sun blinded his eyes, this woman blinded his good sense, enslaved his tongue, and adhered his feet to the earth.

Although born into a different people, she'd been knit together with Totka in mind. And she was perfection, except for the concern marring the space between her brows.

He glided the tip of his middle finger in a line from her forehead down, pausing to iron out the wrinkles, then pausing again at her full mouth. She snagged it between her lips, and his heart took a sprinting leap.

"Ahem." Lachlan Gibb, Scotch trader and long-time acquaintance, pounded a fist against his muscled ribs and cleared his throat with flair.

Totka peered over his shoulder into the murky woods and gave his uninvited travel companion a tart look.

Lachlan's toothy grin, barely visible through his generous black beard, rubbed Totka like sand behind the eyelids. He gave another exaggerated cough. "Must be the moisture in the wind," he said at a near shout. Everything he spoke was overly loud to compensate for hearing loss.

"What wind?" Totka's vexation rang clear. "The Wind Spirit has hidden himself from us."

Lachlan nudged **Micco**, his broad-chested French warhorse, past Totka and Copper Woman. "I could use a breath of wind myself."

The man's **Muskogee**, while bedecked in the more floral tones of

11

the Scots, was impeccable. And well it should be, seeing the man had been wed to a Muscogee for thirteen **winters**. He was a widower now, returning to the Upper Muscogee towns to see if his forge and his wife's trading establishment had survived the war.

He dipped his head at Copper Woman and raised a finger to the hatband of his woolen bonnet. "Miss McGirth, 'twas a pleasure." After a brief exchange with her in English, he switched back to Muskogee and gave Totka a pointed look. "You will find me waiting on the other side. Restless to move out."

Totka stared back, impassive.

It was no coincidence Lachlan chose to leave Mobile for Creek country the morning Totka set out with Copper Woman. Her father was to blame for their obtrusive escort, but he was also responsible for the supply of maize—enough to take Totka's family through to harvest. And enough seed to stock every storehouse in Kossati by winter. The reminder spurred a respectful nod. "Give me but a moment."

"Eh?" Lachlan showed Totka his ear. "Speak up."

"I *said*, give me a moment. I'm eager to take to the path as well. My sisters will be anxious and looking for me already. But I will have these moments with my woman. Alone."

Lachlan raised a disbelieving brow, chuckled, and applied his heel to his horse's black flank, leaving them for the trail Amadayh had broken through the meadow.

"Eager to leave me, are you?" The teasing twitch on Copper Woman's mouth begged purging.

Unfortunately for Totka, he was a man of his word and would not satisfy himself with so much as a simple kiss unless she gave him leave. As if there were such a thing as a simple kiss with this woman. Best he not enter the comfort of that lodge lest he become careless and burn it down around them.

"Not a bit," he said. "But it got us out from under his hawk eye. Was I not convincing?"

"Not a bit." Her chesty laugh did him in.

He wrapped his arms around her and drew her to him in a crush. "What will I do without my little **Red Stick**? You are my smile, my life."

She clung to him, and when a silent sob convulsed her, he pressed his lips to her temple and wished he'd been more firm with her in Mobile.

That night in the white chief's garden while standing toe-to-toe with her father, McGirth, he'd collected the fortitude to leave her, but the following dawn she'd asked him to escort her home ahead of her father, sister, and infant brother. McGirth should have protested, but when he hadn't, Totka discovered he was a weaker man than he'd always boasted to be. Like a cave to earth's tremors, he'd given in to her soft-eyed plea.

When they'd arrived yesterday, she'd revealed that her motives had been twofold. In addition to McGirth's gift of maize, Copper Woman handed over the reins of her horse Wind Chaser as well as her mother's holy writings, insisting the woman would have wanted him to have it. It rested now inside his saddlebag. He would treasure it, even though it was widely thought that all things written were disputably evil. And even though the odd black markings on its talking leaves were about as clear to him as a mule's bray.

Soundless, she clung to him with a fervency that outmatched his own, fingers attached to his shirt, body trembling, lungs frozen. If she kept it up, he would never bring himself to leave her. He would find the nearest secluded spot and show her the kind of freedom unwed Muscogee women enjoyed. Then, he would take her home to Kossati.

He tsked. "Where did my warrior go? We'll be apart but a little while. A few seasons." An eternity. He pulled her face free of his shirtfront.

She dragged in a chest-shuddering breath as he cleared away hair stuck to her mouth, in her tears, blocking her eyes.

"Are you afraid?" he asked. "Tell me you are not afraid."

"I am not afraid." She scrubbed at her tears and shook her head inside the bowl of his hands, filling him with reassurance and pride.

Perhaps *she* was all the sign he needed.

"My insides are already torn apart from missing you, but I am not afraid. Creator brought you to me once. He will do it again. What is there to fear?"

What was there to fear? Now that he knew his soul mate—separation, death, sickness, loss. He feared everything. "Nothing. We have nothing at all to fear." Was his smile telling? It must have lacked a certain element, because she leaned back into his hold and searched his face, eyes warbling with doubt.

Perdition take his inability to lie!

Arms snaking about his neck, she raised up and gentled her cheek against his. "Come back to me." Her whisper was a demand hot in his ear, and it carried far more meaning than a trek back through Creek country. There were conditions to be met before she would bind herself to him.

Her father's, Totka could meet: a lodge, a crop of corn.

Hers was another matter altogether: an acceptance of her Jesus as Creator, perhaps even abandonment of a portion of the **Old Beloved Path**.

But meet them or not, he *would* be back.

His hands settled on the outward curve of her waist. "Spoken as if I could choose. I'd carry you away now if I had even a pebble's weight less honor." He brushed a kiss across her forehead and made himself put distance between them by going to retrieve Wind Chaser. "You know I cannot help but come back to you."

She followed him and whispered in the horse's ear as he mounted with a springing leap off his good leg. The animal nuzzled Copper Woman's neck, chest quivering with an extended nicker.

Totka patted the horse's broad shoulder. "She agrees with me. You should come away with us."

"It is as it must be." Sadness shadowing her smile, Copper Woman flung the closed reins over the mare's head and moved to place a hand on Totka's thigh where the flesh puckered over his old musket ball wound. Even under the spell of her touch, the ruined bone continued its constant, dull throb.

She looked at him through eyes magnified by tears. "Push too hard, and you will regret it. Kossati will be waiting for you whether you arrive in four sleeps or five. Conserve your strength for planting, for rebuilding."

He grazed her cheek with his knuckles, loving her more by the moment.

She tipped into his hand. "My prayers go with you, Totka. Send Singing Grass and the children my love. White Stone as well." She hastily tacked on the last with a charming touch of color to her pale throat.

He laughed and tightened the rein to keep Wind Chaser's eagerness in check. "White Stone would let me hear of it if she were forgotten and —"

A low moan accompanied the first breath of wind he'd felt all morning. The wall of pines behind them whistled and rattled as a great gust swept in, whipping their hair and clothes into a frenzy.

Wind Chaser loosed a nervous whiny, and Totka cooed to quiet her. The wind rolled over the field, laying low the grass and startling a doe, which sprang from her hiding place and bounded into the cover of the woods.

Wind at last. Powerful, alarming, unusual. Not a life-giving wind from the East nor a disaster-laden wind from the North. No, this wind came from the **West**.

The land of the dead.

He had received his sign. And it was a clear one. Fear seeped into every bone. And accompanying it, a chill. It clambered up his back and dug its claws into his neck. A menacing **Shadow** crossed over his soul, shrieked in his mind. The ghost was there, and in the next breath, it was gone.

"Are you all right?" Copper Woman asked.

Grimacing, he massaged the base of his head, floundering for his previous line of thought and not getting any further than one word. *Death.* No, he would not allow death one more victory. But if it could not be avoided . . . In the name of all that was unpolluted and good, he hoped it was his own.

"Totka Hadjo, are you listening to me?"

"Yes. I am fine. A cramp. Just a knot in my neck. Nothing a long day in the saddle cannot fix." He forced a chortle and rotated his head in a slow arc, more to stall for composure than to release the kink.

"Would you like me to knead it?"

"Hmm, I would. My neck and a few other places." This time, the grin came without difficulty.

Contrary to pattern, Copper Woman did not flush but leaned into his leg. "I might do that and with pleasure." The sultry slant to her lips widened his eyes, until she gave way to laughter. "Twelve moons from today."

"Ach!" He shoved outward with his foot, clearing her of the horse and making her safe from him. But she came right back, laughter still burbling out of her. Unable to resist, he joined in. "You are a shameless tease." And so alluring he knew she would spend the passing seasons fending off the advances of other men—white men. Men more suited to her than himself.

The thought sobered him. "And it is eleven moons and twenty-six sleeps from today, not twelve. I'll count every one of them. In the meantime, men are sure to bid for you. Tell them you are spoken for by an Indian to whom the fearsome **owls** report." He added a grin to the statement but let his Red Stick blood take over his eyes. "Tell them my sight reaches far, that my jealousy runs hot, and my revenge is not mild." If anyone harmed her, if the **Master of Breath** decided to take her—

He hacked off the thought and instead filled his head with her image, one last picture to carry him home: hair battling for freedom from her grip, shapely legs outlined through the skirt plastered to her by the wind, an attractive reprimand twisting her mouth.

"I mean what I say, Copper Woman."

All gaiety gone, she backed away, letting her hand trail the length of his leg. "I believe you and love you for it. Go then. We will meet here next spring, at the new blackberry moon."

He nudged the horse forward and, while passing by, ran his fingers over her hair in a parting kiss. "Only the Master of Breath could keep me away." Without another glance, he released Wind Chaser and let her fly into a gallop that devoured the pasture and thundered through his bones.

But no matter their speed, the Wind Spirit drove against them from the west, hard and persistent, screaming *death* in his ear.

Gray and white ash soiled Totka's moccasins. It coated his airways

and reeked of ruin. Like heaps of dirty snow, it covered the plot of earth Lachlan Gibb had once called home. The lodge, the forge, the storehouse, even the potato bin—gone. Only the horse shed remained untouched.

Anger reddening his features, Lachlan bumped his boot through the scraps of his cabin, creating white billows of soot that settled to his Scotsman's kilt, his Indian leggings, and to each of the many black hairs on his stout arms. "Nothing. They have left me not a thing to call my own."

"The anvil survived and some of the tools."

With a grunt, Lachlan bent and picked over the skeleton of a lamp, kicked it aside, and moved on.

Totka abandoned the lodge for the horse shed, passing Amadayh who tended the animals. Three sleeps had passed since they'd left the McGirth child with the new wet nurse, and still, the childless **widow** carried herself delicately, painfully. Her body missed the boy, and peering from her eyes was a heartache Totka understood all too well.

The battle was a constant one to keep loneliness from knotting his throat and his thoughts. Even when his mind was fully engaged in activity or conversation, the ache was there, like a stomach satisfied too fully. But he would not wish it away for all the corn in Creek country, for he would rather be crippled by longing for Copper

Woman than return to the emptiness that had been his existence before her.

When he arrived at the creaking gate to the open-sided stall, his gaze fell upon marks in the straw-spattered dirt. Footprints. Fresh, not smudged by the wind.

Senses on alert, Totka slowed his approach, grasped the haft of the knife at his belt. With an experienced sweep, his eye took in the yard and the **Federal Road** running alongside it, then the horses, ears relaxed and muzzles buried in vegetation, followed by the wall of surrounding forest whose bowels were as thick and dark as the foreboding that tightened Totka's own.

The prints led both in and out of the enclosure, and the ones leading out had been applied in a hurry.

No fire had been struck in the courtyard pit for quite some time. A glance inside the shed revealed a mound of moldy hay partially covered by a tattered blanket. In its center, a man-sized indention.

The scent of sour clothes preceded Lachlan's arrival. "Visitors dropped by, eh?" He spoke loudly from over Totka's shoulder. "Must not have found the excellent accommodations to their liking."

"It is us they do not find to their liking. Keep your eyes open. They'll not have gone far. My guess is fugitive Red Sticks." Those unwilling to surrender to Old Sharp Knife at the newly erected Fort Jackson, that symbol of conquest strategically constructed in the heart of the **Muscogee Confederacy**. "They will be looking for food. Weapons, ammunition. Anything to hasten their flight to Spanish Florida."

"They have already taken it all." Lachlan spread his hands wide.

"Not everything." Totka leaned in so he could speak low on the chance their voices carried into the trees. "And I will not lose a single grain of McGirth corn to a band of warriors too thick-skulled to lay down the club." A man should know when he'd been bested.

Rhythmic creaking and clattering pulled their attention to the road and the matched team of gray oxen that lumbered toward them, pulling a covered wagon. A bearded man, staff in one hand and musket in the other, walked beside the beasts. On the wagon's bench sat a woman, the broad brim of her bonnet moving with the cart's sway.

"What sort of man brings his family into Red Stick country before peace has been signed?" Lachlan scratched his beard and rained ash onto his grease-stained shirtfront.

"The sort who has a rock in place of a brain."

"Aye, aye. Good evening to you!" With a song in his Scots, Lachlan hailed the traveler. "The name is Gibb. Lachlan Gibb."

Happy to let Lachlan deal with the fool, Totka crossed the dreary lot, exhaustion matting his body like sweat. The day had been long, but now it dimmed to a blue-gray haze, and the night creatures were beginning their meditative chants.

A flash of red, human in its irregularity, whipped Totka's gaze to the tree line twenty paces to his left.

Nothing. Not a shivering bush or swinging leaf, not even birdsong. Only eerie silence.

Nerves raw, Totka continued on to Amadayh. He would not be lured into the dark.

She laid more kindling atop the fiery stack, distrust shifting her eyes to the wagon. "They will ask to share our fire." As though angry at the idea, the flames lashed out at her skirt, and she hopped away.

"Not likely. Such an arrangement would make too much sense." At her dry laugh, he smirked and nodded toward the trees. "Stay out of the woods. Someone is prowling."

"These days, there is always someone prowling." Eyes setting up like mortar, she fed the already oppressive heat with an aggressive jab. Sparks hissed and flew into the purpling sky. "But I am done cowering. If I need to use the cover of a bush to relieve myself, I will." She lifted her face, a twinkle in her eye. "But you must promise me— when you haul my dead body home, do not tell my mother what I was doing when I was freed of my scalp."

Totka struggled to keep a straight face. "If you get yourself killed while behind a bush, I will tell your mother where she can visit your rotting corpse."

They laughed—the first in many days—and Totka was pleased for it. Perhaps the lonesome seasons would be more bearable than he'd thought.

"Come, boys." The stranger spoke, and the oxen obeyed, applying their bulk to the yoke and setting the wheels to rumbling.

Moments later, Lachlan joined them, bringing his nose-wrinkling odor with him. Totka appreciated the man's taste in headdress and his dislike of trousers, but he had yet to see him go to water.

"They'll stretch out their blankets closer to the pond." Lachlan yawned.

"Closer to the mosquitoes," Amadayh muttered while spooning a powdered substance into a small, long-handled pot.

Lachlan lowered his mass to the dirt and began rummaging through their sack of provisions. "The man needed an iron worker. That musket he brandished was useless. Warped barrel." He wagged his head and produced from the sack a wheat biscuit, one of the dozens Copper Woman had packed for their journey. "Shame I could not help. A true shame. Tell me, why would they take my bellows? What would any Red Stick want with it?"

Totka flipped open his saddle bag. "Same thing a white man would want with it. To mold iron. Doubtful they possess the skills though." The writings, wrapped in soft, cream-colored flannel, peeked up at him from the bag's depths, and his lungs constricted.

Lachlan buffed his teeth with a scrap of fabric, eyes going to the blackened posts of the lodge. "My wife, Two Spoons, always said I should move the forge to Tuckabatchee. Coweta maybe. Said I would find more business there than I did here on the Federal."

"That is especially true now that so many are rebuilding." With a grimace, Totka sat, placed his bow and quiver within easy reach, and stretched out his cramping leg. "At present, iron is a luxury few Indians can afford. But you might find that over the winter, after crops have been harvested and the hunts have brought in skins to trade, they might be eager to stock their cookhouses with kettles and pans." Singing Grass would be.

Writings in hand, he propped himself against his saddle.

"Hmm." Lachlan became pensive, allowing Totka to descend into the aching cavity in his chest.

Flannel removed, the writings' leather gleamed in the firelight. Totka traced the curious symbols indenting its cover, then with a flat palm, he caressed the surface, patterning his touch after the reverent strokes Copper Woman had made when she'd spoken of its strong **medicine**, its sacred words.

It did not feel powerful or sacred, but Totka trusted his woman. If she said it was sacred, then it was. Its age alone was enough to demand respect.

He opened the stiff cover and released the scent of dust and time and love. For hadn't she loved him much to entrust him with it? The leaves crackled as he turned them one after the other. Black markings, like tattoos, filled the white space in neat rows and columns. At first, they overwhelmed him, but then, he began noticing repetitions.

His eye ran down the width of several rows until it became ensnared on a familiar symbol.

"You read?" Lachlan's gruff voice severed his concentration.

"No, but I know this mark." He stretched the writings toward the man and underlined it with a fingernail.

Lachlan drew the writings closer and squinted. "Oh, aye. It is called *eff*."

"The markings have names?"

"Each is identified by a name, and when joined, they create words." Lachlan paused, leveled an empty stare at the fire. "I have had this conversation before with Leaping Waters." He cocked his head at Totka. "Were you not wed to her at one time?"

Amadayh removed her bubbling pot from the fire and gave a sharp clack of the tongue. "Worse than a meddlesome woman, you are, Lachlan Gibb."

Her stance in Totka's defense was endearing, but not

surprisingly, the question held little sting.

"Eh? What am I?"

"Meddlesome!" Amadayh said, then muttered, "And deaf as a rock."

Lachlan's smile showed off a set of carefully groomed teeth. "I have had *this* conversation before as well. With Two Spoons." His jovial laugh ebbed into a melancholy sigh, and Totka pitied him.

"What is this symbol?" He indicated another letter. "Tell me its name."

"That one is *ah-ee*. How is it you've seen them?"

Totka's thoughts took wing and deposited him in Singing Grass' courtyard before it had been touched by war. The ground was hot beneath his moccasins, his skin hotter yet for the glancing touch of Copper Woman's arm against his bare thigh.

Her slender finger, white as dandelion milk, brushed furrows into the earth. Red dust marred her nose, her chin. The urge to wipe them clean had been tempting. He should have given in to it. Then, she'd suggested she teach him more. He should have given in to that as well.

No, he should have given in to Leaping Waters. Her offer of instruction had come many winters before he'd tripped over Copper Woman and dropped his heart in her lap.

"Eff, Ah-ee." He reproduced the sounds and a smile warmed his face. "Copper Woman showed me the four symbols of my English name."

"Fire. Mad Fire, aye? A strong name."

"A spirit's name." He had always strived to live up to it.

Totka turned another page and trailed a finger along the scrawled markings at the edge. Someone had applied quill and ink to the sacred object. An incantation of sorts? Like a **medicine bundle**? He touched the one hanging from a cord about his neck. It included a wolf claw—a representation of himself, of his role in the tribe, and of his spirit helper.

Lachlan reached for the writings. "May I?"

Hesitantly, Totka handed it over. "Be prepared to sleep with one eye open should you damage it."

"That grin of his means nothing, Lachlan Gibb." One brow hiking, Amadayh poured the contents of her pot into a wooden cup. "He will do as he says."

Lachlan laughed, flipping through the pages with less care than Totka would like. "The advice is much appreciated, but Leaping Waters warned me about him when she was still a little thing. Said he was a guard dog without a tether."

Amadayh swirled the cup to cool the liquid while putting on a sassy smile. "And his bite is every bit as ferocious as his growl."

"I am Wolf **Clan**. What do you expect?" Totka grunted, pleased at their assessment. They'd easily identified the role Creator had given him. Why could Old Grandfather not see it? "More than one person has thanked me for my growl. Although, it has not always served me well." He massaged his thigh with the heel of his hand.

Amadayh's face gentled, then firmed when she studied the curtain of darkness. A hush settled over them as Lachlan searched the pages and Totka, following Amadayh's cue, tuned his senses to the woods. They were equally quiet. He felt for his bow and was reassured by the sturdy feel of black locust wood against his palm.

"Ah ha!" Lachlan angled the writings toward the firelight. "Found it. Come look."

Ear still on the trees, Totka complied. There, above Lachlan's dirty fingernail was the word *fire*.

"What has he found?" Suspicion flattened Amadayh's mouth.

"My English name." In more precise form than what Copper Woman used but clearly the same. Of all the writing on all the pages, Lachlan had been able to find those four symbols joined together. Astounding, really. "Does it speak of the Fire Spirit? Tell me what it says."

"If I remember the story correctly," Lachlan began, settling into position as Old Grandfather often did before making a speech. "It tells of a great prophet. The queen of the land was evil and wished him dead, so the prophet ran. He prayed and Creator sent a messenger to tell him to stand on a mountain."

"Why would he do that?" Amadayh brought Totka the steaming cup. "Chicory for your leg."

"*Maddo.*" He thanked her.

"Look left," she whispered and skipped her gaze to the blackened forest.

As Lachlan continued, Totka put the rim to his lips and examined the outline of each tree and shrub until he spotted an abnormality, the partial figure of a man—Muscogee, by the silhouette, a silhouette Totka knew well. Tension eased from his bow arm but did not leave him completely. It was never wise to relax in his cousin's presence, and if Tall Bull wanted to speak, he would have to show himself.

Lachlan cleared his throat and brought Totka's attention back to the tale. "These are the words written down: A strong wind ripped the mountains and broke the rocks before Creator, but Creator was not to be found in the wind; after the wind came the earth shook, but Creator was not in the shaking; and after the earthquake came the fire, but Creator was not in the fire; and after the fire a still, small voice. And Creator said to him—"

"It says there were no spirits in the elements?" Amadayh cleared rocks and sticks from where she would arrange her bedding.

"Who am I to know these things?" Lachlan said. "But perhaps it is showing that Creator is mightier than the elements, that he does not require them to speak to man."

Amadayh considered a moment and tossed away another rock with a little flick of her wrist. "It is true enough that Creator can do as he wishes."

"The words put down here are from his very mouth, or so my mother told me." Lachlan shrugged and returned the writings to Totka.

After Totka shared a quizzical glance with Amadayh, he closed the book with a snap, then wished he hadn't. He would never find his name again.

From the darkness, a horned owl swooped low over their camp. Amadayh ducked and grumbled something about the writings and witchcraft. She unfurled her blanket with a rigorous snap.

Lachlan went for his own rolled blanket. "So if I were to put up the forge in a Muscogee **talwa**, which would you recommend?"

"What about Tuckabatchee, as Two Spoons said?" Amadayh suggested.

Totka slurped the scalding concoction. "Maybe. But Hawkins will probably supply the Tuckabatchees with craftsmen before any of the other talwas." The treaty promised skilled craftsmen for a number of villages, and the agent to the Muscogees had a soft spot for Tuckabatchee.

Tall Bull's wolf call rang out through the clearing.

Totka sneered through another bittersweet gulp of chicory, happy to keep his cousin waiting.

Eyes jumpy, Amadayh fidgeted with her bedding, unwilling to settle. "There is always Kossati. It sits at the joining of the rivers and is stomp grounds for several villages."

Lachlan scooted toward her, sleep forgotten. "I like how you think, woman. Tell me, do you agree that to avoid becoming overrun, the Muscogees must assimilate some of the white man's ways by learning new skills such as iron work, or by making paper talk with symbols?"

"English symbols," Amadayh said, voice flat.

"Yes, English, but to defeat his enemy, a man must *know* his enemy."

Lachlan could be Leaping Waters speaking — except for his odor, furry legs, and . . . everything else.

Totka slung out the dregs from his cup. "We are at peace with the whites. They are no longer our enemy. A treaty is soon to be signed. Are you suggesting rebellion?"

"Defense, Totka. Against invaders."

Sheared hair, oily from several seasons of neglect, fell across Amadayh's ever-sharp eyes. "The **Muscogee**s must make themselves a confederacy worthy of respect. We must make ourselves equal to the pales faces in knowledge and craft. We should begin at once, as soon as —" She huffed, stood, and lifted her voice to a near shout. "As soon as our skulking guest removes himself from the shadows."

Lachlan glanced about, confused, while Totka choked over contained laughter.

Moments later, Tall Bull entered the circle of their light, but Amadayh's hurled stone thudded off his chest and stopped him just inside the far reaches.

"Close enough," she snapped.

Lachlan bounded to his feet, kilt askew, wide-eyed gaze split between Tall Bull's appearance and Amadayh's performance. Had Two Spoons taught him no woodland skills at all, or did his hearing loss make him inept?

"Your aim has always been shy of the mark, Amadayh." Tall Bull brushed imaginary dust from his shirt.

Quicker than the Thunder Snake flashes the sky, she threw another, but Tall Bull's reflexes served him well enough to avoid a braining. The stone skimmed the side of his head and sent his red feather swirling.

Chuckling, he straightened and unhooked a lock of hair from his nose. "Better."

Lachlan ran a flustered hand over his beard. "Great stars in the sky, woman, you can put a man to shame with that arm."

Ignoring him, Amadayh dropped to her backside with a redoubled huff and directed a fractious look at Totka. "It is only your slippery clansman. Make him go away. He attracts pests." The woman was relentless in her anger and loyalty. She would never forgive Tall Bull for his theft of Copper Woman, for threatening to defile her, for having sent her to the slave post in the freezing rain.

It was an anger Totka supported, encouraged wholeheartedly. "I thought it was clear you are no longer welcome at my fire, Cousin." He propped an arm on his raised knee in a lazy pose.

No need to ask why Tall Bull could be found at Lachlan Gibb's burned-out forge. Leaping Waters would have suggested they seek refuge here, which meant she was near. Totka felt the touch of her eye—gentle, inquisitive, faithless.

"The fire is there"—Tall Bull pointed—"and I am here. Will you give us a portion of the grain you carry?"

"No. The maize is for the People."

"Am I not a Kossati?"

"You are a fugitive. And you have my answer. Go away."

"Broken harmony in the clan?" Lachlan asked. "Sounds like a story to keep my ears occupied on the path to Kossati."

"Tall Bull is not worth the use of my breath." Totka picked at a hole in the toe of his moccasin, one of the many things that would need replacing with supplies he no longer owned.

Tall Bull spoke. "My cousin is tight-fisted with his bitterness, but vengeance is a beautiful thing. If he would look up, he would read my eyes and see that I have had mine. And it was sweet. *She* was sweet."

Sweat broke out of every pore on Totka's body. Slowly, he got to his feet and, breath blowing through his nostrils like a gale, stalked to where Tall Bull stood as arrogant and handsome as always, even in his emaciated frame. "The next time you speak of Copper Woman in such a way," he said through his teeth, "it will be your death song."

Tall Bull shifted away, his tone amended, yielding. "If you want me gone, give me what I need."

"Take this." Lachlan tossed him a biscuit. "Please, put something into your stomach. Your bones are glaring at me."

Tall Bull began devouring it, and Totka curled his lip. "Will you not save any for your wife?" There would never be a day Totka did not feel some measure of responsibility for the woman. Long Arrow, her brother, had bred it into him.

"She is not here." Food clogged his speech.

"How smoothly he lies," Amadayh said.

Tall Bull's chilly glare only made her chin tilt higher. "Watch how you accuse me, woman. I would feed my wife before myself."

"Take her home to her mother," Totka said. "In case you've not noticed, the Red Sticks are defeated. The fighting is done. Quit while you can."

"I would sooner die than surrender!" Crumbs spewed onto his lips. He ridded them with a rough swipe of his wrist.

"Keep up as you are, and you will get your wish. Stop running. Your clan needs you." Totka needed him—the old version. Not the haggard stranger who stood before him barely visible through an impenetrable wall of distrust.

"I *am* seeing to their needs by fleeing to **the Floridas** where we will join the British and the **People of the Point**." The Seminoles. Wild men, as they were called for their appetite for trouble. Fitting that Tall Bull should join them. "There is also a rumor of an army of runaway blacks. We have another chance to whip the pale faces, Totka! To drive them from our borders. Clear to the Great Waters if we choose. In Spanish country, we can rally, gather weapons, come back for a final blow. We can defeat them!" His eyes blazed with vision, but it was a dream made of smoke and empty thunder.

Totka narrowed an eye. "Who is *we*?"

"Hillis Hadjo leads a body of Red Sticks, three-hundred strong, maybe more. Join us."

"Not even my **ghost** in its wildest travels would conceive of joining that crazed **knower**." The prophet, also known as Josiah Francis, was a liar and a lunatic.

Disappointment, thick as clotting blood, sagged Tall Bull's shoulders. "*Tohopeka* is not the end."

But the Horse's Flat Foot, the battle that had slain the Red Stick forces, *was* the end, for all Indians owning half a brain with which to think.

Tall Bull's line of sight, bald in its hunger, traveled to the sacks of grain. He removed the limp pouch slung over his shoulder and extended it. "If you will not join us, will you at least feed us?"

Totka crossed his arms. "No."

"A handful of seed. No more. We are Wolf, you and I. Clan first.

Always. Come, Brother, be reasonable."

How dare he try to resurrect that term? "We are not brothers!" Totka's shout drew a startled whiny from Wind Chaser and propelled Tall Bull back a half pace. "As I said, a waste of breath."

Intent on soothing Wind Chaser, Totka tromped toward the horses, fanning his fingers wide to release tension before arrival.

"Tell Ayo that she will not see her daughter for some time. Leaping Waters will be coming with me." Tall Bull's statement arrested Totka's retreat.

He spun back, but Lachlan was already in Tall Bull's face. "You will not take that sweet girl into the swamp to be hunted like an animal!"

And Lachlan called Totka a snarling watchdog?

While the man continued to berate Totka's flinty cousin, Amadayh snatched the pouch from Tall Bull and marched to the sacks of grain.

With a resigned sigh, Totka went to seek out Wind Chaser.

The animal plodded to him and bumped the flat of her skull against his chest. Totka tangled his fingers in her coarse forelock and scratched behind her ear. "I miss her, too, but don't worry. She is safe."

From hunger and war, from Tall Bull. Leaping Waters was not, however, but Totka refused to care. She had constructed her own rickety **couch**. Now, she must lie in it.

How times had changed. There had once been a day the talwa expected them to grow old together, he and Leaping Waters, but that had been before the war, before he'd lost full strength in his leg. Back when Tall Bull was called Lance, and Totka was called Leaping Waters' future . . .

Chapter 2

Kossati Village, Upper Muscogee Nation
Big Spring Month (April) 1802, twelve winters earlier

In the murky, predawn light, Totka Lawe could just make out Leaping Waters' sleeping form through the curtain of wild grapevines. The spacious sandstone den she occupied was situated in an embankment of the Coosa River.

He propped his boy-sized bow and quiver against the craggy trunk of Old Man Oak, an adjacent tree. Then, on panther's paws, he scampered up and, bobbing under tangled nets of moss, walked out onto a branch that stretched over the gentle river. As he'd done many times before, he dangled his feet and waited for the girl to wake.

Three winters junior to Totka's fourteen, she was his best friend's little sister, and the talwa's child of pity. Not that either she or her brother would accept a morsel of it.

Fingers of fear pinched Totka's insides. He would lose her today, to the Scotsman downriver who'd agreed to accept her labor. But unlike his mother and grandmother who had taken the journey to the spirit world, Leaping Waters would return.

Squashing a gnat that bit into his thigh, he straightened his spine. He *would* see her again, and in the meantime, she would be safe from an aunt brazen enough to whip a girl with thistle stalks, cane, whatever her drunken hands came across.

The grapevine rustled, but it was only the wind. He lifted his face to it, closed his eyes, and smiled because it was an east wind. The girl could use a bit of blessing.

Who would have guessed that over the course of these sporadic quiet mornings spread out over many moons, Totka would learn to enjoy her company? She was young, a scrawny thing, rather pathetic really, with her large, fear-filled eyes and her mousy voice heard by a select few.

Totka would miss the little creature.

Before long, her stirrings reached his ears: the rustle of her bed of leaves, a squeaky yawn, the scrape of her soles against the tree trunk. She crawled up beside him, sat with her shoulder against his arm, and set her short, knobby legs to swinging in time with his.

Conscious that she would not want him studying her, he kept his eyes on her dirty bare feet. He withdrew a corn pone from the pouch slung across his chest and listened to her devour it then lick her fingers. How long had she been hiding this time? Long Arrow should have come to Totka sooner, but then, even with Totka, Long Arrow was greedy with his sister's care.

And proud, too proud to let her stay at Singing Grass' lodge—or anyone else's—when Strong Deer, their aunt, became violent with **tafia**, the white man's evil brew. He would rather no one know of their ongoing shame. The punishments the clan mothers inflicted, harsh though they were, did little to keep Strong Deer from reaching again for the keg. They should banish her and be done with the woman!

Leaping Waters' uncle, her **Pawa** Nokose, who was also Totka's brother-in-law, did all he could to protect the girl, but he could not be at the lodge every moment. This time, he was in Tuskegee, finalizing **stickball** negotiations for an upcoming match. He would not be back for several sleeps.

Long Arrow, whom Strong Deer did not dare touch, had assumed the role of protector, but even he—three seasons into manhood and living now in the warriors' lodge—was unable to shield Leaping Waters. Today, he was under the tutelage of an elder, learning to brew the ceremonial tea, the **white drink**. Which was why he'd woken Totka, the only other person he trusted with his sister's whereabouts.

And there it was again, that rock-hard pride of his. He would rather squirrel his sister away than admit his elder had shamed them once again. Why that was, Totka didn't know, but he also didn't dig too deeply. Long Arrow had always been a puzzle, an old spirit in a young body, but Totka was honored to help. If not for the risk of his own cousin's displeasure, he would find the task enjoyable. As it was, he lived in dread of discovery.

Before most boys had thought beyond mastering their blowgun aim, his cousin Lance had set his sights on Leaping Waters, and Totka would sooner skip his rites of passage than do anything to cause a rift between himself and the boy who was more a brother than a cousin.

But Totka had made his own vow—this one to Long Arrow. He would be there for Leaping Waters when Long Arrow could not. And he would not reveal her place of refuge.

She picked crumbles from her skirt, ate them, and gave a long sigh of satisfaction. "Thank you. It was delicious." Her voice was as soft and tender as always. Would her trials never spoil her sweet disposition?

"Would you like more? Singing Grass said if you needed anything to—"

"No." Her reply was swift. "I need nothing more." Only a sober aunt and the ability to accept help when it was offered.

He huffed. "You are too proud."

"And you, too stubborn." She knocked shoulders with him, and he heard the smile he would not look at. "Spare your breath. I know you want me to go to your lodge tonight but—"

"You will no longer be in Kossati tonight," he blurted, then cringed. Why in the name of all that was pure and balanced had Long Arrow asked this of him?

"What? Not be here?"

"Nokose has found a place for you with the iron worker at the trading post on the Federal Road." The white man's road that had split the confederacy and made his pawa grouse and swear. "You will work for the Scotsman Lachlan Gibb and his wife. In return, at season's end, you will bring home trade goods. Food only or cotton cloth. Nokose will not accept tafia as payment." She would have no trouble remembering the last.

At the tremble of her lip, he rushed on. "It is labor any girl would be proud to have. Think of the things you will see and learn." That she would also be out from under her aunt was a detail that, for its flagrance, need not be voiced.

Leaping Waters plucked moss from a branch overhead and picked at it a long while before speaking. "And the iron worker, he is a-a good man?"

"Would Nokose send you to a bad man?" The answer was obvious to Totka, but Leaping Waters hesitated. To a girl who knew violence at the hand of the one who should protect her, the answer was not so straightforward.

She gave none. Instead, she asked, "I will be gone a full season?"

"Until the frost month."

With a little snort, she let the moss fall into the river and be swept away. "I will miss my Wolf."

A lump formed in Totka's throat so that he didn't trust himself to reply. He must practice being a man, but could form words, he would not. Admitting to friendship seemed a betrayal when Lance could not even get her to look at him. It was not Lance's fault nor hers. She looked few villagers in the eye.

"Long Arrow asks that you remain here until he comes for you," he said, "but do not expect him before the sun has passed its peak."

"It will be a long, lonely morning. Will you stay with me?"

Totka lifted his gaze to her and wished he hadn't. Even in the fledgling morning gray, purple and red slashes were visible on her throat. Acid burbled up his own, and when he discharged an abrupt growl, she shrank away, ever the skittish mouse.

He swiveled his head away but found her hand and held on until

34

he sensed her posture soften. "You need never fear me."

"I-I know, but sometimes . . ."

He gave her hand a squeeze. She needn't say more. "I would stay, but Old Grandfather expects me at the maize field. Lance as well."

"Then you should go. The sun will show herself soon." But instead of freeing him, she tipped her head onto his arm. Her hand settled on his lower back and before he could decide if he should do anything about it, she shoved him hard.

Through his bark of protest, he flailed for balance but went down just the same. His belly met the water first with a stinging slap, and he barely managed to suck air before water closed over him.

Her full-bodied laughter tickled him over the river rushing in his ears. He smiled, and the river engulfed his mouth. When his feet hit the rocky bottom, he propelled himself back up and broke the surface with enough force to bring his fingers within reach of her ankles. He clamped on, cutting her laughter short.

Wildly, she beat the air and landed on him with a shriek. They went under together, a tangle of hair, limbs, and bubbles, and emerged laughing so hard Totka took half of the Coosa into his nose.

They were still laughing when they hauled their sodden bodies through the rushes and up the vertical embankment. An awkward moment passed as they stood facing one another, catching their breath, and creating twin puddles at their feet, suddenly aware of the need to say goodbye.

Looking him dead in the eye, she smiled, creating matching dimples and emphasizing the moon-like quality of her face: large eyes, rounded cheeks, and on the rare occasion that they appeared, perfectly circular dimples. A cool breeze enveloped them, and her flat chest rocked with a shiver. "Will your pawa make you continue training with the musket?"

"No doubt he will." Even though Totka hated the noisy, cumbersome thing. They bruised the shoulder and belched smoke that stung the nose. An arrow's reach was shorter, but it was silent, swiftly ready, and not cowed by rain.

"It's good he does." She smiled, and Totka could not be piqued. "Keep up your ball practice. When I return, I want to see you hit the pole left-handed from ten rods."

"All right. You will." He grinned and did an overhead fling with an invisible ball stick.

"Beautiful form, my pawa says."

"And what do you say?"

"I say that when you are grown, you will be as renowned a player as your Pawa Cetto Imala. My pouch will fill with wagered trade beads, because you will win every match."

"How do you know?" His voice cracked, and he shuffled his feet in embarrassment.

"Everyone knows you do all things well, Totka Lawe." She'd always called him by his full name, pronouncing each syllable with care. And she'd always believed in him.

She was a generous girl, sweet as a honey locust pod.

To thank her, Totka the boy, would embrace her, let his eyes water, and tell her he would miss her while she was away. But Totka was closer to being a man than a boy, so he backed up a step and cocked a half-smile. "Everyone? I think not."

She shrugged. "All that matters is that *you* believe it."

How was it this runt of a girl could make him feel so much bigger than his fourteen winters? He crooked a finger and popped her under the chin. "Sit under the sun until you are dry. The Scotsman's wife will not care to play nursemaid to a sick girl."

She nodded. "Thank Singing Grass for me?"

"I will. Take heart, Leaping Waters." He offered a strained smile and left her before he did something childish, like drop a tear.

A good distance away, he glanced back through the trees. She had returned to their perch, but her eyes were not on the water. They were pointed his direction. Her drooping body tugged at his spirit. He should have embraced her.

It hardly seemed fair that a girl not yet a woman should be sent away simply because her aunt could not refrain from putting the mean brew to her lips and because Ayo, her mother, was too weak-minded to stand between them.

Doubting Leaping Waters could see, he lifted a hand in a stiff wave, and when she sat erect and returned the gesture, he blinked back tears.

It would be a long, lonely summer.

Totka raced the sun, bare feet pounding, **breechcloth** slapping. The sun's lower edge had yet to break free of the horizon, but any moment, it would, and then Old Grandfather's myriad wrinkles would deepen. With Totka's initiation into manhood nigh to begin, it would not do to be slack in his responsibilities.

The quiver on Totka's back bounced, and the reed arrows rattled against each other in a discordant tune. By the time he reached the steep lane leading to the maize field, his hair was nearly dry.

He'd gone to water with the dawn and let the pleasant memory of Leaping Waters' laughter carry his smile through his prayers.

Ahead, Lance strode the path to the maize field, his muscular, brown body small against the hill. Same as Totka, he wore only a long-shirt, sash, and breechcloth. Totka gave a shout, and Lance turned and walked backwards. The wind pushed his long hair out behind him like a black ribbon pennant.

He waved his blowgun over his head, and Totka raised his bow in response.

"I waited as long as I dared. Where have you been?" Lance asked when Totka reached him. "Stealing a ride on Leaning Bow's stallion again?" He flashed a grin and perfectly even teeth. Creator had been good to Lance.

Totka's lungs heaved for wind. "Singing Grass sent me with food to a hungry child." He caught the strap of his quiver as it slipped off his shoulder.

"I should have guessed. Your sister cannot stand for anyone to go hungry." Lance patted his flat stomach and grinned. "And it is my great fortune to live one house over."

"Even if you lived across the chunkey yard, you would find a way to eat our grape dumplings the moment they left the pot. The next time you plan to empty it while Singing Grass is away, you'd best find a place to hide."

Lance loosed a goofy chortle and made a soft mound of his stomach. Totka grinned and elbowed it, forcing an *oomph* out of him.

"Next time, *you* should finish off the dumplings," Lance said. "Take them with ginkgo tea. You will need both to reach my great height." He rose up on his toes, a cheeky smirk rising with him.

A scoff on his lips, Totka discarded the exaggeration with a flip of his hand. Lance might best him in muscle, but if he bested Totka in height it was by a hair's width. The two, born of sisters, had entered **This World** mere days apart. They had grown up together like twin fawns, lean and leggy, sharing their mothers' breasts and their grandmother's wisdom.

The one thing they did not share was Cetto Imala's favor. Totka, by no intent of his own, had inherited the full portion of their pawa's approval. Cetto Imala was brother to both their mothers and thus their guardian, disciplinarian, and instructor in all things male.

"Soon, to make up the difference," Lance continued, "you'll need to wear a porcupine roach and walk on your toes." He snorted a laugh.

"The only thing I'll walk on is your grave" — Totka launched himself sideways and hooked an elbow around Lance's neck — "after I've ground you into cornmeal!" He delivered a blow to Lance's middle.

His cousin doubled over and flung Totka across his back, following him to the dirt where they rolled in a red cloud, each demanding the other own to lesser stature. At last, the knee Totka received to his lip knocked sense back into him.

Licking away blood, he kicked to extricate himself from Lance's stranglehold on his legs. "The birds, Lance. Old Grandfather will —"

"Yes, yes. I know." Lance released him. "Anything to avoid a speech from the ancient one." He grumbled and pushed himself out of the dirt, which he immediately set to sweeping out of his silken hair. "We are too old to scare away birds. It is a task for children and old women." He clasped Totka's arm and hauled him up.

Totka brushed the earth from his skin. "Only a few moons more, Brother, and then we'll never again chase a blackbird from a maize field."

Lance gave a grunt of approval. "But first we'll have to pass the initiation."

"You fear you'll fail?" His voice chirped with surprise.

"Fear? What is fear?"

"Why do you ask *me*?" Totka mimicked his cousin's twisting smile, but they both knew it was fear that drove Lance through life — fear of failure, fear of being a lesser man, and most pressing, fear of losing their land and the Old Beloved Path.

It was a man's fear, handed down from his father who'd lost his parents to a white settler's rash musket.

Totka kept his own fear — that of loss — well hidden, but it was no less real. It had been forged in the same fire that had taken his mother and grandmother and left him to his eldest sister's care. The flames had smoked Totka's hair and blistered his skin, but he would have burnt to a char if not for Lance's sharp thinking. Since then, every glance at a fire was a reminder of everything Totka owed him.

But for his father's blind trust in Kossati's knower, the tragedy might have been avoided. Gray Hawk wanted to take the whole family on the great hunt, but the knower had advised he leave them in the security of the talwa since tensions with the **Long Hairs**, the Choctaws, were high. Gray Hawk had heeded the warning.

But while the town was empty of its men, Kossati was raided by Choctaw braves, who were more keen on earning war titles than distinguishing between warriors and innocents. Totka, broken and lost, had sworn to never lift the war club to a woman or a child.

Quietly, Totka and Lance arrived at the field, green with juvenile cornstalks that were loaded with tiny, succulent ears, so tempting to the birds and wild ones. They settled cross-legged on the ground next to Old Grandfather who rested on his usual log.

A stem of sourgrass protruded from his wrinkled lips and dipped with his deep nod, its spikelets bobbing their own greeting. His earlobes, stretched long by the passage of time, jostled under the weight of their silver bangles.

Totka deposited his bow on the matted grass and rummaged through an undisturbed clump for his own fat purple stem. He peeled off the leaves, crushed the shaft between his teeth, and savored its tart juice as he watched the great orb spread his warmth and light over the talwa. Grandmother Sun touched each lodge with her blessing and set the young maize tassels to glowing pale green.

A shadow materialized beyond the corn, loping a casual trot—a wolf, in the meadow on the far side of the field and moving toward the corner nearest them, heading for the woods beyond the field's break. It would spot them within moments.

Remembering to move with the wolf's own silence and grace, Totka set aside his bow, removed his quiver, and gained his feet before his totem animal came into full view, its alert ears leading the way.

The breadth of its shoulders said it was male. It was a thing of beauty and power, held in high regard by his **lineage**, the Wolf Clan.

Lance joined him, eyes wide and blowgun in hand.

The wolf swung his head their direction and froze mid-stride, nose lifting to the wind. Fearless, it gazed at them, panting, hackles smooth, tail hanging straight down in a relaxed posture.

Totka smiled, sensing the connection to his spirit helper.

Then, head lowering, the wolf bared his teeth.

Totka's heart kicked, and Lance jolted and raised the blowgun. Before it touched his lips, the animal whipped about and hurtled into the woods.

Lance followed through and, with a *whissst*, blew a dart into the ground where the wolf had stood. "I daresay he'll not bare his teeth at Wolf Clan again."

A horrifying display of disrespect, but in Old Grandfather's presence Totka would not spout the words heating on his tongue.

Old Grandfather squinted in the direction they'd last seen the wolf. "Lance's aim was not true."

The sleek lines of Lance's face hardened. "But I was not aiming for the wolf. It struck exactly where I intended, and it was a good shot." His tongue rarely differentiated between peer and elder. "A shot no other brave could have made, including my cousin."

Old Grandfather frowned and the sourgrass thudded against his chin. He tossed it aside and directed a bulbous finger at Totka. "Totka Lawe tell your cousin what he should have been aiming for."

Totka hedged, not appreciating once again being compared to his cousin or being dragged into what was certain to become an admonition. He gouged the earth with his toe. "At nothing, Old Grandfather, for to disrespect one's totem animal is to dishonor oneself." He bathed each word—words Lance knew frontward and backward—in passive tones.

When Old Grandfather nodded, his white braids touched his belly. "And why should that concern us?"

"Because it invites the spirits' anger."

Old Grandfather hummed an agreement. "And?"

Totka inwardly sighed and tried to ignore the sting of Lance's eye. "And puts a man at risk of being struck with calamity." It was a fact that had been drilled into them since they could don their own breechcloths, but Lance had never been a boy to take an affront sitting down, not even, apparently, from his totem animal.

"Soon you will begin your final challenges to become warriors. Put away your blowguns and think as men." He split his cool gaze evenly between them, but it may as well have been a single dart to Lance's pride.

Lance glared at Totka. How was it his poor choices often became Totka's fault? Totka corralled his returning glare as Old Grandfather's crinkled eyes shifted to the field and went pensive.

41

Sensing a lecture in the making, Totka resumed his cross-legged position and laid his bow across his knees. The wind whirred through the stalks, rustling their leaves and carrying back the lush, honey-like scent of new corn, of green spring.

"See how Earth Woman provides for us?" The ancient one swept his arm over the field. "She gives us the three sisters, corn, beans, and squash. Always remember that this land is our Mother, and just as her spirits help us every day, it is our duty and honor to live in harmony and balance in all ways, respecting both the red and the white."

Old Grandfather droned, and Totka's mind began to lose focus, but Lance leaned in eagerly. "There is no question I was born red, Old Grandfather, and before my hairs are gray, I intend to be Kossati's **Great Warrior**." Head war chief.

Lips bunching over bare gums, Old Grandfather studied him. "Red suits you. You will be a great warrior, but not the Great Warrior you wish to be. You have not the disposition for it."

A quiet harrumph jolted Lance's torso, and Totka looked hurriedly away, not caring to see the disapproval rumpling Old Grandfather's placid expression. A flock of crows was alighting in the nearby treetops, their black feathers sleek and shiny. Totka would be busy chasing them soon.

"And what of Totka? Will he become the Great Warrior?"

Totka's gaze swung from the crows to Lance.

"There is little Totka Lawe does not excel at," Old Grandfather said, and Totka returned his sight to the birds. This time to avoid Lance.

"His skill with the bow and his steady judgment will make him a worthy warrior, but he does not have the proper fire within to be a Red Stick. He was born white and has yet to bring his energy into harmony with his white tendencies: peace, council, medicine, the care of the helpless ones."

"What?" Totka burst out louder than intended. "No, Grandfather. I am Wolf." Protector, aggressor, hunter. "My color is red. My pawa is a Red Stick, and I will be as well."

"Since when does Totka contradict his elders?" Old Grandfather said.

The disapproval Totka had tried to avoid was levied against him in full. His lashes fell, but before he could formulate an apology, Old Grandfather continued. "You were born a man of counsel, a **White Stick**. Beware of misplaced desires. A warrior's rank will bring you much pain." Without so much as a breath of pause, he directed his attention to Lance. "Before the sun has left the sky, you will purge with bloodletting."

"Yes, Old Grandfather," Lance replied with the requisite submission, but when the aged peace micco bent to search out fresh sourgrass, Lance's face scrunched with displeasure.

Totka harbored a little displeasure of his own. Old Grandfather recommended he become a peace micco? A man of council? Not likely. A knower? Absolutely not. When had Old Grandfather's mind begun to slip?

Totka stood and led the way to the birds, which were circling the corn. Lance walked morose at his side. "It was a well-placed shot," Totka said. "I could not have made it." The statement was only half true; it *was* an excellent shot.

As expected, the concession appeased Lance. His footfall regained its usual spring. "True and true. Race you around the field!" Not waiting for a reply, he took off.

Whooping like the warrior on the rise that he was, Totka took chase. He could leap like a deer, but in a distance race or sprint, Lance won every time. The perfect healing tonic for his wounded pride. Maybe Totka should be a **medicine maker**, after all. His laughter at the idea carried him around the last corner.

The day dragged long, hot, and dull until Long Arrow arrived with a request for Totka to escort Leaping Waters to Lachlan Gibb's trading post.

While pondering it, Totka fingered the prickle of hair on his upper lip. He would rather not see those bruises again or repeat a butchered goodbye. And he would rather not anger his cousin.

He eyed his friend, probing for more, for why he wasn't taking her himself, but before Totka broke through Long Arrow's expressionless mask, Lance spoke.

"Why is she going to the Scotsman's post?"

A hardness came over Long Arrow that protruded his jaw. It would have made Totka shudder had it been directed at him, but it was not. Neither was it directed at Lance but at some distant point only Long Arrow could see. He said nothing, so Totka did.

"She will work for the white trader until the leaves turn color, to bring home trade goods, and to—" He flicked his eyes to Long Arrow and held his tongue until his friend gave the smallest of terse nods. "And to keep her safe."

Lance's shoulders fell along with his expression, but within moments he'd collected both as a series of shifts took place behind his eyes: understanding, surrender, grief over the necessity of it all.

Totka had experienced the same in the dark hours before the previous night's sleep when Long Arrow had knocked on their doorpost and requested help. Nokose was to have taken her to Lachlan Gibb's when he returned from Tuskegee, but her situation had grown dire, and Long Arrow would delay no longer.

Lance set his jaw. "I should be the one to take her." He picked up a small stone with his toes and turned it over in his hand, then forced a laugh and tossed the pebble at Totka's chest. "Because you will lose your way."

With the stone's thump, Totka felt his defenses rise. Once again, he'd become the escape for Lance's embarrassment.

"It's Lance who has lost his way," Long Arrow said, giving Lance his back, "for he believes he will wed my sister when she is of age. I've heard our mothers speaking. I do not like that the women consult each other without asking Nokose Fixico's opinion or my own."

Long Arrow had been angry at Lance since he'd stolen a kiss from Leaping Waters last summer and bragged about it to every boy in the talwa.

44

"It is the way of things," Totka said. Although the women would not be speaking of the children's shared future if Lance had not expressed serious interest in it. "You will not change generations of tradition."

"Can I not?" One of Long Arrow's brows popped skyward, a challenge if Totka ever saw one.

Lance slung an arm across the back of Long Arrow's shoulders. "You will rear her children no matter the man she marries. Would you not rather her husband be your best friend?"

Lashes lifting, Long Arrow pierced Totka with his gaze. "I would."

Totka's heel slid backwards; his head jerked the same direction. "Are we women? Enough talk of marriage. I want my cousin to tell me—when have I ever lost my way?"

Lance's face split with a grin. "You would lose your way in the maize field."

Totka took up the dare. "I could run through the field lengthwise ten times before you could reach a count of fifty."

Long Arrow pushed a fist into Totka's shoulder. "Ignore him."

The statement only fueled Lance's eagerness to compete. "I could do it in a count of forty."

Long Arrow laughed, exposing dimples. Undeniably, he was Leaping Waters' brother. They might be twins but for their gender and age. And where Leaping Waters was gentle and moldable, Long Arrow was flinty.

Totka tossed his quiver aside. "Very well. A count of forty, in nothing but our skin."

The added challenge snapped Long Arrow's jaw shut and protruded his eyes.

The razor-edged corn leaves would leave their mark. Even so, Lance began stripping. "Whoever is fastest escorts Leaping Waters to the trading post."

Long Arrow shook his head at Lance. "Slice yourself to pieces if you are fool enough, but you will not escort my sister."

"You would send Totka but not me?"

"I am a doting brother and like to give my sister what she wants. And what she wants is for Totka Lawe to walk her to the trading post." Long Arrow mimicked her pronunciation of his name, a detail that surely escaped Lance. He looked to Totka. "Will you take her or not?"

Leaping Waters' big brown eyes, rimmed with thick lashes, materialized in his mind. She trusted him, had asked for him. She, a girl who never asked anything of anyone, only to be left in peace.

But clan came first. Always. Forever.

He collected his quiver, took up his bow, and turned his feet toward home. "Tell Leaping Waters I wish her well."

Chapter 3

Little Chestnut Month (September) 1808, six winters later

Fire Maker pulled his pudgy hand from Totka's and trotted to an anthill rising from the roadside.

"Remember what happened last time you disturbed the ants," Totka called after the three-year-old, but the warning may as well have been an invitation.

The boy squatted, breechcloth crimping on the ground, and poked his wooden knife into the center of the hill. In all his winters, had the boy ever heeded a warning?

Totka timed his arrival to give the ants an opportunity to exact their revenge. At his nephew's shriek, he swooped the child up, then picked a few ants from his wriggling toes and two tears from his flushed cheeks. "What did I tell you? It is a good thing I am here to look out for you, little big man, or those ants might have eaten your toes." He buried his face in Fire Maker's plump belly and pretended to gnaw, growling like an angry wolf.

Squealing with laughter, Fire Maker pushed at Totka, then changed tactics, dug his fingers into Totka's **roached** hair, and returned the assault. An admirable response. A warrior's response.

"Aaah! My ear!" Totka said. "What have you done to my ear? You are too vicious a beast. We must shake the animal out of you before you reach your grandmother's lodge, or she will never allow you near." In truth, the boy's grandmother would sooner go hungry until the corn ripened before denying Nokose's son access to her

47

lodge. Totka flipped the boy upside down and, holding him by the ankles, gave him a good shake. "Is the animal out yet?" he said above the boy's peals of laughter.

Fire Maker gasped but found the power to give another wolfish imitation.

"No? Perhaps I should *fling* the creature out of you." He made good on the threat and swung the child like a pendulum.

Raining drool, Fire Maker chortled and snorted so hard he could scarcely breathe. Yet he found the presence of mind to snatch for the tasseled sash about Totka's waist. Feminine laughter joined theirs, causing Totka's head to whip about.

Leaping Waters and Lance, who endlessly, agonizingly teetered on the edge of binding their lives, had come up behind them and were watching the creature-extraction with a mixture of delight and boredom.

Totka chose to ignore his cousin's mood, which had been dour for more moons than Totka could recall, and focused instead on the woman—the sunshine in her smile, the sweet innocence in her eyes, anything other than the soft curves of her figure. "What say you, Leaping Waters? Have I succeeded in making him a boy again?"

Her forefinger landed on her chin in a thoughtful pose. "Hmm. It's hard to tell. That might be a tail I see tucked between his legs."

"I am a boy again! I am a boy!" Fire Maker said, arms flailing, fingers snatching for Totka's shirt.

Totka's muscles burned, but he lifted the child higher to look him in the eye. "Are you certain? If I must, I'll find energy enough to swing through the evening and into the night."

"Yes, Pawa." He huffed through cheeks that hung the wrong direction and turned his watering eyes into slits. "The beast . . . fell out."

"I see it!" Leaping Waters pounced and made a squashing motion with her heel. "There. We are free of it."

Totka set Fire Maker on his feet and laughed with Leaping Waters while the boy teetered with dizziness. Her laugh was a beautiful tinkling sound, like the waters for which she was named. It was a rare sound too; although, since last spring when Strong Deer fell over in a drunken stupor and never rose again, it had become more frequent.

Lance, however, did not appear to appreciate it for what it was. His pinched expression was a damper to her spark. His mind was clearly elsewhere, then she noticed his aloofness and her dimples dissolved.

When Fire Maker had regained his balance, Totka pointed down the path. "Do you see Leaping Waters' lodge, there? The one with the rooster strutting the storehouse ridgepole?"

"It is Grandmother Kit Fox's lodge, Pawa."

"Indeed, it is, but does not Leaping Waters live there as well? Now, I'll let you run ahead, so long you promise to stay on the path and out of anthills."

"I promise!" Fire Maker's shout trailed him as his stubby legs churned.

"He speaks to his elders as though he were their equals," Lance said, watching the boy. "You give him too many liberties."

"A more tender spirit you'll not find, Lance." Leaping Waters' rebuke was softly spoken and administered with an intimate look that unsettled and confused Totka.

The submissive downward tilt of Lance's chin, however, was not surprising; she had a soothing way about her, taming even Totka's bullheaded cousin who, nevertheless, shook his head. "He will grow into a willful man with little regard for others."

Totka straightened the flap of his breechcloth and began rolling the sleeves of his long-shirt to give himself time to cool his response. "When you become a pawa, you may demonstrate the proper way to raise a boy. Until then, I will do as I see fit with Fire Maker." He tried to meet Lance's eye, but it was fixed devotedly upon Leaping Waters who crossed the road and stepped into the forest of cattails filling a water-logged ditch.

She collected her full blue skirt in her arm and slogged through knee-deep water and shoulder-high plants. A frown creased her brow. While she moderated Lance's temperament, he agitated hers. But she could rid herself of him if she wished.

Last spring, when she reached marrying age, her lineage had given Lance permission to wed her, but the process had gone no further than his request because she neither accepted nor rejected him. To accept him, she must put out a bowl of **sofkee** and allow him to come up and drink from it.

Then, gifts would be exchanged, and even though she would still live with her mother until he finished their lodge and brought in evidence he could keep their storehouse stocked with meat, they could be intimate. To set out the dish and shoo him away from it would be to signal her disinterest, but she kept her sofkee bowl on the shelf in her grandmother's lodge and kept Lance in the pasture like a hobbled stallion.

Totka believed it was inner frailty that controlled her, and it aggravated him almost as much as it did Lance. He alternated between protecting her broken spirit and goading her to thicken her skin.

Long Arrow had confided that she simply followed his counsel above their mother's, above Nokose's, above even their clan mothers'. Why he would counsel her in such a manner, he wouldn't say, but in all the seasons he'd been her guardian he'd done well by her. Nokose had been a token authority figure, for Long Arrow saw that his sister lacked for nothing.

In a moment, however, she would need a knife to harvest the shoots. Palming the handle of his blade, Totka gave Lance the opportunity to notice her need, before giving him up as too distracted. He reached Leaping Waters in the exact moment she realized the plants were too mature to yank from the mire.

They exchanged smiles, but as the knife swapped hands, they took care not to touch. With the Muscogee-Choctaw stickball match only eight days away, he could not risk having his masculine strength and skills diminished by the power of a female.

"Are you on your way to see the progress we've made clearing the land?" Totka's thumb went to his hand where the skin had roughened from the use of ax and saw. They were white man's tools, and it had been difficult to convince his traditionalist cousin to use them. But he'd wanted Totka's help desperately enough to relent.

Leaping Waters' hesitation notwithstanding, Lance was pressing on, moving forward as though she were as eager as he to join their lives. As always, Totka stood at his cousin's side, supporting, encouraging; although, each new moon, it became more trying to do so.

And more painful, for the further he and Lance drifted apart, the closer he became to Leaping Waters. A most inconvenient development and one that could not possibly be escaping Lance's notice.

She dipped her arm into the water, and the stalk swayed with her sawing. "We are. Lance tells me he'll soon begin the lodge." That telltale crease deepened as her eyes darted to Lance and away. "May I keep the knife until I see you again?"

He nodded. Did she know he meant to wait for her in her grandmother's lodge? The subtle tilt of her lips satisfied him that she did.

Chiding himself for the small betrayal, he removed his ball, the *pokko*, from its pouch and lobbed it at Lance, who sparked to life and snatched it out of the air.

"Last ball practice at sunrise," Totka said. Eight cane slivers remained in Pawa's **broken days**, a way to track time. When the last sliver in the counting bundle was snapped in half, the assigned day for the match that would settle the land dispute with the Choctaws would have arrived. "What do you think? Are we ready?"

Lance flicked the soft, palm-sized pokko high into the air above his head. "The Tuskegee players still buck Pawa like unbroken ponies." The pokko landed with a smack in the cup of his hand. "If they cannot learn to play as one body, we may as well shake arms with the Long Hairs and bid Beaver Lake farewell."

Totka glanced down the lane at Fire Maker, who had become distracted by a patch of fluffy dandelions. Leaping Waters had been about that age when the Choctaws stormed Kossati. Shortly after, his father and grandfather had returned, and not waiting for Totka's Pawa Cetto Imala, they pursued the Choctaws to their village where they were told the guilty party had intended only to plunder, that the deaths had been a tragic, drunken mistake.

Lies.

Totka's young eyes had watched the torch being lit, seen the black evil on the face of the one who'd hurled it. But Totka's grandfather, Wild Edge, had thrown Wolf Clan into disarray by, without due authority, showing mercy and cancelling the blood debt. Despite his grief and anger, Gray Hawk had supported the decision, and Wolf, to not stir up war, let the ruling stand.

Pawa Cetto Imala, Totka's mother's brother, had not.

Over the moons following the tragedy, Gray Hawk returned to his tribal talwa a widower, and Pawa and Totka had clung to each other through their mutual hatred for the Long Hairs, hatred as broad and miry as the Okefenokee Swamp.

Totka clapped arms with Lance and pulled him close so that his hard eyes could not be avoided. "The day I shake arms with a single Long Hair is the day I take the spirits' path."

Lance pressed the pokko into Totka's palm with a savage smirk. "Then we had better whip these raw players into submission and teach them the correct way to smash an opponent. What do you say to that, Brother?"

Contentment washed through Totka's chest. How many seasons had it been since Lance used that term? Too many. He increased the crush on Lance's arm and contorted his lips into an equally devious grin. "I say we use weighted sticks and aim for the Long Hairs' skulls."

They shared a laugh before Totka sobered. "In truth, what Muscogee warrior enjoys submitting to the headman of a different fire? But the Tuskegees are no fools. They understand what is at

52

stake. Tomorrow they'll come around. Watch and see."

"Let's hope you are right." Lance jutted his chin toward Leaping Waters' compound. "Your gunpowder of a nephew has abandoned his seed blowing and is chasing a cat."

Totka left at a trot, rescued Fire Maker from the hissing feline, and entered Nokose's clan compound. He swatted the boy's rump to usher him through the doorway to the summer lodge.

Ayo, Leaping Waters' mother, worked the small family garden. Totka lifted a hand to her as he ducked inside the lodge. It was empty except for the **Beloved Woman** who occupied her little corner of the room, a duffle blanket draping her shoulders despite the warmth in the spring air. Her protruding cheekbones gave way to cheeks sunken into a toothless mouth.

"Grandmother Kit Fox." Totka raised his voice to make up for her lack of hearing "You have an important visitor."

She spread the blanket wide and welcomed her grandson's child with a merry cackle.

"A tale, a tale! Give me a tale, Grandmother!" Fire Maker chanted as he snuggled onto her lap.

Totka picked up the gillnet Long Arrow's father had begun weaving. Itco Fixico wouldn't mind Totka occupying his hands while the boy visited his grandmother.

"Which tale shall I tell my warrior child?"

"The bear and the night and the day."

"You wish to hear about your father's namesake yet again? Very well, I begin. Nokose, the bear, presided over the animal council. The elders debated how the day and night should be divided."

The tale continued, but Totka focused on the nettle-twine web that expanded between his hands. He tuned out the story, as well as the next and the next, hearing nothing but the rasp of cordage against calluses until the breeze passing through the sparsely slatted walls carried Leaping Waters' voice to him.

Judging from its direction, he decided she had gone to Ayo in the garden, but she would come to him soon. His lips curved. She always did.

The women entered together, Ayo's smile only slightly smaller than that of her daughter. Her eyes were small and closely set; they missed nothing and kept a world of schemes stowed behind them. "What quick work you've made of that net, Totka. My husband will be pleased." No matter her mood, the woman's voice was always a scratchy whine.

Leaping Waters knelt before him and began straightening the knotted cordage that ran over his bare leg and fed into his hand. "Grandmother Kit Fox has about put Fire Maker to sleep." She spoke in wistful, hushed tones.

And she was correct. The old woman's wrinkled voice purred low and hypnotic, and Fire Maker's lids sagged. He would be drooling on her bosom before long.

Totka settled in for a lengthier stay than planned. Far be it from him to wake a napping child or cut short time spent with Leaping Waters. "When do you leave for Lachlan's place?"

"Are you fretting I'll not be in attendance at the ball play?"

"Of course, I am fretting. You are my *sabia*, my magic amulet."

She chuckled and unwound another length of twine. "Will you set me on a post under the sun?"

"Only if you promise to sparkle. I would be loath to tell Pawa that Grandmother Sun has chosen to keep me out of the game."

Ayo began removing limp nettle fibers from where they soaked in a wide clay vessel. "No fear of that. Leaping Waters sparkles every time you are near."

Neither of them could deny it. "Twinkling sabia or not," Leaping Waters said, "the game awaits you, and I would sooner spit on the fire than miss Kossati's champion ball player dominate the field."

"Kossati's? Try the confederacy's," Ayo said as she arranged the drenched fibers into neat rows. "I hear Pauwocte's Great Warrior would not proceed with game negotiations until Cetto Imala, Lance, and Totka had been assured participation."

"Very well. The confederacy's champion," Leaping Waters

amended with an airy laugh.

"Hardly." Totka looped the twine around the mesh stick and, with practiced speed, created another knot in the chain. He tamed an impish smile. "There's no denying Kossati loves me. And now that I think on it, I was the top pick for the Ockchoy chief." The next loop formed under his quick fingers. "There are also those in Tuskegee who think I—"

The skein of cordage hit him square between the eyes, and he laughed, rubbing the spot with the heel of his hand and lifting his brow at Leaping Waters in playful admiration. "A fine arm you have there. Perhaps you should take my place in the game as lead shooter."

The **Upper Town** chiefs—amid much debate—had selected only their most valued players to represent the Muscogees, and it was no surprise to anyone that Totka and his kinsmen had been numbered among the thirty to take the field.

Some said their bones were made of ball sticks and their blood, the ceremonial white drink. Others whispered sorcery. Their proficiency, however, lay not in the medicine herbs tucked inside the hide-covered pokko but in their years of dedication to practice and their use of stratagem.

Before agreeing to let his household join the team, Pawa had laid out his own stipulations: every player must commit to a full month of intense practice on Kossati's ball field, and the team must have a chief—himself.

The concept of naming a chief for a ball game created a stir, but Pawa's confidence and initiative had won them over and not a man of the remaining twenty-seven had refused.

Leaping Waters retrieved the uncoiled skein and began winding it anew. "Me on the ball field? That would be a sight! No, no. Keeping Fire Maker out of my trade beads is plenty enough sport for me."

"You never said when you plan to leave."

"At the next full moon."

Ten sleeps hence.

"So soon? It feels as though you've only just returned."

"A full six moons have passed, Totka Lawe."

His hands stilled as he let the sound of his name on her lips linger at his ears. He would miss it. He always did when she went away.

She looked at him with her usual serene expression, tenderness in her eyes. It was the same look she'd given him since they were children, but it wasn't until last spring that it had started to have an unnerving effective on him, and when she left, he would miss that too.

"You speak the white man's English well enough," he said, "and Nokose and your father make no demands of your labor. Must you continue to leave us?"

A shadow of humor softened her mouth, and when he tugged for more twine she resisted. "Why should they demand anything of me when they have you to do the work for them?"

Weary beyond patience of her coming and going, he snorted and hauled at the twisted fibers. "*Someone* has to be your backbone."

The twine gave way, but her expression fell. "This will be my last season at the trading post."

"Good," he barked out.

"Lance does not approve of my interest in the ways of the pale faces."

Was that why she'd chosen this as her last season at the trading post? Angry heat flushed Totka from the chest up. His instinctive response confused and embarrassed him, which only furthered his agitation. "If you were a stronger woman—as I've pushed you to be time and again—you'd do as you pleased, not as my irrationally traditional cousin dictates."

"Forgive me, Totka Lawe. I-I know I can be . . . I try to be strong, I do, but . . ."

Remorse needled his conscience. At times, he forgot her spirit still flinched from the abuse Strong Deer had inflicted. A stronger spirit would have borne it with fewer scars, but Leaping Waters was not strong.

She was a polished bow, curved and beautiful but whittled too thin and harshly bent one too many times. With each reminder of her fractured spirit, Totka chided himself for failing to guide her properly in repairing it.

"I was cruel," he murmured, then bent and wished it wouldn't sap his strength to touch her. Instead, he captured her eyes until she blinked away her instinctive withdrawal. There was no counting the number of times they'd done the same.

Sensing Ayo's curiosity, he pulled away and chose a safer topic; although, English markings were barely that. "Tell me. Do the symbols still daunt you?"

Chin tucked, she busied her fingers in the twine. "They do. The counting symbols, I've mastered as well as the spoken language, but the speaking symbols, ack. They mock me. I interpret them with no trouble, but to reproduce them . . ." She sighed. "They must be arranged in special order, and there is no true guide to follow. No sooner do I remember one than I forget another."

"You're too hard on yourself. Who else in Kossati can interpret talking leaves? Besides your pawa Nokose, that is." Although, he never exercised the skill for fear of being branded a witch.

"No one, but"—she lowered her voice to a harsh whisper—"the fear and willful ignorance of our people should not sway my own convictions. And yes, I include you in that group." The tease resurfaced and twitched her lips.

He shrugged. "I have no use for English. Will it make my arrows fly straighter or strengthen my senses on the hunt? No, it will not. And forming a word perfectly with ink will not make your squash grow faster or your corn sweeter. So explain again why you put such weight in the white man's markings."

The answer, he knew well enough, but her passion in the telling was something to be enjoyed repeatedly. He often contradicted her solely to see her light up and twinkle like a sun-blessed sabia, as she did now.

"We are at a disadvantage to the whites. Their resources are vast, and their knowledge of manufacture, especially weapons, is frightening. The timepiece alone is a marvel." She leaned in and gripped his legging, and Totka knew in his gut she'd never spoken of these things with Lance. He wouldn't stand for it, and it gave Totka smug satisfaction to know she shared her deepest feelings with him alone. "Have you seen a timepiece? It is a tool that divides the day into every breath a man takes."

Totka smiled at her exuberance and goaded her to stoke her flame. "And why would I care to do such a thing? Sunrise, high sun, sunset—they are all we need."

She swiped the air between them, erasing his argument. "But one of the whites' greatest powers is talking through paper over long distances. The Great Father in Washington can make powerful speeches to us without ever leaving his lodge."

"Witchcraft!" Ayo rasped and put a palm to her forehead, fear shrinking her voice. "The knower portends illness on those who make the leaves talk."

"The knower is a fraud," Totka mumbled.

Leaping Waters caught his eye and hummed agreement, prompting a questioning cock of his brow.

Trapping two plies of fiber between her fingers, Ayo seemed to hear only the worry spinning inside her head. "Why have I permitted my daughter this practice? One day, it will be her ruin."

"It will give me freedom and respect among the whites, Mother. If we are to understand our neighbors, if we are to be their equals, we must learn to talk with parchment and ink."

Ayo clicked her tongue in reproach, and Leaping Waters fell silent.

To rekindle that smile, Totka gave a playful tug of the cordage, but without looking up, she released it and smoothed her skirt over the tops of her thighs, her mind some place other than Grandmother Kit Fox's lodge.

The rumbles of sleep—from both child and old woman—

58

dominated the room until Leaping Waters ventured to speak again. "Lachlan Gibb's apprentice has taught me more than symbols."

"Oh? Are you studying to be an iron-beater?" With his mesh stick, Totka poked at the slender muscle of her arm and donned a corkscrew smile. "No, that cannot be it."

The banter was lost on her. "He has writings, a good and sacred writing. One created long before the time of the Muscogees. Its teachings say —"

"Ay! Daughter, you weary me," Ayo said in as firm a voice as the woman was capable.

Grandmother Kit Fox snorted awake, but Fire Maker slept on.

"Forgive me, Mother. I do not mean to be wearisome."

Part of Totka wanted to urge her to speak on, to tell him what it was about this writing that fascinated her. She'd never spoken of it before, and he'd been confident there was nothing they'd not shared.

The other part of him withdrew like a crayfish to his rock, pinchers facing out and snapping. If he suspected correctly, Leaping Waters had been listening to a pale-face holy man, and nothing healthful could come of such wonderings.

It was good this was her last season with Scotsman Lachlan Gibb.

"Help me, Leaping Waters. Twist these." Ayo passed her a handful of fibers. "Long Arrow's wife was here a short while ago."

"Was she?" Since his friend had wed and moved to his wife's tribal talwa, Totka rarely saw him. "And how is your son?"

"He's been struck with fever," Leaping Waters supplied. With her fingertips, she twisted a single fiber in opposite directions until the tension created an eye.

"Is he in danger of death?"

"It is hard to know," Ayo said. "Dove was fretful, but she is often overly concerned. Leaping Waters hoped to visit him this afternoon, but it is a long way for a woman's arms to row." Her voice rose with blunt suggestion.

Leaping Waters kept her face in shadow and rolled faster.

He would love nothing more than to row Leaping Waters upriver to Pigeon Roost, but he knew better than to feed his desires. "Shall I fetch Lance? He would be happy to—"

Leaping Waters' head popped up. She slammed him with the hurt in her brimming eyes, then stood abruptly. Her newly twisted cordage and bundle of fibers fell to Totka's feet.

His mouth dropped open, and he shot up. "Leaping Waters, wait."

But she was already in the yard, creating a cloud of dust and holding up a silencing hand.

He stared after her until she disappeared around the corner. The weeds in the garden would feel the aftermath of her hurt. They could blame him for their untimely deaths, but what else was he to do? Betray his cousin?

Never.

If she would only reject the man, free his heart to seek a partner elsewhere. No, that would make no difference. Leaping Waters was off-limits to Totka whether she rejected Lance or not.

"Your cousin has thrown poorly." Grandmother Kit Fox finger-combed Fire Maker's sweaty hair off his forehead. "His stick has not struck as near the **chunkey** stone as yours."

The woman spoke in riddles. Did she mean Totka was competing with his cousin for Leaping Waters' affection? "I've thrown no stick." He wasn't even in the game.

"Totka Lawe's stick was cast long ago, before the stone began rolling. I wagered on yours being the one to strike nearest and win her heart, and I have come away the richer for it."

Sticks, chunkey, wagers. Had age finally caught up to the elder? Totka frowned, plopped back onto the bench, and picked up the net.

"Imagine a life without your cousin." Kit Fox's challenge was presented slowly, deliberately. "Where would your heart lead you? To whom?"

His hands fell limp to his knees, and his eyes wandered to the spot he'd last seen Leaping Waters. The dust had settled, but it was just beginning to stir inside him. On the battlefield of his mind, he faced an old palisade—one he'd erected around Leaping Waters. Its pickets were meant to keep him out, to protect his cousin, their bond, their lineage.

But if his cousin were no impediment, if there were no pickets, what would Totka do? Would he have escorted Leaping Waters to Pigeon Roost? Would he have gone after her just now? Would the field he and Lance were clearing be his own?

The thought was a tomahawk blow to the palisade. A ray of light shone through the fissure. Light so pure and sweet and right it burned his conscience.

Troubled, he told himself to shrink away from it. Then, in direct disobedience, he took to his feet and pointed them toward the garden. He was stooping to exit the lodge when Grandmother Kit Fox spoke again.

"Take my granddaughter a digging stick. She will have forgotten it."

"Yes, Grandmother Kit Fox."

"And Totka Lawe?" She adjusted the boy's flumping body. "Love her if you must, but be warned. If you bring her anything other than a digging stick, your cousin will raise the red club against you."

"Do you mean if Totka brings her a buck?" Ayo's tiny eyes went wide.

Grandmother Kit Fox rolled a hand in the air. "A buck, a bear, a lodge."

If she had been anyone other than a Beloved Woman, a revered elder, Totka would have burst out with a laugh. "If I chose to pursue Leaping Waters, my cousin would not kill me for it."

Thick lids pinching, Grandmother Kit Fox grunted. "He would try."

He hated to contradict the elder, but she was quite wrong.

Ayo tsked and splashed water while swirling an arm through the vessel for more fibers. "Lance and Totka are as close as brothers. There would be no killing."

"Ayo is right. Lance would never lift a hand against me. Not for a woman, not for anything."

"Ignore the warning if you wish, but I say your love for him has blinded you to his ways. The many winters you have spent in the shadow of his resentment has made you like a potted frog to a boil. Today, you feel no pain, see no danger. But tomorrow, you will be dead."

He wanted to argue with the old woman, but his breeding and respect for her won out. "Maddo, Grandmother Kit Fox. Your warning is heard. I will think on it." It would be a pointless exercise, though, because there would never be a day he would provide Leaping Waters a buck, a doe, a plot with a lodge.

A child? His blood floundered in his veins, betraying him. He snipped off the thought and left to find the woman.

She was as he'd suspected—on hands and knees, ripping weeds from the bed with a cyclone's efficiency. While he regretted being the source of her distemper, he couldn't help but applaud her courage to display it. On his way to her, he collected the hoe from the storehouse.

A hearty tug released the root she labored over. "It's too late, Totka Lawe. Too late." Fists filled with weeds, she sat back on her heels and looked up at him, lower lip trapped between her teeth, big brown eyes bright with tears.

His chest constricted. My, but she was beautiful. She'd always been a pretty girl, but it was not until recently he'd allowed himself to appreciate her loveliness as a woman. Now, it took every effort not to.

"Not too late at all. I'll take you." Lance would be angry, but he would recover. Eventually. "If we leave now, we can arrive in Pigeon Roost with the setting sun," Totka said.

Her lip went pale with the force of her bite, and instead of recognizing the offer, she continued weeding more furiously than before.

He eased himself into a squat before her, struck a flint in his mind, and let the sparks ignite. For once, he considered his own

62

wishes, considered what might be, what *could* be if he were a more selfish man.

Where would your heart lead you? To whom?

Where? Nowhere, for he'd already arrived. If there were no impediment, he would have his clan mothers bid for Leaping Waters before this moon gave way to the next.

He gritted his teeth and strangled the digging stick he held erect between them. "Have you changed your mind about visiting your brother?"

With a long exhale, Leaping Waters sat back again on her calves. "You were right to suggest Lance. Best I go with him or not at all." She loosed her weeds and rubbed his taut, white knuckles, disquiet boring into the smooth skin of her brow.

He should pull away. He should *run* away. With her.

Straight and sleek, her hair fell about her shoulders like black silk. It veiled all but the edges of the serpentine tattoo that wound down her neck and had the young men in the warriors' lodge lusting.

He'd shouted at the lot of them and threatened even the brawniest with a severed nose should he think to besmear her name again.

But in truth, he knew that longing. Better than all the rest, he knew what it was to want her. Telling himself he had yet to begin his three-day purification and thus would be unharmed, he reached out, brushed her hair aside, and traced the swirling indigo line from her ear to the hollow at her neck. As he touched her, he could find no rebuke strong enough to stay the hunger. It was an old, gray hunger, one long suppressed and eager to fly from his tongue. With a swig of reality, he washed down the beautiful things he wanted to tell her and satisfied himself by reversing the trail.

She held perfectly still, allowing him this liberty, and he knew, like the earth beneath his feet, that he could carry her to the shelter of the cornfield and touch her to his heart's content, and she wouldn't utter a peep of protest. She never did about anything.

The need to protect her from those who would take advantage of her submissive nature rose up within him like hot tar, as it had since they were children. Presently, she needed protecting from himself.

He withdrew and tilted the digging stick her way. "Spare your back. Take the hoe."

Lashes falling, she took the stick from him. "They speak of us, you know. In the square, in the fields. The whole of Kossati."

A shot of nerves zipped across him. "And what is the whole of Kossati saying about you and Lance?"

Standing, she slipped him a piqued look and used the pointed end of the digging stick to attack the base of a weed that invaded a pumpkin vine. "And I'd always believed you to be an intelligent man."

"No need to bare your claws." Chuckling, he thumped her foot with a clod of dirt. "All right, so tell me. Why do they speak of *us*? What do they say?"

She grunted through the next jab. "Does it matter? You are as silent as rock on the matter of *us*. And equally dumb."

His knees snapped with his quick rise. "Why so testy?"

"Because my patience is spent, and because I am afraid. Afraid of-of . . ." The forceful shake of her head swished her unbound hair about her face. "It no longer matters." She rammed the blade into the soil, missing a weed and severing a vine. Seeming not to notice, she worked on, digging rigorously.

He gripped the rod, stilling it midair. "It does matter. What are you afraid of?"

Her sod-encrusted fingers came to hover over his cheek and filled his nose with the sharp scent of pigweed and the comfort of moist earth. "Of being without my Wolf." Lance was Wolf same as Totka, but if her eyes had a mouth, they would speak Totka's name.

"Am I going on a journey? No, that would be you. It is your choice to leave." His deliberately evasive answers made him the dumb rock she accused him of being, but what good would it do to speak of what could never be? "Set aside your fears, Leaping Waters. They consume you and make you a lesser woman. And while I am

64

being silent and dumb on the matter, I'll add that you cannot continue to drag my cousin along like a puppy on a tether. Put out your sofkee, woman. Choose. Either let him drink or set him free."

"Choose? I have no choice. If I deny him the sofkee, who do you think he will blame?"

"If my cousin makes you fearful of anything, then you are right. You have no choice—turn him away. I am man enough to handle whatever consequences may come."

"Man enough? Why speak of my fear, when it is your own that's kept you from acting on your love for me?"

Love? She was becoming bolder, forcing him to face the truth.

But he couldn't dwell there, so he let anger burn a path through his middle and up his throat. "You would accuse *me* of fear? The gate to the spirits' road has become familiar to me. I've faced it many times, and never once have I cowered or trembled in its presence. I have taken six scalps. One more and I'll be a ranking warrior. No, woman. You are wrong. It is love for my cousin and his happiness that has kept us apart. Not fear!"

By the time Totka was done snarling, he had reduced her to a mess of tears. Confronted with them, he was unsure whether to give himself a whipping or shake a measure of sense into her.

She lifted poignant, damp eyes to him. "Not fear of death, Totka Lawe. Fear of loss."

His insides jolted. The talwa's most skilled bowman couldn't have shot a straighter arrow than Leaping Waters. But why was he shocked? No one knew his soul better than she. Not even the cousin he called *brother*. She knew his old nemesis like it was her own. In truth, it had become just that.

She sank to her knees and began pulling up the weeds she'd loosened before.

Propped against the tool's handle, he watched her tidy a sweet potato mound and tried not to envision her working their own garden while swollen with their child.

She swiped the back of her hand over the moisture dotting her hairline and left a streak of dirt. "My clan mothers would have accepted you as readily as they have your cousin. Any connection with Wolf is a good connection. Our only trouble, my love, is that you fear losing your cousin more than you fear losing me." The tear-filled smile she hoisted sent a pang through him, but he could not contradict her.

"Lineage above all," he said. Above talwa. Above marriage. Above a man's will and wishes. Always.

Lineages had segmented over far less than love. And if he could help it, he would not lose one more member of his. Not to death, not to strife.

She nodded, tears slipping. "I have always known it was so, have I not? We would be better people without our fears. Happier. Do you know what I fear most? Making the wrong choice and losing you both." The dirt beneath her nails held more interest than Totka's eyes. "But you make it easier for me. Tell your cousin there will be a bowl of sofkee by the corncrib at sundown. I'll let him drink, and when I return, we will wed. It is best. For all his crafty ways, Lance loves me and will make an agreeable partner."

So, she would finally bind herself to Lance. The knowledge, the finality of her tone, struck him harder than he'd anticipated. Mouth agape and throat drying, Totka stared at her, trying to process all she'd said. "When did you say?" Never?

"Sundown."

At sundown. Lance would be pleased. There would be no long wait for the cover of dark when a maiden snuck off to share her blanket with her intended.

A crushing weight settled on Totka's chest as though Grandmother Kit Fox's chunkey stone had rolled into it and Leaping Waters' hoe had pierced its center. "Wait on the sokfee, Leaping Waters. Put out the bowl the morning you leave." At her series of blinks, he rushed on. "He will expect to lie with you right away."

And he would succeed because he was single-minded and commanding and she, easily bent to another's will. Totka couldn't image Leaping Waters brave enough to rebuff unwanted advances, much less give herself freely.

Lance had never understood how fragile she was, that she required a gentle voice and a gentler touch. He was a needy man, often impatient. And he would frighten her, bruise her spirit, if not her body.

Blushing like the dawn, Leaping Waters climbed off the ground and stood hunched, arms curled around her middle. Her eyes went distant. The clouds behind him floated across her glossy eyes as she stared into the sky just over his shoulder, unblinking.

Was she afraid? She'd called Lance crafty. Had he hurt her? Taken advantage of her? Or was she referring to his silver tongue?

Totka stood as near as he dared. He'd already put his stickball performance in jeopardy and would risk no more. "Are you certain this is what you want? No one will compel you to wed him or any other man. My cousin could find no better wife, and I've always wished the best for him, but if he frightens you, do not tie your body and life to his. You would live in misery. Gifts can be returned. Marriages can be dissolved. Do you hear me?"

She was lost. Buried in . . . yes, it was fear. Totka saw her future with Lance stretching out before her, one blank-eyed day after another. And it grieved him.

"Leaping Waters, what are you doing to yourself?" He whispered her name again, and this time her eyes focused and shifted to him.

She touched her lower lip with the tip of her middle finger. Dirt from it crumbled down the front of her. "He loves me. Dearly. I think . . . more than you do." There was a good chance that she, a poor judge of how love behaved, was confusing obsession for love. There was also a chance she was right.

When moisture swamped her eyes, Totka looked away. He did love her. But he loved his cousin more.

"The bowl will be by the corncrib the morning after we return from the ball play. Will you tell him?"

With a longing for her warm in his chest, Totka formed a bleak smile. It would have to be answer enough. He could manage no more.

Chapter 4

For the fourth time, Totka plunged into the **long snake**'s soothing embrace, ending his night-long purification and ritual scratching, washing away the blood that oozed from neat rows of four score marks that ran diagonally across his back, chest, and limbs. The water cleansed but left myriad stings as a reminder that he was strong and impervious to pain, and that the stickball match with their old enemy lay just the other side of the ridge.

The match was to be played on neutral ground in an unused field near the Muscogee-Choctaw border. Louder than the river's chant, Totka's blood thumped in his ears, eager for the heady rush of the game.

Twelve summers ago, Totka had sworn he would hate the Choctaws until the Master of Breath took him from This World, and that he would defeat as many as the spirits allowed.

He'd had raids in mind. Bloodshed, death, war. But the **little brother of war** would have to do for now. Besides, stickball would give plenty of opportunities to draw blood.

He emerged from the water facing east at the precise moment Grandmother Sun revealed her curved edge. A good omen. Something to counteract the powerful curses coming Totka's way. Beyond the ridge, the Choctaw conjurer was surely mentioning him by name and clan, invoking the blackest regions of the **Under World**.

Totka might distrust knowers, but he was not fool enough to make light of their incantations. Then again, he had his sabia, Leaping Waters. He imagined her wrapped in pure white hide and nestled in his pouch, and he grinned into the faithful sun.

Pawa grabbed a handful of the hair at the back of Totka's neck and gave him an affectionate shake. "What has you smiling, apart from the fact we're about to send a herd of Choctaw swine running home to their sows?"

"Thoughts of the Black Fog they're wishing upon us."

"What kind of player finds a plague humorous?" Slim Face, one of Pauwocte's defensemen scrubbed dried blood from the scratches on his arms.

With a scramble for breath, Lance surfaced beside them. Water sprayed as he flung his unshaven hair.

"The kind who has a secret amulet," Totka said.

"An amulet? Who?" Blinking away water, Lance skimmed the naked bodies of those standing nearby. "Is it powerful enough for us all?"

Pawa waded toward the bank. "Your cousin claims to have one. He has yet to reveal where he's hidden it."

Grin reappearing, Totka followed his pawa, wrung out the flap of his breechcloth—the only article of clothing allowed on the field— and let their imaginations do their worst.

His sabia would be standing on the sidelines.

Coyote, one of their most skilled stick workers, smacked Totka's hindquarters. "I bet he'll show his woman after he excites her with his stunts."

Leaping Waters' dimples came to mind, and he failed to keep the side of his mouth from twitching.

Lance sloshed noisily up from behind. "Vulgar of you to speak of sabias in such a way. And have you not heard? Totka has no woman. Maybe the game will win you one though, eh, Cousin? One of Red Thunder's daughters would be a choice celebration tonight. They've both come to watch."

"No woman?" Slim Face stopped, and Totka and Lance looked back at the confusion scrunching his skinny nose. "What of the little one who comes to watch our practices? She has ink here." He twirled his finger down the side of his neck, sending Totka's stomach on a similar trail.

Inspired by the hole Lance's gaze bore into the side of his head, Totka hurried to amend Slim Face's not-so-incorrect assessment. "You speak of Leaping Waters. My brother-in-law's niece. She comes for Lance. He and I are clearing land for their lodge."

"Oh?" Slim Face thumbed an oversized ear, looking less than convinced. "My mistake."

"A stupid one," Lance said, his voice flat. "But mistakes are allowed, so long as you make them here and not on the field."

"Excellent advice." Totka drew a deep breath and pushed against the current to begin again toward shore. "It's challenge enough to keep focus on the pokko without the complication of females."

"Agreed." Lance pounded him on a back made raw by a hundred scratches. "How is this target feeling?" Every Choctaw player would be aiming his hickory where Lance's hand now rested.

"As though it's been kissed by Grandmother Sun." And it had.

"Then we'll paint her mighty image right here, so the Long Hair fiends will think twice before striking you."

"Will you have your usual entwined snakes?"

Lance slapped his chest where the red serpents would soon reside. "A game without them would be only half a game."

"Totka! Lance!" From the grassy bank, Pawa held up their pot of slippery elm unguent. "We have prime hunting lands to take back. Finish your women's chatter later and come apply your grease."

They hurried to shore and did as instructed, applying red paint and black ash—the colors of war—and lathering on the slippery elm to make themselves more difficult for their opponents to grasp.

"Coyote," Pawa called. "Having trouble?"

The Tuskegee player, along with Crazy Stone, stood from where they'd been crouching and drawing figures in the sand. Coyote rubbed the flat of his hand over his mouth. "Remind us what the signal is to form the arrowhead play. We cannot recall."

Lance swore beneath his breath, and Pawa looked askance at the man. But Totka, who was closest, caught the edge of a smirk hidden behind Coyote's fingers. "The signal is 'your sister is a fat hog.'"

Coyote threw his head back in a laugh that sprouted tears and smeared the wet *V*s painted beneath his eyes. "Take my bear grease, Brother. Your tongue is not slick enough."

The team's cheery banter dwindled to silence as they gathered their ball-stick bundles and lined up single file to enter the field under the guidance of their medicine maker and to the booming cheers of hundreds of Muscogee spectators. Four Upper Creek talwas were represented, but visitors had come from as far as Coweta, a principle town of the Lower Creeks. If the spirits smiled their way, they would have a favorable report to carry south with them.

In all the players' preparations, none spoke of the possibility of loss. The consequences and humiliation were too terrible to vocalize. The lake and surrounding lands along their western border were too valuable to lose. Muscogee hunters had already gone on several great winter hunts in which they'd been driven off land that had been theirs for generations.

Indifferent to time-honored borders, a large band of Choctaws had crossed the Oaktebbehaw River and erected a village they'd named Beaver Lake Town. Even after several heated parleys initiated by the Upper Creek war chiefs, the Choctaws refused to withdraw to the established boundary. They claimed they had equal right since it had been theirs before Muscogee slave hunters had depleted their numbers and forced them to withdraw into the west.

This day's match was a last resort before battle; although, neither Totka nor Lance would have been put out by the opportunity to take hair.

Amid much chanting and singing punctuated by war whoops, Totka's team circled their goal post. It was a Choctaw goal, a single pole twice Totka's height driven into the ground ten strides from the field's eastern end. The players would be restricted to either throwing the pokko against the pole or touching the pole with the pokko enclosed in the pockets of their sticks.

Across the eighty rods of trampled grass, their enemy replicated the parade. Horsehair tails streamed from their breechcloths, they beat their chests with their sticks, and their ten defensemen were as large and snarly as bears.

Totka's stomach, long empty from fasting, twisted in his center. A glance at his cousin in line before him affirmed Totka was not the only one wearing tension like white paint.

Beyond them both marched Pawa. Thicker of midriff but broader of shoulder, he was every bit the seasoned, unblinking warrior—to include, expert shooter, capable defenseman, and brilliant strategist. A stick resting on each shoulder, he moved with the confidence of a man who had already won, injecting strength into Totka's blood.

White drink blood. The reminder set Totka up with a haughty smirk.

Four summers running, Kossati's team had been undefeated in the entirety of the Upper Creek towns. Totka didn't intend to break that boast here. He clacked his sticks above his head and flung a shriek into the sky loud enough to startle the **Upper World** beings. Other players followed his lead and sent the Muscogee onlookers into a frenzy of shouts and chants of victory.

They met the Choctaws midfield in two parallel lines that ran the width of the expanse. Through much taunting and cursing, they laid their sticks between them so the ball witch could assess them for equality. Once that had been determined, he spoke in Choctaw trade jargon, reminding them of the game's single rule: the hands may never touch the pokko. When he was done, he threw the pokko in the air and leapt out of the way.

Totka fell back with Pawa and the other shooters as the centers of both teams—twenty in all—collided in an elbow-throwing, knee-jabbing scrum. At the first clash of hickory, Totka's mind sharpened to a point that teetered on the location of the pokko.

At the moment, it was impossible to track.

Lance hovered on the outer edge of the struggling pack. Doubled over, sticks at the ready, he sent a constant shouted report of his position until the pokko came flying out from between Coyote's feet.

Almost faster than Totka could register, Lance had clamped the pokko between his sticks and was flying down the field, making good on his name and the swift legs Creator had given him.

The scrum broke apart too slowly for the Choctaw centers to intercept him, and their heavier outlying defensemen were as ineffective as wintering bears in pursuit of a sprinting buck.

Totka ripped a whistle through his teeth and coursed down the alley on the opposite side of Lance's zigzagged path.

While all eyes were on Lance, Pawa and his shooters formed a discreet defensive ring around Totka. Lance twisted left and hurled the pokko. Not a precision shooter, he made up for his lack of accuracy with his strength. The pokko sailed the entire width of the field and thudded to the ground five strides closer to the goal than Totka.

While the mass of defensemen and straggling centers dug in and changed course, Totka completed a running scoop, clapped the cup of the left stick over the right and shadowed a lean Pauwocte shooter who led the way to the pole. But Totka lost his leader when the man threw himself like a shield into a frontal hit.

His body flipped around and over a larger opponent who staggered and keeled, slamming to his knees, then hands, then chin.

Another Choctaw was coming full speed from the left. He hurled his stick.

Totka ducked and darted right. He leapt onto the back of the Choctaw that the Pauwocte player had taken down and flung himself into the wind. At the peak of his flight, he honed in on the pole.

Too far, too far.

But his arm thought otherwise, for it had already begun its forward motion. Committed, he followed through and snapped his wrist early to give the pokko more height. For an instant, it was a black speck against the blinding sky, then Totka was falling and his eyes filled with the Choctaw defensemen stampeding toward him.

Through their joint-rattling collision, his ears picked up the satisfying *thwack* of pokko against wood.

The sting weed he landed in pricked at his back. He kicked to free himself of the lumbering, ranting Choctaw, then noticed the near silence that blanketed the field.

Had he missed the pole? Not possible. He was as intimate with the sound of reverberating wood as he was his own voice.

"Remove yourself!" He applied the heel of his hand to the man's throat, dodged the returning blow, and bounced to his feet.

Pawa hailed him, but Totka's eye was attached to the game witch, or referee, who held his rod above his head and pointed it toward the Muscogee side of the field.

A great roar of applause raised the hair along Totka's spine and brought a sweet whiff of vindication. But he wanted to taste it, to get a mouthful. He wanted to fill his belly with it until he was sick.

Out of nowhere, Lance smacked chests with him, bumping Totka backwards several curt steps. "First point in the game is ours! And so fast they're still wondering what happened. Ha!"

Totka glanced over the tract. The Choctaw players were scattered, confusion thick in their faltering movements. Several of their shooters stood, hands on hips, staring at Totka and talking amongst themselves.

Excellent. Let them worry. They had good reason to.

Totka picked thorns from his shoulder as the game witch strode back onto the field and called for the next toss and scrum.

Lanced hooted and trotted to rejoin the centers. "Nineteen more and we send these lizards back to their holes!" The first team to drive twenty stakes into the earth would own Beaver Lake.

Over the following nine scrums, the Choctaws were like ripe berries — easily plucked and quickly devoured. By the tenth, they had found their rhythm as well as the key to weakening the Muscogees; they planted a wall between Totka and his kinsmen. But Totka took it in stride, letting them believe they'd found a solution.

The stakes in the dirt were ten to one in favor of the Muscogees and spirits were high, but he sensed an undercurrent brewing. The

Choctaws were being beaten too harshly, and they wouldn't stand for it.

But as men who had likely never applied strategy to the game, they couldn't counterattack carefully executed plays that had been drilled for precise execution. The best they could hope for was brute strength to keep the pokko out of Muscogee sticks and to keep Totka apart from the others.

But Pawa had anticipated the shift and changed tactics to compensate. Coyote and Crazy Stone were only too happy to lead the charge and take the glory, while Totka played a lesser part and rested his muscles.

The Tuskegee shooters awarded them another three stakes, but the Muscogee defensemen were tiring, and the Choctaw shooters were becoming driven by blinding anger. One put himself out of the game with a broken ankle, and another's mad drive for the pole could only be stopped by a six-man tackle that rendered him unconscious. It was paying off, however, for they each nailed a pokko to the Muscogee post, bringing the game's numbers to fourteen and eight.

When the Choctaws relaxed their guard on Totka, Pawa signaled for another shift in play. Anticipation squirmed in Totka's middle. His bruises and contusions burned like hot ash, but his legs felt as fresh as when he'd circled the goal post, and he was eager to race.

In the next scrum, Coyote gave him the chance.

Pokko nestled in his sticks, Totka sprinted for the goal. Forced to the right, he faced a loose line of Choctaws headed straight for him. Pawa rushed in from behind them and leapt onto the back of one, sending him face-first into the grass and opening a gap.

Totka hurdled his wrangling pawa, twisted away from the reaching grasp of the next nearest opponent, and kept going with hardly a beat missed.

The Muscogee shooters and several defensemen had corralled the Choctaw defensemen against the post, leaning into them and creating a ramp-like human wall. At a dead run, Totka scaled Coyote's broad frame in three strides—calf, hip, shoulder—and, with a shriek, cracked his sticks against the top of the pole.

The Choctaw players broke his fall and would have broken his nose if the game witch hadn't applied his rod and driven the brawl apart. Pawa reached him at the same time and helped him to his feet.

Blood fogged Totka's sight, but he barely registered the pain. Only the lacerating glares of a dozen battle-starved Choctaws.

Pawa gripped Totka's elbow and tramped with him through their midst. "Put pressure on that cut over your eye until the next ball toss. We cannot have you running half blind."

Totka did as told, ramming shoulders with a menacing defenseman who'd imbedded himself in their path. "Will it end in battle?" Totka spoke low between them.

"If battle breaks out, we are ready."

Totka pinched his stinging wound. "Good."

Weapons of any sort had been forbidden on the ball field or among the spectators. Totka had hoped the Great Warrior would flout the rule. If he hadn't, at least Pawa had. Better to be prepared.

Another scrum was overdue to begin when the Choctaw chiefs shouted for a brief council. Their players, casting darts of repugnance at the Muscogees, began migrating to their sideline.

"What is this?" Coyote threw up his arms and shouted, "If the weaklings need a reprieve, they should admit to it."

Unease crawled like centipedes under Totka's skin. He said nothing until a passing Choctaw defensemen ejected a wad of spittle at him. Totka left it on his arm and levied the full blaze of his hatred, not bothering with trade jargon. "A reprieve will do them no good. They should admit defeat and call on the buzzards to carry their carcasses home, for they are already dead."

Their Muskogean dialects were similar enough that Totka was confident the man understood. If not his words, then his meaning. But true to the code of manhood, the pock-faced Choctaw kept his temper in check, sneered, and kept going. "Your limbs are mine, Kossati," he replied in smooth Muskogee. "Next round, I will break them from your body."

"Come and try, if you dare." Totka tensed his striking arm, but a vise on it held him back.

"Leave it for the scrum," Long Arrow said from behind.

Blood sizzling, Totka spun about. "What are you doing on the field?"

Long Arrow crossed his arms and cocked his chin. "I've come to warn you. Our Long Hair informer tells us they're determined to expel you from the game."

Totka eyed the edgy circle of chiefs and officiators. "Is that what their council is about? Expelling me? What grounds do they have?"

"They'll find grounds. If the game witch deems their reasons sound, I advise you not to contest it. Walk away. You've done your part. They will be hard-pressed to win whether you are on the field or not."

"Walk away? And be named a coward?"

"If that beast tears into you" — he jabbed his thumb at the back of the retreating defensemen — "he'll leave nothing for the birds."

"Do I look frightened? I can take care of myself."

"See that you do. My sister will be inconsolable if you're harmed. As it is, she shudders with every hit you take." The man knew no bounds when it came to protecting his sister. "She loves you too fiercely."

"Did she send you? Where is she?" Briefly, Totka scanned the sea of faces but gave up and swung back to Long Arrow. "There is far more at stake here than a woman's delicate spirit."

Long Arrow moved his focus to whatever unfolded behind Totka. "They've finished their talk."

"Best go then. And if Leaping Waters cannot stomach the blood, take her home. But tell her to meet me at sundown. Our usual place."

Forming a terse smile, Long Arrow nodded. "I will."

"Your . . . usual place?" Lance's halting voice came at Totka from the rear.

Totka swiveled to find hurt and confusion swirling in his cousin's eyes. Dread slammed his ribs like a rogue ball stick.

Lance's jaw hung open, but after two sharp inhales, anger snapped it shut. "Have you taken her to bed?"

How could he even ask?

Motion caught Totka's attention. The game witch, Kossati's Great Warrior, and Pawa were crossing the field, coming Totka's way. "This is not the time to—"

Lance's fist flung Totka's head to the side, darkening the world for an instant. His accusation, though, sounded as loud as a conch shell call to arms. "You have! How could you?"

Head ringing with fury and pain, Totka curled his fingers, shook off the biting memory of Grandmother Kit Fox's warning, and leaned into his rebuttal. "Are you insane? Save it for the Long Hairs!"

"Tell me you do not love her." At Totka's clenched jaw, Lance attempted another cross jab, but Totka blocked it. "Say it!"

Long Arrow wedged himself between them and shoved Lance back. "Everyone knows what they feel for each other. Are you blind that you cannot see it, or simply an imbecile?"

Lance threw himself at Long Arrow, but Pawa hauled him off. "Enough! Lance, behave like a man and curb your temper. You shame yourself and your people. You shame *me*."

Nostrils bulging, Lance swept his tapered gaze between Totka and their pawa. The entwined serpents on his chest twitched and heaved, but he contained himself and backed up enough to allow the game witch to step into their circle.

"Totka Lawe, the Choctaws have a quarrel against you." The old man, bedecked in paint, medallions, and nose ring kept a wary eye on Lance as he spoke. "They claim you are a sorcerer, that you invoke the owls to put wings to your legs."

Totka's blank stare morphed into a snorted cackle. "A sorcerer, am I? And when have I had a spare breath to utter formulas or sing a sabia song? And tell me, who here has not invoked the spirits to give him agility or speed or stamina?"

Sweat pooled in the Great Warrior's wrinkled neck, unease in his hooded eyes. "There is more. Their fallen player is taking the journey. They say his head wound was not serious enough to cause death, so conjury must be the cause. And because of the bitterness you harbor over your mother's death, the conjury has been done in the spirit of vengeance." The worst sort of witchcraft.

"According to tradition," the game witch continued, "they will not seek **blood vengeance** for deaths caused on the field. They ask instead that Totka Lawe be replaced with another player."

Totka's glower cracked his scabbing laceration, and red dripped onto his lashes and wet his cheek. "This is nothing more than a spineless attempt to—!"

Pawa's sharp look and grip on Totka's arm bound his tongue. Vying for control, Totka breathed deep through his nose and sought Long Arrow's eyes.

But his friend, lips white around the edges, was studying Lance, who studied Totka with the reckless fierceness of a brave seeking first blood.

Totka huffed through a split lip. He had no time to coax Lance out of one of his fits. He forced a casual dismissal and directed his attention to Pawa.

"Our formidable enemy has come prepared with knowledge of our players." Pawa addressed the game witch. "But if the Choctaws were truly informed, they would know that the blood debt against my sister was forgiven long ago by our father, Wild Edge. They would also know that my nephew's skill stands on its own. It requires no incantation."

"May I speak?" Totka waited for Pawa's curt nod. "Any informer worth his silver bits would have learned I hold little respect for knowers and would never seek their power. I regret the loss of life. But what player picks up his sticks and tells himself there is no risk of death?"

The game witch grunted what might be interpreted as agreement. "Allow me to deliberate with the other officials."

Giving Lance his back, Totka picked up his sticks, reclaimed his position at the three-quarters field mark, and firmed his stance. They would have to beat him off the turf.

But there was no need. The Choctaws' grievance was declared too weak to stand, and the match resumed.

The pokko kissed the wind once again, the centers clashed, and Pawa loosed a trilled whoop. Four Muscogee defensemen left their goal, spreading out and skirting the melee. A hazardous move, especially if the Choctaws got their cups around that pokko.

Pacing within his shooter's position, Totka spat blood and wiped the dribble from his chin with the back of his hand.

His defensemen were nearing too quickly, so Totka lifted discreet fingers to slow them. It might be some time before the scrum broke apart.

But it was mere heartbeats.

A Tuskegee player broke free, his sticks clamped and held aloft. At the signal, the Muscogee defensemen charged. The Tuskegee cocked his arm, but mid-throw, he was tackled. The pokko soared but landed centerfield.

Totka and Lance sprinted after it, each from his side of the field. Totka was closer, but the earth was already rumbling with the Choctaws' approach, from the rear and side. Were all ten Choctaw defensemen on his tail? Their panting chuffed at his neck, closer each moment. He would go down.

Lance. Get it to Lance.

Unable to afford slowing, he dished for the pokko in a bounding dip. The sidewall of his pocket grazed the leather, sending it on a wild spin.

In the next breath, a Choctaw stick slapped fire across his back.

The player, like a charging bull, rammed low and flipped Totka into the air. The sun glinted in his eye, then gave way to a massive chest pursuing him to the sod.

Wind whooshed from his lungs, and the snap of a rib echoed agony through his body. He had little time to nurse it as new pain exploded from every angle.

Fists, sticks, knees—they swarmed him as one. Fury tore from his throat as he bucked and buffeted, but it was little use. There would be no escape, not in his own power.

Slim Face's shouted voice registered in Totka's brain. As did the screams of women and the taste of dust and blood.

Where was Lance? He should have been there by now. Had he been trampled as well? A window opened in the wall of attackers, and Totka blinked through a veil of blood out across the grounds.

On both sides, the spectators were scattering. Women away from the playing field. Men toward it.

Ball stick cocked like a tomahawk, Pawa galloped into the fray of players. His mouth moved with a bellow directed at . . .

Totka's sluggish brain followed Pawa's line of sight to a short ways off where Lance stood observing, sticks hanging limp at his sides and satisfaction cool in his eyes.

A stick connected with Totka's chin, and he clawed at the grass in a mad scramble to reach his cousin, to prove that what he was seeing was not abandonment. "Lance! Lan—" A blow to his side sent him into a humiliating curl.

The assault lessened as his teammates arrived, turned warrior, and took the heat onto themselves. As Lance should have done. Battle din filled Totka's head as did the ache of betrayal.

Then, he spotted his father, running at the bystanders, waving his arms. Gray Hawk would get himself killed trying to stop the unstoppable.

Totka dragged his knees beneath him and pushed up, but the hot poker in his chest and the spinning in his head buckled his elbows and brought a cry to the back of his throat. His forehead dented the earth. Yellow, sun-parched blades of grass poked him in the eye as he gagged on nausea and warded off edges of black creeping in around his vision.

To the scent of warm hay and the sight of Crazy Stone bending over him, he lost the battle with consciousness.

"Well, Brother? Has our cousin finally broken you?" White Stone's nasally voice shattered the numbing black that shrouded Totka's mind.

Lance? Ah, yes. The treacherous snake. The same snake who thought he deserved the woman Totka loved, had long ago vowed to protect.

Camp noises hemmed him in. A fly buzzed around his ear, and from somewhere above, a catbird repeated its mewling cry.

The sounds brought with them pain he wished he could leave in the depths of unconsciousness. Failing to muzzle a groan, he eased apart crusty eyelids and squinted into needle-sharp daylight. By the slanted rays, it was evening. He'd lost half a day?

His eldest sister stood over him, hands propped on ample hips. A canopy of trees towered over her, casting her in mottled shade.

Totka moistened his lips. "Do I look broken to you? I am perfectly whole." The last word left his dry throat on a croak.

"I meant your loyalty. Not your body." She bent and backhanded his thigh. "Enough lying around."

Where was Singing Grass when he needed her? Home, unfortunately for him, with a belly as big as a watermelon.

White Stone bustled to retrieve the drinking gourd. "A man plays half a stickball match, gets the breath beat out of him, and expects to be babied while the rest—"

"The game!" Totka launched into a sitting position, then held his burning sides as the earth rotated around him. "Or should I say . . . battle?"

"Game." Gray Hawk approached from the right, but Totka dared not open his eyes lest nausea get the better of him. "The chiefs from both teams intervened and put the match back on its feet. The backup shooter from Ockchoy stepped in for you."

"Mink? The war woman?"

Gray Hawk grunted. "Vicious lefthanded swing, that one."

"The perfect ending, I say." White Stone snorted a laugh. "Even our women are better than those insolent dogs. But never better than my brother." The affectionate jostle she gave to Totka's shoulder released the groan building in the back of his throat.

Stiffly, he leaned away from her. "Your praise is . . . excrutiating."

"Hands off, woman. Give him the juice." Gray Hawk's command cracked Totka's eyelids. His father rewarded the effort with a flash of a smile.

"Mink played well then?"

"Scored the last point."

"The perfect ending indeed." Totka's swollen lips worked to form a sneer. "How much did we beat them by?"

His father's chortle was salve to his pulsing brain. "Eight stakes."

Finding his grin at last, Totka nodded and took the cup White Stone offered. "A good number." And the lake and surrounding tracts of land were theirs once again. Tragically, according to the agreement, the Choctaws would be allowed to stay on until they'd harvested the season's second crop of corn.

He drank, and the mouth-puckering crabapple juice made a cool trail to his stomach.

White Stone snorted. "It would have been a better number if they'd not throttled our best player."

"We won, Sister." The scent of roasted meat roused Totka's hunger. He embraced his tightly bound ribs and winced through the effort to rise.

Pawa, battered and bruised but damp with a fresh cleansing, approached and assisted him.

"Pfft!" White Stone rolled her eyes. "As if it is a little matter that your ribs are broken or that your brain is corn mush. Or that they would have killed you if Slim Face had arrived a moment later!" She steered her anger to their pawa. "And what of Lance, Pawa? Will he receive no punishment for surrendering his kinsmen to the enemy?" A pertinent question.

"Watch how you speak to your elder."

She blew air threw taut lips and swatted at gnats. Or was it at the rebuke?

Where was Lance anyway? And Leaping Waters? Totka perused the camp and stopped on Nokose striding through the trees toward him, relief clear in the crinkle of his smiling eyes.

"Good to see you up," he called.

Totka hiked his chin in response and continued his search. The thirty or so Kossati residents who had accompanied the players to the game occupied the immediate forested area. Among them, Leaping Waters and Long Arrow.

Kneeling before her fire, feet tucked, she had yet to notice Totka was awake. It was just as well. Long Arrow paced nearby, beating at swaying weeds with a ball stick; in such a mood, he wouldn't allow her to move beyond the confines of their camp. The man could teach a mother bear a thing or two.

Totka's teammates, laughing and filling their stomachs with the boar that smoked over their fire, lounged in the clearing that bordered a thready creek. Not surprisingly, Lance was absent.

In the pear grove beyond the clearing were those who'd come in support of the Tuskegee players, and farther yet, the representatives from Ockchoy. The camp extended a ways down the stream until it left sight.

Lance could be anywhere. Celebrating. Hiding his shame.

Totka's breath came fast and shallow as anger and hurt contended for dominance. His head went light, and he doubled and supported himself on his knees, grinding his molars through the agony. Every twinge of pain was one that might have been avoided if Lance had been the brother he claimed to be.

Nokose sidled up, squeezed Totka's shoulder, and spoke in his ear. "Unfold your backbone. Fallow Deer is watching."

Gingerly, painfully, Totka straightened and spoke so none in his circle could miss it. "You may tell Fallow Deer to get her sport from my cousin. He should enjoy himself one last time before he meets the point of my arrow."

Pawa's head wheeled about, and White Stone's jowls slackened. Gray Hawk gave an understanding nod, and Nokose snickered.

"Sheath that tongue, Brother," White Stone said. "The only place those words belong is beneath the crush of my pestle. Fool he may be, but Lance is clan."

Clan, yes. But what care had Lance shown it? He had good reason to be angry; he'd been betrayed, albeit not to the extent he believed, but did his anger justify abandoning Totka to a pack of frenzied Long Hairs?

Totka braced his ribs and tried, through the hurt, to find his old loyalty and a desire to repair the rift. If either still existed, they refused to be found just yet. "May the Shadows take that man!"

The curse lured Long Arrow's attention, and Leaping Waters began to rise. At a word from her brother, she sank back down.

Her hands were relaxed on her thighs, but her eyes were troubled. They found Totka's, and even from this distance, their puffy rims were unmistakable.

Her posture sagged. Weariness? Relief? If she returned his smile, it was too small to detect.

Ball stick in hand, Long Arrow loped across the gap, his eyes every bit as disturbed as his sister's. "You look as though a herd of buffalo has used you as a stomp ground."

Totka fended off a laugh his ribs would chide him for. "That about describes how I feel. How is Leaping Waters?"

"Sick with worry and completely crazy. She speaks of putting out her sofkee the morning we return, of letting that coward drink from it. Even after"—the sweep of his stick encompassed Totka—"after this."

"I cannot have you speak so of my nephew." Pawa Cetto Imala's words were surely meant to sound threatening, but his voice lacked conviction.

Gray Hawk gave Pawa a doleful look, and Totka's heart smarted for the man whose humiliation was now complete.

"Forgive me, Cetto Imala," Long Arrow said. "My respect for you

86

cannot be measured, but I have none to spare for Lance. Totka, though . . ." He turned back to Totka, a fierce look in his eye. "He will do what is right."

"And what would that be?" Totka asked.

Long Arrow jerked his head at an isolated stand of shrubs, then stalked to them and continued pacing until Totka, sluggish and riddled with pain, caught up. The stick beat a nervous rhythm against Long Arrow's calf. Upon closer inspection, it was one of Totka's sticks, looking rather worse for the wear. Like himself, he imagined.

"What has you riled, besides your sister challenging you for once?"

Long Arrow rounded on him. "He has had her," he spewed on a hiss.

An ominous feeling, like a leaden weight, plunked into his stomach. "What do you mean?"

"My sister has been used. She is with child."

"With . . . what?"

"A child, Totka. There will be a child. You may thank your conniving cousin." Long Arrow jabbed the ball stick in the general direction of the creek. "You and I both know that given a choice, my fear-riddled sister would have no man touch her but you. And *I* knew the day would come in which Lance stole more than a kiss! He is your clansmen. I expect you to make this right."

Totka shook his head, denial heavy on his brain. As his heel slid backward, it collected a damp mound of forest litter. When the other foot followed, he tripped over a stick and jolted every screaming rib. But he would take a solid twelve moons of agony if Long Arrow would tell him it was a lie, a cruel jest. That Lance wasn't the monster Long Arrow described, that Leaping Waters hadn't been ill-used.

Totka scrutinized the man for a teasing smile but found only anger growing breath by noisy breath.

Long Arrow neared, lips curling. "She would *never* have gone to him willingly! Besides, I forbade him from so much as touching her without my permission."

Totka had been present the evening Long Arrow, still a brave with blowgun in hand, had laid down the law regarding his sister. The many passing seasons had changed nothing; Long Arrow had persisted in his expectations.

But as persistent as Long Arrow had been in protecting her, Lance had been more so in obtaining her. Would he go so far as to force her though? Was he capable?

Totka might not have thought so yesterday, but today, the image was as clear as the tendons protruding from Long Arrow's neck — that of Lance coercing Leaping Waters, who would sooner wilt that resist. Like the butt end of a Choctaw ball stick, the image rammed Totka's chest. He gasped and bent, clutching his ribs. "She . . . told you this? That he . . . forced himself on her?" What payment would Beaver require for such a trespass?

The scoffing toss of Long Arrow's head unsettled his turban. "She'll not accuse him of anything, which robs me of retribution! But she need not form the words. Lance may or may not have pinned her down to have his way, but he is a schemer. Worse than the Trickster Rabbit. He wields words like a weapon and can bend my sister against her will with less thought than it takes to snap a chicken's neck."

Long Arrow's expression darkened to a shade Totka didn't recognize. "Trust me, if you had seen her eyes when she told me, you would not question whether she'd chosen his repeated attentions."

Totka had seen it, her blank-eyed mask of fear. Bile scorched the hollow at the base of his ribs. He pressed a fist against it. "How many times has he done this? How long?"

"Long enough to hit the mark." The tap of stick against flesh increased in tempo.

And Totka, Long Arrow, her pawa — all clueless.

Totka scrubbed at his sweaty forehead, eyes clinched shut. "Why did she not tell me?"

"Shame? Fear?"

Shame of proving she continued to be the mousy, brow-beaten child the talwa had always pitied. Fear of Long Arrow's volatile reaction. True to the woman her aunt and brother had molded her to be, she'd gone into hiding, buried her face, chosen to live in fear. Totka glared at the man before him, but Long Arrow was too agitated to notice the censure.

"It was my mother who told me, and only after Lance dishonored himself by striking you. She demanded I seek you out. Leaping Waters begged me not, thinking to marry your cousin and be done with it, but I knew when you learned of it, you would feel differently about letting Lance have her without a fight." Long Arrow gazed at him as though expecting an answer to an unasked question.

But Totka, acutely in tune with the man's line of thought, would not satisfy him. "If you want something more from me, you'll have to speak it."

"Wed her, but do so aware of her condition. I would not have you deceived as you drink her sofkee. But"—his eyes cut to Pawa who observed them warily—"that is not to say others cannot be."

"Lance does not know?"

An abrupt shake of Long Arrow's head clarified his intention—deceit. "There is not one good thing about that man, so I'll not stand for him to be lauded among the clans as having good seed. No one else knows. She is not far along. If White Stone begins negotiations now, you could have Leaping Waters within days." He threw his hand up. "Take her this very minute! I defy any clan mother who stands in your way." And he would.

Mouth tightening, Totka permitted himself a long look at her.

Her posture remained as before, dimples nowhere to be seen, large eyes on him. They radiated youth, vulnerability, fractured innocence, need.

He longed to fill that need, to love her as a man does a woman, but was he willing to deceive his cousin, his clan, to do it? True enough Lance did not deserve her. He didn't even deserve the honor fathering a child would bring. It was also true that the child did not belong to him at all, but to Beaver. He had no rights.

"Why do you hesitate? Do you not want her?"

Totka's head veered back. "A man would be a fool not to want her! But the greater fool would lay claim to another a man's seed."

"Regardless who is named the father, the child will be Beaver, raised by me. I decide what is best for Leaping Waters and her children. And I have decided that what is best for her is *you*. Not the scoundrel who abused her weak nature and shot her through with fear," he said, rapping his chest and flying in the face of clan mothers who, fortunately for him, would likely agree with his judgment.

Long Arrow stepped so close his heat penetrated Totka's skin. "The same scoundrel who abandoned you to your worst enemy."

The anger that was banked in Totka's belly kindled to life, pounding blood through his body and setting fire to every wounded nerve. A breathy laugh escaped. "And you call Lance the manipulator?"

Long Arrow's point, however, was well taken. Totka's gaze drifted to Leaping Waters' midsection. Pregnancy before marriage was nothing to be ashamed of. Children were always cherished, no matter when or how they made their appearance. But Totka would never abandon Leaping Waters and her child to such a man, for as sure as vengeance was red, Lance would continue to hurt and terrify her. As long as she filled his selfish desires, he would wring them from her.

"Consider the simplicity of it, Totka. Take a moment and consider. Please." Long Arrow backed away, hands held wide, eyes beseeching.

When it came to his sister, the man was a disaster, but Totka did as asked and allowed the process to play out in his mind. Since marriage was more of an arrangement between clans than individuals, and since Wolf and Beaver had already exchanged gifts, marriage would be a simple matter of the clan mothers agreeing which cousin should have her. After what had transpired on the ball field, there would be no contest. She would go to Totka.

Assuming she was willing . . .

"What of Nokose?" Totka asked.

"My pawa trusts my judgment, as does my sister. If I tell her she must, she will have you this very afternoon. But there would be no need to constrain her. Because she loves you. She always has, always will. And together you will love the child."

True. All true. And still, Totka hedged.

It wasn't right, this. Talking marriage, conspiring behind the clan mothers' backs. But from the start, Long Arrow had never intended to let them have any say in his sister's life.

And then there was Lance. He'd once risked his life to save Totka from the Choctaws. What had gone awry between them? Their love for Leaping Waters couldn't be blamed for the lot of it. No, Lance's spirit had gone rancid, and none but he could salvage it.

Not Pawa, nor Totka. Certainly not Leaping Waters, and Totka would sooner hang from a white man's rope than watch the black plague of Lance's heart bleed over into hers.

You fear losing your cousin more than you fear losing me — Leaping Waters' words. But in one afternoon that fear had reversed.

"All right, we will say the child is mine, but I cannot deceive Nokose. Your pawa must agree to the plan, and you must swear to me none will know but us four. If Lance learns of it . . ."

"I know. And I do, I swear it. Brother." Long Arrow grinned. "And Nokose will be agreeable."

He was.

Long Arrow's tongue was yet wagging with the predicament when Nokose eagerly proposed Totka as the solution. White Stone was less agreeable, spouting that no man had any business meddling in the affairs of women. When her rant was spent, she stated that of course she would arrange the marriage. With pleasure.

Pawa listened to the exchange without comment, but when Totka put Leaping Waters in his sights and began toward her, Pawa Cetto Imala caught up and stopped him partway there. "Think, Nephew, before you do this. Lance's actions are inexcusable, but robbing him of the woman he loves will drive the wedge further between you."

Totka cringed at Pawa's anguish, and hoped he believed the expression due to cracked ribs, not pity. "Lance crafted the wedge. It is his to do with as he pleases."

"He will make amends. I'll see it done. Abandon this pursuit of Leaping Waters, or you will lose your brother forever. If Rain Falling were alive, her heart would split."

"My mother was an advocate for peace, but she also spoke on behalf of the weak. She would judge in favor of Leaping Waters' safety and happiness. And that of her child. They will find those things with me and only me."

Pawa seized Totka's arm. "You have none other but him!"

"I have Nokose. He is my true brother." Totka unhooked Pawa's fingers. "And yes, Lance *will* make amends. By giving up this notion of Leaping Waters, by giving her to me."

Chapter 5

Little Spring Month 1809, five months later

From beyond the curtain of budding wild grapevines, in the predawn gray, a red bird whistled its two-part song, ending in a slow trill. The first birdsong of the morning.

It might have woken Totka if the night hadn't already been a sleepless one.

Leaping Waters stirred, gave a hummed exhale, and lifted her head.

"Sleep," he whispered, sweeping back the hair tangled about her throat. He rested his mouth where her pulse drummed a lazy rhythm. "Not time to wake."

There was yet a short while to hold her. Then, three days in the **Warriors' House** participating in war dances, death songs, and rites of purification.

Then battle.

She sighed and snuggled into his chest, nestling her arms and rounded belly between them. He tucked the blanket around her back to keep out the spring chill.

Over the last six moons, despite his cousin's near-violent protests, Totka's love for her had become a living thing. It inhabited the cavity of his chest, straining so hard against his ribs that, at times, it pained him. As it did now.

Relishing the ache, he rested his chin on her crown, and with a finger stroked the silky curve of her hip until her breaths came even again.

Stretching his toes, he touched the end of the sandstone den that had first been hers but now was theirs. Theirs since the previous autumn, since the afternoon they'd exchanged gifts in the presence of their clans. Soon — by early summer — Totka would present meat he'd hunted as proof he could provide for her. Those acts would seal their commitment and release her to him. Until then, her brother and uncle would be her sole providers.

Although she had yet to share a lodge with Totka, in the eyes of their clans, they belonged to each other and were at liberty to spend their nights anywhere they chose so long as she was home by daybreak. Except for the most bitterly cold, they'd spent every one of them together beneath the knobby arms of Old Man Oak.

The river's unceasing gurgle usually lured Totka into a drowsy stupor, but at the moment, it was powerless against the burden of Old Grandfather's repeated admonition and Leaping Waters' advanced condition.

He glided his hand over the bulge of her taut abdomen. Lance's doing but Totka's blessing. He cherished the child already. Almost as much as he did its mother. A heavy breath jetted from his nose. In her state, she should be on a couch in her grandmother's lodge, not on a pallet in a cave. Devoted thing that she was, she chose seclusion with him over the extra comfort of a lodge. He saw to it she stayed plenty warm.

The chores of clearing land, erecting a shelter, and hunting had been far greater without his kinsmen's help. Lance wouldn't speak to him, much less swing an ax beside him, and Pawa was sometimes reluctant to lend a hand and further estrange his nephew. Totka would have liked to make it easy on the man and relieve him of the duty, but he needed the help, even if it came unwillingly.

Thanks to extended clan, as well as Gray Hawk and Nokose — neither of whom was obligated, not being clan — Leaping Waters would have a home by the time the spring corn had ripened.

The construction was being delayed by their upcoming foray to

Beaver Lake, but he would return. Portents be slain. He'd defeated the Choctaw once before. He would do it again, this time with tomahawk and bow. And his plunder? Scalps, overdue blood revenge, and the promise of a ranking warrior's name.

While he was away, the child would grow strong and Leaping Waters would love him more for his absence. But he wouldn't be gone so very long—ten, twelve, maybe fourteen sleeps—but each one would feel like a moon and a half.

She'd become his heartbeat, his tafia.

Panic choked him at the thought of ever having considered leaving her to his cousin, of how close he'd come to not fully knowing her—body and soul. He buried his nose in her hair and exercised restraint until the sun tinted the sky. Then, he kissed her awake and expended himself loving her.

"Would you like me to ask my father if he's willing to work on the lodge while you're away?" She spoke against his mouth and ended the question with a kiss that made him forget she was expecting an answer. "Totka Lawe?"

"Hmm? Your father? No. Do not ask." It was his responsibility to raise the lodge. Beaver Clan wouldn't release her until the last shingle was secure. "It must wait until I return."

She pushed up from his chest and traced the meandering pattern of ink she'd pricked into his neck—an exact replica of hers. "Until you return, then." Even clothed in shades of silver and black, her face showed signs of anxiety.

He braced her cheek and smoothed the line traversing her forehead. "Tell me you are not afraid."

A loud swallow worked through her throat. "I *am* afraid."

His chest deflated. How could she not know he needed her to be strong? To at least try, so he could do what he must with a smidgen less worry?

"Come. Rest your head here." Guidance brought her ear to his heart. "It will beat equally strong next time you see me, if not stronger for having survived the lack of you."

"My Wolf is too good a man for me. Too good to waste his life holding me up."

"Shah. What nonsense. And what use is strength if kept locked away? I will gladly spend my life with you, plus another after it."

She nodded and bumped a fingertip along the length of his ribcage, but the cool drip of her tears said he'd not convinced her.

Could a man breathe his strength into a woman? If it were possible, he would fill this one with his. Since he couldn't, he wiped her tears; as quickly as they touched her cheek, they were gone.

She sniffled and kissed the palm of his hand. "My prayers will sustain you. The Master of Breath is gracious toward me. He will listen."

A smile touched the corners of his lips. It was an attempt at strength, if a weak one. The satin of her jaw occupied his thumb until she broke into his thoughts.

"Will you burn Beaver Lake Town?"

His thumb stilled. "If we leave it standing, they will reoccupy it as soon as we've turned our backs."

"Their corn as well?" Compassion softened her voice.

"They were warned. Many times." At each instance, they'd claimed favoritism on the stickball grounds and an unfair ruling. And so, they'd harvested their fall corn, stayed at Beaver Lake through the winter, and with spring's first warm breeze, they had sowed a new crop. When Beaver Lake Town's maize dotted the ground with green shoots, the Tuskegee chiefs had distributed the bundles of broken days to key Upper Creek towns. The last stick in Kossati's bundle would be broken four sleeps hence.

On the morning of the fifth, Kossati's warriors would meet the rest of the war party where the Black Warrior River spilled into the Tombigbee.

"If you meet the bully who gave you this"—she pecked the nick of a scar on his chin—"put an arrow through him for me."

His chuckle rocked her body. "And here I was, thinking you are a meek little thing." With a deft twist, he swapped positions with her and silenced her laughter with a kiss he made certain would haunt her every night he was away.

Then, ever so reluctantly, they went to water, dressed, and faced the day.

The path to Totka's compound was cold, hard, and silent. Leaping Waters' breath trailed her in white streams, and her nose was mulberry red. More from tears than cold.

Dismayed, he looked away, then caressed the haft of the knife extending from his belt and replaced her image with that of the pock-faced defensemen who'd applied his hickory to Totka's chin. Leaping Waters might walk beside him wrapped in his bearskin, but his mind was already two **sights** beyond them at the Warriors' House, his bow arm already rigid with anticipation.

Despite that, Totka was unprepared for the vision of Lance, framed by the full quiver over one shoulder, musket over the other, sitting astride a bay stallion in Singing Grass' compound. The animal, ears perked Totka's direction, stood at attention in the sunlight that crawled in a westerly direction between the winter and the summer lodges. Lance, as erect as ever, with his full head of hair astir in the breeze and his finely chiseled features made more rugged by the harsh light, created a stunning image—one any woman would look at twice.

And Leaping Waters did. Her step faltered, and her fingers fluttered to her hair, reminding Totka she would have married the man if not for his insensible jealousy and her brother's uncompromising refusal to support such a decision.

Totka recognized that look. Attraction. He told himself it was a natural response. Leaping Waters' soul had been knit to Totka's during childhood, but his unrefined nose and more brutish ways couldn't compete with Lance's hypnotic eye and inbred sensuality.

She might bear Lance's child, but he didn't bear her mark in his skin. Totka did. Even with that reassurance, darts of insecurity drilled his insides.

Stopping, he placed himself to block her view of the man, then tugged the bearskin around her distended middle and smiled into her tear-reddened eyes.

She displayed her dimples in a weak smile. "You want me to go home now."

"I do. Always best to pull the arrow out quickly," he said even as his fingers dug into the fur hide framing her chest.

Her eyes swelled with fresh tears. "Then kiss me and let me go."

He did, savoring both her mouth and the daggers Lance's gaze bore into his back. Forehead resting against hers, he tapped his lips against the tip of her nose and pulled back. "Stay away from venison. It makes you skittish like the deer. For that matter, avoid rabbit as well." She was troubled enough without adding those animals' edgy qualities to her disposition.

"Very well, Totka Lawe. Anything else?" She blinked up at him, open-faced and trusting. If he told her to fast for the duration of his absence, she would likely give it serious thought.

But there was only one other simple thing he wanted of her. He worked his mouth into a brash grin. "Miss me."

On tiptoe, she spread her arms, enveloped him in the warmth of her animal hide, and emptied her lungs against his ear. "I already do."

Tomahawk in hand, Totka jogged through Beaver Lake Town's empty lanes. Despite being nearly deserted, the town was still replete with battle racket. Cries carried through the village, coming from women and children being herded at musket point across the ball ground. Muscogee war whoops, meant to terrify and propel, punctuated the wailing of Choctaw innocents.

But they were receiving a mercy that Totka's mother and grandmother hadn't been granted. And where was Gray Hawk? In his sister's lodge in Tuskegee, taking herbs and recovering from a vision he claimed had warned him to stay away from battle.

Totka's father had such poor timing.

If Gray Hawk had heeded his dreams when Totka was a boy,

Rain Falling would still be alive. Now, he chose to listen and painted himself a traitor before the people, for not a warrior in Kossati was unaware of Gray Hawk's perplexing amicable relationship with the Choctaws.

The morning was bright with fires that consumed every thatched dwelling. Its orange glow howled and toasted the otherwise frigid air.

Totka rounded a blazing hut and singed the delicate skin inside his nose. He went wider, squinting against eye-drying heat toward the town's square grounds and the last untouched structure—the winter council house.

The majority of Muscogee warriors were either prodding the helpless ones toward the Oaktebbehaw River or were finishing off the few Choctaw warriors who refused to surrender. Tuskegee's Great Warrior, the head war chief for this battle, had timed their raid to coincide with a grand council that had taken the main body of warriors to Pascagoula, so that Beaver Lake Town's removal was swift and almost bloodless. The lust for vengeance would be faint in their hearts, and all-out war might be avoided.

A wise approach, but one that left Totka without a scalp to carry home. His ranking title would have to wait for the next raid, whenever that might be.

He neared the cylindrical council house, shoddy compared to Kossati's more established structure. Its cone-shaped, straw roof towered the thick waddle-and-daub walls, and its single doorless entryway led into a murky interior that produced a child's wail and an old man's warbled death song.

Pawa and several others, Slim Face included, stood outside it, conversing and studying the entry. One held a flaming torch recklessly close to the feathers adorning his hair, and another poured powder into a musket's firing pan.

Totka had yet to greet Slim Face since he'd met up with the Pauwoctes the previous morning. He clasped arms with the man and smirked. "Did you bring your ball stick? We scattered the Long Hairs with plenty of time for a game before sundown."

"Are you sure your ribs can handle it? Last I saw, you were hunched like an old woman on the verge of death."

Totka rapped his knuckles against his chest. "My ribs are made of iron."

Slim Face's teeth, too large for the size of his slender face, protruded with his immense smile. "And your blood is made of the white drink, I know. As do the Choctaw cowards."

"Not all are cowards." The warrior with the torch brandished his war club at the lodge's interior. "One remains, protecting their **sacred fire**."

"I spit on their Fire." Pawa hawked a wad of spittle onto the building's exterior, but Totka doubted he would be daring enough to anger the Fire Spirit, even that of the Long Hairs. Even if it resulted in vengeance for his loved ones' stolen lives. "Let me burn it and be done with this place." He held a hand out for the torch. It was given over without argument.

Totka flung a sharp eye at his pawa's back. "Wait. Has anyone spoken with him, tried to reason?"

With a grimy fingernail, Slim Face chipped dried blood off his tomahawk's blade. "Wild Cat told him to collect his fire and leave, but either he is deaf or he refuses, for he shoots upon any who comes within his line of sight. It would be a disgrace to kill the aged."

"Let me try." Totka moved around Pawa to the doorway's edge and directed his voice inside. "Listen, Grandfather," he spoke in halting Choctaw trade jargon. The singing ceased. "Gather your fire and join your women. They await you across the lake."

Lengthy moments passed, enough for the man to have done as instructed, gathered the child, and made his exit. The singing didn't resume, but neither did he make an appearance at the door.

"Shall I help you with the child?" Totka waited a beat, then stepped into the opening. The twang of a bow string sent him springing back. Heat raked his cheekbone. He slapped a palm over his face, and it slicked with blood.

Pawa cursed and cursed again. "May the Black Spider wrap up the old man's soul and consume it!"

"Quite an aim for one so gone in years," Slim Face observed.

Totka pinched his slit flesh. "Perhaps he and the child are not alone." Sticky wet streamed his neck.

The quavering strains of song, mournful in their intensity, joined the young one's howls of fear.

"May the Fire Spirit consume them all." Pawa stalked away, one hand swinging his club, the other empty. The torch?

A mighty *whoosh* yanked Totka's eye skyward to the mountain of flame devouring the straw roof.

Instantly, he was transported to his childhood home, his own choking screams, his mother's lifeless eyes and the blood draining from the hole in her skull, to his cousin's strong hands hauling him away from his grandmother and the burning rubble that covered her.

The Choctaw child's high-pitched screech dropped him back into Beaver Lake Town. The wall at his back was heating. Glowing embers, tatters of sizzled straw, whipped about in the fire's wind.

"Stay out. It will go down in moments!" Until he heard Slim Face's warning, Totka didn't realize he'd entered.

He crouched below the smoke and scorching heat and scoured the interior.

Against the far wall, the old chief sat cross-legged on a stack of furs. His dark eagle feathers contrasted with the whitewash behind him, and his skin, heavy with age, folded over his eyes. Although his posture was relaxed, a sizeable knife rested against his knee. As Pawa had said, the old man would die. Totka would let him.

The child. Why had it stopped crying?

Totka hadn't made it three more steps when he spotted a brave, too slight of frame to be a man, stationed in the shadows to Totka's left.

"Come," Totka shouted and reached for him. "You will die for—"

Too late he caught the dull gleam of an iron muzzle. Its close-range report exploded against his thigh. The blast took him off his feet. He landed on his shoulder, agony ripping through his leg.

Beneath the blinding canopy of smoke, he felt for the wound. His fingers, shaking uncontrollably, found the bare flesh mauled and unrecognizable. Mind-numbing pain clenched every muscle into unresponsive steel.

Think, think. Death hovered. He must move.

The little one's cries, weak now in the suffocating heat, beckoned. It came from behind the brave whose scrawny arms now brandished the musket like a club.

Lungs seizing, eyes burning like the Fire Spirit itself, Totka gathered his good leg beneath him. How much time did he have? A glance at the smoke-blanketed ceiling revealed nothing, but the groaning was ominous.

Desperation carried him hobbling and crawling back to the boy who swung his makeshift club. Totka caught the meager blow across the forearm, then with a swift twist and yank, disarmed him and reached for the smaller child squalling behind the boy.

The girl was so small she couldn't have completed three winters, but she was strong enough and smart enough to cling to his neck. He crammed her wriggling form against him, snagged the boy by the hair, and began hauling them both toward the exit.

The useless limb dragged and threatened to bring him down. A disorienting wall of black descended over the path to the doorway, but Totka forged on. With each fiery inhale, his chest lurched with uncontrollable coughs.

He thought of Leaping Waters and her promise to utter supplications on his behalf. Adding his own frantic plea to the Master of Breath, he stooped and followed nothing but instinct.

The fire sucked and pulled and deprived him of air, eager to usher them into the West where the Milky Way touched This World. Enshrouded by smoke, thick and impenetrable, Totka forced his feet to move, yet braced for death.

I am Muscogee. I am not afraid to die. I am a Muscogee —

Cool air burst over his face and into his lungs. He banged his head on the upper door casing and found enough sense to duck and throw himself out.

Rough hands covered him, dragged him, plucked the children from his grasp. Shouts of alarm, questions, demands—they came at him from all sides.

Unable to clear his vision or his brain, he shook his head and curled into a barking cough. Water splashed over his nose and mouth, preventing his half-choked attempts to regain his breath. He angled his head away and fought to see through baked eyes.

A jolting crash burped stinging air over Totka and signaled the end of the council house.

"You left him! You left him in there to die!" Someone shook him harshly by the shoulders, screamed in his face.

Totka squinted. "Lance?" Why did he care about the old chief? "What are you—?" His scratched throat refused to function.

Water was put to his lips. "Drink. Talk later," Slim Face instructed.

Totka complied, then pushed the water gourd away and groaned through the effort to sit up. The fire still raged—in the rubble, in his leg.

Lance, streaked with soot and speckled with blood, stood before him, shaking with a fury Totka didn't understand. His black eyes beamed with hate so strong, they could have carried the battle alone and come out victorious. And the full of it was directed at Totka.

"Where is"—Totka glanced at Slim Face and swallowed painfully—"Cetto Imala?" Lance needed their pawa's stability to regain his composure.

When Slim Face made no response, Totka gave the man a longer look. His eyes would not settle but flashed from Lance to the destroyed council house and back to Totka, apology and sadness softening their edges. "He . . . went in after you."

Totka's brain tripped over the words. "After me?"

"Did you not see him?"

"See him? I saw nothing." Totka's head wagged, eyes pinned to the inferno. "Only the children, then black. Only black."

"Children. You went in for children. Choctaw children!" Lance sprayed Totka with saliva. "And now my pawa is dead. You have taken everything from me! Everything!"

Lance came at him, but out of nowhere, Nokose appeared and restrained him, shouting and swearing vengeance if Lance harmed Totka.

Was it true? Had Pawa gone in? No, he'd set the place aflame and walked away. Totka had seen him. But as he gaped at his enraged cousin, at Slim Face's sorrowful eyes, at the hungry fire, ugly reality sank in.

The Fire Spirit had spared Totka and the children, but he'd required steep payment.

Totka's pawa.

The grueling trek from Choctaw country ended with Totka spotting Singing Grass beside her compound fire, then slipping senseless from his horse.

Somehow, Nokose broke his fall. His brother's fear-stricken face hovered above Totka's, Grandmother Sun directly behind him, mocking Totka with her blinding light and burning rays. Clothes soaked through with sweat, Totka panted for water but couldn't form the words. It wasn't enough for the sun to let the Fire Spirit take yet another of Totka's loved ones. No, she must also suffocate Totka with heat from her terrible blazing eye.

A chill wracked him shoulders to hips. Or was it fever that scorched him?

Cool wet touched his lips, but his fuzzy vision was growing dark. Water flowed over his teeth and gurgled in his throat; he coughed it out. Then Singing Grass' cry of alarm accompanied him into an unconsciousness that could not fully obscure the agony.

Time passed, broken occasionally by the medicine maker's

healing songs, pursued relentlessly by pain. It woke him periodically, seizing his body with tremors and heat and delirium so intense that, at times, he thought himself still in the council house, trapped beneath the collapsed roof. Other times, he saw his mother again, doused in flames.

And in his worst moments, horrifying, other-worldly beings screamed in his mind. The beings must be the ghosts of those lost in battle. Or emissaries of the owls, those fearsome spirits of the night. But who would have sent them? Embittered Choctaws perhaps. There was no identifying the creatures, but they were demanding, grasping things that struck at him as though greedy for his soul.

Occasionally though, Leaping Waters' voice, sweet as sycamore sap, would caress his ear, bringing with it a stronger Presence that settled about him like a mother's embrace. It was not a resident of his mind, but he sensed it just the same. It had no shape or form, unlike the beastly **Shadows** that haunted him, but its light was unpolluted, and where it was, the Shadows were not. Totka's floundering awareness grasped for it but couldn't take hold, and when Leaping Waters left, so did the Presence.

Then, before he could remind himself he was Muscogee and unafraid to die, terror would consume him again.

At times, he would break free of the binding illness, and his eyes would sluggishly lift to view the underside of Fire Maker's lofted couch. Or a flutter of wind would rustle his hair and kiss his hot, dry skin. Or the scent of White Stone's herbs and poultices would override the sickly-sweet odor of putrid flesh.

And he would know he was yet alive.

Again and again, he cycled through the dark, the confusion, the ceaseless river of agony that flowed through his veins. Until, at last, he found the strength to think a clear thought. His first belonged to the condition of his leg—the pain had become almost bearable. His second belonged to Leaping Waters.

He blinked gritty lids and spoke her name on a hoarse whisper.

Singing Grass was beside him in an instant, stroking his cheek, lifting his head. "Stay with me, Brother. Drink. Please, drink."

He did. Voraciously. "Where is she?"

She mopped the puddle he'd created on his bare chest. "At her grandmother's lodge. Dawn is yet afar off."

Dawn? He scanned the lodge. It was submerged in night. He hadn't noticed, but then, he'd lived one perpetual night for . . . "How long?"

"You reached home thirteen sleeps past. Until yesterday when the fever broke, I was certain we would lose you." Her voice cracked, but she remained erect and purposeful in her ministrations. She left and returned, then put a spoon before his mouth. "Have a bite for me. Just one."

Although he had no appetite, he appeased her and forced down a mouthful of gruel, then let his head drop to the pallet. Sleep gave an insistent tug, and he knew he wouldn't be able to fight it. Would he be trapped again, subject to the Shadows' torment? "I need her, Singing Grass. Bring her. Make her . . . stay."

"Leaping Waters is heavy with child, Totka. It is difficult for her to move about. At first light, I'll send Nokose for the knower. He should be able to—"

Totka shook his head with such force the room began to spin. "Keep him away. Keep him away."

Uttering soothing noises, Singing Grass combed massaging fingers over his scalp. "The medicine maker then. He will bring something for the pain. No need to distress yourself. Sleep and when you wake, I'll see about fetching Leaping Waters."

But the following day, when he opened his eyes again, Leaping Waters wasn't there, and when he sent word for her, Ayo came in her stead. The woman examined him, her close-set eyes taking in his weakness, his uselessness, his broken body. Then, she excused her daughter from visits, owing to a need for bed rest.

A new variety of fear set in.

As soon as the hem of Ayo's ribboned skirt had disappeared around the doorpost, Totka sat up and swung his strong leg to the floor. A knife gouged his thigh, and the room tipped. His fingers strangled the edge of the couch.

White Stone shrieked and bullied him back down with surprisingly little effort. "What are you thinking? That bone was destroyed. If you have a hope of ever walking again, you will lay there until I give you leave to rise. Understood?"

Destroyed? Not walk again? Nausea fisted the back of his throat. "The lodge, Sister. I should be working on it. Leaping Waters will—"

"The lodge will wait, as will Leaping Waters." Her retort was firm, but if she thought Totka too ill to notice the dubious look she exchanged with Singing Grass, she was wrong.

The lodge would not wait, the buck would not hunt itself, and Ayo would not allow her daughter to become attached to a man incapable of providing for her.

Totka had been a fool to join the war party before the marriage process had been completed. Before he'd left, he'd taken death into consideration, but the possibility of being rendered invalid had never occurred to him.

Well, he refused to lie on his couch and be denied the woman he loved. Broken bone, destroyed bone—it made no difference. He would heal; he would walk; he would hunt and fish.

One day drifted into another until he could count them by the moon instead of the sleep, but although his pain had decreased, he felt no perceivable change in his body. No renewal of strength. And no Leaping Waters. She'd not returned, stirring up greater anguish than his ruined limb. It wasn't *her* doing though—he was certain of it. Someone held her by the bit.

Her pawa Nokose, grim-faced and surly, would not speak of the goings-on of his clan, but Totka knew it was Ayo who manipulated Leaping Waters. What surprised Totka most was Long Arrow's lack of influence, for Totka refused to believe his childhood friend had given him up for hopeless.

After some time, news arrived that Leaping Waters had given birth to a son. It was then Totka decided he was done being

107

worthless. Singing Grass, eager to please, retrieved arrow-making supplies from the storehouse and set them beside him on the floor. He dismissed her attempts to make him comfortable, and after he insisted she get on with her day, she made for the river with Fire Maker at her side and a basket of soiled garments on her hip.

It felt good to do more than lie immobile, but perhaps he should've chosen a different task. Each bite of his knife into the end of the cured river cane brought Pawa to mind. Each sharpening stroke of whetstone again garfish scale, each application of pitch paste, and each wrap of sinew was a whispered memory of Pawa.

But there was hardly a chore Totka could've chosen that would not have done the same. A pang attacked his chest as though he'd driven one of his new arrows through it.

Pawa had been everything to him, to his sisters, to Fire Maker. Now that he was gone, Totka's authority figure was his mother's elderly father, Grandfather Wild Edge who lived with White Stone. But for day-to-day decisions, Singing Grass' compound would defer to Totka. There was no other, and the burden of responsibility — the need to get well, to provide — was a boulder to Totka's shoulders.

He rummaged through the basket of cleaned scales, selected one, and scraped his thumb over its jagged tip. Like his guilt, it needed little honing.

Gray Hawk and Nokose had both assured him Pawa Cetto Imala had made his own choice. That he'd not been ignorant of the powers of the fire. He'd entered the council house aware of the risks.

All true, but he wouldn't have entered at all if Totka had not gone in first. Lance was accurate in his anger.

Grief pricked Totka's eyes. He blinked it away and reached for a new length of cane, knocking the ball of sinew with his elbow. It rolled off his lap, across the floor, and under the table. Totka glared at it, knowing the discomfort it would require to retrieve it. But retrieve it he would.

He had yet to walk unassisted, but if he couldn't take a few unsupported steps, he may as well have lain down next to the old

Choctaw and let a death song carry him on the journey.

After two shuffled steps, a sheen of cold sweat broke out over his body. He clung to a peg in the wall, his good leg—weak from inactivity—trembling like a newborn fawn's. The binding rested three steps beyond him, and he would need to drop to his knees to reach it. A daunting feat.

But if he could not collect an item from the floor, how in the name of manhood would he provide for his sister's home?

Nokose would lend aid, as he'd done since the Beaver Lake raid, but supplying Ayo's compound kept him busy enough. He shouldn't have to concern himself with his wife's as well. The strain of it was already hollowing ditches into his brow.

Soon, if Totka could not get back on his feet, he would have to call on extended clan for help.

Shame and anger flushed Totka with heat. It radiated from his skin in waves and gave him the fortitude he needed to put weight on the broken bone. He tested it tentatively, discouraged by the instant wobble and throbbing protest. But there was no help for it.

Freeing the peg, he plunged ahead but was falling before he'd completed the transfer of his weight. His right knee took full impact, followed by the undignified slap of his palms against the dirt. The wounded limb, he somehow managed to spare from the shock.

The outline of a man darkened the flapless entryway. Totka lifted his head to find Lance looking down on him as he might a wallowing hog.

Disgust drew Lance's lip into a sneer, or was it humor? "How appropriate. The perfect position to beg forgiveness for your thievery."

Totka's heart burst into a thrumming war dance and propelled him off his knees. Single-legged hops took him the remaining distance to the table, which he used for support. "I am no beggar," he said through the cage of his teeth. Whether he should ask forgiveness, though, was debatable.

"You will be when I take Leaping Waters from you. Along with my son." Lance's cool confidence said this was no test to determine the truth. He already knew it.

Totka's breath backed up in his throat, rendering his tongue a useless flap of muscle. From the start, Long Arrow's scheme had been destined for discovery. But so soon?

Totka's future with Leaping Waters dimmed to a nebulous form, but he wouldn't let it disintegrate without a dogged attempt to hold it together. He thrust his torso across the table; it rocked beneath his mass. "Your words are a pierced gourd. They hold no water. Ask Ayo. The child is mine. As is Leaping Waters! If you go near either of them—"

Lance's contemptuous laugh cut him off. "Why do you even try to lie? I can read you like the noonday sun. Besides, Ayo was the one who told me." He flicked an insect from his shoulder. "It would appear she has tossed you into the fire with the weeds and rotten vegetables."

Of course she had. Ayo had always done what was best for her. A woman who cowered while her daughter was abused would not think twice about breaking a vow of secrecy, if she believed that doing so would protect herself.

Lance neared, his gait as smooth and arrogant as a stud stallion's, his bow arm solid and stable, not weakened by disability. His hair flowed about his becoming face, and Totka knew, like he did every curve of Leaping Waters' body, that she would be sorely tempted. Like her mother before her, the woman was a slave to security. Love, consideration of others, her own happiness—they all took second wife to self-preservation.

Totka's arms began to quake alongside the remnants of his hope, but his voice was strong, uncompromising. "Leaping Waters deserves better than you, a man who would force himself on a woman—"

"Is that what you think?" Lance's chest jolted with his derision. He slanted forward and met Totka in the middle of the table, invading his breathing space, begging for that perfect, slender nose to be made crooked.

"She would have you no other way," Totka spat.

"Does the truth hurt so badly, Cousin?"

Totka straightened, balanced on one leg, and elevated his chin. "The truth is you have always been a spoiled child, willing to go to any length to get what you want."

"That may be, but it does not change the fact she came to me willingly. Many times. That she enjoyed it." Lance took a deep, relaxed breath as though savoring the memory.

Fury shot through Totka with the strength of the Thunder Snakes. His double-handed slap of the tabletop rammed splinters into his flesh. "Lies! You terrify her. She would never go to you!" This was manipulation, plain and simple, a desperate attempt to crush Totka, to shred his dignity.

"What are you doing here, Lance?" Gray Hawk's barked question entered the lodge in advance of the man himself.

Totka looked around Lance's suddenly stiff form. "Father?"

Lance put distance between himself and Totka as Gray Hawk filled the doorway with his powerful presence, hurling Totka back to his childhood, to the times his father had pulled Lance off him in a brawl that had gone several shades beyond playful. But Totka didn't need rescuing this time.

As if the lodge were still his wife's, Gray Hawk dropped a pair of reed duck decoys by the door and tossed his turban on top the pile. Then he moved aside for Nokose to enter behind him.

With a black bear snarl to his lip, Nokose assessed the situation. By the twitch in his cheek, he found it wanting.

Lance's discomfort was evident in his high-pitched chortle. "What say you, Nokose? Am I lying or did your niece bear me a son?"

"The child belongs to Beaver." The snarl traveled to Nokose's voice. "Gray Hawk asked you a question. Either answer it or get out."

Lance pitched Gray Hawk a lazy glance. "I came to tell your son that I know he is a lying thief."

Gray Hawk didn't reward Lance's affront with so much as a blink. "Now that you've told him, you will leave." He stretched his pointer finger toward the exit, and Lance, after a sidelong gander at Totka, moved to do as instructed.

Nokose sidestepped into his path, slamming shoulders with him. "Do not return. This is no longer your home."

The brash poise that, over the years, had become branded to Lance's person slipped and revealed a glimpse of the tender boy Totka once knew. His bare feet hissed as they skated backward. "You would banish your wife's clan from her own compound?" His cousin's quivering brow struck Totka dead center.

It did nothing for Nokose. "No, I would *beat* my wife's clan from her compound. In the council square, I will be cordial. And on the battlefield, I will watch your back, but in this compound, the man who violates my niece is my enemy." Nokose cleared the doorway. "Now be gone. Go scratch your fleas or eat your vomit or do whatever it is that dogs do."

Lance's scales—as sharp and impenetrable as any garfish's—fell back into place. His posture solidified, and his chin jutted. "They mark their territory," he said with one last fierce look at Totka. "And the stronger dog always wins."

When Lance was out of earshot, Totka's elbows collapsed and thudded onto the table. "He will take her from me."

His father came to him, draped his arm over Totka's shoulder, and assisted him back to his couch. "Not if you get well, and you will never accomplish that if you persist in rising before your bone is mended. Soon it will be, and when it is—when White Stone gives you leave—rise like the man Cetto Imala reared you to be."

Totka lowered himself to sit on the couch and snuffed out a sigh of relief. To his shame, he let his father lift his leg and swing it up.

Bending, Gray Hawk gripped Totka behind the neck. "Fight for what is yours, Son. Hold onto it as you would life itself. Release it to none other than death." His smile went distant. "You have your mother's pure spirit, her strength, her passion to share that strength with others, with the weak. And you have her eyes."

After all these winters, Gray Hawk still grieved. It hung from him now, ripe and heavy. After Rain Falling's death, he'd never been the same and he'd never remarried.

"But he has your stubborn tenacity, Gray Hawk." Nokose stood at the sofkee gourd, grinning around the ladle he slurped from. "What was it she likened you to? Popped corn between the teeth?"

"I remember it being a tree stump," Totka said.

"No, no, Totka. You are thinking of yourself." Nokose bellowed with laughter.

How very true. If Totka had inherited anything from his father it was that streak of obstinacy as wide as the Coosa. And loyalty, fierce and unending. Just as there was no one else for Gray Hawk but Rain Falling, there was no one for Totka but Leaping Waters.

He could not lose her.

Gray Hawk joined him, wrinkling the faded red hunter's Vs painted beneath his eyes. "She accused me of both, and I can deny neither." He gave Totka a firm smack on the arm and stood. "I put a brace of ducks in your storehouse. Smoked this morning with Applewood, skin on." Duck, to give flight to Totka's healing. Cured the way he liked it.

"Maddo, Father."

Gray Hawk gathered his things and invaded the afternoon sun. It glimmered against the silver that raked his roached hair. "Thank me by displaying that stubborn tenacity we so prize, you and I. We will shingle Leaping Waters' lodge with the next moon. I expect you up and walking by then."

"I will be." And he would shingle the lodge himself.

Chapter 6

Big Summer Month (July) 1809, two months later

Totka arrived at Leaping Waters' compound in great pain, out of breath, and in sore need of a dip in the river to rinse off his sweat.

In the shade of the storehouse, she lugged a deer hide from a bucket, suspending it over the container to let it drip. Even unkempt from laboring in the heat, she looked good, like the sight of home after battle.

When she noticed him leaned against the side of the winter lodge trying to appear composed, the hide slipped from her grasp and fell back into the bucket with a burp of air and a geyser of mashed corn and deer brains.

Leaving it as it had fallen—half in, half out—she removed her apron, then wiped her face, her neck, and every finger twice before setting the apron aside and turning to face him. Her sleeves were rolled past her elbows, and even though the day sweltered, she rubbed her arms. She was nervous.

Well, so was he.

They'd not spoken for over three months—apart from those moments her voice had reached him through raging delirium. His last clear memory of her was the feel of her warm lips the day he'd left for Beaver Lake Town.

Earlier, Totka had heard Leaping Waters' son was feeling a little poorly. Knowing she would not be at the stickball scrimmage with the rest of the talwa, he made his way to her compound where he hoped to find her alone. Grandmother Kit Fox could be heard humming inside the lodge, but she would not deny him access to Leaping Waters. Unlike Ayo who'd turned him away repeatedly.

She approached on silent, bare feet, eyes large, apprehensive. "Why have you come?" Her blunt greeting stung despite being cushioned in her gentle tones.

He pushed off the house and balanced discretely on one leg. "Why else but to see you?"

She motioned to the trestle bench stationed before the fire at the center of her grandmother's courtyard.

Totka hobbled toward it, brushing off her offer of assistance and trying not to appear eager for a rest, but when his backside landed, a heavily expelled breath escaped him. He grimaced, more from shame than discomfort.

At least he'd arrived still on his feet. He'd considered riding the short distance, then scoffed the idea. He would walk and without aid. He'd done it, but his bone rebuked him for it. A muscle cramped in his inner thigh. He stretched out that leg and bore the heel of his hand into it as Leaping Waters, with her usual stealthy grace, walked to the water pail and plunged the dipper.

For having borne a child, she was thicker around the middle, but it lent her an air of maturity that made her all the more attractive. And her hair, draped alluringly over one shoulder, gave Totka hope. She remained unbound to a man, specifically Lance, who was now called Tall Bull—thanks to his accomplishments during the Beaver Lake raid.

Totka had been holed up in the lodge for far too many sleeps. Any news that reached him came through his family, and at times, he'd doubted their truthfulness. They wished to protect him, and their loyalty was appreciated, but he was man enough to face any hard-to-hear facts head-on.

When she returned, he asked. "How is the baby?"

"Better." She offered him a tin cup. "My mother would fly into a rage if she knew you were here. She forbids me to see you or speak

116

with you."

Totka's grin lacked humor. "Fortunately for us, she is not the final authority in this compound."

"Fortunately? Your presence will cause trouble." Those were Ayo's words, and they sounded foreign on Leaping Waters' tongue. She'd tried to sound firm, but she'd revealed her heart by collecting her hair over one shoulder and exposing the design that said they belonged to each other.

Totka drank. The water cooled his mouth, throat, stomach. He took his time draining the cup, watching her from over the rim.

Eyes lowered, she braided and unbraided her fingers before her.

Compassion welled within him. Ayo, Tall Bull, and a host of others had exploited her moldeable nature, warped her thinking, but Totka could straighten it. He'd always been her stabilizer; she, his purpose, his dearest companion. Nothing would ever change that.

"Since when has being together not done us both good?" He reached to stroke her arm.

"Since this very moment," she snapped, eluding his touch. "I cannot bear it. You should leave." *Those* words were sincerely spoken. Achingly so.

But it had never been in his nature to coddle hurt feelings. "No," he said, hammering his cup on the bench. "I'll leave when I choose. And before I go, I will hear from your mouth that you'll bind yourself to me, that you will wait."

Instead of caving, she bristled, eyes sharpening and rising to meet his. "So, you've joined the ranks of those who would badger me." Skirt twirling, she stalked off only to spin and return as irritable as a cat rubbed the wrong way. And looking all the lovelier for it. "Would you like to know what the other options being presented to me are? Mother says I should look to my storehouse. 'What?'" She imitated her mother's raspy whine. "'Totka cannot bring you meat? Then forget him!'"

Leaping Waters thrust her arm in the direction of Singing Grass' compound. "Pawa Nokose tells me if I wed Tall Bull, I am a greater fool than he'd believed me to be, and Long Arrow—" She gave a short, mocking laugh. "Would you like to know my darling brother's advice? He recommended I leave Tall Bull's offspring in the woods to die. Of course, that was before he laid eyes on the child. Now, he would give his life for his nephew's, but still he insists that you will not heal and that I should look beyond Wolf Clan for a husband, for he is far too tempted to pin Tall Bull with an arrow."

Long Arrow's betrayal was a digging stick to Totka's confidence. It unearthed the shallow roots of his belief that he could recover. If Long Arrow, his closest friend, didn't believe in him . . . No, the man was only protecting his sister. In his place, Totka would do the same. Would he not?

Leaping Waters was still speaking, and Totka mentally scrambled to catch up.

"My mother is the worst. She berates you day and night for expecting me to wed half a man, but Grandmother will not listen to her. She honors your offer and says you need nothing more than time and much patience. That as sure as you have always loved me, you will mend and hunt and prove yourself capable." The fight petered out of her, left her slumped arms hanging. "Grandmother tells me to look to my heart, to have faith." She shrugged as though such a suggestion were ludicrous.

Totka gaped at her, stunned as much by the hateful words she'd repeated as by the fiery way in which she'd said them. And by the dreadful knowing that she believed them. At least Grandmother Kit Fox still cast her lots on Totka's chunkey stone. It was something, but would the ancient one have enough sway?

Totka beat road dust from his leggings. "You have yet to mention Tall Bull. How does my despicable cousin try to manipulate you?"

The bench shook when she sat back down and pasted her gaze to the hide slumping over the bucket's rim. Had Tall Bull brought her that animal? Nausea sent water to Totka's mouth.

"He states the obvious—that he is whole and strong, a more capable provider. And he—" Undertones of red darkened her cheeks.

"He asks me to recall the passion we shared."

Totka loosed a derisive snort. "Passion! Is that what he calls violating a woman's body?"

She whipped her head around, confusion swimming in her eyes. "Tall Bull never violated me. I have told you this before. Indeed, he is quite . . . persuasive, insistent. But I knew at every moment I was free to walk away."

Totka had always been adept at lying to himself, but Leaping Waters' skills at that game made his own laughable. "I know my cousin. He could convince a hog at slaughter that it had a choice to live or die. And Long Arrow was certain you had been used against your will. He said you were distraught and—"

"If anyone was distraught, it was Long Arrow." She flipped a dismissive hand. "He is too possessive, too protective. He sees evil intent in every odd look sent my way."

"That I cannot deny." Totka forked fingers through his roach, then did it again and again, but for all his stalling, his mounting frustration and injury didn't abate. He'd suspected she was attracted to Tall Bull but had persuaded himself it went no further than any other female who laid eyes on the man yet was smart enough to know the difference between a scarlet snake and a coral snake.

He shifted, pitted the edge of the bench with his nails, resisting the urge to shake a brain into her skull. "Think for a moment, and be honest with yourself. Now that you know what it is to be loved, *truly* loved, can you tell me that what you had with Tall Bull was acceptable?"

Her expression went cloudy, her eyes distant. For many heartbeats, she sat rigid as death, saying nothing. Had he lost her to her world of fear? He hoped so. Perhaps when she found her way out, she would remember how purely Totka had cherished her.

From the lodge came a baby's soft mewling, then Grandmother Kit Fox's droning song.

Leaping Waters blinked and sucked at the air. She let it out with a slow shake of her head. "You ask an unfair question. Earth and fire

119

cannot be compared. Fire is beautiful and bright, and its dance is mesmerizing." Her eyes settled on the fire crackling near their feet; her breathing picked up tempo. Was she recalling their hollow by the river, their first night together? How pristine and right it had been? "Fire is all-consuming, intense, hot. It demands much, and those who are careless are burned, even scarred. But in the end, fire is essential to life."

Totka sat forward, perplexed. "How have I ever burned you?"

Eyes glossing, she took his hand between both of hers and drew his knuckles up, rested her lips against them. Moist warmth blew between his fingers. "Dear Totka, I was not speaking of you."

What? No. She would *not* give Tall Bull, of all people, Totka's designation. He yanked his hand away to thump his chest. "I am fire. I am Totka Lawe." Hungry Fire.

Wet brimmed her lids as she leaned in and touched his neck with cotton-fluff fingers, trailing his tattoo, eliciting familiar responses that begged attention.

His heart broke into a canter, and his skin broke out with heat. But underneath, deep inside his bones, he sensed this was no prelude to intimacy, but a farewell to it. Fear fisted his stomach.

"Tall Bull is my fire." The series of quick nods she gave continued overly long as though to convince herself, to strengthen her resolve. "Earth, though, she is strong beneath my feet, nourishing and sustaining. Predictable, faithful. She makes few demands, gives generously to those entrusted to her care." With the heavy drop of her hand to her lap, she formed a smile that didn't match the pain swelling her eyes. "Yes, Totka Lawe is fire, but he is not my fire. He is my *earth*."

No, he was fire. He felt it in him now, sizzling in his center, building into a mighty storm. "Strong, you say? And nourishing, sustaining. Predictable? All good. Except I am no longer *any* of those!" They'd been taken by a single, perfectly placed musket ball.

Bitterness grabbed him by the jaw, set it to trembling. It warped his voice into that of a man he didn't know. "To you, I am the dregs of a tea sucked dry, a useless lump of a man no longer able to fulfill your *many* needs. You are a weak spirit, Leaping Waters, blown about by every foul wind. But you spoke true on one count—I am faithful. Today, tomorrow, a hundred winters from now, I would be by your side, giving myself to you. Because above all, I am faithful to those I love!"

"I know, Totka Lawe. You are more loyal than any other. It is what I hold dearest about you, but there is more to consider than loyalty. Please, do not hate me!"

"Why would I hate you? What are you saying? That you have chosen him over me? If so, tell me plain!"

Her shoulders jolted, but her parted mouth remained silent—as he'd known it would. The words had become stuck in her throat because they weren't hers; they were Ayo's. Tears, though, she had in abundance. Always. A river of them coursed down her neck, brightening her beautiful indigo spirals. And it irked.

"Enough tears! I am *through* with them." With a growl, he launched to his feet and, ignoring the agony striking his thigh, paced away to regain a level head. He would get nowhere intimidating her.

After a time, he returned and carefully lowered himself into a squat before her. Pain seared a warning, but he disregarded it and steadied himself by capping her knees with his hands.

He looked up at her, those round cheeks glistening in defiance to his command, and then, he took a moment to usher a four-fold prayer.

Bless me. With wisdom, with understanding, with compassion.

He breathed deep to stabilize his delivery. "Whatever you might call me, *you* are my fire. Likely, you will never understand what your presence does to me or how the thought of you makes my insides sear with need. But I am no Tall Bull. You are more to me than passion, than a thousand nights of it."

"You only think I'm your fire, but I am no one special. There will be another better than I. When you find her—"

"Stop it!" He pressed fingers into his pricking eyes. "We've

121

shared a love since we were children. How can you think there might ever be another who could replace you? Never, *never*." He whispered through a narrowing throat, then tapped from deep within to put devotion into his expression. Could she read it there, or was she too blinded by her tears?

They continued to fall, heedless of his sudden dislike of them. "You are much too good to me. Too good *for* me." She dabbed at her nose with the wrist of her sleeve. "I am what you say—weak and needy and selfish—and I will always be those things. You deserve better."

"How wrong you are!" She satisfied him completely.

"You deserve a woman who is your equal," she continued, unhearing, "who requires less and gives more. Much more. A woman who challenges and sharpens you, for you are capable of much greatness."

She loved him. He knew she did. Why did she deny herself?

"You have always believed in me, Leaping Waters. Now, you must believe in yourself." He seized her upper arm, pulled her downward, desperate. "Grow some courage, woman! Wait for me. Is it not true that Mother Earth is not always steady? At times, she trembles, but those times are brief, and soon, she is stable again. Trust me, dear one. I *will* recover."

His legs warbled. Sweat beaded and cooled on his hairline and temples. It trickled into his eye, its sting mocking his assurance that he would mend.

"Wait? But how long? Mother pressures me, and Grandmother chides her for it, and Father chides them both. It is unbearable!"

"Ignore them. Until spring when I am whole again. And if you cannot find the strength to wait, then take mine!" The fingers of one hand tightened on her arm; the others dug into her knee as though to fuse themselves to her. "I have stores of it, enough for us both with plenty to spare. Come away with me. Choose a **Lower Town peace talwa**. Any of them will do. We will hide there until the next Green Corn." When all elopements were forgiven, assuming the guilty couple was not caught first. But would Long Arrow or her father even pursue them? Totka doubted it.

A despondent cry trilled from her throat. "And how do you plan to run the length of the confederacy when you can hardly walk to my grandmother's compound?" Abruptly, she stood, knocking him off balance.

He flung an arm behind him, catching himself, but his depleted legs lacked the strength to push up without him first flipping to his hands and knees. Like an animal.

She backed away, shaking her head, oblivious to his struggle and humiliation. Or hoping to emphasize it?

The baby's fussing increased. Her eye flitted that way, softened. "I will always love you, Totka Lawe, but it is Tall Bull whom I've chosen. I love him too, in my own way." Her quiet confession gouged, seized him by the lungs, incapacitating his speech.

Benumbed, he floundered for the bench, wounded leg refusing to function. It dragged behind him. Through ache worse than any musket shot, he began hauling himself up. The world swam. He blinked hard and angled away from her.

It is Tall Bull whom I've chosen. It is Tall Bull, Tall Bull, Tall Bull . . .

That wretch of a kinsmen had thrown a final punch and knocked Totka out cold, but this was no game. This was his life. *She* was his life. And while Totka was down, Tall Bull had taken her just as he'd threatened, as he'd always intended.

Totka had known better than to go up against his cousin, but he'd never believed he could lose. Not when it came to Leaping Waters' heart. Lose his cousin, yes. Lose Leaping Waters? Never.

Totka was the one she'd called for time and again, season after season. Totka was the child, then the man, she'd shared her heart with, her dreams, her fears. One of which was Tall Bull himself. But now she *loved* him? How was that even possible? Was the man so beguiling that she no longer understood the difference between love and lust?

The child bellowed now, demanded his mother.

"We are right for each other, he and I, each of us flawed." She spoke through the muddle of Totka's thoughts. "And he's the father of my child. We will be bound within days. It is done. Now go, and do not come back, I beg you!"

The patter of hurried footsteps led to the lodge. The babe's cries hushed, but those of Leaping Waters did not.

He stared after her at the dim interior and moved his sluggish eye to the tanning bucket. *It is done. It is done.* "It is done." Totka's voice was that of a dead man.

Eyes unseeing, he turned toward home, barely making it to the nearest cover of trees before collapsing, fire clawing up his throat. He lay there in a pathetic heap, physically drained, mentally incapacitated, grief demanding release yet being denied. Had he not said he was strong? He was.

He would not cry like a woman, and he would not be defeated. And one day, he would march back into her life a complete man, a warrior worthy of rank. By then, she would have seen his cousin for who he really was, and she would divorce him. She *would* have Totka. Eventually.

Utterly exhausted, he slept. Until a strong hand shook him by the shoulder, smacked his cheek.

"Totka. Totka! Wake now."

He stirred, swallowed a stale taste from his mouth, and squinted up into the night. Pinpricks of light painted the black dome above Nokose's bending form.

"Come. Up with you." He hooked Totka under the arm and hoisted him to his feet.

"Leaping Waters, she —"

"I heard. Let your dog of a cousin have my niece," Nokose growled. "I'll get you home. And I'll get you well. Then you will find another woman, one who is more worthy of you. Now move those legs."

Chapter 7

Totka Hadjo swung the sledgehammer back, level with his right ear. Ribs expanding, muscles hardening, he focused on the softened block of iron, on the spot indicated by the tap of Lachlan's smaller hammer, then delivered another ear-ringing blow. Red sparks scattered, chased by a lick of flame. He directed the sledgehammer's bounce onto the anvil and lifted to repeat the process as Lachlan flipped the block to be struck on the other side.

Perspiration rained down Totka's bare chest, and his muscles burned like the bellow-blown fire in the stone forge, but being an iron worker's striker was satisfying work, a skill he was pleased to acquire. And Lachlan, a man with a slow burn, was easy to work with.

"One more should do it." Lachlan spoke in English and gave another tap to indicate where to apply the hammer's weight.

Totka drove the head once more, set the tool aside, and studied Lachlan's precise chiseling technique.

Beneath Lachlan's expert hand, the metal, yellow as the sun, flattened into the beginnings of a blade. With his long-handled tongs, he buried the misshapen iron in the coals.

Totka pulled the bellows cord. The fire leapt and reached for the shed's rafters. All four law-giving spirits were present in this craft— Wind in the bellows, Fire in the forge, Earth in the iron, Water in the cooling bucket. They worked in beautiful harmony, yet everything they did was at Lachlan's thankless bidding.

The white man's myth of the garden named Eden came to mind, as well as the command Creator had given the first man. Creator prized the man above all else, above the earth, the water, the plants and animals. Man was given precedence over the rest of nature. More shocking than that, he'd been instructed to subdue it.

Little wonder the pale faces walked with a conquering air, taking from Earth Mother with little consideration or gratitude.

Lachlan never prayed to the elements he used, nor did he provide offerings in exchange for their sacrifice. But for all his carelessness with the spirits, no disaster had befallen him. Not yet, anyway.

Copper Woman's urgings came to Totka often. Especially in the night when her absence was most sharply felt. It astounded him that he could so keenly miss the body of a woman he'd never experienced. But then, their souls were one. Their bodies should be as well, tet he was in Kossati, and she, a good five sleeps distant. Because of an insane vow he never should have made, a vow he likely would be unable to fulfill. But, may the spirits help him, his word would not be brought to question.

Every sunrise, Totka went to water and prayed to Hesagedamesse, asking him to protect Copper Woman, to spare her whatever ill that West Wind had forewarned. Every sundown, Totka went back, washed off the day's labor and, as he'd promised, he prayed to her Jesus.

It was always the same prayer — the demand for a vision, a sign. Or, as with the prophet on the mountain, a small voice. Anything that might prove Jesus was Creator as she claimed him to be. So far, he'd learned no more than ancient stories meant to inspire.

They did little to compensate for other, more disturbing stories, those spoken by his own people.

The passing of three hundred winters had not hushed the tongues of the elders who continued to hand down tales of brutality and slaughter so thick, the Floridas were still a barren, almost peopleless

126

land. The cross, the symbol of the white man's Jesus, had led that bloody trail—a truth Copper Woman had not denied and Totka would not forget.

Lachlan withdrew the bright axe head from the heat and returned to the anvil. "Will you have time tomorrow to fashion the handle? Red Cloud said he would be by in the evening to pick it up. The cracked shovel set me behind today."

"I begun yesterday."

"Began, lad. You *began* yesterday."

Four moons of nothing but English with the man had filed Totka's brain to a dull nub. At the end of each day, it felt as pounded as the iron wedged between Lachlan's tongs. When Copper Woman was learning Muskogee, she hadn't seemed to struggle—nor had she lost her patience—to the extent Totka did.

He mumbled the corrected phrase and switched to Muskogee. "The roof of the winter lodge needs minor patching, but after that I am free to work."

Sweat from Lachlan's brow sizzled against the hot metal he bent over. "Are we moving into the winter lodge already? A bit early, is it not?" Mercifully, he allowed the reprieve from language lessons.

"It is. **Wind Clan** warns of an early frost."

"But the Green Corn Festival is still five sleeps away, and I like my couch where it is."

Totka's lips twisted. "Above White Stone's you mean. Do you gaze down at her while she sleeps?" He yanked on the rope, and the fire blazed lemon yellow.

Lachlan bellowed his own roar and slapped the front of his blackened apron. "Guilty. But I am a man with needs, same as any other, and your sister is fine company, a fine woman."

"A fine cook," Totka said.

She had refined the art of snoring as well; though, man had ever accused her of being a beauty.

"That too." Lachlan looked up from his work, eyes twinkling, shaggy beard hanging dangerously close to the sweltering iron. That

White Stone seemed to return the Scotsman's interest was almost as bewildering as Lachlan finding her harsh disposition a thing to be appreciated. But then, Lachlan's presence *had* mellowed her. A little.

Like a stray, the man had followed Totka home and, after one evening with White Stone, had found a reason to stay. But the arrangement was mutually beneficial. Three moons past, after helping plant McGirth corn in the community maize field, he and Lachlan had rebuilt the summer lodge. The storehouse went up in days. Finally, with permission from the clan mothers, they'd erected a shed for the forge near the Coosa on the outskirts of the talwa. While Totka's sisters had labored over their family garden, he, Lachlan, and Little Warrior had hauled stones from the river and constructed an air-fed forge.

After the forge and its shed were complete, Lachlan had taken a barge downriver to Mobile for iron and additional supplies, and Totka had joined others in repairing the communal granary, all the while envying the man his proximity to Copper Woman.

Lachlan, however, had likely been pining for Kossati and a certain rotund widow of Wolf Clan. A year remained in White Stone's required widowhood, but if he wished to wed her sooner, Totka doubted anyone would begrudge the couple premature happiness. Far too little of that was to be had these days. There were too many other concerns, such as overcoming grief, surviving the coming winter, and bringing Muscogee babies into the world. White Stone would happily oblige the last.

If they wed soon, he would suggest they use Copper Woman's lodge until she arrived. A duplicate of Singing Grass', it lacked only a roof and sat so close to his sister's their eves almost touched.

The courtyard was more cramped with two summer lodges, but Copper Woman would prefer it to the plot of land had Beaver offered Totka on her behalf. She had no real ties to the clan that had adopted her, and because the war robbed them of Nokose, Totka was reluctant to leave his sisters.

"Pawa! Mr. Gibb!" Little Warrior's naked feet kicked up dirt as he ran full speed down the lane. He'd used the man's English title from the day he'd learned it. "Mother found—"

"Stop." Lachlan held up a stiff hand. "In English."

Brightening with the challenge, Little Warrior began again. "By the river, Mother found . . ." His eyes shifted right as did the tip of his tongue. "Grapes?" He drew out the pronunciation.

"That's right. Grapes." Lachlan quenched the completed axe head in the water barrel. Steam clouded his face.

"They're ripe, and she's made . . ." The tongue reappeared.

"Biscuits?" Totka proposed.

"He means dumplings. And it sounds heavenly." Lachlan continued in English.

"Dumplings!" Little Warrior trounced on the word as well as the stack of firewood Totka labored daily to keep in supply. His unshorn hair flapped in the wind with every hop. "Grape dumplings for *everyone*." The wood teetered beneath him, and he flailed for balance, a goofy grin emerging.

Totka snapped his fingers. "Down. Lachlan cannot weld broken necks."

"Are you coming?" The boy leapt to obey, and Totka smiled his approval.

"Wouldn't miss it. Day's about done anyway." Lachlan removed his apron and hung it on a J-hook—the first item Totka had crafted in the new forge. "Run ahead and tell White Stone that if she saves the biggest dumpling for me, I will make her a lantern with the next shipment of glass that comes upriver."

"All right. I'll tell her." Little Warrior, the tail of his breechcloth flapping wildly, began back, shouting as he went. "But if you're slow, you will have to look for it in my belly."

Totka hefted a rod the width of his pinky, judging its weight against his palm. "English sticks to the boy like beggar's lice."

"Leaping Waters was the same, but then most children are quick learners. Be patient with yourself. It'll come. Watch—soon you'll take over the readings."

Totka grunted a laugh. He was doing good to understand, much less speak. Making the paper talk was another matter altogether. But Lachlan was happy enough to translate. He read large portions of the writings every evening, and when Grandmother Sun took away her light, Singing Grass lit the simple oil lamp Lachlan had made and set it on the table beside him.

The writings' legends had begun at the creation of Mother Earth and continued through many hundreds of winters to a faraway desert land that Creator used to discipline his people for their lack of belief in his power.

They were good stories. Entertaining. The children moaned every time Singing Grass clapped to signal bedtime.

"Would you like to try your hand at a few nails?" Lachlan indicated the rod Totka held.

"Now? What of that dumpling White Stone is setting aside for you?"

"English, lad. Or you'll never learn." Lachlan went back for his apron, tossed it at Totka. "I intend to eat it. You've watched me enough. See what you can do with what's left of that fire. Just try not to burn the place down." Humming a Scottish tune, he set off for home, kilt swaying about his soot-streaked legs.

Totka discarded the apron, then began mounding red coals over the tip of the rod and called after Lachlan. "Go to water first, or my sister will beat you from the lodge with that spoon you made for her."

"English!"

Totka growled and lifted his voice another degree. "Bathe, you big oaf!" It was the name Lachlan had given Wind Chaser when her rump had crushed him against the rail of the horse pen. It seemed appropriate now.

Lachlan's returning laughter carried from the direction of the path that led to the river. White Stone could thank Totka later.

Smiling, he set to work angling the rod's blunt end into a sharpened point. Grandmother Sun left him to work by the light of the fire, and by the time the fuel had burned down to a useless temperature, Totka had completed three respectable nails. Tomorrow, when Lachlan saw them, he would flash those perfect teeth and rattle off a string of English that would make Totka's head hurt.

Totka popped the last cooling nail out of the nail header and scooted it to line up with the other two. A scraping noise snapped his gaze to the sea of darkness beyond the support beams of the open-sided shed. "Who is there?" It came again, the shuffle of a careless foot. Eyes laboring to see into the black, he reached for the sledgehammer's long handle.

"Totka Hadjo?" The voice, though meek, was unmistakable.

His hand froze partway to the would-be weapon. "Leaping Waters?"

Wavering like a broken stalk of corn, his cousin's wife entered the fast-dimming light. The shed's front pole caught her shoulder as she slumped into it for support, the cradleboard strapped to her back seeming an unbearable weight. Her traditional buckskin d, once a compliment to her full curves, hung in tatters from a lanky frame.

Totka's heart balked. Except that he'd heard her speak, he wouldn't recognize her. Before he could find a single coherent thought, she lifted sunken eyes, sluggish in their focus.

"Lachlan . . . I heard he was . . . here." Her balance teetered; the cradleboard shifted to the side drawing her with it.

Totka was moving before his brain registered the need. He caught her under the arm, and she hung limp yet fully conscious, crying with not a tear on her filthy cheeks.

He held her aloft while awkwardly working the cradleboard tumpline off her chest and over her head, all the while mentally naming his cousin a dozen vile things. "Why are you alone? Where is Tall Bull?"

"On my trail, probably. I left while he was away with Josiah Francis. A meeting with the British, he said." She lifted a shaky hand, but her attempt to help him remove the board was fruitless. There was no strength left in her. "But he will be here soon. Angry."

"Yes, I imagine he will be." And hurt. As angry and hurt as Totka had been when Copper Woman had left him for Tensaw. But this was a different situation entirely.

Tall Bull was a fugitive, and Totka wouldn't hesitate to turn him into the Warriors' House to be dealt with as such. There was the treaty with the Great Father in Washington to uphold.

Clumsily, Totka's calloused fingers fought to untie the additional strap about her waist. The baby, head drooping, had yet to utter a sound. "The child, is it yours?"

She gave a nod, blinking drowsily.

"Did you find another husband or did my cousin finally call you to his couch again?" A harsh question, but he and Leaping Waters had always spoken plain. This was not the time to begin treading delicately.

"What does it matter, if my son is dead?" Her dull tone carried not a speck of hope. "Have I killed him?"

Totka swung the cradleboard off Leaping Waters and lowered her to the ground, then carried the bound infant into the firelight. He'd never laid eyes on her first son, the one that had almost been his own; the babe had died the next winter. This one looked like his mother — gaunt and pale. A flutter of movement at his shriveled lips drew Totka's fingers to his neck where a fragile pulse could be felt. "He lives, but not for long. Is he ill?"

"My milk ran dry. Several days after I ate the last of the parched corn."

He set the cradleboard on the workbench and went for his water gourd. "You traveled alone? From the Floridas? What were you thinking? Have you no good sense at all?"

"There was no food. People were dying. I knew if—"

"Well yes, they are dying! What did you expect?" Like flames to a bellow's wind, white-hot anger licked up Totka's insides. "You were warned, Leaping Waters. How many times did I tell you to divorce the man? And Long Arrow more times than I. But you would not listen! Because you are drunk on Tall Bull, like a bird gorged on china berries." Fingers shaking, he wrenched the corncob stopper from the gourd. "Have you finally had your fill of him?"

She took the reproof as she always had — eyes downcast, voice tiny. "Don't be angry at me. I-I need . . . I need you." Of course she did. She always had.

And gorged on his own china berries, he'd always been there for her. Until she'd discarded him as she might a cracked vessel. Pain shot through his tight jaw.

"If you will not help me, then help my son."

"Is that not what I am doing?" He filled his lungs with a calming breath and trickled water into the baby's mouth. The act harked him back to his race through the woods with Copper Woman and her newborn brother, Choctaw warriors an arrow's flight behind them. Copper Woman's image cooled his disgust to a workable temperature and cleared his brain.

His hand stilled on the gourd. What was he doing giving water to this child? He should be on his way to Singing Grass. She would share her milk.

He shimmied the tumpline over his shoulders, plucked Leaping Waters off the ground, and left the fire to her fate.

She weighed so little that when he entered the compound at a snappy march he was only mildly out of breath.

At the dog's call of alarm, Lachlan shoved aside the flap covering the entry to the summer lodge. "Totka? Who do you have there?"

Little Warrior darted out from beneath Lachlan's arm. "Who is that?"

"Leaping Waters. She brings an infant. He is near death with thirst. Lachlan, help me. Call my sister."

"Singing Grass, come at once!" Lachlan ran into the courtyard.

"Lachlan." Voice quavering, Leaping Waters stretched an arm toward her old friend.

The moon was slender and weak, and yet Lachlan's eyes became large at the sight of her. With fatherly possessiveness, he pulled her close against him. "What has that man done?"

"Nothing. It is my doing." When Lachlan slanted a deaf ear, she bolstered her faint volume. "I left for the child. He was failing, but now I fear he is—"

"Speak of it later," Totka interrupted. He had no time for her fears. "Lachlan, trouble is coming. Will you stand by me?"

Little Warrior bounced at his heels. "I will!"

"Tell me—what do you need?" Lachlan said.

While Totka walked, Singing Grass wiggled the tight strap off him, all the while cooing to the lethargic infant. Totka untangled himself from the contraption and spoke to Lachlan as they moved toward the lodge. "Stand watch outside. Little Warrior will make a good set of second eyes. But before that"—he took the boy by the base of the neck—"fetch Ayo. And tell—"

"My mother cannot see me this way!" Leaping Waters cried out.

"Then White Stone will feed and bathe you first, but your mother *is* coming. Nephew, no one must know—"

"What are you telling me to do?" White Stone called from inside the lodge. "What is going on out there? You have woken the children with—"

"Quiet, Sister!" Singing Grass commanded. "Slice a watermelon for Leaping Waters." She rushed into the lodge, cradleboard in arms.

With a squeeze of his hand, Totka regained Little Warrior's attention. "Tell no one else Leaping Waters has returned, that she's here. Not until I have dealt with Tall Bull. It would be unsafe for them and for us. Now fly." Instructions complete, Totka released him to charge down the lane, then followed Lachlan indoors.

Rain Child and Speaks Sweetly, eyes round and bright, lay on their pallet as still as frightened possums. Singing Grass occupied the dimmest corner of her couch, coaxing the infant with her breast. If she managed to salvage the boy's life, Totka would attribute it to magic. "See, girls?" she said. "It is only your pawa. Close your eyes. Go back to **hunting dreams**."

Lachlan laid Leaping Waters on Totka's bearskin as Totka

reached for his weapons. "Tall Bull will come, be assured. If he sees her on my couch, there will be war."

"Then I will fight him." Lachlan came to him, battle-fire in his eyes. "Anything else you want me to do?"

"I'll not have my cousin in the lodge or the compound. Beat him back if necessary. We cannot risk being associated with a fugitive. Apprehend him if you can, but if you must abandon Leaping Waters to do it, let him go. Do you understand?"

Lachlan's mouth flattened behind his black whiskers. "And where will *you* be?"

"On my way to Pigeon Roost to fetch her brother." She was Long Arrow's responsibility not Totka's.

"Lachlan, you mustn't let him go!" Leaping Waters tried to rise, but White Stone rushed to her, pushed her back down.

"Hush, girl! You came for help, so let the men do as they see fit."

Leaping Waters gripped the ruffle adorning White Stone's sleeve cuff but pegged Totka with her fright. "Totka, *please*. Wait until Tall Bull has come and gone. Long Arrow will be furious and will fight my husband."

No, he would *kill* her husband.

"Better he than I," Totka said, slipping his quiver onto his back, not bothering with a shirt despite the nip in the air.

The strenuous row to Pigeon Roost kept him warm enough. That, and his anger. She might have been on the hunt for Lachlan Gibb, but Leaping Waters—per her usual pattern—had brought her troubles to Totka's door.

Long Arrow was fully armed and out the door of his lodge moments after Totka uttered his sister's name. When the man's racing legs hit the river, they didn't slow. Water sloshed clear to his turban. "Where has he kept her all these moons?"

"The exact location? There was no time to ask. But she comes to us from Josiah Francis himself." Totka shoved the dugout into the current and leapt aboard.

Long Arrow was already rowing. "Francis, the chieftain knower?

135

What do I care of him? That cousin of yours is the one my scalping knife is after. Josiah Francis is no concern of mine."

Totka couldn't agree and neither would the pale-face soldiers. Half-blood Josiah Francis, Old Sharp Knife's slippery adversary, was the most wanted Red Stick in the territory. If the soldiers learned Leaping Waters knew of the man's whereabouts, that she'd spent the last many moons in his camp, every person she associated with in Kossati might be suspect.

Dawn was nearing when Totka and Long Arrow entered the compound, bows strung. The hide covering the door hung motionless. A weak panel of light shone from the gap beneath the cover and stretched pale across the yard and over the thread of smoke snaking up from the unbanked fire pit.

A strange hush suffocated the deserted courtyard. No Lachlan. No Little Warrior. No dog—not so much as a whine. Even the crickets had abandoned their posts.

Apprehension stole over Totka, alerting every muscle.

"He has already come." Long Arrow's rasp sent Totka's hand to his quiver.

"Pawa, I'm here." Little Warrior scampered out of the winter house shadows. The dog trotted beside him, as silent as the boy. He'd hidden well. The taut string of his bow rested against his forearm, but his movements were agitated, his breath too rapid. "Tall Bull has come and gone."

He was lying. Tall Bull had come, but it was not their cousin's way to go quietly.

"Already gone?" A fount of rank words spewed from Long Arrow's mouth. "Did he take—?"

"Leaping Waters stayed. And her son."

Her brother rushed toward the lodge.

"She sleeps!" Little Warrior whispered the last in a shout aimed at Long Arrow's back.

"Tell me the truth." Totka bent and placed his question square in the boy's face. "Where is he?"

A tiny breath of surprise — or was it relief? — preceded the tipping of Little Warrior's head in direction of the storehouse. "He wishes to speak with you alone. Everyone believes him gone. He said Long Arrow would try to hurt him or —"

"I know. And he would. You did well." He popped his knuckles against the boy's chin and resumed his normal volume. "Was there any trouble?"

"No, Pawa. No trouble."

Well, there was still time for it. Tall Bull was scarcely safer with Totka than with Long Arrow, and if he believed otherwise, he should stop by the medicine maker on his way out of town to see about fixing his head.

Lachlan stepped outside, musket propped against his shoulder in soldierly fashion.

Long Arrow followed. Even after seeing his sister, his carriage retained its combative saunter.

"Glad you're back." The Scotsman took Totka's arm in his blacksmith's crushing grip. "Your cousin could not leave quickly enough for my liking. He's like untempered iron — brittle, unpredictable. It was impossible to tell from one moment to the next whether he would kiss me for feeding his wife or lift my hair for keeping her away from him." His chest shook with a nervous laugh, but Long Arrow folded his arms and blew a gust through his nose.

Lachlan continued. "The women and children are all sleeping. Finally. Ayo came and left to collect a few items for the baby."

"Little Warrior tells me there was no trouble."

"None. I aimed my musket at his belly and told him his wife and son were being cared for. That you'd gone for her brother, and that unless he wanted me to put White Stone to work digging lead out of his gut, he should strike a fire under his feet."

"Lachlan Gibb was as fearsome as a bear, Pawa. Growled like one too. He should be Bear Clan like Father."

The vision of Nokose's snarling lip rushed to the front of Totka's mind and pinched his heart. Totka would give any number of things to have his brother with him now, if even for the next short while. Tall Bull had always deferred to Nokose without question.

Totka forged a meager smile for his nephew. "Lachlan has your approval then, does he?"

Long Arrow snatched the turban from his head and wadded it between his hands. "The Great Warrior will *not* approve. You should have seized him, Lachlan!"

The butt of Lachlan's musket hit the ground as he loosed the growl Little Warrior boasted of.

Anticipating a struggle, Totka nudged his nephew with an elbow. "See to your mother."

Shoulders hunching, the boy plodded away. His back was still visible in the doorway when Lachlan leaned around his weapon's barrel. "The treaty is *yours* to defend, not mine. I'm not beholden to it. So, I let him go. I even gave him a little corn for his journey."

Totka's head jerked back. "You gave him corn from *our* crib?" May as well put the noose around their necks now.

"The man's pouch was empty." Lachlan jutted his chest. "Anything to hasten him on his way. Aye? But he'll be back in the spring, he said, after first harvest." With a snort of disgust, Lachlan stalked toward Copper Woman's empty lodge, muttering as he went. "Plenty of time for Long Arrow to plot his brother-in-law's death."

"Lachlan," Totka called, and when the man looked back, he continued. "Maddo. For guarding my family when I could not."

"They'll soon be my family too."

Totka allowed himself a small laugh and watched the Scotsman until his large, bone-white frame was swallowed by Copper Woman's lodge.

Lachlan Gibb was an unusual white man. Above reproach. Totka turned to his friend. "He did you a good turn. If not for him, Leaping Waters might be gone already." Rebuke sharpened Totka's tone, but from the empty way Long Arrow's gaze scraped the ground, Totka doubted he heard or cared.

"Plenty of time . . . five moons." One end of the turban fell from the man's grasp, dropping before his legs in a long, undulating swath of silk. Slowed by whatever had captivated his thoughts, he began to wrap it around his head. "While apart from Tall Bull, Leaping Waters will listen to me. She will see reason. Spring harvest will be earlier along the coast. That gives us four moons, not five. Plenty of time for us to convince her that divorce is the best—"

"Divorce? Why do you say *us*? Keep me out of your—"

"Forget the white woman, Totka!" Long Arrow's wrapping increased to an agitated rhythm. "She's been nothing but trouble and will bring you nothing but more trouble. Do you truly want white children? Children without a clan to claim them?"

"Copper Woman is Beaver! Our children will be Beaver, same as their mother and Nokose. Same as *you*."

Shortly before Nokose took the journey, the clan mothers had allowed him to bring her under the shelter of his clan, protecting her and indirectly protecting Totka. If anyone had insisted she be adopted by Wolf, Totka's clan, she would have been ineligible to him. Clans were forbidden to intermarry.

"Nokose Fixico is dead." Long Arrow laid the statement out flat and bare and unfeeling.

And what of it? Was he saying he would refuse his duty as pawa to her children? "And you, Long Arrow? Do you intend to be dead? Or perhaps dead only to my white wife and half-blood children." As Nokose's next closest clansmen, Long Arrow should assume the responsibility. The clan mothers would see that he did.

When Long Arrow said nothing, only busied himself tucking away the loose ends of his turban, Totka's innards began to quake, his bad leg to ache with the tension that commandeered his body. He clenched his fists to keep from knocking the man's headdress clean off. "What has eaten into you? Have you forgotten everything I gave up at your pleading?"

Long Arrow's arms fell limp at his sides. "No. And from that day to this, nothing has changed. You are still my choice for Leaping Waters. I never truly surrendered that hope. Not even while advising my sister to seek a man outside Wolf."

"Surrender it, my friend. Copper Woman owns my heart. So then, tell me now—will you be brother to her, pawa to my white children, or has my loyalty and sacrifice these many winters been wasted effort?" McGirth would never release his daughter if he knew Beaver's most influential male balked at accepting her. "Answer me! Will you claim them?"

"I will." Cradling her child, Leaping Waters leaned against the doorframe. The harsh angles of her bones created pools of shadow on her face.

"Leaping Waters! What are you doing up?" Long Arrow hurried to her, but she held up her arm as a bar between them, fending off his embrace.

"Shameful of you, Brother. Copper Woman is our clan sister, and you *will* be pawa to her children." She transferred her son to his arms. "As you are to mine. Look. Is he not perfect? He suckled and has revived. I've decided to name him Journey's End."

Long Arrow went soft and snuggled the infant. "What a terribly slight thing you are, little man. And no cougar skin blanket. Only these rags." He clucked his tongue. "How will you be a great hunter of women with no cougar skin to welcome you to the world?"

Singing Grass came up behind Leaping Waters, rested her chin on the other woman's shoulder but looked at Long Arrow. "Is that all men think of? Hunting? Taking down deer, bear, women?" The smile in her voice shone through the darkness. "A barbaric pastime, but I suppose we will humor you. In the meantime, his grandmother has gone for a cougar skin."

"Ah, there," Long Arrow cooed. "See, Journey's End? We will have you properly clad in no time."

"And his mother properly rested." Singing Grass pulled back the flap on the door, and jerked her head at the dim interior. "Back to bed with you."

Leaping Waters yawned and obeyed without protest. Long Arrow, whose eyes had yet to leave his nephew, disappeared behind her. Somehow, the man had managed to avoid answering the question of Copper Woman, and the fact sat uneasy with Totka.

Singing Grass squeezed the bridge of her nose. "I would hunt a few more dreams myself if the children would let me."

The world had lightened to a dull gray, but sunrise or not, Singing Grass needed her rest, and Totka would rather she not see whatever was about to transpire with their cousin.

"Go back to bed. When they wake, I will see to them as long as they'll let me. Take your pallet to the winter house where you'll find some quiet."

She came and slumped against him, arms tucked into herself. A protracted sigh left her on a hum that might be construed as a sob. "I miss him."

"As do I. Today more than usual." His hand ran the length of her hair, startling when it reached her neck and touched skin. The rough crop was meant to sever accumulated memories, to ease the parting. Little good it did. Six moons later, Singing Grass still clothed herself in grief as though Nokose had been cut down days ago. But once Copper Woman returned, things would be different. Singing Grass would laugh again. They all would. His beloved was good medicine.

Totka held Singing Grass close, kissed the part in her hair. "But we have each other."

"We do." Pulling back, she patted his chest. "And White Stone and the children, and fair warning, Leaping Waters will be staying until she recovers her milk."

Totka huffed. "How long will that take?" The sooner she was gone, the sooner he could breathe again.

"A day? Five days? A moon?" She shrugged and scrubbed her face, lids heavy. "But you are a big, strong warrior. You can bear it." Indulging in a massive yawn, she trudged to the winter house. "Bring Sky to me when she stirs. She'll want to suckle. And you, young man, help your pawa. No complaining." She ruffled Little Warrior's hair in passing.

How long had the boy been sitting there on the bench before the fire pit?

"I *am* helping, Mother." With an affronted tilt of his head, he bobbed away from her affection and directed the tip of his bow at the winter house. "Sleep, before the day grows hot."

"All right." Ineffectively masking humor, she did as instructed.

Arms crossed, Totka towered over his nephew, debating whether to reproach him for ordering his mother about. But at the memory of that ominous westerly wind, he decided to let the boy exercise his role as head of the compound. There would come a day Totka would travel the Milky Way. It might come sooner than any anticipated, but he was Muscogee. There was no fear in death, only in being left behind.

"Quite the stealthy foot you have there."

Little Warrior popped to his feet, beaming, displaying several gaps in his teeth. "My pawa taught me to tread like a wolf." His smile vanished, taking with it the reminder of his youth. "Tall Bull is in the forest behind the storehouse. He has his bow, a musket, a knife at the back of his belt, and a club at the front."

"Maddo. Anything else I should know?" He chose an arrow.

Little Warrior eyed it, licked his lips. "He looks strong. Not weak like Leaping Waters. The British have fed him well, I would say."

"Well done." Totka nodded, impressed. Then, he closed his eyes, faced the eastern wind, and whispered a prayer. "Bless me, Hesagedamesse, Spirit of the Wind. Bless me with a sharp eye, a sharp mind, speed and skill."

He wedged his bowstring into the nock of his arrow and jutted his chin at the lodge. "Go in, Nephew. I will not be long."

Boldness hardened Little Warriors' stance. "Will you take Tall Bull to the Warriors' House?"

"The agreement our chiefs made with the pale faces says I must." Totka slanted a look at the boy. "Should I abide by it, do you think?"

"Tall Bull is clan. Our lineage."

Clan above all. Totka could almost see the oft-repeated line traveling across the boy's mind. "So he is. But there are authorities in a man's life that rise above clan. In this case, a treaty with the Great Father in Washington. It says Tall Bull is our enemy because he refuses to surrender. For the good of the clan, he must be detained and brought before the council."

Confusion flickered behind Little Warrior's eyes. He looked out across the courtyard to the copse of pine beyond their compound. "The talk with the Great Father is too big for me, a boy. But I know right from wrong, and Tall Bull did wrong. He frightened Copper Woman." In a move Totka had seen Nokose make a thousand times, Little Warrior whipped an arrow from his quiver, skimmed the **cock fletch** between his moistened lips, and lifted a determined chin. "I am going with you."

Brows launching upward, Totka shuffled back a step and took in the rigid line of Little Warrior's mouth, the ardor intensifying his eyes, the curl of his lip.

Nokose hadn't left them after all.

Comforted, Totka's heart expanded with pride. Little Warrior's loyalty to Copper Woman was second only to Totka's.

Alone, Totka entered the stand of pines, bow arm leading the way, sinew partially drawn, arrow pointed just below the wooded horizon—to let Tall Bull believe he had the upper hand.

A quail erupted from a shrub and lifted off with a babble of flap and flutter. It disrupted the meandering flight of a bright orange butterfly. Ahead, a rabbit nibbled a twig, its black, seed-bead eye following Totka's movement. It was Tall Bull's rapid emergence from behind a stout trunk that sent the rabbit into a fit of leaps and springs.

His bow was fully extended; the arrowhead centered on Totka's heart.

Totka swiveled and replicated Tall Bull's offensive posture, minus the tight bowstring. "Fitting that you should keep company with a rabbit, tricksters that they are."

"Fitting that you should keep company with a smelly Scotsman."

"That smelly Scotsman let you rummage through my storehouse.

143

He said you needed it, but you look rather fit to me." As strikingly handsome as always.

"The British are excellent hosts. You should visit some time. My fire will always welcome you." His red feather, faded and tattered, caught the wind in a mocking gesture.

But Totka wouldn't look back on what had been, on what the Muscogees had lost: their dignity and pride, their strongest warriors, their hope for an unaltered future, their land—vast tracks of it ceded to the Americans. All that was left was to look ahead, to make the most of preserving what remained of their future, their children.

Totka's laugh was dry and brief. "The only fire of yours that will welcome me will come from that musket slung over your shoulder." He lowered his bow a degree, and Tall Bull responded in kind. "Your family is cared for," Totka said. "Your corn pouch is full. Why are you still here?"

"What? And leave without taking a shot at your heart?"

"So take it. Or tell me what you want."

The shaft of Tall Bull's arrow angled downward, but his fingers retained their straining hold. "I saw Gray Hawk on the outskirts of Tuskegee. Two sleeps past. He still rides with the Long Hairs. I thought you would want to know."

No, Totka did *not* want to know, and Tall Bull was surely aware of it.

Gray Hawk hadn't been seen in Kossati since before the war, the night he'd crept out of town and joined the amassing White Stick army. Totka had seen his father only once since. After that awful day in the woods, when Gray Hawk intervened and spared Totka's life, he had hoped in vain his father might abandon his affection for the Choctaws and come home. If not to Kossati, then to his tribal talwa, Tuskegee.

"My father can do as he pleases."

"Even if that means speaking on the Choctaws' behalf in Upper Town councils? They are negotiating the rights to Beaver Lake hunting grounds."

At the mention of Beaver Lake, a bolt of pain traveled Totka's leg. "You lie to spite me."

"You're right, Totka. I am lying." Ridicule hung thick about his words. "I have waited here, exposing myself to daylight and risking discovery only to spite you. Get your head out of the muck of your own stupidity and *think*. I speak the truth. To prepare you. Your enemy is coming and with your father."

Totka wagged his head. This made no sense. "*You* are my enemy."

Tall Bull's black-as-char eye lashes fell in a sudden sweep. "I have been yes, but I tire of it. I regret our differences."

"Our differences, you say? You must be referring to the fact I have a man's spirit and you have that of a mongrel dog."

"There *is* that little detail. No denying." He flashed a boyish grin. "But can a man not change? I'll call you enemy only if you take my wife and son as that thieving brother of hers would have you do. Little chance of that though, with Copper Woman filling your every thought."

The arrow resting in the crook of Tall Bull's thumb began to tremble from his exertion. "You and I, Cousin, we are clan. And as clan, we watch out for each other. You saved my son. The least I could do was warn you that your true enemy approaches."

What sort of delusion was he under that he thought with a few slippery lines, he could erase everything he'd done? "You could give ten thousand warnings and still our harmony would be broken. Unstring your bow. You are coming to the Warriors' House to be tried by General Jackson's treaty."

Nostrils expanding, Tall Bull heightened his arms in threat. His steps reversed. "Old Sharp Knife is general to you now? I always knew your white insides would bleed through eventually."

At Totka's signal, Little Warrior pivoted from behind the cover of a holly tree and assumed a perfect stance: index finger of his pulling arm under his chin, nose touching the rigid bowstring, right eye following the line of the shaft.

Exactly as Totka taught him.

"Target practice, Pawa?"

From behind his tightening bow, Totka gave rise to an arrogant smirk. "Just so, Nephew."

Tall Bull remained steadfast except for his growing a smile. A genuine smile. "Well done, Little Warrior. You make me proud."

Totka said to the boy, "Our cousin has been away for some time. Tell him how your aim has improved."

Little Warrior bumped a cocky shrug. "I can shoot the beak off a humming bird, a tick off a dog. And I can sure enough shoot Tall Bull's fat haunches."

Tall Bull's shoulders shook with a hearty laugh, tempting Totka until he crackled a chuckle, but in the next breath, he spun on Little Warrior, primed weapon going before him.

Little Warrior jolted. The *twang* of his releasing bowstring stopped Totka's blood mid-flow. The arrow whizzed past Tall Bull's thigh and lanced the trunk of a tree. As the shaft vibrated wildly, Tall Bull leveled the tip of his arrow on Little Warrior.

"Drop it, Tall Bull!" Totka rushed in, bowstring at his lips. He reduced the gap to several strides, arrowhead aligning with the artery pulsing in Tall Bull's neck. "He is but a brave. Your *kin*. Put it away! What are you thinking?"

Blood trickled down Tall Bull's leg, but his trajectory held. "I'm thinking you are as weak as ever I believed you to be, and that in this moment, it will work in my favor."

How had Totka ever wished to be as ruthless a warrior as Tall Bull? Heart in his throat, he deliberated between charging the man and letting him walk free.

Bow empty, Little Warrior glowered at Tall Bull. "I should have put cane in your rump when I had the chance."

Tall Bull developed a corrupt grin. "Yes, you should have. But Leaping Waters thanks you. She will thank you again when you tell her it was your pawa's love of you that allowed me to escape."

More brazen than Fire Maker could have ever hoped to be, Little

Warrior hiked his chin and hurled the blackest of looks straight into his elder's eye. "Yes, she will. Then I'll tell your son that his father is a coward. That to save his scalp, he would draw on a brave half his size."

Tall Bull sucked air, hissing like quenched iron. His jaw muscle flinched along with his arm.

"Go." Totka slackened the string and splayed his hands. The bow and arrow hit the forest floor with a thud that rang of defeat. "Get yourself gone."

Satisfaction tipping his mouth, Tall Bull casually stowed his arrow and unstrung his bow, then landed a light smack on Little Warrior's cheek. "Maddo, little cousin." He tossed a glance at Totka but spoke in false whisper to Little Warrior. "Don't tell your pawa, but he is too gullible. I would never hurt you. We are both Wolf, after all. Could you not see my arrow was pointed to the right of you?"

Doubt shadowed Little Warrior's brow. "Yes, I thought maybe, but . . ."

"Good eye. Better than your pawa's who was too angry to pay attention to details. As I knew he would be. Trust your instincts, Little Warrior. They are sharp. And keep working on that aim. In the spring, I want to see you bring down a humming bird."

Losing the battle to contain escalating rage, Totka collected his weapon and jabbed his arrow at the musket. "Best come with that thunderstick loaded. Perferably, do not come back at all. Leaping Waters is better without you."

A fleck of sadness wrinkled the edges of Tall Bull's eyes, but unmistakable fear soon consumed it. "What will you say next? That she is better with *you*? I won her, Totka. It's time you accept that."

Totka stared at his cousin's perfect face now marred by irrational fear. This was no stickball match, and Leaping Waters was no pokko. Totka was sorely tempted to go back on his word and restring his bow. He chose instead to give the idiot no consolation. "What a burden it will be to carry that question with you for the next four moons."

"If you touch her, you will pay." Tall Bull spat the words and whirled about. His hair spread out like a black cape, then flowed back as he broke into a beautiful, unblemished lope, the red feather catching the morning rays.

Maybe, before he reached Spanish Florida, he would collide with the musket ball of one of Jackson's roving parties of soldiers.

Totka could always hope.

Chapter 8

Big Chestnut Month (October) 1814, four months later

Kossati was an ancient talwa laid out in the old way, with the winter council house atop a circular mound at one end of the chunkey yard and the square ground atop another mound at the opposite end. Banks of earth surrounded the chunkey yard where Totka, at Old Grandfather's request, drilled Little Warrior and several of his peers on their stickball skills.

Despite his advanced age, the **Beloved Man** still made it a priority to foster the braves and their training, but this particular session had more to do with keeping Totka out of the current council meeting than it did refining the boys' clumsy moves. A much-appreciated excuse.

"Canoe Boy," Totka called to the tallest of the four. "Go long! Look up!"

The pokko flew from the cup of his stick before the boy had a chance to break into a run. With a forearm, Totka shielded his eyes from the sun, surprised that the pokko soared higher than usual. His aim had become a little rusty over the bare seasons of illness, war, and reconstruction, but his long-shot was better than ever. Work at the forge had done more than give him an extra skill-set. It had bulked his muscle, strengthened his swing, and apparently, made his pokko fly farther.

Little Warrior whooped. "It will reach Choctaw country before it lands!"

In that case, Totka should have used his new quill and inscribed a message: forget it.

As Tall Bull had predicted, a Choctaw delegation had ridden into Kossati led by none other than Gray Hawk. A township-wide meeting had been called, bringing men from as far as Pigeon Roost. They convened now in the square.

Totka was content to play with the boys while the chiefs sent the Choctaws on their way with a polite kick to the rump. In Kossati, sentiments still ran hot against those who'd pummeled their champion player, reneged on their word, and put Totka out of the game for good. He had no doubt they would do the right thing.

His father, on the other hand, had ceased that attempt several winters past.

Shame and anger sent Totka's blood on a steaming race through his veins. The continual *rasp-rasp, rasp-rasp* of the medicine maker's broom heightened it.

The man swept the hardpan clay of the chunkey yard, working near the **slave pole**, that hideous instrument of torture that would have released his beloved's spirit if he'd not arrived in time. Every swipe of the broom was a grating whisper. *Tall Bull, Tall Bull, Tall Bull*.

Feminine laughter floated down from the embankment behind him. A group of eligible young women had gathered to watch him. If the gossip could be trusted, more than one had voiced the hope Copper Woman would not return.

Canoe Boy lobbed the pokko, sending it wide and forcing Totka to scramble. He followed its trajectory and reached its end heartbeats after the pokko smacked the clay. It was between his cups and out again before his running stride could carry him another two rods. It flew a straight path to Little Warrior. A simple maneuver, but his audience cheered.

He gritted his teeth, then chided himself for being callous of their predicament. They were attractive women, but their prospects were glum. The upcoming Green Corn Festival would probably see several of them married off as second wives to older, established men.

Young men, unwed men, any men at all, were in short supply. The roofless winter council house was proof. As were the blackened remains of the camp houses lining the chunkey yard. All efforts had been put into rebuilding and stocking granaries and storehouses.

The conch shell blasted, and the square bustled with movement and noise as the council came to an end. From all sides, men descended the mound in animated discussion. At the sight of his father heading his way, Totka's stomach hardened.

The sloping set of Gray Hawk's shoulders spoke of the defeat Totka had anticipated.

Totka angled away from his father and looked to the boys. "Walker, your arm is too stiff. Loosen up that wrist. Try again." Totka picked up a spare pokko from the sidelines and hurled it out to the brave. They exchanged several easy throws while that hateful broom scratched and Gray Hawk neared.

Bells jingled with the man's every step. Since when had he taken to wearing Choctaw bells?

Totka tensed, and his next toss lost air because of it.

He heard the hollow clatter of cane on cane as Gray Hawk dropped his quiver at the base of the embankment. Gray Hawk had come to the ceremonial grounds armed while in the role of peace advocate? Some might call it wisdom, but Totka called it fear.

Unable to put off greeting his father, he threw the pokko into the field's center. "Play amongst yourselves a while," he called to the boys. "Work on straightening your left-handed stroke, Candid. It pulls to the right."

He turned just as Gray Hawk reached him and startled to find another man with him. A Long Hair.

Two features on the man stood out—his blue-gray eyes and the set of three white semicircles that extended from them down his cheeks. They were a perfect match to the paint adorning Gray Hawk's face.

White for peace. Replicated by the men to show unity of purpose.

To Totka, an insult of the highest degree. Had his father no memory whatsoever of the Choctaw murderer who'd robbed him of his wife?

Pressure built in Totka's neck. If he could not a bridle his hammering pulse, his veins would burst.

Gray Hawk stood placid before him, mute.

It was Totka's place to welcome him home, to say the first words, but his voice was hostage to his anger. Breathing hard, he clamped his jaw and stared down into the thick folds of his father's eyes.

Gray Hawk formed a flat, expressionless smile. "It does my soul good to see you." He looked Totka up and down, then grunted with a nod. "You look good. Fit."

Totka couldn't return the compliment. The grooves around his father's mouth were deeper; his cheekbones, more prominent; the silver in his hair, more abundant. War had aged him or maybe hunger.

"Maddo, Father," he managed to say without rancor. "The raven of war has spared us both." Although it might have been better Gray Hawk had died rather than consort with the enemy.

With a shriek of delight, Little Warrior thrust himself between them and, as though he were a slip of a boy again, jumped into his grandfather's arms. "Grandfather! You are back!" He squeezed Gray Hawk's neck until his elder pretended to choke. Then they laughed and hugged, Little Warrior giving off not a whiff of accusation for the seasons he'd been neglected.

A pale shade of remorse softened the muscles in Totka's back. Little Warrior had few male elders now. He needed this. Totka could behave civilly for his nephew.

"Are you home to stay?" Little Warrior asked.

Gray Hawk set the boy on his feet with a noisy sigh. "Not this time, my fierce brave, but soon, soon. How are your sisters?"

The boy's bottom lip protruded. "Boring. Have you come to practice with us?"

"For a while, yes. Run out there and show me your overhand swing."

Totka handed Gray Hawk his sticks while the Choctaw withdrew to a solitary spot on the grassy earthwork.

Gray Hawk flicked the pokko to his grandson with an awkward bend of his arm, reminding Totka he'd not gotten his athleticism from his father. "Why is the slave pole being cleansed?" Gray Hawk asked. "Is there to be an execution?"

"I wouldn't know. I was at the forge all morning."

"That was you making such racket?" Gray Hawk hopped two steps right to scoop the pokko off the clay.

"Lachlan Gibb mostly." From his peripheral vision, Totka sensed the Choctaw had anchored his gaze on him. If the man didn't stop, Totka would teach him how unwise it was to gawk at the enemy.

"The hairy Scotsman from the Federal? Here? And you work with him? That explains the extra muscle." He grinned and poked Totka in the chest with his ball stick.

Totka shrugged.

With a running skip, Little Warrior performed a lateral hook that dropped the pokko at his grandfather's feet.

"Well done! Before long, you will be giving me lessons." Gray Hawk laughed and sent the pokko back.

Totka withheld a wince at his father's poor form. He could use those lessons today.

"Iron work is a noble craft. Useful," his father continued, determined to keep up the drivel. "The confederacy needs more men like you. Men with keen foresight who are willing to try something new for the betterment of our people."

This would be the appropriate time for a son to beam under his father's praise, but although sincere enough, it counted for little when delivered by a man wearing the paint of his enemies.

Totka's frustration mounted until it burst from him uninvited. "I cannot understand you, Father! After all they have done, why have you given the Long Hairs your peace bundle? Why do you exchange tobacco with them and speak on their behalf?"

An emotion akin to grief contorted Gray Hawk's features. He

opened his mouth then closed it and dove for the incoming pokko.

Totka slashed a hand through his hair, took a calming breath. "Come back to us. Find a woman. Give the tribe more children. Surely, Tuskegee Deer needs you." If his clan would even have him.

Gray Hawk allowed a respectful lull before responding. "My vision reaches higher than the wattle and daub of my sister's lodge. If you will permit, I'll explain."

Was there any vision lofty enough to justify mingling with the Choctaws? But Totka owed his father a listening ear. The Choctaw boring a hole into his back, however, deserved nothing but scorn.

Totka jumped in front of Gray Hawk and intercepted the pokko as it came in, then spun on his toes and hurled it at the Choctaw. The shot, aimed at his face, was true, but with the reflexes of a bobcat, the man caught it a feather's breadth from his nose.

With a crisp smack, leather connected cleanly with skin.

Brows launching, Totka examined him through a different lens, that of respect for a fellow athlete.

The man was young. Twenty winters at most. His black hair, shaved close at his temples, hung long and loose except for a set of thin braids that framed his pleasant, well-balanced face. A wide strip of blue flannel topped by a silver band encircled his head and housed two pure white crane's feathers that stood at attention above his right ear.

There was a certain familiarity about him, about the way he held his mouth in a straight line while smiling with his eyes. Thick lashes gave those blueberry eyes an effeminate quality, but his broad, rope-thin mouth was all man. As was that catch.

The Choctaw unfolded himself and came to them, setting off the little silver bells lining the sides of his fringeless leggings. He tossed the pokko between his hands and, of all things, smiled. Not the sneer of a man who'd bested another but the grin of a boy allowed on the ball field with the men for the first time.

It was off-putting, as it didn't align with Totka's mean-spirited throw. He would rather be charged with a bill of curses than looked upon with, with ... What was that on the young man's face? Admiration?

Totka frowned, and Gray Hawk chuckled. "Well, Hilaho, you have rendered my son speechless. Perhaps he's met his match."

In height, yes. It wasn't often Totka could look level-eyed at another. Not since Pawa. He made certain to find his tongue. "One expert catch does not make a man an expert player."

"You honor me, Gray Hawk," Hilaho said in unblemished Muskogee, "but the Muscogee Falcon will always be my superior on the ball field."

Muscogee Falcon? He was a flatterer too.

Gray Hawk waved off their protests. "Trust me, Totka. The man is your match. And he would present an interesting challenge for you."

If Totka's pride were not a boulder in the path, he might take him up on it. "There's no time for scrimmages these days."

An understanding nod bobbed the hawk feathers tied to Gray Hawk's hair.

"May I?" Hilaho held out an open palm, a request for Totka's sticks.

Gray Hawk handed them over at once and watched him trot, jingling like a trader's pack mule, onto the yard to join the boys. "Do you remember him? He was with me the day I came across you in the woods."

Ah, that was why he looked familiar. "I was a little distracted by the musket you aimed at my chest."

"A ruse, Son. A ruse. To protect you. I had yet to earn their trust."

Why would he want it? Totka pursed his lips. Gray Hawk had been his and Copper Woman's savior that day, but one favor didn't cancel out the seasons of betrayal between that day and this.

The boys congregated and eyed Hilaho with suspicion, and Totka inwardly applauded. Satisfied, he gave the field his back and his father his full attention. "My ears are open. Tell me about this vision of yours."

Gray Hawk's eyes lit up. "Maddo." He drew out the word with the respect one would give an elder, and Totka's spirit blushed with shame.

He didn't deserve the man's respect. He'd certainly given none; whereas, Gray Hawk was making a concerted effort at cordiality.

"The Oaktebbehaw River Choctaws come from poor, rocky land," Gray Hawk began, his speech deliberate and slow as though he were still at the square. "Its soil was exhausted some time ago and refuses to produce crops enough to carry them through the winter. But they're hemmed in on all sides. By the Chickasaws to the north, the Lower Choctaws and French to the west and south, the Muscogees to the east. None of their neighbors are willing to give up land, so they slowly starve."

Hilaho looked healthy enough. "What of their alliance with the pale faces during the war? Surely, they were compensated for their loyalty."

"Not as profitably as they'd hoped. They received cattle in payment, but they are little experienced with the beasts. Some have died. Those that remain cannot be slaughtered for another four seasons. They are a slow investment that does not solve the problem of the maize that will not grow."

A sizeable problem, too, but it wasn't Totka's responsibility, nor Kossati's, nor Gray Hawk's.

With his toe, Gray Hawk pensively scratched at the hardened ground as though he might unbury the solution. "They have few resources, but they are wealthy in young men." The exact opposite of the Muscogees who had rich land but few men to till it. "The Great Warrior tells me your white woman provided seed corn from her father's storehouse, enough for the entire talwa."

Totka's mouth soften at the corners. "She is a good woman, blessed with beauty and generosity. Kossati's grain bins owe her their gratitude. Another few sleeps until harvest, until they are filled."

"Kossati has fared better than most, but you're still in great need of laborers." Gray Hawk arched an arm across the ceremonial grounds. "The council house is in shambles, widows across the talwa have no winter lodge, and cold weather fast approaches. Even your camp houses are piles of ash."

"We have the winter to finish rebuilding."

"And when will your hands, busy with hammer and saw, be free to pick up the musket for the great hunt?"

A valid question. Meat would be scarce for another couple of winters. If McGirth knew, he might try to forbid him Copper Woman for an extended period. But Totka had fulfilled the man's conditions: a lodge and a full granary. A gracious suitor would insist his intended stay with her father a while more, but when it came to Copper Woman, Totka was hopelessly selfish.

A commotion behind Totka redirected his wandering thoughts.

The boys' laughter and shouting indicated they'd overcome their aversion to their guest. Totka's molars grated. The Choctaw had pilfered not only his father but his pupils as well.

The women on the hill leaped to their feet and applauded. Gray Hawk, looking past Totka, smiled at whatever had brought it on.

Although sorely tempted, Totka refused to become audience to Hilaho's performance. He pegged his gaze to the white kerchief knotted about his father's neck. "Tell me what was spoken at the council."

Drawing a large breath, Gray Hawk began. "They propose that in exchange for permission to move their talwa to the shores of Beaver Lake, they will provide three, unwed men to each of the four townships who share the surrounding hunting grounds."

"Oh?" An interesting proposition.

"They will stay a year in each talwa to build, plant, hunt, and even fight, should trouble arise from outside our borders. When the year of labor is ended, should they find any young women willing to bind themselves to a Choctaw brave, they will erect their lodge poles among us and fill their wives' bellies with Muscogee babies. Future warriors to rebuild our ranks."

"Their situation must be dire indeed to bring such a radical proposal to our councils."

"Is it so strange? For a hundred winters the Muscogee Confederacy has grown mighty because it welcomes into its fold tribes of every variety."

"So long as their intentions are peaceful."

"The Choctaws come swearing loyalty and lasting peace."

Totka gave a breathy, disbelieving laugh, but Gray Hawk had the grace to ignore it and continue.

"They send their finest men. They are skilled and eager to do what they must to better the lives of their clans." He gestured to Hilaho as though he were a prime example. "Their blood would strengthen ours. Their hardy backs would put Kossati back on its feet that much quicker."

Let the enemy into their midst? Totka struggled to harness his contempt. "A decent offer, Father, except we would never be able to trust them."

"The majority of the council takes your position. Pauwocte and Ockchoy agreed to our terms, but without the consent of all four townships, we cannot proceed. We have yet to meet with the Tuskegees. Perhaps if they agree, Kossati will reconsider."

"Perhaps."

His father had earned the right to entertain false hope, seeing he had Kossati's welfare at heart. Although, that couldn't have always been the driving force behind his strange liaison.

Hilaho's laughter mingled with the merry chiming of his bells. It swelled as he rejoined them, then dissolved at the sight of Totka's glower. When he returned the sticks, he displayed humble enough thanks, but men were capable of great deception when necessity required.

He studied Totka with unabashed curiosity. "I watched you play when I was a boy, younger than Little Warrior there." He jabbed a thumb over his shoulder. "Our knower said you used witchcraft to give you flight. Watching you leap, my child's mind believed it. You were the falcon of the field."

158

The Muscogee Falcon, apparently.

Totka smirked. "Until your players took up a battle cry and clipped the falcon's wings. How does it feel to be kin to cheaters and cowards?"

Hilaho's blue eyes turned wintery, but he wisely kept his tongue in check.

Leaping Waters appeared at the rise of the embankment and waved, and Totka jerked his chin in acknowledgement.

"Is that Leaping Waters?" Amazement heightened Gray Hawk's pitch. "Is she ill? She is far too thin."

"Not ill, and not as thin as she was. The war was hard on her, but White Stone has tasked herself with putting meat on her bones." And still she could not give her child suck.

A frown wrinkled Hilaho's forehead. "Is she bound to you?"

Was he a clueless child who knew no better than to pry into a man's life? Totka slid his narrowed gaze from Hilaho to Canoe Boy whose over-handed pass fell shy of Little Warrior. "Choke up on the stick, Canoe Boy! And it hooked around your neck again. Less twisting at the shoulders should help with that."

Gray Hawk answered for him. "Leaping Waters belongs to my son's cousin, Tall Bull."

"Ah, yes. Tall Bull." Hilaho nodded.

Little Warrior, Tall Bull. Did the man know the dog's name too?

"For a moment," he continued with an annoying little smile. "I thought your pretty white woman had gotten away from you."

At least there was *one* name he didn't know. Totka replied for his father's benefit. "Copper Woman will bind herself to me at the next blackberry moon."

That was the hope. If she couldn't learn to forgive their differences in spiritual beliefs . . .

Leaping Waters descended the hill with her lashes low and her footfall hesitant. "Gray Hawk, welcome home."

"Maddo. How is your husband?"

"He is as well as can be expected, I suppose." Her smile was tight.

She skipped a shy glance at Hilaho and at the medicine maker who had moved on to sweep the square grounds. "Singing Grass sends for Little Warrior. The clan mothers are to deliberate on the matter of Water Moon, and she does not want him hearing of it from anyone but her."

"What matter of Water Moon?" Gray Hawk asked.

"Several days ago, he loaned his hunting dogs to Tempest, but the animals turned on Tempest. Got him by the throat in is his own courtyard." A shiver rocked her shoulders. "He was dead before his mother could beat them off him. Rabbit Clan demanded full compensation." Water Moon's life.

Hilaho shook his head. "Who would demand such a thing? If ever mercy was to be shown, now would be the time, when Muscogee numbers are so few."

"It is within a grieving family's rights to request it," Totka said, aggravated at the reminder of their weakness.

By the clan-upheld principle of blood law, Rabbit had the right to demand a life for a life no matter the cause of death, whether by malice or accident, by a man's doing or by his dog's.

In this instance, though, Totka would lay down all the silver he owned that the clan mothers would not allow blood to be shed. They would recommend Water Moon give his life in another way — by filling the hole left in Rabbit, by leaving his clan and becoming the son of the dead brave's mother. Not that Totka would deign to explain any of this to Hilaho.

Hilaho expelled a blustery breath. "To even discuss it is foolishness."

Agree or not, Totka refused to abide the Choctaw's arrogance. "How my father stands your wearisome company is a mystery to me. Take your bells and opinions back to Choctaw country and see if you can come up with a better plan to save your miserable hides than robbing us of our land."

Leaping Waters gasped. "Totka Hadjo!"

He spun to the yard and shouted, "Little Warrior, we leave.

Now!"

The embankment was behind him before he heard Gray Hawk hurrying to catch up.

"Why do you shame me?" he asked, a little breathless.

"Your *friend* is an insolent child."

"Hilaho knows something of blood vengeance gone wrong. His French father was taken unawares, as payment for an accidental death. He speaks from experience and pain." Weariness entered Gray Hawk's voice. "Much as you do."

Totka hated that his father was right, that he knew the man's story, his character, his struggles. But Gray Hawk was *his* father and his mother's great love. For her sake, as well as Little Warrior's, Totka should try a little harder.

He slowed his vicious march. "Do you have lodgings? You are . . . welcome in mine."

"Your hospitality means a great deal to me. Maddo. But we press on to Tuskegee. Let me bid you farewell." He stopped and extended his arm.

Disappointed yet again, Totka gazed down a moment before taking it. His father's grip was as warm and strong as ever it was, along with his smile. Longing crept up Totka's throat and behind his lids. He blinked it away, resigned to carrying the burden of family headman alone.

His elder was halfway back to the chunkey yard when Totka lifted his voice. "Father, what of the debt owed them, for sparing my life?" Shouldn't Hilaho have made mention of it, lorded it over him? He had the right to.

Gray Hawk tossed up a shrug and grinned. "Haven't you more pressing concerns, such as preparing a lodge for your woman?"

Totka couldn't help the smile working its way up his cheek. "The lodge is complete. All it lacks is filling."

"Then get to it."

Chapter 9

*H*ugging the writings under his arm, Totka climbed the four-rung ladder to the elevated storehouse. His little oil lamp led the way into the musty, black interior. At the far side, he assembled a pile of husked corn into the semblance of a table, then placed a slab of wood over it and balanced the bowl-shaped lamp on top.

The maize reached halfway to the rafters along the back wall, but here, in the front of the pile, it rose just high enough to serve as a table before the stack of duffle blankets and oilskin tarps he used as a seat.

This wasn't the first time he'd been woken from a dead sleep by Copper Woman's whispered, insistent call. *He has promised He will show Himself to those who seek Him.*

There was no escaping his vow, nor did he wish to; however, the number of sleeps he'd been seeking without response blurred into a frustrating mass of futility.

With a sigh, he set the writings on the improvised sideboard, opened its stiff cover, and settled in. Instead of going to where Lachlan last read—a story about a king who rebelled against Creator—he aimlessly flipped the pages.

Perhaps he would stumble upon stories of the god-man. Even if Totka found them, there would be little reading. He could name all the symbols and create their sounds. Putting them together and coming up with something that made sense was almost more work than it was worth, but he sensed that, like a sabia, the writing itself would provide the magic to interpret its message.

He hoped. If not, he was out of luck.

Lachlan had yet to answer even one of Totka's questions, nor did he seem to understand his driving curiosity. To Lachlan, the writings were a grand tale. Nothing more.

But Copper Woman was convinced the words on the pages were those of her Creator. Totka had to admit they drew him in like flotsam to a whirlpool. If the events told in the pages were even partial truths . . .

He shook his head, afraid to consider what it would mean, how it might transform his life, his beliefs, his traditions. Or would it? The not knowing made him nervous, set his fingers to tapping his knee.

A crisp breeze blew through the widely spaced slats and rustled the writings' leaves. He corralled them, then let cricket song fill his ears. From the rafters, a bat fluttered into the night. A furry moth fluttered above the lamp. He shooed it from the heat of the flame.

To think the little creature had no spirit seemed absurd. It contained special transforming powers, but according to the writings, animals were nothing more than-than . . . What *would* they be, if not spirit beings?

This explained much about the white man, why he took from Mother Earth without offering thanks for the sacrifices made, or how it was he could peel the hide from a deer and leave the carcass to the carrion birds. Totka wasn't sure he could worship a Creator who cared so little about the plants and animals that he would give them no spirits, that he would leave them to man's tending.

Man was flawed. Despairingly so. Even the Muscogees who strove tirelessly to honor nature, to keep it in balance, had to constantly cleanse and pray, for having muddled things. A man could never hope to keep it all in harmony. He could only be diligent in the attempt.

But the idea of a Creator who'd created all three worlds—the Upper, the Under, and the one Totka's feet rested upon—yet worked intimately in man's heart and life was so alluring, he kept turning pages. Hadn't Copper Woman always spoken to her Creator as though he were a pawa from whose loving eye she could never escape?

Call on my Jesus Creator, and see if He does not answer. Her plea was alive in his head. *Seek Him and He will find you.*

He dragged a heavy hand down a column of confusing symbols. "If you are a true spirit, show yourself to me." The prayerful demand was scratched by fatigue but no less insistent for it. He skimmed page after page as lost as ever, until his eyes became unfocused. Then, since he could not find Copper Woman's god-man, he laid his head on his arm and let his mind fill with *her.*

With her laughter, free and easy. The gentleness on her tongue, which stood in stark contrast to her strength of character. The intense look in her eye that said she loved him and only him. The soft curve of her body, the heat of her mouth, the stirring touch of her finger as it traced the winding path of his tattoo. The memory was so vibrant he could feel the cool silk of her finger pad.

A dream. Only a dream.

Even so, his heart quickened. He would stay here in this moment with her all night if he could.

The writings slid from his hold. His lids flew open as he slapped to keep it from falling.

A figure jumped away from him and cloaked itself in the thick shadows outside the lamp's narrow circle. He would recognize that silhouette in any lighting. Her breathing pattern alone gave her away. Shallow, stuttered, rapid.

"Always the same," he said. "Lurking, cowering. Face the light, Leaping Waters."

Instead of insulting her, he should call her wise to shrink from him for having tried to take the writings. He drew it to his chest, closing it as he did.

Her breathing stopped altogether. Then she moved the opposite direction toward the ladder. Since when did she defy a command?

"And now you run?" He stood, drawing himself to his full height, holding the lamp before him.

She'd arrived in his compound five days ago, but they had yet to speak a word to each other since that first night. Artful avoidance.

On the opposite side of the storehouse, she was no more than a blurry form with easy access to escape. But something halted her, brought her back. Had it been the light he'd lifted to his hardened features? The tension pouring off him? The recollection of everything they'd shared?

Whatever the cause, she came, hands knotted before her, lashes hovering above her cheeks. A long-shirt covered her to the thighs; the fabric, worn to a sheer transparency, was almost pointless.

His pulse took flight even as his heel retreated. It kicked the base of the corn stack, causing it to shudder. A cob rolled clumsily down the heap and came to a teetering rest between them.

Even thin as a waif, she was fetching, but to Copper Woman's glorious sunshine, Leaping Waters' russet skin and loose, black hair was night and darkness; the vision of her created the same inside him.

She would come to him like this? Alone? In the quiet of night?

Black anger billowed in his gut, increasing its fury as his eye fell upon the twirling line of indigo that adorned her neck. His hand went to his own throat, to the design that would forever bind him to this woman. The fact had once heated his blood. Today, it heated his ire.

Like a blow, his dream came back full force. It had felt real for good reason. "Have you come to seduce me?"

Her jaw hung suspended by the shame in her eyes. Or was it confusion? "How could you think that?"

"How could I not? You tossed me aside for my cousin. He's now fallen on hard times. Why not reverse the situation to better suit you? As I look at you now" — he swept the light over her — "in your bare legs and unbound hair, I wonder if there was more to Tall Bull's accusations than I'd allowed myself to believe."

"My husband says many things that are a shade off the truth, but I've always been a loyal wife. I would never —"

"You touched me!" And set his skin on fire.

"Forgive me, Totka Hadjo, I only meant to —"

"Be gone! before I send you and your child back to your trickster husband."

Although her mouth trembled, her spine straightened. "No." More obstinacy? Her time in the Floridas had changed her. "Not until you let me speak uninterrupted."

His narrow-eyed silence was all the permission she would get.

"I saw the light and feared a fire, but it was only you, sleeping over the book." She hunched and crossed her arms over her breasts.

A degree of apprehension eased from his shoulders.

"I thought to read the writings myself. It has been so long . . ." Her voice trailed with subtle fondness. "But your hair covered the page. I moved it and-and . . . If I touched you, it was only for that, so I could see." Her throat bobbed with a fearful swallow, filling Totka with regret.

He was becoming like a snake with a speedy, indiscriminate strike.

"You slept so soundly," she said. "I thought I might remove it from under you. But you woke and scared me, and I knew what you would think, how you would see me." Her mouth formed a peevish pucker. "I was right. You've always been quick to judge, Totka Hadjo, and slow to forgive. Far too slow."

Was that censure she was wielding? It looked awkward on her. But . . . she was right.

Even so, it galled that she'd so accurately predicted his reaction — an irksome reminder of how close they'd been. Deflated by niggling remorse, Totka lowered the lamp. Over the dome of its light, they stared at each other until their breathing came more evenly. At length, he said, "You wanted to read the writings."

A furtive nod rippled her hair. "Do you . . . mind?"

"You know I do." His nails dug into the leather.

The writings were intimate, a part of Copper Woman. Allowing Lachlan to read from them was hard enough, but sharing them with Leaping Waters felt a betrayal. His beloved, however, would likely snip at him if she knew he'd denied anyone access. Especially Leaping Waters. Oddly, the women had taken a liking to each other.

As far as he was concerned, the two were white fire and tepid water. Boundless fears hid beneath Leaping Waters' murky surface, but Copper Woman was pure and hot and strong enough to merge with his own flame.

"Yes . . . I do know." She backed up a tiny pace as though seeking permission to leave.

"Wait." The word exploded from him before he knew what exactly he wanted from her.

She froze, eyes wide.

Moments ago, she'd said something. What was it? His gaze floated to the writings locked in the crook of his arm. She'd wanted it. Did that mean . . . ? "Do you understand it?"

"The sacred writings? Some. But . . ." Fear shot through her eyes. She glanced behind her at the ladder. "Tall Bull told me I was never to speak of it again."

So she had some understanding of it. Enough to get herself in trouble with her husband. How many times had Totka prayed to Copper Woman's Jesus to show himself, to send understanding? Was Leaping Waters the answer?

Awe, like the Thunder Man, rolled through Totka's body. There were no coincidences. Fate, led by the spirits, determined every step of a man's life. That Totka's prayer had been answered at all was surprising. That it had come, not through a white man but through one of the People—a woman and his old love—was nothing short of startling. That she shouldn't be in Kossati at all except for a rare display of courage and defiance shook him so thoroughly, the flame in his hand flickered and danced.

But she was more than in Kossati; she was lodging in his sister's winter house.

Totka gathered his scattered wits and swiped a harsh line through the air, spattering the ground with oil. "Forget Tall Bull. He left you. Since you are under Wolf lodge poles, you will do as I say. And *I* say you will teach me."

"To read?"

"To understand." When she simply stared up at him as though he'd asked her to traverse the Great Waters, desperation gripped him. He advanced a hasty stride, sending a cob skittering across the planks. "How much do you know of the white man's Creator? Tell me. Empty your head of knowledge. I can take it, whatever it is. I need to understand, Leaping Waters. I must."

He shoved the writings against her chest, scooting her back a step.

She looked down at it for a moment, then stroked the cover, the words etched on it, the channel where the edges of the leaves met, and when she looked up, tears had clumped her lashes.

"Do the writings mean so much to you?" he asked.

"Yes, but also, I have prayed for you, pleaded to Creator on your behalf, since, since . . . Well, forever, it seems." Her frayed inhale ended in a tearful gulp.

"Why would you do that?"

"Like every other, your soul is unwell and requires a healing song that only Jesus can sing. One he has already sung." She tipped an ear toward the trestle above. "Can you hear it?"

A healing song? A frown scrolled his lips. "All I hear is your babbling."

With the sacred writings hugged against her, she drew nearer, fervency brightening her eyes and voice. "Listen harder. It is here, in every word of the writings. You've had many of them read to you. They are alive, you know. Each one. And they are inside you now, whispering, but you must open your heart and listen." The flame between them shrank under the influence of her rapid breath. "You might not recognize the song, but you have heard it. I know you have. I saw it in your eyes." With a petal-soft touch to his forearm she whispered, "The song is calling to you. *He* is calling to you."

"Who?"

"Jesus."

The firm shake of his head tapped his earbobs against his neck. "I have yet to hear anything read about him."

"Then, come. I will show you." She hurried to the stack of blankets, placed the writings on the wood, and thumbed through it with expert hands.

Totka stood as he'd been, numb and confused. A healing song from Copper Woman's Jesus? Living words? Had the woman lost her mind, or had he lost his for wanting to know more?

"What are you doing over there?" She waved him over. "Bring the light."

For the remainder of the night, to the sweet scent of corn, she read to him from a portion of the writings penned by a man named John. He'd known Jesus, followed him, witnessed miracles every knower would be envious of.

But Jesus was more than the chief of knowers and medicine men. He was a good man, perfect by all accounts. He bore no resemblance to the Spaniards who'd spouted his name and carried his symbol the length Totka's land, enslaving the People, slicing them down like so many nettlesome weeds.

No, the Jesus in the writings was not that sort. Love, kindness, mercy, truth—they were his staples, and despite not being a warrior, he was a man Totka could admire.

But not everyone felt the same. Evil men had earned the ear of the rulers of Jesus' talwa, and through manipulation and deceit, they had him tortured and put to death. At that point in the reading, Totka decided it was a horrible tale. Worse than the ten plagues, worse than Creator teasing Abraham with the sacrifice of his only son. A knot clogged his throat, but Leaping Waters let tears flow unchecked.

"Since the tomb was close by, they laid Jesus in it." Overuse roughened her voice as she made the paper talk. "Early Sunday—"

"Stop. How do you expect me to hear the song of a man who is dead?" Totka cleared his throat, ashamed of the emotion it revealed.

"But the story is not yet through." The base of her nose shone with wet, and she wiped it with a sleeve.

"The papers have said enough. I am tired." He stood, pushing hard off the board.

The corn beneath shifted, but her swift reflexes steadied the writings and lamp. "Leave now and you will regret it." She patted the place he'd abandoned. "The best is yet to come. I promise."

"Well, it cannot get any worse." Scowling, he refilled the lamp and plopped back down, feeling the lack of sleep in his sore leg and burning eyes.

The tale continued. It told of men finding the tomb empty. Someone, it appeared, had stolen the medicine maker's body.

"Mary turned to leave," Leaping Waters read, "then saw a man standing nearby. It was Jesus, but she did not recognize him. 'Dear woman, why are you crying?' Jesus asked."

"What?" Totka sat forward. "He was not dead?"

A sleek smile tugged at her lips. "He was. Then, three days later, he was not."

"Impossible." Derision dripped from his smirk.

The story had suddenly taken on the myth-like qualities of Muscogee legends where the impossible became possible and the unbelievable was a natural occurrence, where spirit creatures from time-before-time roamed the earth. Totka had always been a man of faith, but he'd not expected the nonsensical in a tale with such a lifelike setting.

"For man, yes, but not for Creator. Do you recall that Jesus named *himself* Creator? At the beginning of John's account."

"Copper Woman called him the god-man," he muttered.

"So he is—all the power of Creator in the body of an unpolluted

171

man."

Ah. A flaw. "If that were true, he would not have let them torture and kill him."

"He allowed them to kill him, so his death might cleanse us from pollution."

That made no sense, but what did it matter? It didn't apply to Totka anyway. He shrugged. "To cleanse the white man."

She picked at the bent corner of a page, ironing it flat with her finger. "Lachlan Gibb had an apprentice who once explained these things to me. He said Jesus lived across the Great Waters far removed from the English and Spanish. He belonged to a tribe named Judah, and his skin was probably as dark as ours."

The teachings were not that of the pale faces, but of some dark-skinned tribe in a distant land? Totka massaged his temples. "Enough. My head hurts. You should go before someone finds us together and thinks the worst."

"Of course." Her compliant smile made a reappearance as she rose to leave. She paused and examined the streaks of gray coming through the gaps in the wall. "The dawn has caught us unawares." Rushed steps carried her to the ladder. "Perhaps Journey's End will draw milk with his suckling today."

"And if he does?" She would leave and take her knowledge with her.

On the top rung, she looked back. Daylight tinted the sky and revealed a new softness about her. It smudged the lines of hunger and trouble into a semblance of the woman he'd known before Lance made her a mother against her will. "I am not going anywhere, Totka Hadjo. Not now."

Chapter 10

Mulberry Month (May) 1815, six months later

Totka set down the spade handle he'd been whittling, sheathed his knife, and glared at Long Arrow's back as he strode from their compound.

"Why would the council ask for you?" Singing Grass leaned her shoulder into the tall pestle she rammed into the corn. Over her head, the paddle-like weighted end of the pestle cast her face in shade, but her disgust needed no bright spring sunlight for clarity.

"We'll know soon enough. Best not keep them waiting." He stood and dusted wood shavings from his shirt and the flap of his breechcloth, then went for the sorghum broom leaned against the winter lodge. He swept the shavings into a pile to the tune of grinding corn and Speaks Sweetly's lullaby to her cornhusk doll.

The girl, a mirror image of her mother, sat in the dirt by the mortar, strapping her doll into a minuscule cradleboard. White Stone, after a spat with Totka earlier that morning, had taken refuge at the river with Rain Child who'd begged to try out the little fish trap Totka had made for her.

Leaping Waters, son strapped to her back, entered the compound from the direction of the family garden. Two round spots of dirt soiled her skirt where she'd been kneeling, another smudged her forehead. She'd given up on her milk, and since Journey's End refused to suckle with any wet nurse but Singing Grass, Leaping Waters had stayed on with them, sleeping in the winter lodge.

Totka felt the weight of her eye as he cleaned up his mess, disposing of it properly by burning every shaving in the courtyard fire, but she continued to the winter lodge with no more than a meaning-filled glance that ushered a whisper across his mind.

The blackberry moon approaches.

True, but his curiosity about the writings was having less and less to do with Copper Woman and more to do with sorting out truth from myth. His talks with Leaping Waters had continued; although, several times, he'd become so overwhelmed he'd begged off discussing it for great periods of time.

This was one of those times. He flattened his mouth at her and went for one more quick round of sweeping, the increased rasp of sorghum tassels against dirt his protest to frustration.

"The Long Hairs should have known better than to return." Singing Grass' embittered voice followed him to the fire where he sprinkled in the last of the shavings. She drove the pestle into the burned-out center of the beech log mortar. "If they are the ones calling for you, they're bigger fools than we thought."

"They are probably as irritated as I that I'm being summoned."

White Stone had called him a coward for refusing to attend the council meeting. There wasn't a speck of truth in her accusation. His only fear was in shaming himself and his clan by losing his temper and exacting justice on a Choctaw delegate accepted into the village under the shelter of the eagle feather and pipe. White Stone saw only avoidance of conflict.

"They should be. Murderous cheats, every last one. And our father is playing into their schemes like the thin-blooded fool he is."

She voiced his own thoughts. "Watch yourself, Sister. He is yet our father and elder. Then too, little ears have big mouths." He angled his head at Speaks Sweetly who gazed up at her mother adoringly.

Singing Grass blew air from tight lips while placing the unwieldy pestle on the ground. "So they do." She hoisted Black Sky's cradleboard with a grunt. The girl, despite sharing her mother's milk, was as chubby as they came. Singing Grass crooked a finger at Speaks Sweetly. "Nap time, little one."

Totka untied his knife from his belt. "Take this in."

"Smart man. I would tell you everything will be well, but I am no better a liar than you." Singing Grass gave him a sympathetic smile before ducking into the lodge.

Six moons had passed since Gray Hawk had promised Little Warrior he would soon return to their township to stay. From that day to this, they had yet to see even his shadow. A passing French trader had made mention that a Gray Hawk of the Kossatis was in residence with the Choctaws, that he'd taken a wife with them. Totka could believe it.

Long Arrow had said Gray Hawk was not in attendance this time. Probably couldn't bear to leave his woman or the pleasure of creating a new son. A Long Hair son.

Hostility squeezed Totka's chest and made his fingers twitch for his bow, but he would go in unarmed. He washed his hands and face in the rainwater barrel outside the storehouse, filled his lungs with cool spring air, and let it out with a portion of his anger. It would have to do. He exited their compound and turned onto the tree-lined road that led into the heart of the talwa.

A young woman traveled toward him, chin lifted, eyes roaming, as though in search of someone or something. Although garbed as a man, there was no mistaking her gender. Leggings covered her from ankles to knees, and a long-shirt fell to her thighs. She toted a quiver and carried a man's bow. It was longer than she but not by much, for she was tall, her stride lithe and confident. And she was lovely, with her hair pulled over one shoulder and tied loosely with an unraveling ribbon.

When she noticed him, her eyes lightened with interest and her step quickened. "My name is Polly of the Alabamas. I am Wolf and was told Singing Grass would help me." Blue-flecked hazel eyes blurted her ancestry; the red rimming them hinted at fatigue.

Polly of Alabama Town? Wolf? She may as well have saved her

breath and introduced herself as Josiah Francis' daughter. But she could have lied. Should have.

Totka instinctually took in their surroundings. The lane was empty, but the stretch of woods lining one side of it could hide an army.

This might end poorly for one of them, but he wouldn't hold Polly responsible for her father's actions, and her truthfulness was admirable. "Singing Grass is my sister. Come to your home."

At the traditional clan greeting, relief entered her eyes, dousing them in innocence and betraying her youth. It curved her lips up into a smile that lacked no charm in its modesty. She dipped her head in a regal nod befitting the daughter of a high micco. "Maddo."

"You thank me too soon. I'll not send the daughter of Josiah Francis into my sister's compound without good cause. But I am called to the council square and cannot keep the chiefs waiting. Walk with me. Tell me your need." He set off, not sparing her his long stride.

After a discreet glance into the trees, she came alongside him and matched his tempo and bearing with the ease of one accustomed to the company of men. "Hominy. A journey of many sleeps lies ahead of me, but as you can see" — she patted the flat pouch against her stomach — "I've no provisions."

"Do you travel alone?" Would her honesty hold out?

"There is one other with me." Her thick lashes blinked up at him, eyes open wide, testifying to her rampant honesty. Her mouth, however, was set in a line that would reveal no more.

In short, she expected him to knowingly break treaty and give aid to a fugitive's daughter and to her undisclosed companion — likely a male, the owner of the bow she carried with such familiarity.

The ceremonial grounds came into view, and Polly stopped. "Will you help me?"

Totka retraced the two steps he'd taken without her and studied the determination setting her chin at a slight angle. "You saw which compound I came from?"

She gave a brisk nod.

"If I give you corn, will you promise to feed only yourself? I cannot give aid to a Red Stick on the run."

She blinked again, lashes fluttering like butterfly wings, confidence shaken. But for no more than a bundle of breaths. Another decisive nod restored her aplomb. "I do."

Whatever Josiah Francis might be—crazed knower, relentless Red Stick, deceived visionary—his daughter was an admirable creature.

Totka lowered his voice. "Ask for Leaping Waters. Speak only to her. Tell her I sent you, and take no more than what will fill your pouch."

"You have my word." Polly extended her arm. It was a manly vow and a manly gesture, but the sudden moisture in her eyes said she was woman through and through. "I have only my deep gratitude to give in return. Maddo."

Totka accepted, noting that her strength went beyond her demeanor to the sleek muscles in her forearm. Was she a war woman? "Up river, along the eastern side, there is a hollow in the bank, hidden behind a curtain of grapevine. It makes a fine couch."

Leaping Waters would ask Polly if she had a place to pass the night, and if Totka didn't offer an alternative, he might return from the meeting to find two fugitives bunking down in his storehouse. *That* he would never allow.

They parted ways, and the drone of heated discussion led Totka up the mound to the square. All four sheds were full to overflowing. Totka might have been the only man in the township who'd spurned the Choctaws' invitation to renew negotiations.

His arrival didn't go unnoticed. The chatter intensified as furtive glances were tossed his direction, but he waited in the shade of the warriors' shed until he was summoned.

Long Arrow occupied his usual cane bench in the north-facing warriors' bed. When their gazes snagged, a thunderhead came into his friend's features. After an intense moment, he looked away, leaving Totka to wonder whether the man's anger was directed at him or held on his behalf.

Above, a turkey buzzard silently circled. Totka looked hastily away.

Leaning Bow, Wolf headman, sat on the front row of the elders' shed, but his usual companion, Old Grandfather, was absent. Totka skimmed the beds until he found the ancient one seated in the chiefs' shed to the right of the Great Warrior who sat to the right of the principle chief, Micco Bird Creek Fekseko.

What did that forebode? Totka's already agitated stomach took a dive.

At the chief's left hand, in the place of honored guest, sat a number of Choctaw warriors. Seven, if Totka's quick count proved true. Enemies were often honored for their bravery to come and talk, but the sight of them outfitted identically in white crane feathers, white paint, and white kerchiefs inflamed his ire.

Propping a shoulder on a support pole of the shed, Totka crossed his arms and blew a laugh through his nose. How foolish they were, thinking they could conjure peace by bedecking themselves in its color.

He recognized one among them by the headband he wore— Hilaho, the bell-wearing youth Gray Hawk had taken such a liking to. The others with him seemed at ease, but the youth's bare chest was as rigid as an unstrung bow. He had broadened through the shoulders since Totka had last seen him, or did they only appear so in contrast to his leaner frame?

Shortly, the speaker of the house of warriors rose and addressed all present. "We all know the deeds of the one who will speak next. Even our honored guests know of his skill as displayed in the little brother of war. Every uneven stride he takes is evidence of his resilience and sacrifice."

At that, Totka emerged from the shadows and waited for the speaker to conclude the introduction.

"He has achieved much in his life and has won honor and respect from all the people, near and far. He fought bravely and honorably to protect the lives of our helpless ones while our warriors fought at the Horse's Flat Foot, many of whom have taken the journey onward."

The speaker bowed his head in respectful pause. Then, in a voice strong and perfect in pitch he said, "*Hvo!* It is good. Yes." He signaled with uplifted arm. "Come forward now, Big Warrior Totka Hadjo. Listen to what has been spoken here, then let us hear your words and heart on this matter."

Not bothering to mask his limp, Totka did as told and came to stand before the principle micco, off to the side in recognition of the man's rank.

Avoiding the Choctaws, he adhered his gaze to his chief. Micco Bird Creek Fekseko's steady gaze met Totka's but revealed nothing. The buzzard's shadow ghosted across the man's torso, then repeated, drawing Totka's attention skyward. The bird had become a trio.

He neutralized the acid pooling in the back of his throat and, with as much grace as he could muster, accepted the calumet. Totka inhaled four times, sweeping the smoke over his face and head with each exhale, blowing to each of the four directions. He returned the pipe with a drawn out maddo that settled his nerves.

"Totka Hadjo, the council thanks you for attending our request for your presence." The micco's face and voice were both impassive. "Yatika Mad Turkey will speak on our behalf."

The *yatika* began in the clear, sonorous tones that had earned him the position of orator. "Totka Hadjo, our guests and neighbors, the Choctaws, tell us a tale of hunger. Over the winter, many of their children and elders sickened and took the journey. Their storehouses are empty, their hunting bows stiff with neglect. Their lean faces are evidence of their truthfulness."

Totka could grant them that, but since when did a tribe not rejoice at the trials of its enemies? Perhaps Copper Woman had whispered her crazed notions into their dreams, so that now, they thought they could come among the enemy and expect love in return for hate. The lunacy of it all brought an untimely snicker up his throat. He coughed it into a quick death.

"Our guests have returned with five braves instead of the original three." Mad Turkey swept his arm to indicate the Choctaws. "Each has expressed eagerness to toil alongside us, to pray with us at dawn, and to drive his lodge poles into Kossati's ground.

"The councils of Pauwocte and Ockchoy have accepted the Choctaw braves as payment for the use of our land. Even Tuskegee has softened toward our neighbors' plight and diplomacy."

They'd done *what*? The responses of the first two talwas didn't surprise him. The war had dealt them an exceptional blow. But Tuskegee? Whatever had compelled them to surrender their honor, their livelihood, in this way?

Did it matter? They had, and in so doing, they'd left Kossati as the deciding factor in the fate of the Oaktebbehaw River Choctaws. Not a pretty place to be.

"Our clan mothers are eager to see our young women wed and with child. They are agreeable to the Choctaw braves and would expect each to consider taking a second wife as soon he is able," the orator continued. "The council values their wisdom and thought to the future. However, many of our Red Sticks bitterly recall the Choctaws' accusations of our prized player as well as their treatment of him. They have also made disgruntled mention of the Choctaws' swift submission to the white chief Jackson and of their fight against us in the late war.

"The White Sticks among us would have us lift our eyes to the eastern horizon, which is dark with threat. They wish for peace with every all Natives no matter their tribe, for they say we are stronger united. Those who agree and those who oppose are two bulls locked horn to horn, equally matched in strength, unable to gain or give ground."

It was the age-old division that had launched them into civil war. If Totka listened carefully, he might hear a chorus of war drums beating inside a hundred minds.

Yatika Mad Turkey directed his gaze at Totka. "After much fruitless discussion, our Beloved Man has wisely advised we seek your counsel, Totka Hadjo, for a good portion of the Choctaws' offense is against you. If you are able to look beyond their wrongs to you, the Red Sticks will agree to do the same. The remainder claim you have the heart of a White Stick. They have good faith in your judgment.

"Our clan mothers urge you to accept the Choctaws' offer, but in the name of peace here among our brethren, they will defer to your ruling on the matter." Mad Turkey spread his arms wide. "What say you?"

Stunned, Totka gaped at the yatika, expecting him to list the names of the chiefs who would make the ultimate decision, but Mad Turkey took his seat and fell silent, as did the rest of the square.

They were placing this decision on Totka's shoulders? The council was well aware of his intense hatred for those seated in the place of honor. But as intense as his hatred was for his enemy, his tenderness toward the helpless ones was even greater. According to Singing Grass, that fact was widely acknowledged in the talwa—at times in scorn, at times with admiration. And now, they would put the fate of his enemy's starving women and children into *his* hands? They would pit his nurtured hatred against his inbred benevolence?

As he stepped forward, his old wound reminded him of yet another cost the Choctaws had exacted on him—his mobility, his pawa's life. His chest heated like a furnace. Some might construe it as an honor for the council to entrust him with this level of power, but Totka saw it as nothing short of cruelty.

Worse yet, they'd called him a White Stick. The recollection was a bellow to his fire.

Very well. If the council wanted his opinion, they would get it.

He slid his tongue over dry lips and let his eyes travel to the sky where the carrion birds were spiraling downward. Foreboding sang a death song in his head, but he raised his voice over it. "The Choctaws' behavior on the ball field was deceitful and cowardly, but their greatest offense against me was in the murder of my mother and grandmother. Kossati's wise council members ask if I can forgive

181

such injury." As was customary, he moved about as he spoke, so that all might see him, so that they might know by the rigidity of his face that he was in earnest. "Perhaps they believe me to be my father. If so, they are grievously mistaken. My answer is no. Send the Choctaws, all seven, back the way they came."

Agitated murmurings rose like a flock of crows. Disgust and relief came at Totka from all sheds, but he kept his eye on the deep, drooping ridges of Old Grandfather's face. He hated to disappoint the wizened chief, but his first loyalty was to his lineage, his clan.

Movement caught Totka's eye. Beyond the slave pole, at the base of the ceremonial mound, Leaping Waters, who rode astride Wind Chaser, appeared in the chunkey yard. The mare, ever restless, pranced and skipped beneath the woman whose timid hand was no match for the animal's powerful spirit. How many times had he told her to stay away from the mare?

She dismounted and, shielding her eyes from the sun's glare, looked toward the council square. Something must have gone awry with Polly.

He gave Leaping Waters his back. Whatever trouble was brewing at home would have to wait.

The micco raised his arm until peace settled around them. "Hilaho wishes to speak."

When order had been regained, Hilaho, feathers vibrating and bells tinkling, rose with the somber-faced dignity of a chief, but his taut, unblemished skin gave off the fresh scent of youth and naivety. He moved into the square and pinned Totka with his deep blue gaze, but he spoke to the congregation. "Of all Muscogee warriors, I expected Totka Hadjo to be the first to show mercy, to give sacrificially for the benefit of the weak. Have I been mistaken to believe his White Stick heart is large with forgiveness? Has the strain of suffering and grief so twisted the man he has forgotten who he was created to be?"

His brow arched over those penetrating eyes, and his fellow Choctaws shifted on their bench, nodding and murmuring as one.

Fury whipped up a gale inside Totka. He drew a sharp breath to maintain hold of his composure. "Do not think that because you have shared a campfire with my father, you know me and can predict my actions. You know *nothing*." He took a step back, fearful of the storm within. "I could no more condemn Choctaw innocents to hunger and death than I could my own nephew, but I owe my clanswomen vengeance. Even now, their ghosts haunt the eves of my lodge, anxiously awaiting release to the spirit world."

Between his lungs, his heart rocked and pounded in its cry for blood. "For peace to exist between us, I demand blood vengeance."

Hilaho's jaw sank as the square erupted with the clangor of shock.

Totka shouted above it. "Bring the man responsible for the deaths of my loved ones. If your situation is truly as dire as you claim, his life will be pittance to you." He glared at each Choctaw in turn, ending with Hilaho. "Once I've taken his life with my own hand, then and only then I will bless your request with my forgiveness."

Murmurs of approval rippled through the micco's shed and around the four corners of the square. It seemed they all agreed that someone must die for Choctaw transgressions. Many here, White Sticks included, had lost loved ones, property, and pride to their enemy.

Micco Bird Creek Fekseko, approval ripe in his eyes, addressed the Choctaws. "You have your answer. Take Totka Hadjo's words back to your people. Should you return with the murderer in cords, we will accept your proposal and welcome each of your five braves into our talwa as adopted clan."

Brittle and indignant, the remaining Choctaws gained their feet, joining Hilaho who had yet to recover the use of his jaw.

"A horse approaches," Old Grandfather said, chin raised as though he sniffed the wind.

Moments later, a mounted lookout galloped across the chunkey yard. At the edge of the ceremonial mound, he leapt off his animal and ran into the square, sweating and gasping. "Six Bluecoats. On horseback. Nearing the talwa's limits."

Commotion ensued. Men rose, hands going to empty sheaths. None were armed. Their weapons rested in the shed at the mound's base. .

The Great Warrior darted into the square's center and lifted the voice they'd followed into battle countless times. "Hold your peace! We greet them as honored guests." He pointed into the warriors' shed. "Wind Drinker, Kossati Imathla, escort the soldiers to the square."

While they awaited the Bluecoats' arrival, the conch shell was sounded to signal a decision had been reached. The Choctaws begged leave to begin their journey back, and Totka excused himself to attend a matter at home. As he began across the square, the soldiers, brilliant in their blue jackets, white trousers, and fine mounts, rode into view.

Kossati Imathla directed them to the square grounds, but the lead soldier broke off from the rest. The party halted as the man, without consideration for those behind or ahead, made a new path, then leapt off his trotting horse and kept going, straight toward Leaping Waters.

Did she know the soldier? By the way she stiffened and leaned away, she wasn't pleased with his bold behavior. Wind Chaser, ears at attention, ceased her fidgeting.

Totka began down the ceremonial mound, increasing his pace to a jog.

"What could the soldier want with her?" Long Arrow appeared at Totka's side, worry harshening his pitch.

What did any man want from a beautiful woman? Totka said nothing, only sped up to compensate for Long Arrow's burst of speed.

The soldier suddenly stopped, extended a gloved hand, and spoke. There was something about him—the unusual breadth of his shoulders, the gruff inflection of his voice, the sand colored hair that curled over his collar. And that profile . . .

Low and deep in Totka's mind, an empty power horn bellowed

alarm. No, it couldn't be. This man lacked the element of swaggering self-assurance the other had possessed in overflowing abundance, and . . . was his hand trembling?

"She is my responsibility," Long Arrow said. "Let me handle this alone. Stay back."

It took another few strides for Long Arrow's order to sink in. He was right to put Totka in his place. Many winters had passed since her safety had been Totka's concern.

He slowed to a stop twenty or so rods from the scene and hung back near a burned-out camp house as Long Arrow continued on.

The soldier's spontaneous change of course had halted the rest of his party. They straggled, watching, as he removed his hat and let the sun play in his pale hair. He spoke again and advanced another step.

A friendly whiny peeled from Wind Chaser and she lurched forward, yanking Leaping Waters along beside her. The mare didn't slow until she'd butted her head against the soldier's chest, pushing him back several steps, much the way she greeted Totka.

The white man's laughter and Wind Chaser's nicker of pleasure sent something cold and hard scurrying up and around Totka's spine. Wind Chaser knew that white man. Did Totka? The man held a remarkable similarity to— No, no. It couldn't be. Totka was imagining it.

Murmurings increased from the square, drawing the soldier's attention. He looked over his shoulder, skimming Totka with a careless glance and presenting him with a full view of his face.

Recognition choked Totka's lungs. Even with a mind-cringing scar spoiling half his face, he was undeniably the same—Copper Woman's lover. The dead Long Gun. Who was not dead.

How was this possible? A sea of confusion, Totka's brain churned and sloshed. *His name, his name* . . . What had Copper Woman called him?

Phillip! Her voice, screaming the name, severed Totka's thoughts, drawing blood and reversing his stride.

He'd seen it happen—Phillip crashing to his knees, two arrows

185

skewering his body; a Red Stick bearing down on him, scalping knife at the ready. Totka had spun away then, left the man to suffer whatever end the warrior deemed appropriate.

Yet in the ensuing moments Phillip had . . . What? Overpowered him? More than that, he'd somehow eluded four hundred vigilant Red Sticks and healed of his wounds in a black-water swampland devoid of allies. What sort of magic was powerful enough to extricate someone from such a hopeless situation? And how in the name of every sabia known to man had he retained possession of that scalp of his?

Totka's heel slammed into a scorched log from the camp house rubble, stopping his retreat and bringing his mind back to a sharp point.

Now what? What did Phillip's sudden appearance mean for Copper Woman? For *them*?

In a flash of dread, Totka saw Wind Chaser being taken from him, then Copper Woman, for had she not pledged her life to this white man first?

Long Arrow reached Leaping Waters and nudged her to move back, but she stayed as she was at Wind Chaser's flank, hand clamped to the reins.

Phillip levied a commanding question at her—an indignant question, placed while taking possessive hold of Wind Chaser's halter. The distance and brisk wind made it difficult for Totka to hear, but he dared not draw attention to himself, the warrior who'd hauled Adela McGirth off the slaughter-field and away from this very Bluecoat.

Leaping Waters would know to guide her brother to discretion, wouldn't she?

No, to her, Phillip was simply a soldier who recognized a horse and an opportunity to hang an Indian for theft. She would say whatever necessary to save Totka.

At Phillip's continued inquiry, Long Arrow stepped forward but looked to his sister for translation. Her response brought on another question, this one more demanding. Clearly, Phillip had no idea how Wind Chaser had come to be in Kossati, which meant he probably was unaware Copper Woman was alive. Otherwise, the name of this talwa — and every action she'd taken in connection with it — would be engrained in his mind.

The revelation gave Totka hope. Was there a chance they might keep it that way? There *was* a chance Phillip might not recognize Totka. It was a risk he would have to take. If he left the explaining to Leaping Waters, he might lose more than his life; he might lose Copper Woman.

Blood pumped through his veins in a headlong gallop as he began toward the confrontation.

Just then, Leaping Waters flicked her eyes Totka's direction, and with a knowing look and shake of her head, told him to stay back. He arrested his advance, uncertain. Was she concocting a believable enough lie? Perhaps she knew what she was about. Perhaps he should trust her.

Their heated conversation continued with the square growing more restless and the soldier more shaky. Sweat soaked his hair line, his stiff collar; it trickled over his scar. The shudder in his hand was quite evident now. What was wrong with the man?

The war had changed him and not for the better.

Wind Chaser sensed it as well. She laid back her ears; her head bobbed in an attempt to extricate herself from Phillip's grasp.

Totka knew the instant Leaping Waters revealed Copper Woman was alive.

Phillip's eyes widened, his head wagged. Leaping Waters continued speaking, gesturing to some unknown southerly point, then stroking Wind Chaser's muscled neck.

No, no, no! Again and again, the word thundered inside Totka's skull, but there was no stopping a cyclone, and there was no stopping what Leaping Waters had begun.

At last, as Phillip began to believe it, his knee collapsed. As did Totka's chest, but whereas the white man hastily rectified his stance,

Totka felt he might never draw another full breath. He inhaled sharply, but wind dodged him. His vision went white around the edges.

Time passed, blurred. Voices, English and Muskogee, merged into a senseless hum. Horses clopped past. A blip of a glance told him one of them was Phillip's.

Heat swelled in every muscle, his murderous thoughts teetering on the edge of irresistible. Eyes level with the compounds outlining the horizon, knees locked, he distrusted himself any nearer the man who held the power to ruin his life, to ruin every life in Kossati for having harbored white captives.

Curse that Fort Mims Red Stick! His bones probably baked in the Tensaw sun, and justifiably so for being outrageously inept.

Long Arrow spoke to Totka, touched his arm, spoke again. "Totka, are you hearing me? Go home. The Bluecoat is appeased."

Totka blinked until Long Arrow's sweat-dampened face came into focus. He exuded calm, instilling a bit of the same into Totka. Totka unwound his clenched fingers. "How? What did she say to him?" He darted a glance at Leaping Waters who studied him while scratching behind Wind Chaser's ear.

Phillip had left the mare to them? Perhaps he *was* appeased.

"Leaping Waters credited your sister's husband with rescuing the women, protecting them, and seeing them returned safely home. She explained the gift of the horse, the maize."

"And?" Nothing about Totka? Their love, their arrangement?

"And nothing else." Long Arrow's smile was tight, his words rushed. "I will see what damage I can prevent at the council. You shouldn't come. Take the horse home and stay there." He turned and trotted up the slope.

As clear as broad tracks left by a group of stampeding boar, the next events at the council square lay out before Totka: Phillip would seek confirmation of the facts, someone would unwittingly divulge the full story, then he would spur his mount toward Tensaw, toward Copper Woman, and Totka, bound by an oath to stay away until the blackberry moon, would be helpless to stop him.

Or was he?

There would be no preventing the man from returning for Copper Woman, but Totka could strike first. If Lachlan was willing to help.

Avoiding Leaping Waters' gaze, he snatched the reins from her and swung up.

"Why are you angry at me?" She touched his leg in the exact spot Copper Woman had last rested her hand.

A press of his heel moved Wind Chaser into a sidestep away from the woman. "Because now I must fix what you have broken."

"Nothing is broken. Did you not hear my brother? The white soldier's anger has cooled. Your name was not mentioned. I made sure of it, Totka Hadjo." Why must she continue to speak his name in such a tender way?

Wind Chaser danced in place, and Totka did little to stop her. "If you had not brought Wind Chaser to the square, none of this would have happened. I have warned you to stay away from her! She is too spirited for you. Why did you come?"

Anxiety washed her features, slipped her lip between her teeth. Her unsteady fingers went to her tattoo, and Totka's neck prickled, as though she'd touched him. Oh, to erase those markings from his skin, the memory of her touch from his mind!

"You are too upset. Ask your sister. I-I shouldn't say."

Now he was intrigued. "Yes" — he edged the mare toward her — "you should."

The tip of her tongue swiped the corner of her mouth as she considered. "Singing Grass asks that you go to . . . to Tuskegee. To you father. He is returned from his travels. She-she asks that you question him."

Ah. So, their long-lost father had reappeared at last. Little surprise it coincided with the arrival of the Choctaws. "About what?" he bit out. "Coming to share in a swig of tafia with his son?"

"Have you not heard what the people are saying? Singing Grass returned from the communal granary rather disturbed. The women are saying that your grandmother was a fixed liar. They say your mother was not born Muscogee, but that your grandfather stole her. From the Choctaws." She whispered the last as though it were a foul word. And it was because a man's lineage came through his mother.

Apart from smearing his grandparent's honor with dung, the insult was subtle, for his mother—no matter her birth—had been raised Muscogee. She was Muscogee, as was Totka. To the roots of his teeth. No one would deny that. The implication, however, said he was the offspring of his enemy. Artfully constructed slander it was.

A laugh burst from him so suddenly, Wind Chaser leaped forward. He reined in, then spun her in a tight circle, bringing her back. "The women are saying that? Truly?"

"According to your sister. The Choctaw delegation did not make mention of it in the council? No one did? I assumed the rumor originated with the Choctaws."

Totka had received curious looks, especially from Long Arrow, but he'd credited it to the unique position he'd been placed in. He still did. "The chiefs know better than to entertain ridiculous gossip meant to demean me." He laughed again, almost grateful for the break in tension. "First, I am a **witch** who can transform into fowl mid-game. Now, I am the son of their long-lost daughter. What will the Choctaws say next to manipulate us into getting what they want? Or perhaps the tale was created by the White Sticks who hope to soften my heart toward my enemy's plight. Either way, it is a shameful invention."

Doubt tightened Leaping Waters' mouth. "It might be the truth. Do not be so quick to dismiss it."

In a daze, he searched for his tongue. "You-you've swallowed their lies?" This gullible streak of hers would never cease its destructive pattern. But she'd always believed in him. Always. "Of all people, you would believe such foolish talk?"

Her shrug was nebulous, her tone apologetic. "It explains the many times your father has come to their defense. Perhaps, because

190

of your mother's heritage, he feels a kinship to them."

"Now you claim my father is Choctaw." He put mockery into a dry guffaw. "Who next? The Great Warrior? Old Grandfather?"

Hands held erect before her, she waved to stop his verbal assault. "Not Gray Hawk, no. But if the woman he dearly loved was birthed by them, I might see—"

"Enough!" This time, he held Wind Chaser in position so he might better glare down into Leaping Waters' expansive eyes.

The woman could not be blamed for having been born a weak spirit or for being ignorant of Copper Woman's relationship with the Bluecoat, but those facts were powerless to trim the anger from Totka's voice. "You wound me, Leaping Waters. Deeply."

"That grieves me, and I am sorry for it." Puddles appeared in her eyes, but she boosted her chin and sniffed. "Still, I agree with Singing Grass. You should go to Gray Hawk in Tuskegee. Make him answer for your grandfather. Put the doubts to rest."

"Whose doubts? I have none." The words became powder between his grinding teeth. "And the doubts of others I will not entertain by running to my father as though I were an insecure youth. I know who I am. I am Wolf, Muscogee, bitter foe of the Long Hairs. And I defy any man, or *woman*, who would insult me and my kin with my enemy's cowardly name." He gave Wind Chaser the bit and left Leaping Waters in a cloud of dust.

She could find her own way home. He had a journey to prepare for.

Chapter 11

Totka led Wind Chaser behind him on the paltry deer path that would eventually open up to Zachariah McGirth's Tensaw land. Palmetto fronds sawed at his leggings; ropes of crisscrossing vine reached for his neck.

A maddening swarm of mosquitoes had been on his trail since dawn, their incessant buzzing punctuated periodically by a smack. Spring's extra helping of rain had spawned a double blessing of mosquitoes. The winter's all-too-brief hunt had produced no bear, leaving him bereft of grease, and the dog-fennel weed he'd collected along the road that morning hadn't repelled the winged beasts for long.

Nothing would stick to his sweaty skin anyway. Except, of course, the mosquitoes.

Little Warrior bounded through the thickets toward him, creating enough noise to frighten every animal between there and the Mobile River. So much for Indian stealth.

Through the breaks in the treetops, the high sun flashed the boy's bare torso, brightening its umber tones. The grin that bunched his cheeks filled Totka's insides with the tickle of sweet success.

"Pawa," Little Warrior shouted at the top of his lungs. "Mr. Gibb convinced him. He said *yes*. You can come!"

"Slow down!" Laughing, Totka stopped the boy's flight with an arm across his scrawny chest. No one could appreciate Totka's joy at being received at the McGirth's lodge as much as Little Warrior, nor would any other express it so enthusiastically.

When Little Warrior had learned that Totka and Lachlan's journey to Mobile would include a detour to Tensaw, he'd become relentless in his plea to come along. There was no denying the boy anything, particularly when it came to Copper Woman.

That morning, the other two had gone ahead to seek permission for Totka to speak with McGirth "on a matter of some importance." Now that he'd received it, he could breathe again.

"Tell me everything. Leave nothing out." Totka hooked a thumb under his quiver's strap and cleared undergrowth from before him with his unstrung bow.

Trotting ahead, Little Warrior hiked his own little quiver and mimicked Totka's hold on it. "He is as you described: as wide as Mr. Gibb but with less fur on his arms."

"Forget McGirth. Was she there? Does she look well?"

Little Warrior glanced back and exhibited the gaps in his teeth. "Who?"

Smirking, Totka jabbed the boy in the side with the end of his bow, bringing on a belly laugh and an evasive hop.

"All right, all right. I saw her."

"And?" Totka drew out the word, impatient.

"And I hugged her and kissed her cheek. She smelled like honey," he sing-songed and leapt over a broad, muddy hollow.

"You're a rotten boy." Totka laughed again, but his mind was already working out how he might get a taste of that honey. He crossed the pit with a single lengthened stride.

"She was crying when I left to get you though."

The laughter vanished. "Why? Did her father say something to upset her?" That she would not be allowed to see Totka, for instance. His pace increased.

Little Warrior jerked with a lopsided shrug. "He made her wait in the lodge instead of coming with me as she wanted. Then, Bitter Eyes said Copper Woman should behave like a proper white lady instead of running off into the woods all the time and returning home with muck on her bare feet, like a dirty Indian. And I said, 'Who are you to call *me* dirty? Your hair is so greasy I could milk it for lamp oil.'"

Totka stopped cold, and the underside of Wind Chaser's neck scraped his shoulder. "You did not."

"I did!" The little weasel beamed. "And her cheeks got red, Pawa. Like war paint. Like Copper Woman that time you caught her coming from behind a bush with her dress stuck high in her leggings. Remember?" He chortled and took off on a bounce, hair flipping every which way.

Remember? How could Totka forget? Her blush had been as becoming as red on a peach. He'd come *this* close to taking a nibble— one of the many times he'd grudgingly leashed himself to the limitations she demanded.

He resumed his march, Little Warrior's quick trot putting his aching thigh to the test. "And what did Bitter Eyes say in answer?"

"Nothing. But she made a mean face at me. I saw her smile once. It was nice. She can be pretty sometimes."

"Maybe." He'd not given it much thought. "Lachlan popped your mouth, I hope."

"He pinched my backside and made me apologize for my naughty tongue." He rubbed the spot and scowled. "But Copper Woman smiled at me, and her father praised my English, so I was happy. Mr. Gibb said she'd waited ten moons already and was 'surely lass enough to wait a wee bit more.'" The last was said in perfect imitation of Lachlan's Scottish lilt.

So, her tears were for want of Totka. He could shoulder that.

"Then, I left, and now I am here. And I wonder . . . When we return to Kossati, may I get an inked moon?" The boy's mind was a grasshopper. He hurdled like one, too, from stone to stone over a dry creek bed.

"You want a tattoo?" All Totka wanted was to let his imagination wander to the moment he would lay eyes on Copper Woman.

Little Warrior tapped the side of his head. "Done here like yours."

Nostrils wide, Wind Chaser balked at the stones in the creek bed, so Totka slowed to coax her around them. "Boys do not get tattoos, and they do not shave their heads. After you've lifted a scalp in battle, we will talk of tattoos."

"I've skinned a deer. All by myself."

Back on the trail, Totka's feet picked up the tempo. "Yes, and the work was nicely done, but a deer hardly counts, and you know it."

"Well, my name *is* Little Warrior."

"True . . ." Distracted by images of Copper Woman sifting through his head, Totka craned his neck to see through the tangle of trees. Another bend in the path, and he should see the McGirth's fenced maize patch. His stomach sizzled and flipped like corncakes in a skillet.

On the Federal, a peddler had warned of a scourge of yellow plague in Mobile, so Lachlan had decided to cut their journey short. He would return another time for the order of rod iron he'd placed some moons back. They wouldn't risk contagion at the port city, but nothing could have kept Totka out of Tensaw.

"You will let me?" Little Warrior said.

"What? No."

A pout slouched the boy's shoulders

"Come now, Nephew. You know better than to ask. There should be special meaning—a story—behind every mark, every scar on a man's body. They are not carelessly applied."

Little Warrior began walking backwards, somehow avoiding the mossy roots traversing the way. "And your moon? What is its meaning?"

He touched the place above his ear where Singing Grass' garfish tooth had repeatedly pricked, creating the slender pattern of a new moon. "It symbolizes a new beginning."

"The beginning of what?"

Through the forest's thinning foliage, the bright green leaves of McGirth's corn waved a merry greeting. Totka's heart vaulted, and he forced himself to focus on his nephew. "Of my life without Leaping Waters."

It had been a pivotal point for him, the day of his last failed attempt to convince her to divorce Tall Bull. The swamp sickness that had ravaged Kossati and taken their small son earlier that year, but even without the child to bind her heart to Tall Bull, she'd been unwilling to leave him.

It had driven Totka mad with frustration.

The tattoo had been more symbolic than effective. He had still pined for her at every mention of Old Man Oak, with every casual brush of his fingers against his neck, and in the night when he stopped his ears to the sounds of Nokose loving his wife.

"But that was long ago," Totka said. "Before Copper Woman." His true new beginning. He nailed his gaze to the edge of the McGirth lodge coming into view beyond the corn, then rushed through his next question. "Tell me why you want a moon like mine."

"Because my name is no longer Totka Hayeta, and I miss carrying you with me. And I want a star beside it. For Father."

At the brink of the forest, Totka slowed, waved mosquitoes from his nose, and looked in awe at the child beside him. When Copper Woman gave him a son, would there be any room in Totka's heart for him? Little Warrior already filled it up.

He smiled. "I'll talk to your mother about it." Not that anything would come of it.

Confidence permeated Little Warrior's deep nod. "She will approve." With that, he broke through the tree line ahead of Totka and tore across McGirth land, whooping like a Red Stick on the warpath. If he didn't quiet down, he'd have every white man within ten sights taking up arms before sundown.

Totka cringed but let him go and followed at a dignified speed. He released Wind Chaser to the field near the barn and turned in time to see Copper Woman's yellow skirt brighten the doorway of her lodge.

Barefoot, she stood on tiptoe, hand shielding her eyes. Her beautiful laughter rang out clear across the yard. She hopped off the stoop and welcomed Little Warrior back with a hasty embrace. Then, she set her eyes on Totka and went as still as a rabbit in hiding.

Her father appeared at the door behind her, voice rumbling in commanding tones. Not providing him so much as a backward glance, she began toward Totka.

"Adela!" McGirth's call was clear, but she continued, as deaf as Lachlan.

Totka fought a grin and let his eyes feast on her.

Her figure was fuller, healthier. McGirth's plentiful table had been kind. She wore a gown cut in the style of the pale faces, but it was simple. No lace. No ruffles. In fact, she looked much the way she had at their first encounter. From her skewed apron to the single, thick braid that hung over her breast.

The only difference was the radiance in her eyes. Eyes that had yet to leave him.

His muscles twitched in anticipation, but he moderated his steps, determined not to let his absolute weakness for the woman propel him into an unmanly display of emotion. Especially here, under her father's scrutiny.

She, on the other hand, began a jog. Three stride in, she broke into a skirt-lifting sprint—as she'd done outside the burning fort. Except this time, she was not running to Phillip, and the only object in flames was Totka's throat as it burned with the effort to swallow.

He braced himself to receive her all-out run, but when she loosed his name on a jagged cry, he dropped his bow, quiver, and decorum and hastened to meet her.

She flew hard into his arms, laughing and crying at once, knocking the wind from his chest and the good sense from his brain. His rogue mouth went in search of hers.

Despite her happy little murmurings and the sighs hot at his ear, he regained himself and angled away, pressing his cheek to hers, unable to draw her close enough. Her body was softer than he recalled, warmer, more eager. And Little Warrior was right—she smelled as sweet as honey.

Nose buried in his shirt, she inhaled until her ribs strained against his hold. "Tell me you've come to take me home," she said on a contented discharge of breath.

Just like that? No questioning him about whether he'd found her Jesus Creator? He would certainly not be fool enough to remind her.

His hand filled with the thick of her braid. "You *are* home. Now, with me. It will have to be enough, for today at least."

Hands clasped behind his neck, she leaned back and struck him with her evergreen eyes, their whites streaked red with tears. "Just for today?"

"Unless your father has had a change of heart."

Disappointment drained joy from her, but she recovered beautifully by rewarding him with a tender smile. "For today then, I am home."

Spirits above, she was his very soul. If she extended the slightest invitation, he'd give that mouth a taste of what waited for them beneath the blackberry moon.

Her finger made a crescent track over the moon on his shaven scalp. "We have much to talk about as well."

There it was, her exasperating allegiance to their spiritual differences. "I've done as you asked. Faithfully."

"This comes as no surprise." Eyes brimming anew, she slid her fingers down his jaw in the gentlest of caresses. If she kept it up . . .

"But we have time for that." She sniffled and laughed. "My head aches thanks to the tears you've caused this afternoon. I imagine the sight of us has given my father one too. Does he look angry?"

McGirth remained outside his lodge, arms folded, legs set firmly apart, chin lifted a degree higher than natural. Most definitely angry. "You will need to apologize. As will I, if I do not release you."

When his arms loosened, she wrapped hers around his waist and crammed her ear against his heart. "Not yet you don't."

"This is what I love about you," he said into her hair. "You know what you want and do what you must to get it, no matter the cost." But would she still want *him*? Once she knew Phillip lived?

"This is what you love about me? That I thwart my father's

wishes to hold you?"

"Among other things. Such as this." He brushed a thumb across her mouth and filled his tone with suggestion.

She nipped at him, then giggled, snatched his hand, and gave it a peck on the knuckles. "It's good to be held again."

McGirth closed in. The man clomped like Micco, Lachlan's warhorse.

Totka couldn't help his testy grunt and said lowly, "Before I leave, I want time alone with you."

Head tipping back, she seared him with a saucy smirk. "We are alike in some ways, you and me. We both know what we want. I trust you will do what you must to get it."

"Is that a challenge?"

"Indeed."

"Accepted."

"Totka Hadjo." McGirth joined them, arm extended, obligating Totka to release his daughter. His forearm was thick, his grip firm. "Come to your home." The familiar phrase, recognizing Totka as a clan, instantly set him at ease.

"Maddo. Thank you for receiving me before the appointed day."

"You are clan and will always be welcome in my compound. Besides, I owe you too great a debt to deny you anything."

"Then I will consider these private moments I've stolen with Copper Woman your gift to me. As well as the others you will give me later today, before I set out for Kossati." He cocked a brow at Copper Woman, and she cocked one back, applauding with a sideways dip of her head.

McGirth's chest shook with a laugh. "I'll consider it, but for now, come share my fire." He put one arm around Copper Woman and stretched the other toward the lodge.

Totka followed, encouraged by the longing in Copper Woman's sidelong glance. Her body was tucked beneath her father's arm, but for this moment, her heart was in Totka's hand.

She placed him at their long table beside Little Warrior, who was engrossed in slurping from a bowl. She sat opposite Totka as their black-face servant, Hester, served bread and a generous helping of beans and pork. Lachlan, seated at one end, ripped a bite from his bread, grinned, and nodded support. At Totka's left, McGirth took the head, spreading himself the width of the table.

Bitter Eyes stationed herself in a back corner of the room and rocked her baby brother. The child had grown large, as had the antagonism in his sister's countenance. Totka blessed her with a long, provoking glare, which she enthusiastically returned. Then, he proceeded to ignore her.

Over the midday meal, they reviewed the seasons they'd spent apart. What had filled them—laboring in the compound, building the forge, learning the trade. And what had not—leisure, hunting, peace. Tensions were still high in both worlds. Distrust was thick.

McGirth suggested their peoples might never live together in harmony, but Totka disagreed. He batted at a duet of flies pestering his bread. "Copper Woman and I will prove it, as will our children."

The other man chewed his lip a moment and invited Little Warrior to explore the barn and visit the piglets. After the brave had dashed off, McGirth picked up the discussion. "History has proven that the weaker nation must submit to that which is stronger. By taking my daughter to Kossati to live as the Muscogees, you prove nothing. Many whites—myself included—have done so before her. The true challenge and proof would be for you to live here, as a white man." His knuckles rapped the table. "To assimilate yourself into our society. Could you do it?"

At Totka's ear, a mosquito whirred and buzzed, driving him to distraction.

Was McGirth still referring to the tribes in general with Totka being used as an example, or was the man laying down new terms? Totka got the overbearing sense it was the latter.

He strangled his tin spoon until it bent. "No. And I would fight any man who tried to make me."

Lachlan burst out with a laugh. "The Red Stick awakens!" His fist landed on the table, rattling dishes and startling the baby awake. Charlie's lips turned down in a quivering frown, and fat tears filled eyes as blue as a summer sky.

Copper Woman gave an empathetic chuckle and went to her brother, but McGirth continued unaffected. "The tide comes in swiftly, my son. If the Indian cannot learn to take on the ways of the pale faces, he will be swamped, carried out to sea, and drowned." He leaned closer to Totka, fervency quickening his words. "Along with those he loves." So, it was fear for his daughter that compelled him to speak so boldly.

Totka could appreciate a man's protective nature. With a respectful maddo, he released the spoon to his empty bowl.

Bouncing the babe on her jutted hip, Copper Woman stood near enough to have heard. Although her lips were bent up at the edges, insecurity descended about her like a darkening mist. She believed what her father said. And once she knew that her soldier was alive, she would be confronted with one inescapable fact: life with Phillip would be simpler, safer, more predictable than life with Totka.

Doubt squirmed in his middle like a netted eel. He grasped for the confidence he'd felt outside the lodge, but his hand remained empty. Her heart had withdrawn.

McGirth took the spoon and began straightening its warped handle. "Never lose your fire, Totka Hadjo. It kept my women alive. Brought my son to me. It will carry my dear girl safely through whatever trials lay ahead for your people. I will fear for her, but I trust you." He tossed the spoon back in the bowl and handed the set to Hester as she passed.

Did he really? The words were arranged properly, but they sounded unnatural, rehearsed.

"Enough talk about the confederacy's bleak future," Lachlan said. "Tell them what brings you to Tensaw, Totka. Get it over with. Remove the splinter before it festers."

With a deep breath, Totka ventured into the unknown. The telling was brief, seeing he knew little. He finished with, "The man has a scar here" — he sliced from temple to jaw with a forefinger — "but I knew him almost at once."

"Are you certain?" Copper Woman paced away, landing firmer-than-necessary pats on the baby's back. "You saw him but twice. Neither instance gave much opportunity to truly know his face."

Totka released a dry chuckle. "Trust me. His face is whittled into my memory."

"If he had such a large scar, maybe you confused him for someone else," McGirth said.

"There was no confusion. Half of his face is perfectly whole, and he recognized Wind Chaser. She came to him like an old friend."

At last, Copper Woman ceased her pacing and deposited herself in a chair. "They *were* old friends. He raised her from a foal. Gave her to me not quite a year before the war."

Totka could have done without that bit of information.

"I watched him die," she said. "*We* watched him die."

Bitter Eyes came to stand beside her sister. "You saw Phillip die?" she said in English. How long had she understood Muskogee? However long it was, Totka doubted there would ever be a day she deigned to speak it. She continued. "The last time we saw him was by the woodpile."

"That's not true. I saw him . . . after . . ." Copper Woman's eyes darted to him and away. Her face crumpled, and her eyes went on a journey he'd seen them take before; she'd left the room for Mims' place. What was she seeing? Blood? Fire? Arrows slamming into Phillip Bailey's body?

Charlie yanked on her braid and jabbered in her ear, but it didn't bring her back from the fort.

Totka longed to crouch before her, to coax her back into the present, but fear that she would see war paint when she looked into his face welded his backside to the bench.

The lodge fell into a hush as they waited for her to complete her thought. Hester stilled her clattering over the kettle; Lachlan, in studious silence, traced a wood-grain pattern on the tabletop; even the baby had occupied his mouth by gnawing on the end of Copper Woman's braid.

Her lashes fell in a series of blinks, then slowly lifted to Totka. "Phillip is alive," she said on a breathy laugh. Her face lit with joy.

Beneath the table, Totka twisted the flap of his breechcloth slow and hard until its coarse strouding burned his palms. Had she looked that happy to see him earlier? The instant he made the childish comparison, he chided himself. He was being unfair. She was allowed a moment of happiness at discovering her former lover hadn't been slain in battle.

So long as he truly was *former*.

"Imagine that." McGirth chuckled and lapsed into English. "Those Baileys were always hard to take down. Never could best that Dixon at the turkey shoot. It'll be good to see the boy. Well" — he scratched his bearded chin — "I reckon he's all of a man now. Hard-won, too."

Bitter Eyes dabbed at her nose with a square of linen. "Poor Phillip with a scar like that. He was always so handsome."

Poor Phillip nothing! He was a soldier, doing what he'd been trained to do — defend what he believed was his, same as Totka, and he'd survived the bloody war.

"It's been almost a year since peace was signed." Copper Woman addressed her father, seeming to have forgotten Totka sat an arm's stretch away, perspiring like a boy facing his first ceremonial scratching. "Why hasn't he come home?"

Home? Totka thought Kossati was home. *He* was home.

Phillip Bailey was the privy.

The mosquito landed on Totka's forearm, and with a swift smack, he crushed it.

Bitter Eyes, wearing a triumphant little smile, took the baby from her sister. "Totka here is afraid Phillip will come for you," she said in a mock whisper.

At last, Copper Woman's attention came back to him. Her brows arched.

Through a tense jaw, he replied in Muskogee. "He *will* come for you. As soon as he's completed his business in Kossati." What man wouldn't? "I've traveled fast to arrive before him because I cannot rest until I know whom you will choose."

Chapter 12

Whom would she choose? How could he even ask?

Adela sat back so hard the chair's rail bruised her backbone.

Totka wore an expression of angst she hadn't seen since the Hillabee Massacre. His eyes, those beautiful brown windows, teemed with it.

As a self-protective measure, she'd never been very open with her feelings, but did he doubt them so thoroughly?

He said he'd been seeking her Jesus, and before he'd arrived, she'd quizzed Lachlan. The blacksmith told her they'd read from the scriptures every night for the past ten months.

While living among the Muscogees, she'd spent nearly a year absorbing all she could of their beliefs, embracing practices that honored Creator and deepened her gratitude and worship, so it pleased her that Totka was at last doing the same, meeting her halfway. Yet there was one matter in which she would not budge.

She leaned over the table. "You know the vow I've made to Creator. Do you ask me to break it?"

The instant flare of his nostrils told her that he was. The cluster of eagle feathers tied to his roach flapped with the upward jerk of his chin. "Two moons yet remain for you to consider your error in judgment." His mouth tipped with a cocky grin.

"I assure you I will consider no such thing," she said boldly, returning his expression in full, aiming for that unconquerable warrior spirit he admired.

His eyes retained their inflexibility, but when his lips twitched with repressed amusement, she knew her aim was true.

Tension eased from her back. "We'll speak of it again when that time has passed. But it is one moon and twenty-two sleeps, not two. I have been counting." She found his moccasined foot beneath the table and with her toe drew a line over his arch.

Mr. Gibb chuckled, and Totka relaxed his posture, leaning back, tucking his hands inside his crossed arms. The thick silver bands that strained against the bulge of his arms emphasized his brawn and made her middle glow warm.

Had he been so muscular before? She remembered his strength being subtler, but it had been a long time since she'd seen him out from under the influence of hunger and—

In a single sweep, he locked her foot between his and dragged it beneath his bench's edge, causing her backside to skid forward an inch on her seat. She coughed to cloak a gasp and propped her elbows on the table to give herself more tether. There was no sense trying to free herself, and did she really want to?

He removed a bundle of broken days from his pouch and tossed it onto the table between them. "Twenty-*one* sleeps. I do not count the day you will join me under the blankets." The hairline scar on his cheek nudged upward as he caressed her with a sluggish sweep of his eyes.

Heat crackled in Adela's cheeks. She flinched when Papa cleared his throat loudly, energetically.

"Rather bold of you to speak so at my table and in the company of women."

Totka's lashes dipped in a slow blink before he stored his bundle and directed his gaze at her father. "Forgive me. I have little knowledge of white man's manners." And by his shrug, little desire to attain it. "But why not speak plainly of what I want? Phillip Bailey will, I promise you that."

Naturally, Phillip would. He and Adela had almost become man and wife. An hour from their vows, Totka, in a whorl of flame, had stormed into their world. Two weeks later, he sauntered through his sister's courtyard, spotted Adela shucking corn, and with a lengthy, blood-spiking perusal, he'd told her he wanted her, and as they'd established just now outside the McGirth barn, Totka always found a way to get what he wanted.

A vision of him throwing her over a horse and galloping off to Creek country spurred a nervous chuckle within her. She caught it in the nick of time. The man wouldn't appreciate it one bit. But surely, he knew Phillip didn't stand a chance. If she felt at liberty, she would lift her gaze from the strap of his pouch to his hooded eyes and, with a look, undress her heart.

In that look, she would tell him she wanted him so close that his features became blurred and his breath became hers. She would tell him she wanted to lean across the table, run her lips over his tawny skin, and send to perdition every obstacle that stood between them. Her heart would shout that she wanted him to fight for her, to fight for them.

She would tell him in that glance that she wanted *him*, not Phillip, like she'd never wanted anything before. Instead, she tucked her lip between her teeth and memorized the zigzag pattern of the pouch strap cutting a diagonal line across his shirt.

Papa steepled his fingers and set them before him on the table, heralding a ruling. "Regarding Bailey, when he returns, assuming he does, he will be welcomed, same as you. And same as you, he will be allowed access to my daughter. If she should choose him, you will act with the decorum expected of gentlemen both white and red." His fingers folded and his head tilted back in courtly fashion. "No matter of her decision, this will always be your home."

Pressure increased on her ankle as resolve flattened Totka's lips and the silver bobs dangling from his lobes vibrated. All he lacked was black and red battle paint streaked across his face. Yes, he would battle for her. And his opponent? Phillip, her Jesus, her principles, her father. Any of them. All of them.

Sweet Lord, she prayed Phillip was their sole obstacle, and he was no real obstacle at all.

Abruptly, Totka stood, sending his medicine bundle arching outward. It swung back against his long-shirt with a quiet *thump* that was easily heard in the silence that had fallen. He turned to her father. "Thank you for your hospitality, but the day wanes. I will take your daughter now, as agreed, and return her before the crickets sing."

Papa's chair rocked with his hasty rise. Bread crumbs tumbled down the front of his shirt. His breath came through his nose in a short burst.

Totka, nearly a head taller, met Papa's gaze without blinking. His chest filled and crashed several times fast before Lachlan spoke.

"Why not send the wee brave with 'em, Zachariah? He'll keep the two on the straight and narrow."

Adela bit her lip to keep from smiling. Either Lachlan didn't know Little Warrior at all, or the boy wasn't who she remembered. He was more likely to build them a hut and stock it with cradleboards than curtail any illicit activity.

Papa's ribcage sank beneath his great exhale.

Within minutes she and Totka were riding out, Adela before him on Lachlan's big black named Micco, and Little Warrior on Wind Chaser. Lachlan's stallion could have been a charger in a medieval tournament. Power undulated through him, but the massive animal had nothing on Wind Chaser's spirit and speed. They'd barely cleared the cornfield, and already Little Warrior, hair a rippling black flag, was riding full gallop.

"Too fast," Adela shouted but got only a mouthful of wind for her efforts.

Totka's fist, holding both reins, rested on Adela's thigh. The other wound around her waist and pulled her flat against him. "Better for us if he goes."

She reached back and stroked him from earbob to chin. Because she could. "He'll be thrown."

"On a horse, the boy is a tick. Who do you think exercises her every day? I have not the time, but in the evenings when loneliness is thickest she is a great comfort."

Adela gave a contented sigh and relaxed against him so that their bodies swayed in tandem. "Is it insane to envy a horse? Wind Chaser spends every day with you, and I have only this one."

"Only if it is insane to envy a baby. He is far too liberal with his affection. Does he sleep with you as well?"

She felt the bunching of his cheeks against her ear, heard the tease in his voice, and she laughed. "And if I told you he snuggled at my side every night?"

"Then I would fight him for you. Right after I've defeated Phillip," he stated matter of fact. "Unless you spare his life by sending him away first. Swear to me you will. Swear to me our lives will be bound. I'll not leave without knowing."

Hadn't they decided not to discuss this again for another month and twenty-two—no, twenty-*one* days? She frowned and locked her jaw.

Little Warrior, their inept chaperone, sent Wind Chaser flying over the last McGirth fence in an impressive bound, then spurred her into a body-lengthening gallop that set them on the long stretch of road leading to Mobile.

"Well?" Totka drummed her ribs with his thumb. "If I'd wanted your silence, I would have saved myself the four-day trip and stayed in Kossati."

"Phillip is not the man I love, but I'll make no promise I cannot be sure to keep."

Totka's body took on vague rigidity. "You tempt me to ride north and not stop until your lodge comes into view."

He would most assuredly haul her off like a sack of potatoes if she didn't give him the answer he wanted. Half of her wished he would.

Her itinerate fingers slipped under the thong that suspended his knee-high leggings to his belt. They located the coin-sized scar on his outer leg and traced its circular ridge. "My lodge?"

"Hmm. Your lodge. It stands beside that of Singing Grass. I

decided you would rather sit on my sister's hip than live beside Leaping Waters. The lot Beaver offered stands beside hers. Not that either of them are in it at the moment."

Live shoulder-to-shoulder with Tall Bull and Leaping Waters? Not a chance. "A prudent decision. Singing Grass does not mind?"

"She is delighted."

Adela gave a contented sigh and settled her head against his cheek. It sounded wonderful. A place to call her own. The unhurried, easygoing Indian life. Quiet, solitude. With Totka's arms around her like now, every night.

He rested his chin in the curve of her neck. "It waits for you, beloved."

"You have certainly kept busy."

"All a man needs is good motivation. That reminds me." He switched the reins to his other hand, so he could twist and rummage through the saddlebag, and produced a set of moccasins so new they still carried the sweet and sour aroma of tanning solution.

"They are perfect!" Adela hugged them to herself, appreciating the sacrifice of supplies and time that had gone into them. His own were battered and thin.

"Beautiful moccasins for a beautiful woman," he said in careful English.

"Well done!"

He chuckled. "I practiced."

"Your English is quite improved. Lachlan tells me you've learned to read."

"Lachlan's tales are always three sizes too big. I read the little words. He reads the big ones. Leaping Waters is a stricter taskmaster."

"Leaping Waters? Is she not in the Floridas with . . . ?"

Tall Bull's demanding mouth commandeered her memory, and she braced against a shiver.

Totka's hold on her strengthened. "Save yourself the pain and do not speak his name. It is not worthy of your tongue."

"What happened to bring Leaping Waters back?"

"She found the backbone to leave him. Arrived on foot one night in the little chestnut moon looking more dead than alive. With a cradleboard on her back."

"A child?"

"A son. Not that the scoundrel deserves one." In his most astringent tone, he related the story of Leaping Waters living in his compound, Singing Grass serving as wet nurse to her child. Tall Bull's apparent threat to Little Warrior. The tedious wait for his expected return. Only when Totka shared how Leaping Waters explained passages of the Bible to him did his inflection soften.

Adela should be jealous. If she were smarter, she would be worried that Totka had accepted the woman he'd once loved into his compound, but the abundance of awe and gratitude filling her heart left no room for such triviality.

Leaping Waters was a believer. And she was spreading her faith.

As tears threatened, pain shot between her eyes and traveled to the back of her head where a dull throb pitched its tent. No more crying for her, or she'd not sleep a wink that night. She rubbed the base of her skull, noting her wet hairline.

Despite its downward slant, the sun beat her skin into a flush. From beneath, Micco's massive body radiated heat, and from behind, Totka's warmth mingled with her own to soak the back of her gown. Sweat glistened on his arms and slicked his bare thighs.

With the back of her wrist, she swiped trails of it from beneath her chin. "I should have worn a bonnet." At least the direct sun kept the mosquitoes at bay.

"Grandmother Sun loves your pale skin. If she could, she would set it aflame."

"It feels as though it already is." For spring, the heat was making quite an impression.

He turned Micco off the road and into a field so that the sun was at his own back. "Shall we go to water? The long snake will cool you."

"A dip in the river sounds refreshing. But let me walk a ways."

He lowered her and followed her down. She donned the moccasins and, as they walked, dug her fingers into her lower back, which ached in an unusual way.

Eyes straight ahead, he took her hand and Micco's halter and ambled what seemed an aimless path through the scrub brush of what was once Mr. Ashburn's tobacco field.

She filled her eyes with Totka and let a smile overtake her. His appearance, at once rustic and kingly, was identical to the man in her thousand waking dreams. He wore his hair as he always had—shaven except for the broad, cropped strip running from forehead to spine where he let it grow long and blow free. The same teardrops ornamented his lobes; the same black- and red-striped fletching ribbed the arrows in his quiver.

The array of feathers was new. Two of them were joined at the quill by a beaded leather thong that attached them to the hair nearest his right ear. They'd been Nokose's; there was no forgetting them.

The snippet of Totka's shirt remained where she'd last placed it inside the folds of her bodice. There would come a day she would let it go, but not until she had the man to replace it.

Totka's mouth became a straight furrow, his heavy-lidded Indian eyes narrowed and severe. Whether due to the sun or internal unrest was hard to decipher.

"Are you less talkative than I remember or is something on your mind?"

The question made his mouth go flatter, if that were possible. "Have I been too vague with what concerns me? I beg forgiveness." Definitely not the sun.

"How is it I can love such a surly man?" She smiled, enclosed his free hand within her two. "Would you like to share what you've learned from Leaping Waters?"

He directed his gaze to the world's edge where pine and hickory competed for dominance of the land. Between her and the woodland there lay a flat expanse colored with a tapestry of blooming red clover and towering clusters of dog-fennel.

After some moments alone with his thoughts, he shook himself free of her and thumbed a mosquito against her neck. "We'll not speak of it until the blackberry moon."

She wiped away blood and the sting she was suddenly aware of. "Very well, but in my prayers tonight I will thank Creator for setting Leaping Waters in your path."

He nodded and skimmed her forehead with his lips. "It is good of you to not begrudge me her presence. It was unexpected but not wholly unwelcome."

"Creator often uses the unexpected things, the weak things, to accomplish His purpose."

A shadow crossed over his eyes, as though he'd suddenly recalled something unpleasant. "How true that is, for Leaping Waters is the very definition of weak." He released a scoffing laugh. "The day Phillip Bailey arrived, she informed me of a rumor circulating the talwa that claims my mother was born Choctaw. Which makes my grandparents liars of the greatest sort and in a despicable, roundabout way assigns me on the name of my enemy. The rumor's timing, its stinging, personal nature . . ." Totka shook his head, eyes going hot. "This is no mere uncovering of a family's heritage. No, it was meant to belittle or manipulate. Both."

Adela knew of his past, his uncle, his leg, his hatred. There could be no greater insult than to call him a Long Hair, if even thinly. "Who would say such a thing?"

He stopped and plucked a hairy stem of dog-fennel, then began scouring his arms and neck with it. "Does it matter? The people enjoy a good tale, and this business with the Choctaws has got every society twittering. Each with a different say on the matter. Even Leaping Waters. She probably heard the tale from Ayo, and since she is too feeble to form her own opinions, she was happy to take on her mother's. I thought she had a heart, that she would never stand against me, but I was mistaken. She has aligned herself with those who would call my grandmother a trickster for having deceived the clan mothers." The mangled plant flew from his fingers. He tore off another stalk and began on Adela's arm.

Its nasty odor was almost as unpleasant as Totka's sudden choler. Scowling, he lifted her chin and scrubbed at her throat, coating her in the plant's scent. "I've refused to speak to her since."

Adela ached for him. "Implying you are Choctaw is akin to telling a wolf he's a dog, or . . ." Her lips swung up on one side. "Or telling a Mims captive she is a Red Stick."

His hand stilled at her collarbone. "That is different."

"How so?"

"Because I say it in love and admiration! Because Red Sticks are—"

"Admirable? Honorable? Your Red Sticks have proven themselves the opposite on a number of occasions. But they cannot be discounted as a whole. Same with the Choctaws."

The bulge of Totka's arm hardened as did the muscle of his jaw. He stood at the brink of fury; Adela, of his displeasure.

But there would be no apology coming from her. "That being said, a woman needn't go too far to come upon an honorable Red Stick." She leaned her weight into his arm until he gave way and came within reach of her lips, which deposited a kiss on the speck of a scar at his chin. "Did you know you are quite handsome when your blood is up?"

From between narrowed lashes, he grazed her with a cooling eye. "And you are quite thoughtless. Almost as much as Leaping Water."

Bitten, she unlatched herself from him. To be compared with the woman he resented . . . It stung to the point of thick-throated silence.

"At times, I wonder at my sanity for having loved her so desperately and for so long." He continued swabbing her with the repellant, but his mind had flown a hundred miles north. "I thought the war or perhaps the child had changed her, made her stronger. But hers will be a pale, anemic soul until the day she enters the spirit world."

He went on unbottling stored frustration and hurt, but after the parallel he'd just made, it seemed as though he were speaking about *her*. It wouldn't be the first time he'd called her weak.

"At least she was smart enough not to tell me Tall Bull had returned yet again. He arrived in Kossati the same day as Phillip Bailey. Coincidence? I think not. Lachlan waited with the news until we'd been on the trail a day. If I'd known any sooner, I would have sent the Bluecoats after him, for I had a decent guess where he was hiding and with whom."

She offered her other arm and pounced on the change in subject. "Was that the reason Phillip was in Kossati? A manhunt?"

"It would appear Tall Bull has made such a name for himself that the Bluecoats have set a party of soldiers on his scent. I would expect no less from a renegade Red Stick who keeps company with the daughter of Josiah Francis." Ministration complete, he picked shreds of leaf from her skin.

"Keeping company?" Did he mean his cousin was . . . ? "Oooh. Does Leaping Waters know?" After all she'd been through—the false accusations, the estrangement, her unerring faithfulness—she would be ill.

"It is none of my concern." Yet he relayed the news as if it were a personal offense. He picked up the meadow's path where they'd left it and guided them around a stand of pokeweed, keeping Micco's muzzle clear of its toxic, purplish stems. "If the Wind Spirit blows in my favor, they will both be arriving at the Apalachicola by the time I reach Kossati."

He spoke as he always had of spirits and spirit lands. The chasm between them seemed even wider than when he'd left, and now she feared they might not traverse it. Not in time for the blackberry moon. But as surely as she'd given her soul to Jesus, she'd given her heart to Totka. The blackberry moon meant nothing. She would wait until their faiths aligned. As long as necessary.

"You have so few male clansmen," she said. "With your cousin gone, will there be any left who are your peers?"

"Not within a day's travel."

"As I thought. Since Nokose's death, I've often wished you had a brother. If your mother had truly been born Choctaw, think of the dual kinship you might form. Muscogee *and* Choctaw. There would be new uncles, clan mothers, cousins." She grew excited at the thought.

He discarded her hand as well as Micco's reins. "I would rather have none, than find them among my enemies!"

At his bark, Adela jolted and Micco snorted loud and fluttery.

Totka stalked off, but she followed, undaunted by his temper. He stopped, hands on hips, to look out over the Mobile River valley and the arrow of geese that descended from out of the sun's glare.

She inserted her arms through the loops his had created and ran her hands up his front, appreciating the definition between his lean stomach and muscled chest. The work at the forge felt good on him.

His hair tickled the cheek she rested between his shoulder blades. "But Totka, you strive to bind yourself to a white woman who was once your enemy. What difference is there?"

He didn't answer. Didn't move.

"What? Now you will not speak with *me*?" The wind beat at her back and wrapped her skirt about his legs, fusing them together.

The heat amplified, swelling painfully in her head and settling into a grinding ache in her lower back. In contrast to the sweltering temperature, a scourge of prickles lifted across her arms and neck, bringing to mind the possibility of a fever. She closed her eyes and took advantage of Totka's motionless, solid frame to support her head and wait out the sudden malaise.

A lengthy breath deflated his chest as he trapped her hand against it. "Never for one moment have you been my enemy. I shouldn't have brought up the Choctaws. Why do you badger me about it when you know how I hate them?"

"Because I refuse to let you become devoured by that hate, as my sister has done. I will not abide it in the man I love."

He rotated and looked down on her with brow-wrinkling shock. "I am *not* the Bitter Eyes."

"True. You are stronger—much more so—and if there is an

218

inkling of truth in this rumor, your strength will be put to the test. Forgive them, Totka. Forgive. It is the only way. You must or the worms of bitterness will eat you alive."

"You expect me to forgive." One eye tapered and twitched. "As you have forgiven the Red Sticks who slaughtered your people? As you've forgiven me the part I had in it?"

"I . . ." Where was this coming from? "Yes, you know I have. The Sacred Writings teach forgiveness, and while I am as flawed as the next woman, I do try to—"

"Show me. Prove your forgiveness."

Her heel scooted away. "What do you mean? Have I not shown you already by loving you?"

"*Do* you love me? If you did, you would take me as I am, every part of me. But you refuse to bind yourself to me because you have yet to forgive me for being Muscogee, for praying to the law-giving spirits, for seeking purification from the long snake and adhering to our ancient ways."

He advanced, a towering palisade, flaming with indignation, but she stood her ground, chin lifted, unspeaking.

"In the end, Adela McGirth, it comes back to one thing—my defense of the Muscogee Confederacy. You cannot forgive the fact I warred against your people!" He grabbed her hand and led her at a march toward Micco.

"Where are we going? Stop this. Stop it!" She tugged against him, but his face and grip were set. She seized her skirt and matched his furious stride. "You blabber nonsense. The war is done. Long buried. Leave it there."

"Leave it? It was the pick of your tongue that dug it up."

"When? No, that was only an example, to help you see that not all Choctaws are—"

"You went pale as death, Copper Woman, in your father's lodge. At the memory of Mims' place. Then, you would not look at me. Because you still see me painted in the colors of war. Because you spout forgiveness when you are incapable of giving it yourself!"

Thistles punished her exposed legs. Stones jabbed through the soles of her moccasins. A hatchet pierced her skull with each footfall. "That you believe in different spirits has no bearing on my forgiveness of-of . . ."

"You cannot even form the words!"

She'd prayed tirelessly that God would give her the ability to forgive, to move on. Less for herself than for her sister, and most especially for Totka. That he might see Christ's love in her. Her breath came in snatches. "We *all* need forgiveness. From each other. But mostly from Creator."

They'd reached Micco, but the horse was leery of Totka and swung his head away. Totka lurched for the reins and blew hard through his open mouth. "Does your tongue know only one path, woman? Again, you cower behind your sacred writings. How much easier it is to love a god-man you cannot see or a white man who shares your beliefs, than to love an Indian whom you must forgive again and again, with each memory of a day that will *never* leave your mind."

"You cannot see into my mind! Who has been whispering such insanity into your ear?"

Instead of answering, he fisted Micco's mane and took a mighty leap that smoothly seated him. He thrust his hand down at her along with a glare that could light his sacred fire four times over.

He wanted proof that she'd forgiven him? Very well. She would oblige the man. Although how, she couldn't imagine.

She smacked her hand against his arm, toed the stirrup, and let him hoist her up in front of him. Before she could swing a leg over the horse's neck he cinched her about the waist and kicked them into a thundering gallop. Her stomach instantly churned into a fit of nausea.

She clung to him as he skirted McGirth land in a broad arch, delving deep into Bailey property to do so. Then he continued east toward home, never slowing. They passed the burned-out hull of Davy Tate's cabin, then Cornell's decrepit trading post. Little use for trade goods with no settlers brave enough to rebuild this close to the Indians and no Indians willing to build this close to grounds desecrated by war.

This Indian was the exception. He tore across Verna Bailey's abandoned potato field as though he owned the place. Disturbingly, the lay of the land was no stranger to him. When he veered a sharp right onto an overgrown road, Adela became uncomfortable at the dawning awareness of their destination. This path ended at Tensaw Lake and the one-time home of Samuel Mims.

An overhanging branch sliced at her cheek. She emitted a cry and didn't refuse her smarting eyes.

Totka hauled the reins and brought the animal to a trot.

Out of breath, trembling, and still jouncing with the horse's less-than-smooth gait, Adela pulled hair from her mouth and swallowed to relieve her dry throat. "Where are you taking me?"

"You know where."

She did. Although why he would do such a thing . . . "I've no desire to go back. None." If that were the case, she would have done so already. "Why would you force me to see that place? Totka, *please*. Do not do this." Fear gripped her, shook her from the inside out.

His muscles hardened around her, and the horse plodded on.

They rounded a bend and Mims' dock came into view. It appeared as it always had, a half-rotten collection of boards stretching from the lake's swampy rim and through a patch of water-logged cypresses. Some broken at the knees, some towering, they were moss-laden witnesses to the horrors of that day.

In a macabre reverie, the memories began sprouting before her, brilliant in every hue, ghastly in their vibrant red.

Major Beasley writhing in the sand, a tomahawk buried in his back. Lucy's beautiful blue eyes, frozen in shock. The white of Verna's skull, the gray of her entrails.

Adela choked down a scream. She tasted blood where her fist crushed her lip against her teeth. She couldn't go back! Heart pounding a warpath up her throat, she grappled for the reins but was too clumsy for his quick reflexes. "I am no longer a captive to be forced against my will. Turn away, turn *away!*"

Sounds assailed her. Whoops, shrieks, ceaseless musket fire. And flames. Always the greedy roar of flames. She hunched into the shelter of him and clapped her hands over her ears, but her eyes refused to close.

Totka's soothing, cadenced speech penetrated the din, but it was muffled, indecipherable.

Micco carried them at a walk into the clearing where the Red Sticks had first appeared. She'd spotted them through the negligent, yawning gates. The earth had teemed with their vermillion bodies. They'd raced across this very ground screaming for her blood, and Totka had been one of them. He'd stormed the pickets that were now no more than smeared lines of ash.

The horse's hooves stirred the remains and released its stench into the air. She whipped up her apron to cover her nose and quell building illness. The ache in her head increased as the grounds opened before them, wide, flat, and clear of corpses. It was her shock at the absence of the dead that made her realize she'd expected to find the place as she'd left it — body heaped upon body.

But it was calm. Peaceful. Free of violence and death.

The din inside Adela's mind abated to a hum. She slowly lowered her hand and gave the lot a skittish rake of her eyes. Except for patches of black where buildings had once stood, the dirt was its usual reddish brown, sprinkled with pine needles and sun-bitten grass.

No blood.

The only red in sight was the pair of cardinals that hopped along the upper edge of the bastion's wall. They sang a loud string of happy whistles, bringing a hint of normalcy to the abnormal.

The bastion alone remained on its feet, its wide door in splinters outside it. Why had no one torn it down? It seemed a dishonor to those who'd died there to leave it standing as a heinous memorial. It was sentinel to broad, shallow mounds of dirt topped by a carpet of cheery dandelions and several shoddily constructed crosses.

Sudden squeaking and clambering made Adela jump.

A squirrel, only a squirrel.

It scampered up and around the scorched trunk of a pine.

Her chest shuddered with a convulsive breath as she gradually straightened and flattened herself against Totka as they moved away from the graves.

Micco kicked a tin cup. It pinged and shot out before them. Little was left as evidence that nearly five hundred people had once lived here: the bones of a wagon, crushed pottery, a crippled chair.

But if she held her breath, she might hear old Hansen's harmonica and the girls' giggling through their chanted ditties. Phillip had sauntered through those cypress trees there, headed straight for her. He'd died opposite them, just yonder by that thick stand of rushes. Or so she'd thought . . .

They were at the fort's center now, stopped before the largest square of rubble. Ash lay in heaps of white and gray around hunks of blackened wood. Not a beam remained erect, but the cabin's door . . . It had once stood right there, where the hewn-rock stoop squatted.

Mama! Open the door! Elizabeth's muffled shouts swept over Adela. Tears surfaced, but she refused them, making her throat cinch painfully. "Beth," she whispered.

"What is Beth?" Totka said.

She gave a start, having forgotten he was there, then shook her head, unwilling to find her voice.

He looped the reins over the saddle horn, and even as she honed into the site of her sister's death, she became keenly aware of him. Of the nudge of his war club against her hip, the brace of his arm about her, the ripple of power in his legs as he shifted, the sticky heat that soldered her to him, and she wasn't afraid. Not of this place, nor of him or of what he'd done.

Only grieved.

He stroked the hair from her damp forehead. His hand smelled of warm leather. It was tender, understanding. Then it stretched and took in the acreage with a ponderous sweep. "Look there, at the bones of your people made ash by mine, and tell me you have truly forgiven me." His breath warmed her ear, but his words, though spoken softly, cut her to the quick.

He was so lost, so buried in hate he couldn't accept forgiveness when it was freely given. Nor did he seem to comprehend that it even existed. All he knew was vengeance. It shattered her, but maybe he'd been right to bring her here. What better place to confront their unsightly past, then bury it once and for all?

"My sister's name was Elizabeth, but we called her Beth." The feel of her sister's name leaving her mouth was achingly beautiful. "She was tall and slender but often harsh. Her love was deep and steadfast, if now and again frenzied. At times, it controlled her, causing trouble, but you'd have found none more loyal than she." An irony-laden chuckle barely made it past the fist that clamped onto her windpipe. It created a strangled sound. "Much like you in so many ways. And as you would do, she died protecting me. Here, under the hatchet of a Muscogee warrior, who thought nothing of cutting down a fleeing woman."

His fingers returned to her hair. Brushing it aside, he laid a gentle kiss at her ear. "I grieve with you, beloved, but that is not forgiveness I hear in the telling."

"Then keep listening. Will you let me down?" Gaze affixed to the ugly patch of earth, Adela squirmed until he sighed and eased her to the ground. On numb feet, breath coming with effort through a throat knotting with tears, she trudged to the ruins, her destination its very center.

"No! Stay out!" Totka's rushing tread sounded behind her. She felt the swipe of his hand against her gown, but he missed because he'd drawn up short. His gasp was a tight hiss. "This is burial ground. You will desecrate it!"

She shook her head in tiny jerks. No, she would honor it. By weeping over those she'd loved and lost, by moving beyond the hate that festered between their peoples, by proving life could go on. That it *would*. She would kneel here among those she'd cherished, and God help her, she would forgive the man who'd had a hand in their deaths. Then, she'd love him until he believed it.

The ash she kicked up clogged her already struggling lungs. Gasping and coughing in bursts, she kept on and sank to her knees. The ground was soft, a cushion beneath her, but it couldn't touch the ache that pierced her middle.

The anguish was oblivious to her purpose. It reared and thrashed inside her as acute as ever, set on having its way with her.

From somewhere behind, Totka issued a command to return to him.

Not yet. She shook her head as a sob rose. It grew until it bulged painfully, but she would not let it emerge as she guided her finger through the ash, forming wobbly letters.

A fearsome trio—tears, cinders, and encroaching panic—tightened her throat until she couldn't breathe. Leaned forward, nails digging into the ash, braid dragging through it, she abandoned her letters and sucked in a long, grating breath, but her throat remained in knots.

She waved off Totka's continued coaxing, even as she swayed with the wail that would not be set free. Overcome with it all, she dropped her forehead to the baked ground, then her shoulder. Heat came off it in waves, singeing her.

Totka repeated his order, shouted it. He shouldn't see her like this, defeated by the memory of the deed she'd sworn she'd forgiven. *Sweet Jesus, give me strength. I've not finished.*

The sight of his moccasins, rushing into view and obliterating her scrawling, loosed the belt on her airways.

"What is it? What's wrong?" His hands were on her, pushing her, pulling her toward him. "Can you not breathe? Speak to me!"

Blessed air entered her lungs. "Back away," she rasped, batting at him, not recognizing her own voice through the ring in her ears. "I . . . need only . . . a moment."

His fingers dug into her shoulders. "The Master of Breath is stealing your wind. It is a warning. We've disturbed the spirits of the dead and should leave."

Breath coming a mite cleaner, she sat back on her thighs, lifted her eyes to him, and blinked. "Ghosts? Here?" Her swallow made her wince. "But I do not believe in them."

He hunkered before her, forearms on his splayed knees, hands fisted. "Deny their existence if you will, but they are real enough." Obstinacy bore a vertical groove into the span between his eyebrows as he clothed his face in steely purpose. His knees cracked as he straightened, hauling her up by the arm.

Once outside the perimeter of the Mims' cabin, he dropped her as though she were contaminated with the dreaded pock. Her legs buckled, and she sank back down. Breath now a manageable wheeze, she was able to fully appreciate his odd behavior.

He stalked off a distance, then spun and peered at her as he might a corset, a foreign object he'd rather not handle. Was treading a grave so awful a thing?

Fear crept in. "Totka . . . ?"

He turned from her, hands on hips, shoulders rising and falling in exaggerated fashion. A minute passed, maybe more, and for its entirety Adela felt the anxiety Lillian had displayed when she'd tossed water onto the fire and cowered under Totka's wrath.

At last he returned, limp more pronounced and gaze unresting, scanning, searching for an enemy she could not see. When he stood before her, he spoke low and intense. "You are covered in death." No accusation could be found in his tone, only quiet horror.

She looked down at herself, at the mess that she was. Dust stained every part of her in various hues of gray. Her breath hitched and erupted in the sob that at last made its escape. "These are my sister's bones," she wheezed out the words.

The fiery swipe of his hand scraped hair from his face, revealing a suspicious gleam of moisture in his eyes. "Why, woman? Why?" Sorrow rent the last word.

She shushed her weeping with a gulp. "Did you not ask for proof?"

At the crinkling of his brow, she began again to write in large, clear symbols in the dirt. Tears fell, making craters around them, but she thanked God her movements were firm and unflinching. When she'd finished, she gathered shaky feet beneath her, stood beside him, and peered down at her work, satisfied. There, proof.

Could Totka read it? Did he understand the words, the meaning behind them? He studied the ground, then slowly crouched. "You have . . . put your name in the earth."

"I have. Ill-fated though it is."

In one swift move, he stood and swiveled, head tipped. "Your *Muskogee* name."

"Yes."

One step brought him to her. One touch to her chin nearly crumbled the walls that held her together. "Why? Why here?"

There had been a day she'd refused to claim it, and it hadn't sat well with him. Now, she more than claimed it; she inscribed it into the ground where her sister's life was taken by Muscogees.

"Why should I not? I am Beaver." She prayed steadiness into her voice. "You are the other half of my soul, Totka Hadjo, and I hold no anger for what was done here."

Chapter 13

As Copper Woman gazed up at him, the wind continued its course. It was a bland wind, but there was no mistaking its point of origin. The west.

And here they stood beside an improper grave, defiling it and themselves. The dead had not received a correct burial, so their spirits likely roamed lost. Threat loomed, yet Totka could not tear his eyes from Copper Woman nor his mind from the inescapable truth.

The evidence was in her eyes, her voice, and it was written in the dirt at his feet—somehow, she had forgiven the Red Sticks. More than that, she'd forgiven him, which meant it was possible to forgive such a grievous debt. It also meant she didn't withhold herself from him out of bitterness but for the reason she claimed: she loved her Jesus Creator more than she loved him.

Bitterness, he could have dealt with. He'd planned to. Here, on this battlefield. But a spirit? One great enough to create the world, command every element, and defeat death? There was no competing with such a being.

His hand fell to his side and exposed the smudge on her neck. It complemented the ash that was pasted to her damp forehead and hairline. An ugly shade of gray, it marred what should be perfectly white skin.

These are my sister's bones.

Horror came back for another shocking blow. Regaining his senses, he madly wiped at her chin, smearing the stain, adding to it.

The wind nibbled at his mind and prickled his skin.

He'd erred greatly in stepping foot on this ground. When Copper Woman teetered on the edge of collapse, he'd been certain he would be dragging her unconscious body off this accursed plot. But she'd recaptured her breath in time for him to resign himself to doing what it would take to set this offense straight. Offering a blood sacrifice. His own.

Would the spirits require the same of her? She was ignorant of the gravity, a mere child when it came to these matters. The spirits would see and know, but he would bleed doubly, on the chance they chose to be unforgiving.

Frantic, he beat at the ash smothering her skirt, but that dreaded west wind blew the cinders into her face, coating her tacky skin, giving it a mottled-gray tone.

She swatted at the haze, coughing roughly again. "What are you doing?" Her retreat stirred up more billows.

He pursued her, removing his shirt as he went. "I should not have brought you here. I've roused the ghosts and defiled us both."

For what? For proof that she'd forgiven him? Why had he refused to believe her? Because of a pale-face soldier named Phillip Bailey, because of the threat he was.

Totka found the cleanest section of his shirt and scrubbed at her face. "Stand still! You make it worse." A grunt rumbled his throat. This was pointless.

To her squeak of surprise, he scooped her up and made for ground beyond the fort's boundary, but once there, he thought better of it and kept going, straight into the lake. It was brown and thick with decay, but it would have to do. Warm water swamped his moccasins, instantly filling them with muck.

"Is my offense so great? What will you do to me?" Another cough seized her. She sounded like her mother! But the Master of Breath would *not* take her.

"Whatever needs doing. First, you'll cleanse."

He splashed and shuffled to frighten off snakes and terrapins. An alligator, mouth agape, sunned itself on a nearby bank, as unconcerned with Totka as Totka was with it. All that mattered was doing what he could to set this right. She certainly wouldn't do it herself. Not properly. Not soon enough.

Her skirt dragged the surface, and she whipped it up. "The water is filthy. May I cleanse at home?"

"You'll cleanse now. Grab a breath." Breast-deep in water, he plunged to his chin, taking her all the way under. She thrashed, but he held her down, letting the water soak her through.

He brought her up spluttering, spitting muddy water, flailing for his neck, scoring him with her nails. Before she could attach herself, he spotted ash still marring her throat and dunked her for a second round.

This time, though stiff, she didn't fight him, so he scrubbed at her neck before lifting her to the surface.

She twisted and gripped his arm with both hands, head shaking in a ceaseless wag. "Leave me alone! There are no ghosts, Totka."

"Indeed, there are. I have met them and would not wish the same for you. You still have ash in your hair. Hold your nose." He pushed her under again, forked his fingers into the hair at her temple, and rubbed vigorously.

When she broke the surface the third time, she was sobbing. "No more! Please, no more. You frighten me!" Limp in his arms, she let her forehead fall against his chest with a dismal *thunk*.

If ash remained on her, it was buried by the sediment and plant matter that painted her hair a foul brown. A twinge of regret touched his tongue with a sour flavor, but he spat it out with the grit that had collected between his teeth.

"You are not frightened nearly enough. What you've done is no trifling thing. If we are careless in setting it right, you'll fall prey to disaster." Did she not see he was trying to protect her?

Mud dribbled from her hair onto the back of her neck. "Release your fear and let me go."

"I'll not deny it. I am afraid." Morbidly so. Afraid for her life. Totka gazed over her head, watched the alligator skid into the water and leave a bubble trail going the opposite direction. "But I won't release it. Not until we've restored balance and I am assured of your safety. You should have minded my warning, Copper Woman, and trusted me. Since you have not, we might both pay."

The gravel in his timbre expanded her luminescent eyes until his chest ached with the thought of the price the spirits might exact. "Have you an inkling of the lengths I would do to spare you?"

"Some, yes. Enough to make my heart swell," she said, "but you fear punishment, Totka, which tells me you do not know perfect love, that of Jesus Creator. If you knew him as I do, you would not live in dread."

Not following the transition, Totka stared down at her, neck angled awkwardly.

She spoke an unknown language that he might never understand, no matter the number of evenings he spent hearing from the talking leaves. He felt like a prisoner, chained in a cave of confusion. No matter how far he stretched toward the dim light at the entrance, he never managed to reach any closer to understanding.

"I have seen his work, Totka," she continued as warm water lapped at them, bathing them in its musky odor. "Felt him, His power. And He assures me I have nothing to dread."

She'd seen this spirit? Had she taken a vision journey? Totka would not call her a liar. Many Muscogees experienced such visions. He'd had one of his own, of Wolf, his spirit helper. But the message she'd received contradicted what Totka knew to be true. There was much to dread in breaking the sacred law, but for now, he would let her believe whatever brought her peace. If his predictions were accurate, there was a good chance it would be ripped from her soon enough.

"Then you are truly blessed." His smile felt stiff and grim.

"I am. Abundantly." Wiggling, she unpinned her arm from between them, then wrapped it around his back and over his shoulder. She pulled herself flush against him, nuzzled her face in his neck, and released a sad sigh. "No more dunking. Please."

If she knew he intended to bleed for her, she would thank him for the dunking.

He adjusted to get better footing. One moccasin slid in the mire that nearly sucked the other one off his body. This lake was a pit of filth.

"You have cleansed enough for now. The river is near. I'll take you there to wash out this mud and any ash that remains."

"Take me to the Mobile, if you will. If it comforts you, force me under, but go back to Kossati knowing that I do not fear punishment."

Oh, but she should! He closed his eyes and drew a slow, patience-sustaining breath. Never had their differences in spiritual matters been so starkly opposed, so downright alarming.

Long Arrow's words returned to haunt him. *Forget the white woman, Totka! She's been nothing but trouble and will bring you nothing but more trouble.*

Trouble. Yes, that's what this was. A heaping, malodorous pile of it.

With a mouth-puckering turn of his stomach, Totka wondered for the first time whether her insistence on aligning beliefs had a measure of worth. Could he truly spend a lifetime with this woman, wondering at every moment when her next unpredictable carelessness would rain down trouble?

His heart still raced at the strain she'd placed him under, and even once it slowed, he would continue to worry until he'd done what he could, given of his own lifeblood to restore harmony and earn the spirits' mercy. There was no doubt he would drain his body to the last drop for this woman, but how much easier it would be if she would embrace a healthy fear of the spirit world. By the set of her mouth, that would not happen any time soon.

But this mishap was ignorance, pure and simple. With a bit more instruction, whether she believed or not, she would respect his ways. As she'd always done. They could make it work. They would.

For the moment, Totka didn't know whether to growl at her

impertinence to the spirits or applaud her reckless courage. He settled for a meager smile. "Ever my little Red Stick. The things I most love about you are my worst enemies."

Her tenacity both exasperated and bewitched him, as did the feel of her wet body against him. So close, yet so eternally distant. Why could love never come easy for him?

He pulled her to him, savoring her, wishing he'd done as threatened and flown like an arrow for Kossati.

Plant debris slid past them in its sluggish journey toward the cane-lined creek that eventually emptied into the river. In some hidden covey, hatchling alligators began a series of grunts, calling for their mother. Copper Woman alerted to the sound, angling her head sharply toward it. While her ribs suspended beneath his hand, he counted her increasing heartbeats and fought to rid himself of apprehension at what might become of her once he'd left.

The placement of his mouth at her temple put her ribs back to work, and she relaxed against him. Smiling, he ran his hand from the back of her head, down her snarly braid, and over the curve of her hip. Then, at his flare of desire, he regretted it. The shiver that rocked her made matters worse by draining his self-restraint to a pittance. This woman was powerful medicine. May Hesagedamesse give him strength.

Smart enough to know better than to play with fire, he transitioned and moved his thumb in deep circles at the base of her head.

She relaxed and emitted a little sound that made his blood run faster, hotter. How simple it would be to turn her head, find her mouth, and fill it with his.

"Keep going. A little higher."

He put his forgetful fingers back to work, grateful for the distraction. "Does your head still ache?"

"Mmm." A laugh rumbled deep in her throat.

"Are headaches amusing?"

"I was imagining my father's face when I show up smelling like a swamp."

"The river will rectify that."

Her eyes slid closed, and at the roll of her head to expose more of her neck to his kneading finger, he sighed. "I envy your god-man."

"Why is that?"

"He has your complete devotion."

Against his command, his hand wandered to her jaw where the nudge of his thumb directed her face into the path of his mouth. Her back bowed and tensed, but he recalled she responded well to coaxing. More than well. The day she unleashed herself, would be the day she would swear off this stringent lifestyle she led. Perhaps this was that day.

With unapologetic suggestion, he held her jaw and placed his words at the corner of her lips. "My love might not be perfect, but if you would allow yourself to experience it fully, you would give *me* complete devotion as well." In anticipation of her assent, he stilled the wind in his chest.

Each of her ten fingers bore into him, but her lips were white with the exertion to keep them closed. As clear as war whoop, a battle played out within her. Beautiful, stubborn woman!

He prodded her cheek with his nose, blew cool air over the droplets on her neck, and watched chill bumps form. "Yours, beloved, is a generous spirit with enough love for both your Creator and myself. I ask only for my portion."

She lifted wet, trembling fingers to his mouth, angled it away from her. "To place hominy before a man during a purification fast would be a cruelty. It would dishonor him and his vow of restraint. You are my hominy, Totka. Savory and inviting, but not to be partaken of. Not yet." The rebuke was mellow but effective, delivering its intended sting.

It was also a fresh reminder of her unshakable loyalty to vows. He should praise her. Instead, with a resigned exhale, he removed himself, setting her on her feet and putting a bumper of distance between them. That cooling plunge in the Mobile would be appropriate now.

He wrung brown water from his hair and strove to dispel the crushing weight this battlefield had levied against him. "Do you think your father will notice if I do away with a few cane slivers from my counting bundle?"

Her genial laughter did fine work smoothing a few of his spirit's rough edges. "It is worth a try." Eyes filling with alarm, she gasped. "Totka! There was an alligator on that bank. Where did it go?" She spun a circle, scanning the water's surface.

Joining her nervous survey, he injected tension into his body. "We should get out. It could be anywhere." Discreetly, he lowered his hand into the gloomy water behind her. "It could be . . . *here*." He roared and clawed the back of her leg.

She squealed and leapt so high her knees cleared the water. Even when his uproarious laughter made it evident he feared no attack, she continued her scramble and didn't slow until she'd reached dry land. Huffing and steaming, she rammed her fists on her hips, looking less than fierce in her muddy, sopping clothes. "Totka Hadjo, you-you wolf!"

His sides ached with laughter by the time he sledged up the swampy beach. He was still chuckling when he finally reached Micco. The animal grazed in the ravine Totka had crouched in before the assault.

The reminder was sobering. It goaded him back to Copper Woman and onward to the river. True to her word, she cleansed again without protest, praying aloud to her Jesus as she did. It suited Totka fine. His sole complaint was that she asked not for her own cleansing but for his. To maintain proper balance, while he plunged, he asked for hers.

Mindful of the need to get her home, he kept a diligent eye on Grandmother Sun who perched on the horizon, announcing the day's end.

Copper Woman went solemn. The ride back was quiet save for the continuous clicks of innumerable cicadas. When they reached their meadow, they dismounted and walked its width hand in hand.

Little Warrior would be about, somewhere in the fastness of the woods, waiting for Totka to say his goodbyes. The moon had yet to show himself, but the evening's first fireflies had already begun their display of light. He caught one in his palm and chuckled at the tickle of its feet. When he offered to pass the little creature to her, she gave a strained smile, shook her head, and looked away.

Either she was already mourning the loss of him, or she'd finally come to understand the gravity of her actions. Both were appropriate, so he said nothing but kept her in the corner of his eye.

Her clothes, though rumpled, were dry and, for the most part, clean. At the long snake, she'd unbraided her hair. The heat had sapped it of moisture some time ago. It billowed about her now in glorious copper waves, accented by the sinking sun. Although he was sorely tempted, he wouldn't touch it. Instead, he stroked her knuckles.

"Singing Grass is finger-weaving a sash for you," he said. "She would like to know which colors you prefer, blue and yellow or blue and white."

"Umm." Her throat bobbed with a hard swallow. Cherry red patches had come into her cheeks. Her lips matched the lush hue and were so full as to appear swollen. The splashes of color were stunning, beckoning, but her eyes were squinted, and her jaw was tight. "Blue and . . . white, I think. Thank her for me."

"I will." He grazed her chin with the back of his fingers, warily examining her. "Are you well?"

"When I see you again, I will be." She squeezed his hand, the instant cheer in her voice setting his mind at ease.

And did that mean she would turn Phillip away, that she'd wait for Totka? He chose to believe it did. Otherwise, he would be unable to pry himself from her hand.

He let his smile be his response.

"You'll not stay the night? We have plenty of room."

"And break my word?" The condition for seeing her had been to stay for a day, not a day and a night. There was light yet. They would travel a short ways before bedding down.

Little Warrior on Wind Chaser emerged from the trees on the meadow's northern edge and waited. Lachlan, kilt rippling, stood at the mare's shoulder. At Totka's side, Micco lifted his muzzle to the wind and whinnied a greeting.

"They will be eager to get home. Go to them." Copper Woman raised an arm and waved at the two. "But come back to me. One moon and twenty-one sleeps from now." Her smile wobbled as she lifted on her toes and brushed her lips against his cheek.

He pulled her in for an embrace, brief yet bold, and hauled himself onto Micco's broad back. Her eyes, shining with an unusual gloss, embedded themselves into his brain as he retrieved his broken days and snapped one sliver in half. He tossed the bundle to her and lifted a brazen grin. "The day is done. Make it one moon and twenty."

As soon as Wind Chaser's chestnut coat dissolved into the murky forest, Adela went headlong into the shelter of the nearest thickets. She'd not made it twenty strides when her stomach upended itself. On her knees, she heaved until the muscles in her back screamed for reprieve.

Trembling and sweating, she pulled herself out of a prickly bed of pine needles and felt better. She breathed a prayer of thanks her insides hadn't declared all-out war until Totka was out of sight—he would've blamed the spirits.

Nausea had been compounding since their meal. Typically, she had a strong constitution, but Micco had joggled her something awful, and it *had* been an emotion-packed day.

It was over now though.

Make it one moon and twenty. That lyrical intonation of his lapped at her mind like a gentle tide. She would smile if it weren't for the claws burying themselves in the back of her neck. Agony ran the length of her backbone, increasing with each step down the path and across her vacant yard.

Noise in the out-kitchen tugged Adela that direction. She stopped in the doorway and slumped against the jamb. The fire had already been banked and no lamp was lit. If not for the white of Hester's apron, her black skin and brown dress would have blended into the dim room. It was one of her rare moments of relaxation. She sat perfectly still, one elbow on the table, mug frozen at her lower lip, feet propped on the chair in front of her. Her youngest filled the kindling bin.

The lingering scent of beans scrambled Adela's stomach. "Where is everyone?"

"Well, there you is!" Hester's bare feet hit the ground. She clunked her mug on the table, sloshing coffee. "Your papa's in the barn saddlin' up old Henry, rifle loaded. Never seen that man in such a state. Givin' you to Jesus one minute. Takin' you back the next. If you ask me, he's tryin' to pick up the war where he dropped it. Mitchell, scoot on out to the barn and put his mind at ease."

"Hey, Missy Adela," the boy said as he skittered out the door.

"Get on in here, girl. I'll fix you up something to fill that belly." The chair groaned with the release of Hester's weight. She went to the breadbox on the sideboard. "Hungry?"

Adela trudged inside. "Not really."

The lid to the breadbox slammed shut. "Saints in glory, child, have you seen yourself? Where did that man take to you?" From the wash bucket, Hester took up a bar of soap and a wet rag, then bustled over to scour the pale red blemish along Adela's hem—remnants of caked mud.

"We went for a swim."

"Where? The pig trough?"

"Don't ask." No reason to dredge up Tensaw Lake.

Hester harrumphed. "At least you done kept your clothes on." Her attempts at scrubbing were pointless, but Adela didn't have the energy to stop her.

She drooped over the table and rested her head on her arms. "I could use some mint tea."

"Stomach upset? Love can do that to a woman." Hester brushed Adela's arm, then touched lips to her forehead. "How long you been hidin' that fever?"

Totka spoke into her mind. *You should have minded my warning, Copper Woman . . . we will both pay.* She flapped a loose hand, dismissing him. The malaise had begun creeping in before they'd even reached Mims' place.

"A few hours maybe." A shiver wrung her spine, and her thoughts went hazy.

"A little white willow with that mint then. Small wonder you got fever with all your traipsin' about in this heat. That Indian done wore you out." She collected the hair off Adela's burning neck and began braiding. "A good night's sleep'll make you right as rest on Sunday. Tea, then to bed with ya."

But Adela never heard the kettle boil. Sleep overtook her.

She woke in her papa's bed to the sound of chickens squabbling and Charlie practicing the word *no*. The misery in her back and head persisted. Throughout the day, Lillian kept water trickling down Adela's throat, then held the bucket for her when it came right back up. Hester, permanent scowl affixed, fussed over cool compresses, and scolded anyone who dared utter the words *yellow jack*.

Periodically, Adela found a quiet corner of her brain in which to wonder about Totka's trip home. Prayers for him put her to sleep that night, and visions of bronze skin stretched smooth over hard muscle danced through her dreams. The next morning, Hester palmed her forehead, examined her eyes, and applied another wet rag and kissed her cheek. "I'll get over to the kitchen to see about your breakfast."

If Adela's eyes were anywhere near as yellow as her skin, Hester would be carrying the words *yellow jack* herself this time.

Adela dozed until Lillian came in bearing a steaming bowl of porridge and a smile that was a shade too bright. The porridge went down thick and unsettling.

With an unsteady hand, Adela set the bowl on the bedside table. "Has anyone heard anything about Phillip?"

"Not a peep. But he'll come." Lillian picked up the dish and scooped another bite onto the spoon. "Your Indian called the soldiers Bluecoats, so Phillip must have gotten a commission in the **Regular Army**. He'll have to wait for leave to be approved." Unlike the **standing militia** in which a man could come and go with little fuss.

Adela shook her head at the spoon Lillian raised.

"Eat." Lillian nudged the air with the utensil, but Adela turned away.

"Best make sure what I have inside will stick around first."

"We'll wait for Hester. She'll whip you into shape." The chuckle she gave sat wrong with Adela, but when Lillian abandoned the bowl to the nightstand and reached for the brush, her smile was its usual brittle self.

Too weak to help, Adela let Lillian pull her hair to the front where she dragged the brush through it with long, even strokes.

"Won't it be good to see Phillip again?" Lillian asked.

Adela swallowed bile. "It will. But Totka says he's changed."

"Pfft! What does *he* know? Phillip will come back to us as charming and brave as ever, and he'll sweep you off your feet all over again." Her voice went dreamy.

Only one man had ever swept Adela off her feet, and he wasn't Phillip. But she didn't have it in her to argue. "I'm sure you're right. He'll always be charming and brave."

Lillian's eyes sparkled with hope. "He could show up any minute, you know. Would you like a bath today? I could have Caesar bring the tub in."

Pain ripped through Adela's center. She gasped and pulled into a fetal position only to fling herself over the edge of the bed and aim for the pan on the floor. A torrent of red spewed from her mouth, spattering the bed, the ground, her dangling hair.

Lillian's scream escorted Adela into a black fog.

Time became marked by periods of less pain, of dark and light, of

241

confusion and clarity. Through the sluggish blinks of semi-consciousness, morning became night, which in a storm of misery, became day again. The process repeated countless times, and at some point in the endless nightmare, she realized she was dying. And the knowing came over her like a call to battle.

Death was good. The natural progression of things. Her suffering would be over, Jesus would greet her, then Mama and Beth, but Lillian would lose her mind, and Totka's beliefs would be validated. He would seek blood revenge, and finding no man to blame, he would exact it on himself.

Adela filled her waning lucid moments with prayer for healing, but every time she peeled back her lids it took more effort. And every time, Papa was there, rooted to the stool by her bed. This time, moonlight outlined his massive figure. He leaned forward on his knees, head supported by his hands.

"Papa," she whispered, through a tortured throat.

He was beside her at once, stroking her hand. "I'm here, sweet girl." His touch was balm to her fears, but sandpaper to her sensitive skin.

The terror on his face blurred, and as she lost focus, she wondered if it would be the last she'd see of him. Some indecipherable amount of time later, his voice came to her again. "You'll dry up if you don't drink," he was saying. "Take some water. If only a swig."

She placated him, but without the strength to swallow, it dribbled down her chin where it heated to the sizzling temperature of her skin. Time was slipping away. "Get parchment." The act of speaking drained her. "I need to write. To Totka."

"Write Totka? Why?" In his haste to rise, he knocked something from the nightstand. "No, I will *not* let you start saying goodbye."

"Now, Papa. Call Lilly." If she didn't do it at once, she might not get another chance. She was already losing the tug of war with consciousness, and death, she sensed, lay just the other side of it.

Chapter 14

The Upper World spirits were in a tempestuous mood, and they were heading Totka's way.

A mass of dark gray clouds rolled toward Kossati, covering the flake of a moon and cloaking the world in bleak darkness. Silent Thunder Snakes whipped their tails in menacing flashes of light the length of the northwestern horizon and charged the air with expectation.

Wind Chaser slurped at the water bucket Totka placed before her. Tail and ears twitching, she fidgeted in place. The cause of her unease might have been fatigue or the lowering weather, but most likely it was Little Warrior's muffled cries coming from the lodge.

The brave had fallen ill. His distress, however, seemed prompted not by discomfort but by a sudden irrational need for Copper Woman. He'd shed not a tear but called out for her again and again.

Totka finger-combed the horse's mane, raking out leaves and twigs illuminated by the Thunder Snakes. "Shah, shah," he comforted. "It bothers me too." More than he would ever be able to express. Remorse was a suffocating, mettlesome thing.

He retrieved the scraper from the shed and set to work flinging sweat from her coat. She swung her head back and thanked him with a dribbling kiss at his ear.

A couple firm slaps to her neck conveyed his mutual respect. She'd done well, gone beyond her limits, pushed herself for him. For Little Warrior, really.

The boy quieted, and Totka breathed easier.

If ever Totka might be called a coward, this was the moment. The wailing had pierced him clean through. If the child cried for Copper Woman one more time, Totka might saddle this poor beast and hit the trail again.

The tromp of Singing Grass' feet against dirt signaled her arrival. She sniffled boorishly, and Totka tensed.

"Can you hear him? It is endless! He lies in misery while guilt hangs from my brother as heavy as a woolen blanket." She shook his arm. "What did you do to bring on this illness?"

The nasally question did not catch him off guard. His sister knew him like her own child. That didn't give her the right, however, to address him as such.

"Am I a brave that I cannot walk my spirit path unassisted? Leave off your mothering." He shrugged out of her hold and slashed the rag over the mare's hindquarters. A violent flick of his wrist flung lather near his sister's feet.

He went next for the hoof pick, but when she snatched for the tool, he let her have it. It hit the side of the shed with a clatter that propelled Wind Chaser, tail high, to the other side of the pen. "Tell me." Her voice was a stone wall.

His molars chafed. "I trod burial ground. Mims' place." He would not lie to her, nor would he involve Copper Woman. This was his fault. His alone.

"You did *what*?" In a dozen uneven flashes, light burst across her contorting face. From the distant hills, Thunder Man replied. His voice grumbled in Totka's chest.

"I cleansed immediately after." In muddy water, crawling with decay and pollution.

"What were you thinking? You have no care at all for the sacred, and now my son, whom you insisted on taking with you, suffers for your contempt!" Her fists lashed at him.

The bruising blows to his chest and arms were only the beginning of what he deserved. When her anger was spent, he picked up the bucket Wind Chaser had kicked over and deposited it with a

244

resounding *clonk*. "I've begun a fast." And he would continue to offer his food to the spirit of the wolf until harmony within him had been restored.

"It will not be enough."

"I know." His offense was too grave, the consequences already evident. "When I have finished with Wind Chaser, I'll go to Old Grandfather. He will guide my sacrifice."

In preparation, Totka had run a great portion of the trail home, run and prayed until his leg had refused and he'd dropped time and again. With every fall, the Shadows had been there to mock him. He'd felt them. Felt their fury, like the bite of pepper grass on every surface of his body.

However, he would take their gnawing presence for a year of moons if it meant they would loose their hold on Little Warrior. And what of Copper Woman? What of that blush on her cheeks that hinted of fever? She'd said there were no spirits. How wrong she was! Old Grandfather would help Totka make amends. He would teach the songs to guide the wandering ghosts back on the path to complete their journey.

Singing Grass sniffled and brought Totka's mind away from what lay ahead for him. For long, silent moments, they each stared at the other's black face.

At last, Totka said, "How is he?"

"Bad. I fear for his life. He is delirious. I have told him repeatedly that Copper Woman is no longer with us, but he insists I bring her to his sickbed. He says he must speak with her before he—" A hideous sob wrenched her. She clawed at her blouse and doubled as with pain.

Totka made himself iron against the urge to comfort her. She would only refuse him.

Death had been on Little Warrior's mind from the morning they'd suspected his illness. "There is no way he can know for certain he will die." The odds were evenly split. Even a brave knew this.

"Tell him then, for he'll not listen to me. And he will not let me hold him! He intends to die like a man, he says. Not a child."

He was a gem among braves. Not fit for death but for greatness, for chiefdom. The spirits knew this. They would spare him. "Let him believe himself a man."

Totka went for Wind Chaser to complete her grooming, Singing Grass pecking at his heels. "Where does he get such bravado? Sick two days and already dying like a man! Next, he will ask to sleep with his bow in case the Master of Breath comes for him in the night. Far be it from any proper warrior to die without his weapons in hand!" The laugh that ripped from her was that of a crazed woman.

Totka would speak with White Stone about administering a calming herb to their sister. "Are White Stone's treatments helping at all?" At a touch from him, Wind Chaser plodded at his side back to the shed.

"Too soon to know. The medicine maker has come and gone, but I've sent Rain Child for the knower. When he arrives, you will welcome him as a guest and pay him whatever he requires." The statement was sheathed in a coat of arms, brooking no argument.

At the stall, he grabbed a rope halter from a peg, slipped it over Wind Chaser's head, and shoved the end of the rope into his sisters' hands. "The only payment he'll receive from me is a sour look. If you want him welcomed, do it yourself."

He tromped to pick up the hurled pick, but her little sob broke him. When he returned, he took the rope from her and, sighing, brushed the jagged hair from her neck. "But if it pleases you, I will bleed until my nephew is well."

The fast, he'd begun yesterday at dawn when Little Warrior woke with an ache in his head so severe it wrung tears from his eyes. Before the sun topped the trees, the boy had worn dual splotches on his cheeks. Cherry-red. By noon, he'd not had the strength to hold himself upright in the saddle.

Totka had held him close and pounded their four-day return trip into three. His body still quivered with fatigue, but the boy had needed his mother's love and the medicine maker's **herbal warriors**.

If it was the yellow plague, as Totka suspected, neither of those things would make any difference. Little Warrior would either live or die. As the spirits judged.

"Do that. And while your blood is flowing" — she hiccupped — "consider the ways you might beg his forgiveness and mine."

She left him to finish Wind Chaser's rubdown in silence, but guilt kept him company, as well as the mental image of Copper Woman's squinted eyes, the unnatural hue of her skin. He crammed his lids together to expel the vision, to refuse it consideration. Even so, a creeping vine of fear slithered up his body and embedded its tendrils in his brain, crimping one hand around the horse-blanket rag and the other around Wind Chaser's mane.

"Totka Hadjo?"

He spun at the sound of his name on Leaping Waters' tongue.

She came toward him, Lachlan's little oil lamp hooked on a finger. Tenderness colored her eyes in the deepest shades of sympathy, sweeping away the angry seasons, making him crave the innocent comfort of her embrace. He would indulge if not for the man who loomed over her from behind, leading that abhorrent speckled mare.

The light played around the chiseled contours of Tall Bull's face, recalling the boyhood nights they spent in the woods telling ghost stories and daring each other to affront the owls.

Totka met his cousin's black eyes. "I was certain you'd be in the Floridas by now." Taking a second wife.

"My wife refused to leave until your return. Something about begging your forgiveness. Now, she sends me away to Tensaw to fetch your *beloved* Copper Woman for Little Warrior. Because I am sick in the head, I do as she bids."

Tall Bull would fetch Copper Woman over Totka's scalped head! Totka threw his rag down and his shoulders back, then thrust himself into their space. "And you are sicker yet if you — if *either* of you — thinks I will allow it." The lamp's flame singed his bare chest. "If anyone fetches her, it will be me."

"Sparring stags, the both of you!" Leaping Waters applied the flat of her hand to Totka's belly, driving him back. "I am ashamed of you, Totka. So busy locking antlers with my husband that you would leave Little Warrior to suffer without his pawa! Tall Bull has nothing better to do than dodge my brother's musket balls." She drilled his chest with a rigid finger. "You will stay. He will go, and he will do it because he is Wolf."

The drop-jaw shock on Tall Bull's face must have reflected Totka's own at the anger she wore. And she was right. It would be heartless of Totka to leave his nephew.

He huffed anyway, refusing to admit Tall Bull was the man for the task. Long Arrow might go, but in the time it would take Totka to reach his friend's village, Tall Bull could already be ten sights beyond Tuskegee. Lachlan would go if he hadn't decided at the last moment to carryon to Mobile to finish his business.

Leaping Waters rounded on her husband next, skewering his ribs with her finger. "And you will go because, admit it or not, you have committed grievous wrongs against us. You have made me an adulteress before the people, while bringing another woman under my roof and knowing how you would hurt me. You terrified Copper Woman with your advances only to spite your cousin and left her to the whim of the elements." She emphasized each point with another poke. "And your offenses against your cousin are such a mass of evil, I would be here till dawn sorting through them!" She threw her arms wide and almost extinguished the flame. "Today, you will begin to repay your debt."

Tall Bull snorted. "You ask the impossible! The woman will take one look at me and run the other way."

Leaping Waters turned to Totka. "The writings should go with him. As proof he is your messenger."

Balking, Totka crossed his arms, making himself large and unbending. The last thing he wanted to entrust to Tall Bull, besides Copper Woman, was the writings.

She spun back to her husband, a growl in her throat, this one directed at Totka. "Swear to us you will not molest her." When Tall Bull did not respond fast enough for her, the lamp's flame wobbled with her furious tremble. "Swear it!"

He laid a fist to his heart. "I swear it. I have only ever wanted you."

"A lie. You've wanted your revenge more and your precious cause, your dreams."

"And the pretty daughter of Josiah Francis," Totka added, his tone dry. "Where did she go? Did you send her on to the Floridas ahead of you?"

Leaping Waters hissed a gasp, but Tall Bull merely crinkled his nose. "Polly Francis? I've not seen that child since before the Horse's Flat Foot. No one has. Her father gave her up for dead."

Totka narrowed his eyes, weighing the sincerity in Tall Bull's tone. If not the truth, it was deceit at its finest. "Not dead by far."

"You saw her then? She's well? Francis will wring me for information." Spirits above, the man was good.

But if he was telling the truth that meant Polly's companion was another. In which case, the Bluecoats might not have been searching for Tall Bull, after all.

Totka shrugged. "Well enough to warm a man's couch, I wager."

With that, Tall Bull leaned in, his curled fist going before him. "Not *my* couch. And I'll advise you to squelch that bit of slander, unless you have a yearning for loose teeth."

Totka backed off, convinced but unwilling to give the man any credit. "Perhaps it is your history of molesting women that has me wary."

Tall Bull angled his head away in the closest form of shame Totka had ever seen the man take. "It was a game gone sour. Nothing more. A ploy meant to make you feel the sting of betrayal. I have regretted it." With that last line, he lifted eyes flickering with exactly what he claimed — regret.

Totka blinked stupidly, unable to absorb the notion of Tall Bull regretting anything.

"Never mind my cousin." Tall Bull turned to his wife. "He has confused me with another. Since the day we bound our lives, I've lain with no woman but you." He stroked her cheek with his knuckles, but if she softened at all, it escaped Totka's notice.

She looked to Totka. "He's sworn not to harm her. It is enough."

"No. It is *not*." But McGirth was there. He would see to Copper Woman's safety. Of that, Totka was certain. "But it will have to do. I'll get the writings." Weariness bore down on him as he began toward the lodge.

She snagged his sleeve. "It is wrapped in layers of cotton and leather and stowed in his saddlebag." Was there anything she had not thought of?

Tall Bull looked to the threatening sky. "I'll be chastened by wind and rain the entire journey, and for what? To be turned away with a laugh."

Not true. Heedless of her own security, Copper Woman would move all three worlds if Little Warrior asked it of her, regardless who the messenger was. "She will come." Unless she was flat on her back with the plague.

Those flushed checks and overly bright eyes had been so becoming on her. Now, they haunted Totka's every waking thought and invaded the few snatches of sleep he'd managed to achieve. He'd wracked his brain trying to remember whether she'd felt feverish when he brushed a kiss across her forehead, but the day had broiled. Naturally, she'd been warm. He should have pressed her, stayed to make certain she was well. He was in torment not knowing and assuming the worst. But in a few days' time, his cousin would rectify Totka's ignorance.

"Her father might accompany her, but she will come," Totka repeated, more to assure himself than his cousin.

"Her father?" Tall Bull's pitch hiked in the first display of alarm he'd shown. "I plan to go in an out like a ghost. Not announce my presence to the Long Knives!"

A fugitive Red Stick did have reason to worry. "McGirth is a reasonable man. The sister is the one you should avoid. Do not doubt she will call the dogs of war on you in a heartbeat."

"The sister . . ." Tall Bull rubbed his jaw, eyes going pensive. "I had forgotten about the dark-haired one."

"Totka Hadjo is right. Stay out of the sister's way. She will give you trouble. Oh, and best leave this here." Like a snake strike, Leaping Waters ripped the feather from his hair.

Tall Bull should have glowered at her, given her the blackest of looks. But he made no response apart from nodding. Had she always had such control over him, or had their time apart steadied the flow of their relationship? Perhaps he was simply dumbfounded, or perhaps, he truly was trying to change.

She continued, brandishing the feather like a knife. "And if I learn you've touched one copper hair, I will crop that perfect nose from your face with my own blade." If the whetted edge in her voice were any indication, she meant what she said.

"I'll do as you ask. I will go, but I cannot promise to bring the woman back."

"Find a way, Husband. Bring Copper Woman back to Little Warrior, or do not come back at all." She let some moments pass before unwinding the tension in her back and turning to hold the light to Totka's face. The strident lines around her mouth and eyes melted away. "You're exhausted. Finish with horse and come inside. I'll see that you are fed."

Behind her, Tall Bull shifted and drew himself taller.

Her "sparring stags" accusation still stung and kept Totka from replicating Tall Bull's stance. He picked up the rag, folded it into a square. "No need to worry yourself over me. I am holding a purification fast for the boy." For them all. "I will be with Old Grandfather for several days."

A shroud of sadness fell across her eyes. "Spare yourself. Blood has already been spilt."

"Not mine."

A glance at Tall Bull pulled her lips taut. She touched Totka's chin with the cool tips of two fingers, whirled, and swept past her husband and his mare. She scurried back to the lodge, casting furtive glances at the Thunder Snake displaying his power above them.

The spirit released another round of crackling light, exposing the animosity lurking behind Tall Bull's penetrating glare. Truly, Leaping Waters should know better than to touch Totka. It was a cruel blow, and in Tall Bull's place Totka would glare too.

Just the same, turmoil brewed in Totka's gut. His fist strangled Wind Chaser's halter line.

The man had shown clear regret over his theft of Copper Woman, and he'd vowed not to molest her. But he'd broken that vow before. This one had been made to Leaping Waters, the sole person who had any sway over him. Would it make enough of a difference?

As clear as Thunder Man's voice from above, Totka knew it would not.

He spun to retrieve Wind Chaser's saddle when Little Warrior's cries began afresh. The courage-shattering sound hobbled Totka's steps, and while he stood—his two greatest loves battling within—he listened to the jangle of the speckled mare's tack, the soft grunt Tall Bull released as he swung up, the clop of restless hooves.

No! He couldn't allow it. He twisted back in the same instant Tall Bull laid his heel to his horse's flank.

A slap of thunder drowned Totka's shout, sent Wind Chaser darting across the pen, and spurred Tall Bull's horse into a frenzied gait that carried them out of the compound.

Totka darted after him, screaming his name, but his weary leg refused the demand. He came to a limping halt in the middle of his deserted lane. From just ahead, a quiet roar met his ears and increased with each of his chuffing breaths. The next lash of the Thunder Snake's tail unmasked a solid wall of rain that advanced at a gallop. It hit Totka with the power of a thousand blowguns.

There was small comfort in the fact Tall Bull would pass a miserable night. But it would be nothing compared to Little Warrior's. Or Totka's.

Chapter 15

In the seclusion of the woods, at the Coosa's brim, under the influence of Old Grandfather's guidance, Totka sang for those who'd died at Mims' place; he sang for the little people to come and guide the lost spirits to the Milky Way.

When he finished, he dove into the Coosa and scrubbed himself with the sands from the bottom. Then he stood before the dawn as a newborn babe and sacrificed his flesh to all four directions. To accomplish that, Old Grandfather scratched Totka with wolf's claws until his blood flowed freely and his guilt began to seep away. The blood, he offered to the fire. Along with prayers for forgiveness and cleansing, for renewal and restored harmony. Prayers for pity from the spirits and mercy toward Little Warrior and Copper Woman, toward every life his affront might harm.

The fast he'd observed since Tensaw had been only the beginning of his journey to forgiveness. The black drink had purged and cleansed him from the inside out. Then, the symbolic burial in which he'd lain covered in a pit, breathing through a length of cane as a fire was kindled on wet palmettos above him, giving a taste of the suffering and deaths of those who had lost their lives. Upon emergence, he'd been administered specially prepared teas to assist him on a final vision quest to meet the spirits of the deceased whose resting place he had disturbed.

His wise elder ended the ceremony with the admonition to live life in beauty, balance, harmony, and to adhere to the sacred law, loving it always.

They sat now at the river's edge, having just gone to water, Old Grandfather beside him, both of them watching the sky drip with endless rain onto the river's turbulent surface. For the ordeal's entirety, Grandmother Sun had hidden her face behind a curtain of dreary gray wet.

He felt shunned, preferring that she would scorch his wounds instead of turn away from him. Arms hooked over his raised knees, he hung his head and longed more than anything, more than food and rest, for good news from home.

Leaping Waters had promised she would bring word should Little Warrior take a turn one way or the other. So far, all Totka had heard was the river's song melding with his own.

Weariness pervaded him, dulled his senses. He felt nothing but pain. From his face to his calves, it struck every raw cut, assuring him he'd given his all.

"The spirits are pleased," Totka said as firmly as he could muster. "I feel it."

Old Grandfather studied him through the day's gloom. His thoughtful hum filled the air between them. "Your purification and sacrifices are complete. Go to your sister's son. Eat. Strengthen yourself for whatever may come." He unfolded his legs, teetered to his feet, and rested his hand on Totka's river-drenched hair like a blessing. "You are an oak. This storm will not break you."

Did the Beloved Man think Totka cared one whit for himself? "And what of Little Warrior? He is but a sapling."

A long breath left the elder on a groan. "The spirits will look upon your sacrifice, whether it was from a true heart. Then they will determine his fate and yours."

In that case, all would be well. He'd been true. Had he not? His foray into the writings would not be held against him. In all his sacrifices, though tempted, he'd not beseeched Copper Woman's Jesus on her behalf. He'd remained true to the ancient ways.

As Old Grandfather left him, Totka said not another word, nor did he budge from his position before the river. Eventually, though, he would need to unpaste himself from the earth and face whatever Singing Grass' lodge held for him.

"Totka Hadjo, why are you still here?" Leaping Waters called as she approached, a certain edginess to her voice. "Old Grandfather met me on the path and—"

"Is it Little Warrior? How is he?" Heart going riotous, Totka reached for his clothes and stood.

She averted her eyes as he dressed. "Frail and tender in his belly, but asking for you."

Still tugging the front flap of his breechcloth through his belt, Totka gripped the nearest tree to keep from crumpling with relief. "He's well?"

Her nod was slight, but her dimples were deep, her smile the loveliest he'd seen since Tensaw, though it dimmed as she let her gaze travel his shredded body. No doubt he made a gruesome sight, but his sacrifice, his prayers—blessedly, they'd been found worthy.

She neared, reached as though to touch the wounds on his face, but stopped short. "Totka . . ." She breathed his name on a pain-filled whisper. "They are deep. You'll scar."

"Save your pity," he said softly. "I've gotten all I need from the spirits. They spared my nephew." Relief washed over him, drained into the ground, and left him a lighter man.

Rain or tears, likely both, dribbled down her chin and onto the indigo that had once made her his own. Her sopping dress stuck to her legs, and her hair was plastered to her forehead. Lips firming, she shook her head with the nearest to reproach she would come.

Then she cracked a little smile. "Don't dress until you've stopped bleeding, or Singing Grass will peel your hide for staining your clothes."

Singing Grass. She would forgive him now.

Totka's laugh was liberating. "That she would. And look at you, mud up to your knees and half the forest in your hair." He dug a twig from her disintegrating bun and a pine needle from her crown. She'd come a long way with this message.

"Perhaps, but your roasted acorn bread is still dry and in one piece." She removed it from her beaded pouch and handed it to him still wrapped in a scrap of duffle.

"Maddo." The blessed scent alone made him feel like a new man. He began toward home and broke his fast by shoving half the bread in at once.

She sidled up and slogged through the mud with him.

Since the night he'd arrived home, rain in various intensities had pelted them unceasingly. The ground had soon become saturated, and now, water coursed through ditches and collected in the low areas. Leaping Grass filled his ear with how the deluge had converted the maize field into a swamp and Singing Grass' garden into a tangle of rotten vegetables. The talwa spent yesterday morning harvesting green corn before it could mold, and Wind Chaser was in fits over Thunder Man's continual argument with the Thunder Snakes.

Their lives had turned into soup, but Little Warrior was well again, and Tall Bull should be home within the next two sleeps, toting Totka's beloved. Fear tried to creep around the corners of his resolve, but he hacked it off at the feet. She would come, and they would celebrate with suckling pig and dried apples.

"Much happened in the night after Little Warrior's fever broke." Leaping Waters held her bespattered skirt over her arm and leapt the expanse of a stream that had not existed that morning. "We spoke, he and I, of his incessant pleading for Copper Woman."

Totka swallowed the last of his bread. "And?"

"And as it turns out, it was not Copper Woman he wanted so much as her knowledge. He feared taking the journey without her Jesus Creator."

"Truly?"

"Yes, truly."

Quite odd. "We have spoken of the god-man only a little, but perhaps Copper Woman did more."

"She did."

They were close, those two, like a bean vine around a corn stalk, and the brave was as likely to speak of his fears with Totka as he was to play cornhusk dolls with his sisters.

As Totka's thoughts wandered, his tread took up a stuttering tempo, and with a touch to his arm, Leaping Waters stopped him altogether. "At my husband's insistence, I've hidden my trust in Jesus of the writings. From all but you. I have hidden it so well Little Warrior did not know I share Copper Woman's beliefs. But in the dark hours of this morning, I spoke to him of Jesus' sacrifice." Her lashes swooped downward, and she shrugged. "I . . . wanted you to know."

Globs of rain fell from the leaves, shaken loose by the wind. Totka wiped his face, welcoming the burn of calluses against open flesh. He schooled the impatience from his tone. "Is that all?"

"And he put aside his doubts and trusted. As we all must do in our spiritual journeys, for we will never fully understand the mysteries of the spirit world or the universe."

How very true. It was beyond any man of any faith. Totka blinked to clear rain from his vision, but gave up and lifted his face to the downpour, to the water that should be a spirit for its life-sustaining abilities.

"Are you angry?" she asked quietly.

He should be furious—at Little Warrior for disparaging his mother's teachings, at Leaping Waters for leading the way—but he'd come to realize no man should force his beliefs on another nor should he forbid another from exploring new ones.

As a freed woman, it was Copper Woman's privilege to hold to her staunch refusal to accept Totka. Her duty as well, seeing she'd made a solemn vow. There was even, he was loath to admit, some wisdom in it. Regardless, to Totka's heart it was a thousand scratches of the wolf's claws. He would not do the same to his nephew.

"Little Warrior has made his choice. Angry? No, I will not be angry. But perhaps . . ." He closed his lids and let his mind soar to the woman who was perpetually just beyond his reach. "Perhaps I am a little envious."

"Well, young brave, Leaping Waters tells me you are on the mend. You must be, for I hear you've been arguing with your sister." To the clatter of rain, Totka settled onto the edge of his couch—Little Warrior's sickbed.

"Not arguing. Correcting." Little Warrior wriggled away to give Totka more room. "She said it was the man John who had walked on the water, but I said it was his brother James."

"It was Peter." White Stone said, not looking up from shelling moldy beans.

Totka cocked a brow at her. She'd never appeared interested in the stories before.

She and Singing Grass straddled the bench cozied up to far side of the rotund lodge. Singing Grass wore a dour expression; White Stone, a cat's impish grin.

Something was different about his eldest sister. Her hair. Though still dirty, it was longer. Tied back with twine. She looked pretty.

The lean winter in the woods had thinned her, unveiling a womanly figure Totka had forgotten she owned. He'd expected the padding to make a reappearance in the moons since, but so far, the extra work around the place had kept it off. Lachlan's keen interest might have had a hand in it as well.

She looked up at him, both shoulders hiking. "What? I listen too."

Totka grinned. "So you do." He went to the shelf on the wall for his razor and leather strop, stepping over a snoozing piglet, an bobbing clear of water that dripped from the ridge board.

The summer lodge, as well as the animal pens, had become swamped. Even though they'd moved into the dryer, more spacious winter lodge, it was crowed. Three children, two babies, the women, and half a barnyard. Totka was outnumbered.

Lachlan should have been home two sleeps past. He must have holed up somewhere to wait out the weather. Either that or he was down with the plague. None of them had put voice to that very real concern.

Relentlessly, the rain beat the gabled roof and seeped through in several places. To keep standing water out, Totka had stacked boards and sacks of dirt across the doorsill. The oiled skins covering the opening were saturated and streaming.

Piglets ran amuck, returning on occasion to the fat sow stretched out at Singing Grass' feet. The dog, swollen with pups, blessed them by keeping to herself under the table.

"Peter . . . yes, perhaps it was Peter." Grimacing, Little Warrior pushed up into a sitting position. "Either way, Jesus calmed the stormy lake by mastering the wind."

Razor and strop in hand, Totka stopped and stared at his nephew. Breath, wind, air—all the same element, all the same spirit. Did Little Warrior realize he'd just called Jesus the Master of Breath?

Totka flicked a glance at Singing Grass who was already boring into him, brows lowered, as though she expected him to put a stop to the nonsense. So long as the boy broke no sacred laws, Totka would not interfere in his spiritual explorations.

"That was not the same story, but yes, he did." Leaping Waters' eyes twinkled from her place on Singing Grass' couch. In her arms, Journey's End gnawed a corncob.

Little Warrior yanked free his turkey feather, bringing up hair by the roots. "And he is the rock, the light, and the water that lives." He said it without hesitation or stumbling, and with his few words, knowingly or not, he tagged the writings' medicine maker with the title of every element spirit.

Singing Grass tsked, as Totka returned and sat beside him, pensive and a bit flustered at having Copper Woman's Jesus given such a lofty position, as though he reigned over every element, as though he were . . . "Creator," he muttered, running fingers down the scabbing lines on his cheek.

A hen darted between his feet and, clacking and flapping, awkwardly winged her way to the rafters. He batted floating feathers from his face, spat one from his mouth.

"There's one on your ear." Little Warrior giggled. "You look silly."

Totka smacked it off and playfully shoved his nephew in the shoulder. "We'll see who's laughing when I tell you I've changed my mind about that tattoo."

The boy sobered in an instant. "Is the razor sharp enough?"

"Not quite." Totka went to the door and hung the strop on the peg that kept the covering in place. He peeled back a corner of the flap, and as he drew the razor's edge back and forth over the supple leather, he watched the rain. It fell in a steady torrent.

While Rain Child and Speaks Sweetly squabbled over who would hold the runt of the piglets, Black Sky howled, and Singing Grass bemoaned the weather, Totka whetted the blade and pondered Little Warrior's statement.

One after the other, the passages he'd referred to filed through Totka's mind. They ended on the one that boldly proclaimed Jesus as master over man's greatest enemy — death.

A flash lit the courtyard reflecting in a million drops of falling rain. With it came the light echo of Copper Woman's voice. *I've seen his work, Totka. Felt him. His power.*

That was well and good for her, but what of Totka? What of his prayer for a vision? Wolf, Totka's spirit helper, had eagerly revealed himself. If it was true that the god-man equaled the power of even a single spirit, then he should be able to do the same.

Before long, light drained from the earth. Totka hooked the flap back on its peg, removed the strop, and used his sleeve to wipe rain from his face. "Have you ever seen such a thing as this rain? It cannot go on." He went for the lamp and set to work shaving a narrow strip of hair from above Little Warriors' ear.

He held perfectly still until Totka raised the lamp and inspected his work.

Little Warrior slumped back with an exhale and explored the smooth skin. "You missed a spot." There was something about his voice . . . Tension? Pain?

Totka neared the light under the pretense of studying the boy's scalp.

The brave smiled up at him, weary yet content. The shadows under his eyes were deep, and his fingers were balled over his stomach, but his face reflected peace.

Totka breathed easier, smiled back, and ran a gentle thumb along the spot Little Warrior indicated. Whiskers nettled his skin. "That I did."

The night passed with so much noise and so many awful smells, Totka might have done better out under the weeping sky. But Little Warrior made not a peep, and every time Totka felt his skin, it was cool.

Something heavy and nauseating escaped from Totka's every pore, leaving him feeling lighter, albeit exhausted. It wasn't until near sunrise, Totka realized it was fear that was fading from him.

While it was yet dark, he unfolded himself from his station at the boy's feet and stretched cramped muscles. There was no point clothing himself. Everything he owned was damp and crusted with mud. At least the rain's incessant pattering had ceased.

Little Warrior rolled over. "Where are you going?" he whispered.

"To the storehouse for the garfish teeth. For your tattoo."

"Will you bring me my bow?" His voice was reedy, weak.

Totka's heart kicked, then went deathly still. "No. Today, the inked moon. Tomorrow, we polish your bow."

"Quiet, Brother," Singing Grass hissed. "If you wake the babies, I will put them to your breast to suckle!"

From the bunk above Little Warrior's, Leaping Waters snickered.

The boy edged up on one elbow. "Please, Pawa?"

"Would you like to begin crafting another?" Totka said to deflect. "You've grown and could use a larger one. There is a cured black locust rod in the storehouse loft. I have saved it for you."

Black Sky fussed and Singing Grass groaned a complaint. The canes in her couch rattled.

With a sigh, Little Warrior eased back down and curled into himself, hugging his middle. "There is no time to make a bow. I want my old one."

Leaping Waters' breath hitched. She lifted her head from where it rested on her bent elbow. Her eyes were round and black.

Totka yanked his gaze away, unable to bear the weight of her alarm, so burdened he was with his own. "We have all the time in the world." He injected levity into his tone, but it came out strained. "Especially if this weather persists." A tremor shimmied through his bones so that he struggled to unhook the flap's corner loop.

First, cowardice. Now, trembling. What was happening to him? Phillip's unsteady hands came to mind. Totka shook off the thought. He was *not* Phillip Bailey. He was Muscogee. Fearless.

White Stone heaved her feet over the side of her couch and stepped on a piglet. It shrieked and hurtled across the lodge, trampling the girls and setting the dog to howling.

The solitude of the storehouse called to him. He would stay a while, collect his thoughts, and not return until he was composed enough to face whatever lay ahead.

Leaping Waters was suddenly behind him, touching the small of his back, drawing close, presumably to secure the flap as soon as he stepped out. "Come back to us soon. We are stronger together." Her soft voice flowed over him like honey over a sore throat. How well she knew him.

He pulled back the covering and froze at the sight of Tall Bull slumped in the saddle.

Leaping Waters loosed a sound like a strangled bird cheep.

Tall Bull's mare stood broadside before the lodge. Sludge coated her from hoof to shoulder. It weighed down her lifeless tail and dripped from her mane. Tall Bull was spattered with it clear to his stringy hair.

And he was alone.

Heart climbing into his throat, Totka flitted his gaze around the courtyard. It was empty. Quiet, save for Wind Chaser's nervous whiny from the paddock. "Where is she?" He splashed into the yard, shouting. "Why did she not come with you? Where is she!"

Tall Bull lifted his head. A strand of hair covered one eye, but the other took in Totka's scored body. "In a grave under an apple tree."

Totka's eyes tightened; his lips hardened. "You are lying."

"That has been true in the past, but not today." Not a shred of humor or guile lurked behind his dead eyes, but trusting this man came like corn in winter.

"Enough games. What have you done with her!" He seized Tall Bull's legging and told himself not to rip the man from his horse.

"I told you—I am weary of our feud," he said, voice maddeningly level, controlled. "I went to Tensaw because I wish to snuff it out, not kindle it." At last, his features sparked to life. He bent and gripped Totka's shoulder, jabbing a thumb under his collarbone and giving a shake. "I swear to you on the Old Beloved Path and the soul of our pawa, I speak true. Your sacrifice was not enough. Copper Woman has taken the journey."

The world shifted beneath Totka's feet. He clung to his cousin's leg, slapped at the saddle horn for a handhold.

That lovely face, flushed with fever, absconded with Totka's mind. Left him bereft, grasping for air. "What . . . what happened?"

Tall Bull straightened, eased his grip but kept hold. "The dark-haired sister met me in the compound. She had a rifle. Cocked. Her father was away, she said." He swallowed, seemingly to gather his words. "I told her everything and gave her the talking leaves as proof. She pointed to a grave freshly dug."

A growl cut from between Totka's clenched teeth. "The girl is a viper. She would say anything to keep me away."

"I think not this time. Her eyes were red. Swollen, as with much grief." Tall Bull withdrew a square of sloppily folded parchment. "She gave me this."

Totka snatched it from his cousin's soiled fingers and ripped a corner in his haste to open it. Handwriting trailed the page in uneven lines. The letters were irregular, distorted. Even had they been tidy, Totka would have been unable to read for his trembling. His vision clouded over the writer's signature. "I-I cannot, I cannot— It is—"

"Let me." Leaping Waters spoke from behind. He must have passed her the page, for she said, "The writer was . . . Copper Woman."

Tall Bull firmed his possession of Totka. "The Bitter Eyes said her sister put quill to paper the morning she released her spirit." There was no victory in his voice. No goading. Only pity.

Totka shucked off Tall Bull's hand. "Read it, Leaping Waters."

She began in English. "To Totka Hadjo of Kossati."

"In our tongue." He would not risk misunderstanding.

"Time has blurred since you left me with your broken days, but my father tells me six have passed. I have been ill, beloved. Gravely. Yellow plague has swept through Mobile, sparing not even Tensaw."

No, no, no. Denial welled within him, but the facts compounded: the ache in her head, the peculiar blush, her own sweet voice coming to him from Leaping Waters' mouth.

His chest screamed in pain, as though something were within, ripping him apart. He recognized it for what it was. Grief too vast to contain. Before it was fully grown, it would tear him straight down the center.

She continued in halting fashion. "Should you hold this letter, it is because my spirit has passed into the loving arms of my Creator, but I would not leave This World without—"

"No!" He pivoted and jerked the page from her hand. "I cannot hear any more!" It would take him down. Right here.

"Pawa, why are you shouting?" Little Warrior stood in the doorway, slouched against the post, cradling his stomach.

Leaping Waters gasped.

Dawn's clean light exposed a yellow tint to Little Warrior's bare chest. But his eyes, his eyes! Totka gaped at him, unable to comprehend why they were solid red.

The boy gave a sluggish blink and a tear tracked his cheek, leaving a scarlet trail. Blood seeped from his nostril, began a slow drip over his lips. "Is it Copper Woman?" He sniffed and swiped, smearing it to his ear, appearing barely strong enough to support his own weight.

Death. He looked two steps from it.

Was this how Copper Woman had looked in the end? Had she wept blood? No, he could not lose them both!

Leaping Waters' mouth moved, but Totka heard only the mad *ker-thump* of his heart. His legs became pulp. He found himself careening toward her, sliding down her front. His knees slammed into a puddle. Water splashed his face, reviving his senses.

When he looked up, Little Warrior was beside him, leaning on his shoulder, hand in Totka's hair. Singing Grass filled the doorway, horror contorting her features, mouth open in a silent scream.

"Is she unwell, like me?" Little Warrior asked.

Totka wrapped his arms around the boy's slight frame, buried his face in his feverish chest. "She has left me." He choked on the words. "For the spirit world."

Little Warrior stroked Totka's scalp. "No, Pawa. For Jesus. But she will not be lonely. She has her mother and her sister. And soon, she will have me."

Totka hauled back and directed his fiercest glower into Little Warrior's bloody eyes. "Copper Woman is strong. She has no need of you!" He pounded a fist against his chest. "I need you! Enough talk of death. Do you hear me?" He shook the boy by the arms until his head bobbled. "I will not hear it. And I will *not* get your bow!" The sob broke free then and wracked his body with a ghastly bray.

Little Warrior, red streaking his face, bunched his lips in disdain. "You are Big Warrior. Let the women keen."

The reprimand was sobering, and reminded Totka that Little Warrior was a chief in a child's body. He could not die. His people needed him.

And Totka needed to be strong, to refuse the boy these thoughts of death. Not everyone who succumbed to the relapse died. He had a chance, if only a small one.

With his thumb, he wiped blood from Little Warrior's cheek. "And you are a brave with a rogue tongue. Back to your couch." Totka climbed out of the mire, picking Little Warrior up as he did. "You will rest, and you will heal. And you will *not* leave me."

But for all Totka's demanding, three sleeps later, Little Warrior with his bow in hand, left him anyway.

Chapter 16

Blackberry Month (June) 1815

Totka tapped the side of the nail header against the anvil. The nail popped out, hot and black, its head a perfect square. Using the tongs, he tossed it across the shed, landing it in the tin can with precision aim. It clinked against the other hundred or so he'd made over the last moon of sleepless nights.

The task occupied his hands and required just enough thought to occupy his vagrant mind. The unruly thing persisted in returning to those he'd loved and lost, robbing him of sleep and appetite.

White Stone had dropped a handful of parched corn into the pouch that now hung on the J-hook by Lachlan's apron, but the only thing Totka would eat this morning would be the metallic scent of hot iron that coated his tongue with the taste of blood.

Currently, the ache in his stomach paled next to the one that gnawed at his spine. When he set aside the tongs and hammer and arched his back, the sun lanced his eyes. It had climbed a good hand's width above the horizon.

He'd missed the dawn and his prayers, but it was a chore finding the energy to care. His mind was engorged with loss and counting down the days until the change of moons. Five remained. On the fifth, as promised, he would stand in the meadow with his beloved's spirit and let the new blackberry moon wash them both in his dim, cold light.

Then he would do as Copper Woman asked. He would let her go.

Or try to.

Her letter washed up before his mind. *Do not let grief crush you. Mourn a little while, then put it away. You have many winters ahead of you. Love me by loving again. I am yours. Copper Woman.*

Put it away, put it away. Her unthinkable plea haunted him.

And it wasn't the only thing she'd asked him to do . . .

The forge's heat chapped his skin and made raisins of his eyes. With calloused fingers, he rubbed his lids and cringed against the burn, then against the memory of Little Warrior's bloody tears.

He opened them to Lachlan topping the rise that led to the forge. The man was leaner of frame, thanks to the illness he'd suffered, but he'd survived and brought White Stone to her knees with relief the day he'd ridden back into Kossati.

Next to him walked Gray Hawk. Despite advancing age, Totka's father still moved with the grace of a stag: chin high, eyes alert, each footfall deliberate and silent. Footfalls that tended to wander.

On Little Warrior's last evening in this world, he'd cried for his grandfather, but he'd been denied. Gray Hawk had charged into Kossati the following morning, missing the brave by a handful of heartbeats. He'd been stricken with regret. Rightly so.

The man never said where he'd been. Only that he'd ridden hard the moment he'd heard Little Warrior was ailing, but there was no canceling his negligence.

In the twenty-odd sleeps since that grim morning, Gray Hawk had reestablished himself in his tribal talwa across the Coosa, visiting their lodge every few days, playing with his granddaughters, befriending Lachlan. Making himself annoyingly useful.

He'd mended the shingles and helped the women salvage remnants of their flooded garden. Replaced the shredding straps on Black Sky's cradleboard and added a side of smoked venison to the storehouse. He'd even trimmed Wind Chaser's hooves. Too little, too late.

Clan or not, he should have been there for them. For Little Warrior, for Totka.

Totka yanked the iron dowel from where it heated in the coals. Its tip glowed marigold orange—peak forging temperature. Mercilessly, he beat its end to a fine spike until his father stood before him. Then, he beat harder, snapping the fledgling nail from the rod a finger's length from the point.

Lachlan tipped the nail can to peer inside and petted his beard. "You'll keep the town in hardware for a year at this rate. Slow down, lad."

"I told you. No English." He rammed the butt of the nail into the header and shoved the remainder of the rod back in the fire.

"Like it not, you'll hear it anyway." Lachlan let the can drop with a nail-rattling clunk. "That was the deal. You help in the forge. I help with the English. Your need for it doesn't end with Adela McGirth."

"Copper Woman." The hammer landed with ear-biting precision. Twice. "Her name is Copper Woman, and from here out, it will not be spoken again." Not even in his thoughts.

Gray Hawk lifted the tongs, then opened and shut them with childlike curiosity much the way Little Warrior had done. Sparing his father a tart remark, Totka took them back and used them to steady the nail forming beneath his hammer.

"He is in a foul mood today, Gray Hawk." Lachlan switched to Englished and inspected the saddle buckles Totka had made in the night.

"Why wouldn't I be?" Totka said. "I come here to be alone, yes I am not." The forge was the ideal place to escape a courtyard devoid of his nephew yet filled with the presence of a man he could not forgive.

Gray Hawk pulled the bellows cable, and the flames clamored and reached, reflecting off his polished silver gorget and framing his face in fire, giving him a ferocious bearing. "What I have to say cannot wait for the blackberry moon to end your time of solitude."

"Then say it." *And be gone.* Totka nabbed the hot iron with his fingers.

"The rumors are true. Your mother was born Choctaw."

The statement caught Totka's arm mid-toss. The nail missed the can by a foot's length. It pinged off the shelf and fell at his father's feet. Totka stared at him, speechless, as the man bent and picked the pin out of the dirt.

Gingerly, Gray Hawk passed it between his hands until it cooled enough for him to enclose it in his fist.

And still, Totka had not found his head, much less his voice. His mother was . . . ? The gossip. It was . . . ? No. It wasn't true.

It wasn't *possible*. Not in a village such as Kossati where every resident knew every other's family history like his own. More than that, they'd experienced it together. An unsightly fact, such as a woman owning Choctaw heritage, would never have stayed buried. And certainly not for so long.

The steady look in his father's eye, however, and the earnestness with which he'd spoken . . . His father had never lied to him before nor did he have reason to now.

A frigid hand took possession of Totka's heart. He leaned over the anvil, gripped its horn and heel.

"She was taken at a young age by your grandfather, Wild Edge," Gray Hawk said, tone softening. "In a raid as revenge for having lost his own children to a Choctaw blade. Her uncle came after her, but Wild Edge and his wife fled. They came to Kossati—"

"Why are you doing this to me?" Totka's voice was strangled. "Now, of all times?" When his fortitude was at its weakest, when one more blow might turn it to dust.

Unshrinking, Gray Hawk withstood Totka's steely gaze. Met it. Returned it. "Because you have been summoned to the council square. The Choctaw delegation has returned. They've met your terms and have brought a man willing to fulfill blood law."

Hope sprang up as did a sneer that was salve to Totka's raw heart. "Excellent. A gift from the spirits after all they have stolen."

It had taken close to thirteen winters, but his mother's spirit and that of his grandmother would at last be led to the path so they might complete the journey. Totka shoved aside the echo of Leaping

Waters' voice reading from the writings, but he could not ignore the suspicious connection of his father's revelation to this latest development.

He pushed off the anvil and straightened his spine. "You hope I will change my mind if I believe she was once one of their tribe."

Gray Hawk's chin descended in a reticent nod. "Their deaths were satisfied. Payment was received. Let this quest for revenge rest."

"Grandfather was not clan! He had no right to make such a decision without Wolf approval. The clan mothers never would have surrendered the debt! Not without proper payment." Pawa Cetto Imala would have insisted upon it.

"Wild Edge was in the wrong to steal her in the first place. Then to demand blood when one of them returned and took her life? Unthinkable."

Totka flung up a dismissing hand as the ache in his back embedded itself in the base of his skull. Every tribe demanded a life for a life. Even, sometimes, among clan. "And what of Grandmother? Did her life have so little value it could be exchanged for deerskins and trade goods?"

In the silence that swelled the air between them, Lachlan's rustling kilt was a clap of thunder. "Scrub up, lad. Collect your bow from the lodge and get yourself to the square, so you can be done with your ill-conceived deed."

Ill-conceived? Betrayal, isolation, confusion—they took turns washing over Totka. Was he the only man in his compound with enough courage to take a life in order to safeguard the spirits of those he loved?

Lachlan's mustache drooped with reproach. Gray Hawk pointed his gaze at the distant square, disappointment marring his features.

Well, then. So be it.

Totka wrenched off his apron, dumped a bucket of water over his head, snatched up his shirt, and stalked toward home and the bow collecting dust on the pegs by his couch.

His mother and grandmother deserved to have their murders avenged. Balance must be restored and preserved. It was expected. Law. A matter of high honor. Totka *would* see it done.

In the courtyard, he ignored Singing Grass' evil eye; in the lodge, Leaping Waters' piteous glances. The woman had refused to return to the Floridas with Tall Bull, then she'd refused to leave Singing Grass' courtyard. Not until she knew Totka would be well, she'd said.

Without a fight or hardly a word, Tall Bull had vanished to only the Shadows knew where, leaving Totka to deal with his wife, their child, and her useless attempts at comfort.

Using the aplomb of pre-battle ceremony, Totka mixed a batch of red ocher paint and stamped his face with a handprint. It covered his mouth and cheek, representing the hand that would speak for the People in seeking justice. He selected an arrow from his quiver. One was all he would need.

When his fingers hooked around his bow, White Stone took hold of it as well, lifting puffy eyes to him. Her hair hung behind her in a short but tidy braid, and she wore her heart in her soft, imploring eyes. "Don't."

He tugged the bow, but she was anchored. "You would judge me as well?"

"What our father tells you, it is true. I asked Old Grandfather. Our mother was born Choctaw." The quaver in her eyes was the very image of Totka's soul—shame at their grandparents' deceit, turmoil over what to do with this unwieldy information.

Do? There was nothing *to* do, but proceed as planned.

His innards roiled as the horrible truth landed its final crippling blow. If Old Grandfather had affirmed it, it could no longer be denied.

Totka staggered back. This changed nothing. Wounded his pride, slashed it to pieces, but little else. He was Muscogee, painted with the power of his people. They supported him.

Did they not? His gaze darted to Leaping Waters, and she was on her feet in an instant. Panicked at the thought of receiving her pity, he shot her through with a scowl.

Hands folded before her, she plopped back down but remained perched on the edge of Singing Grass' couch. Why, oh why, had he exposed his heart and looked at her?

Because she'd perceived the truth from the beginning. Because he'd berated her for it. Because he desperately needed someone to believe in him. Instinctively, he'd looked to her. But those days were far behind them.

White Stone was speaking. "It feels a betrayal that Gray Hawk has chosen a Choctaw woman as bride, but I sense there is more to this than you or I know. Store your vengeance, little brother. For a time when it is truly needed. Trust him."

Trust the man who would rather consort with the enemy than be at his own grandson's deathbed? "Would you have me abandon *your* ghost to wander the eves of this lodge? Free me to care for this family as I see fit."

Gaze skipping about, White Stone whispered, "Are you certain that is necessary? What of . . . the writings?"

Breath lodged in Totka's throat. Would she follow the path Little Warrior had blazed?

Totka cupped his sister's shoulder. "They have value, but do not forget the price exacted when I scorned our sacred law. Watch me suffer, Sister, and be warned."

Behind him, Leaping Waters made a clatter in her haste to leave the lodge.

White Stone's eyes followed her trail, then came back to Totka, brimming with worry. Head tipping, she touched the back of her hand to his forehead and frowned. "Hurry back."

"It should not take long."

The north, south, and east sheds in the square were sparsely occupied. The Choctaws' arrival had been unexpected for everyone it would seem.

In the westerly shed, along with several men from Raccoon and Turtle, Old Grandfather and Lachlan conversed in terse tones. The east-facing shed housed Micco Bird Creek Fekseko, his Second Man, and the yatika, Mad Turkey, along with the headmen of Wind and Deer. Fierce Raven, the Wolf elder was away, leaving Totka as sole representative for his clan.

Singing Grass, who'd deigned to walk beside him through the talwa, waited below the square. Being a woman, she was to remain outside the mound's perimeter.

Rigid as slave poles, three Choctaw warriors shared the micco's bench. At Totka's entrance, they stood and faced him. The jangle of bells identified one of them. No great surprise Hilaho was back.

Impulsively, Totka's eye sought his father.

Gray Hawk remained outside the north shed's far corner, watching Totka from the tops of his eyes, one fist tucked behind a folded elbow, the other raised and covering his mouth. How difficult it must be for a man to watch his son come to heads with those he was suing for peace. The price for splitting loyalties.

After being introduced, Totka traversed the grounds and swiftly assessed his opponents. They were heavily ornamented in silver, the burliest wearing discs so large they touched the tops of his shoulders. The men stood as one, elbows touching.

The wall they formed rattled Totka, disturbed him in an unexpected way. There had been a day he, Pawa, and Lance would have stationed themselves just so, but today, Totka entered battle alone. No matter. He was warrior enough for it.

Back straight and chin high, he left his gait at off-balance and slowed it to give the illusion of self-assurance.

Hilaho tipped his head at Totka. Center of the three, he was dressed the same as before, except for the addition of an elegant white ostrich plume in his headdress. If his height and bearing hadn't already given him a princely air, the plume would have served the purpose nicely. There was no denying he had noble blood. Strangely, his gaze was as open and passive as before. Except for the sweat glistening on his upper lip, he would have no visible sign of stress.

At his right was an elder, likely a chief, or *minko*, by the elaborately wrought silver gorget covering half his breastbone. The half-rings of white paint radiating down his cheeks matched that of the other two, as did his headband—a swath of blue fabric topped by a silver tape.

The broadest stood to Hilaho's left. He'd positioned himself like a defenseman guarding his goal: legs splayed, body slightly hunched, meaty arms bent and at the ready before him. His deeply pocked face triggered a memory.

Totka had seen this man before, confronted him on the ball field and dared him to make good on his threat of dismemberment. The man had taken up the challenge and might have achieved it if Totka's teammates hadn't unsheathed their inner Red Stick.

Totka thumbed the divot of a scar on his jaw line and singed Pock Face with a white-hot glower.

A smile, hard as old-growth cypress, rearranged the craters in the man's face. The scars made it difficult to assess his years, but Totka would put him a good eight winters beyond himself. About the age of the man who'd tossed that torch onto Totka's lodge roof.

Totka came to stand off-center before the micco. He dutifully shared from the white drink gourd, then puffed a pipe and bathed his head in gray clouds of peace.

Formalities behind them, Micco Bird Creek directed Totka's attention to the eldest Choctaw. One of his eyes appeared to be in a permanent squint, but the other shone with the commanding luster worthy of a chief. Unfalteringly, he leveled it on Totka.

Micco Bird Creek spoke. "**Minko** Yellow Tree comes to us from Reed Clan of the Divided People. He is husband to two wives. Father to seven children. Brother to four sisters. And he has exchanged tobacco with the great white chief, Jackson. He led many warriors to battle at the Horse's Flat Foot where his eldest perished under Red Stick fire."

Totka refused to utter false condolences but, during the respectful silence that followed the pronouncement, granted the minko a civil dip of his head.

Micco Bird Creek motioned to Pock Face. "Beside him, his nephew Rainmaker. He has begun raising beef for food and leather and has been a generous source of knowledge to our Deer Clan."

Rainmaker gave a polite enough nod, but by the hate making arrows of his eyes, he would snap Totka's neck at the first shift in the wind.

Decade-old anger licked at the hollow beneath Totka's ribs, breaking him into a sweat. He'd left his bow with Singing Grass, or he would put a swift end to these droning introductions.

Clan members were responsible for carrying out blood revenge, which meant Minko Yellow Tree should be the one taking the knife to Rainmaker's throat. But Totka had been specific in his demand. He would end the murder's life himself.

The micco shifted their focus to the youngest. "You will recall Hilaho from our previous gatherings. The stories of his bravery precede him. We are honored by the presence of so great a warrior."

What stories? Totka had heard none. A great warrior? The man's skin was tight with youth and unblemished by the sun, and he wore no scars, not a single tattoo. What could he have possibly done in his few winters to deserve such praise? Slain Red Sticks, most likely. There had been abundant opportunity at the slaughter pen the pale faces were calling Horseshoe Bend.

Mad Turkey, the micco's speaker, gave Minko Yellow Tree the floor.

The squint-eyed chief nodded and rose, flinging his silvery queue over his shoulder. Although advanced in winters, his posture was firm, unbent. It demanded respect. "Allow me, your humble guest, to speak on the condition of my people." He addressed the square in a voice powerful enough for a yatika. "The deer is gone from our forests and our corn and few beef cattle struggle to thrive on the rocky, dry grounds allotted us by the Upper Choctaw Council. Totka Hadjo hears the cries of our hungry children, and his heart expands with pity toward them."

Totka conceded the truth with a downward tilt of his head. But the survival of the Choctaw women and children was merely the honey glaze on the bear ribs of his vengeance.

"However, he demands a hard thing of us—the blood of our clansman in exchange for the use of borderlands. Not a warrior among us will deny that Choctaw offences against this warrior are many, the most grievous being the murder of his clanswomen by Four Bears."

Rainmaker was not the murderer?

Minko Yellow Tree angled his body and gaze at Totka. "Four Bears' youthful, drunken transgression was unsightly, a mark of shame against us. Wild Edge and Gray Hawk took the red path of vengeance and hunted him to his very lodge, but when they laid eyes on Four Bears, their mercy was stirred. The debt was settled without lifting the tomahawk, and they parted ways in peace."

He redirected his one eye, sweeping it over the chief's booth. "Gray Hawk's son claims his grandfather negotiated outside the bounds of clan authority. What a burden it is for a man to barrel resentment and carry it upon his back. Totka Hadjo has toiled under his burden many seasons, and he claims he will not rest until further payment has been made. But Four Bears, my own nephew, rests on a scaffold outside my lodge. Soon, his flesh will be picked from his bones." The minko's voice cracked, showing the first sign of emotion.

Totka hardened himself to it and fed from the tension rolling off Rainmaker. It made no difference the man was not the murderer. One Choctaw death was as good as the next. Blood vengeance was not a picky eater—so long as balance was restored, it would be satisfied.

"Grief has made my stomach a stone," the minko continued, "but it will be made heavier yet. For another of my nephews has offered his life in ransom for that of his people. He gives it to Totka Hadjo to do with as he desires. But should Totka accept and take his life, we will require the assurance that the terms of our earlier agreement still stand and that once it is done, Totka's Hadjo's anger will be directed toward us no longer."

After a yielding glance from their micco, Yatika Mad Turkey

spoke. "The terms continue as they were spoken in the little chestnut month, and you have Kossati's solemn vow they will be fulfilled to the word."

Micco Bird Creek turned to Totka. "Old Grandfather, as Beloved Man, has overridden the council and given you final say in this matter. It is a grave thing the clan mothers and council have done entrusting you with such a weighty decision. Do you accept Minko Yellow Tree's blood substitute, or will you reconsider?" The slight inflection in the final question made his preference known.

Gray Hawk, Lachlan, now Micco Bird Creek. Who else?

If Totka looked behind him at the opposite shed, what would he find on Old Grandfather's countenance? How would the ancient one advise? The sentiment of the day seemed to be mercy. Had his people's defeat in the war so thoroughly wounded them that they would leap to take up white man's ways and abandon blood law? Shameful to give up so much so quickly! But Totka had not been reared to buck the advice of his elders, and the fact that three of them respectfully opposed his actions . . .

Then again, not a one of those men was responsible for the welfare of his family — of both the living and the dead.

Totka crushed the doubt as he might an ant beneath his thumb and gave a curt nod. "I accept."

Rainmaker made to rise, but at the slight turn of Minko Yellow Tree's head, he stilled. "My nephew makes his own demand," the minko said. "Before the next blackberry month, Totka Hadjo must come in peace to the new Beaver Lake Town to meet his kinsmen and see the good that has come of this sacrifice."

Totka seized a rogue snort. Vow to meet the kinsmen of the man Totka would skewer with cane? So they might return the favor? Come in peace, Yellow Tree had said. Did they take Totka for an imbecile? Expect him to be fool enough to lay down his weapons and walk into a pit of vipers?

Totka let the scoff in his eyes travel from Yellow Tree to Rainmaker. Then, they brushed Hiloha's and became ensnared.

Unlike Rainwater, whose barely contained aggression heated Totka's skin, Hiloha was a rippleless, glassy sea. Clear, placid. His wide-eyed, steady gaze held what seemed unquestioning compliance, leaving Totka almost powerless against the pull of surrender.

In all fairness, these men had the right to make a demand of their own. Besides, what other choice did Totka have but accept their terms?

Forgive . . .

Totka closed his ears to his beloved's ghost. If she were beside him now, she would understand that justice was long overdue, that it must be served. Trade goods were laughable payment for such a heinous crime.

Later, he would worry about the journey to Choctaw country. Later. After harmony had been restored. "I accept your terms and wish this business done immediately."

Minko Yellow Tree sat as stoic as before, but Hilaho flinched, shock wrinkling his brow. He truly was a child if he'd thought Totka would turn down such an opportunity, even with the added condition.

Rainmaker burst to his feet. Rudely, without ceremony or dismissal, he marched across the square toward the pole at the far corner. Eager to get it over with?

Very well. Totka could accommodate. At his chief's consenting nod, he followed, fingers pining for the feel of the nock between them.

The scuffle of feet behind him said the chiefs' shed was being emptied. The other sheds came alive with movement, but Totka's attention was affixed to Rainmaker.

The burly Choctaw surprised him by veering toward the weapons piled outside the western shed. He was checking the priming on his musket before Totka reached him.

"Put that away," Totka said, remembering the man spoke Muskogee. "This is an execution, not a duel."

Singing Grass spotted him and hurried up the mound to hand off his bow. She graced Rainmaker with a disdainful sneer before stepping into stride with Lachlan who passed by, eyes affixed to the pole. The councilmen, accompanied by the Choctaws, did the same, casting hardly a glance at Rainmaker or his weapon. Gray Hawk alone hung back, surveying from a distance.

"It is a precaution," Rainwater said, "should your aim be as bad as every other Red Stick's I've come up against." He used his teeth to pop the cork from the powder horn.

Totka snorted air. He needed no back-up shooter. "Ironic it will be a Red Stick who ends you." He butted the end of his bow against his foot and arched the upward end so he might hook the eye of the bowstring over it.

A cockeyed leer smudged Rainmaker's scars. Black grain poured from the horn to the pan while he peered at Totka from the side of his eye, as though he were the bearer of a secret.

Heart jolting, Totka nocked his arrow. His bow arm popped into extended position. What element was he missing? While in tune with Rainmaker's actions—the corking of the horn, the click of the frizzen closing—he skimmed the grounds.

Villagers were straggling in from the fields and lanes. They gathered in clans at the mound's base, maintaining respectful distance. Those from the council had congregated in a loose circle around the slave pole.

Stripped to his breechcloth and leggings, hair riotous in the breeze, Hilaho stood dead center, the pole at his back. Minko Yellow Tree gripped him by the back of the neck, forehead resting against Hilaho's. Mouth moving, he drew the younger in for an embrace so desperate it made Totka's head buzz with the intensity of an oncoming swarm of locusts.

Hilaho was the volunteer? The blood substitute?

Sweat slicked Totka's hands. His half-stretched bow lowered of its own accord.

Rainmaker watched its descent with interest. "Did it not occur to you that with four sisters, my uncle might have more than one nephew?" He shouldered his weapon and looked out on the scene that shot holes through Totka's resolve.

Not Hilaho. Totka could end either of the other two but not the able young athlete whom Gray Hawk adored, the young man who displayed not a hint of guile.

The plates hanging from Rainmaker's ears swayed violently and sagged his lobes. "You call this justice, blood law, a righteous execution. In truth, it is abuse of power. The vilest form of contempt." His nostrils broadened. "And still my cousin holds you in high esteem. But neither his sacrifice nor his generosity of spirit surprises me. For you may search in every tribe, white and red, and nowhere will you find a warrior with a purer soul nor one his age with wisdom rivaling that of a beloved man. He is the pride of our people, and *you* wish to snuff out his life!"

That wasn't true at all. Totka had no desire to see the youth fall under his arrow. Frustration mounted, burned the knuckles clasping his bow. It made his brain swim and his breath come hard.

Why Hilaho? It was customary for elders to offer themselves in place of their younger clansmen. And it was within Totka's rights to take the guilty party's life or — should he not be found — that of the first of his clansmen he came across. Without warning, without ceremony, without fear of reprisal.

He should take Rainmaker's this instant and be done with this spectacle!

Rainmaker, with the arrogance of a man flaunting control, walked backward toward the pole, heightening his chin in challenge. "Now that you know the full price of your hatred, tell me, Totka Hadjo, son of the Choctaws, what will you do?"

What would he do? Drive a length of cane through this man's snarling throat before he could even think to swing that cumbersome musket off his shoulder. Totka's arms shook with the want of it while his head battled the vow he'd made to abide by the agreement.

Curse his own stupidity! He'd been so eager for blood he'd not paused to clarify the details. Now, he would be forced to kill the unpretentious young Choctaw or be branded a coward and a man whose word did not stick.

Son of the Choctaws . . . spoken with contempt like the profanity it was.

He would always be Muscogee. And a coward he was not.

And though still green with youth, Hilaho was not a helpless child. He stood as tall as Totka, his broad, bare chest sculpted with the full strength of manhood. A great warrior, Micco Bird Creek had called him. If so, then his noble death would increase his renown, and he would live on in the legends of his people.

Totka would help him along that path, and he would do it without hesitation. Without regret.

No regrets. No regrets. If he said it enough he might convince himself.

Blood law aside, the young man's death would secure lands for his people and husbands for Muscogee maidens. It would also abate the bitterness that had festered in many Kossati hearts. This was right.

Resolve coiling his muscles, Totka advanced, twanged his bowstring, and spat at the man's feet. "What will I do?" He hardened his voice, hoping the river of sweat soaking his shirt didn't make him appear as weak as he felt. "What else, but spill your kinsman's blood?"

Rainmaker's confident backward swagger faltered.

Taking advantage, Totka swept past him down the mound and didn't slow until he collided with the mournful strains of a death song.

Hilaho's clear voice lifted to the Master of Breath. The song sent Totka back six winters to a flaming council house and an old chief who refused to abandon his sacred fire.

The ring of onlookers parted for Totka. His leg creaked and twinged as though it too recalled that life-stuttering event. It buckled, and Totka misstepped.

Hilaho's tune hiccupped in response, but he continued, face angled skyward, arms lifted loose at his sides, a white wampum belt draped over one palm, a medicine bundle clutched in the other.

Where were his weapons? No musket or bow? He would die without even a knife at his belt? It was unseemly. A warrior should enter the spirit land armed. Totka's unease compounded; his pulse spiked.

No regrets. None. Not a one!

Ten paces away, he stopped, facing Hilaho as well as the land of the rising sun.

Hilaho had done this purposefully—laid aside his defenses, forced Totka to face the source of all blessing and life. Wise as a beloved man, Rainmaker had said. Indeed.

And Totka would be wiser yet to eliminate such a shrewd enemy. He nocked his arrow and waited for the death song to end.

Totka, son of the Choctaws . . . Rainmaker's voice came to him like a storm and, on its heels, that of his beloved. *Forgive them, Totka. Forgive. It is the only way.*

His beloved lifted her ashen, tear-streaked face to his memory. Below, peering up at him from the dust, was her Muskogee name etched in earth that stood guard over her sister's bones. She'd proven it was possible. For her.

Beside him, Rainmaker jammed the butt of the musket stock against his shoulder and stood ready to finish what he perceived would be a messy execution. His rapid breath, the click of his rings against the iron muzzle, the anger radiating from him like steam from a kettle—it unsettled Totka's already tremulous nerves and wrung sweat from his brow.

It dripped and smote his eye. He licked salty lips and mashed his eyelids.

When they opened again, he saw not Hilaho's outstretched arms but those of another man. This one, neither red nor white but swarthy brown, save for the blood painting his tortured flesh and dripping from his scraggly beard. The man's body was deeply lacerated, as though he'd endured a hundred scratchings, then submitted himself to a hundred more.

Stomach going caustic, Totka blinked again, and the vision was replaced with Hilaho's calm demeanor. Rattled, he flitted his gaze over those nearest him, but he knew without study that they'd not seen the eerie transformation.

He also knew who it was he'd seen. But why? Why had he shown himself? Totka's heart pounded a mad rhythm against his ear drums.

A vision. He'd received a vision. And a warrior who received one while not on a quest was surely favored. Totka would not even try to shake it off. Far from it. He must decipher the thing.

It was a blessing on this sacrifice. Was it not? Why else would the writings' medicine maker show himself dying?

"May my blood satisfy the debt owed." The song had ended, and Hilaho was speaking. Too steadily for one standing at the brink of the journey. "May it bring lasting peace between our people. May it be a seal between us that cannot be broken."

Peace. Was there such a thing?

Arms lifting and hardening, Totka drew the bowstring to his ear. The fish scale aligned with Hilaho's left breast, which swelled and went still.

Totka's did the same.

It was time, but the apparition . . . Was it a blessing or a warning?

It flashed again before his mind's eye, bold and revolting. Like a glimmer on a rippling lake, it was there one instant, gone the next. But it was enough to cause the arrowhead to waver.

"Big Warrior Totka Hadjo," his father spoke, his tone gentle, pleading. "Will you not forgive them, as I long to do you?"

His father wished to forgive *him*? For what? Totka kicked the question aside. The vision, what to do with it?

His muscles burned; his lungs demanded a resupply. But his father's voice, spoken with love and longing, came back through his mind for another pass, accentuating the cavity that yawned in Totka's chest.

Leaping Waters had spoken true when she'd said his soul was sick. He was a black pit of bitterness and hate, and although surrounded by his village, he felt utterly alone.

And his beloved's Jesus, the one who taught that man should live peaceably with others, would never approve of this killing.

Totka let the string uncoil from his sweaty fingers. It snapped, burned the length of his bow arm, and reverberated clear to his aching backbone. The arrow shot straight and true, burying itself in Hilaho's thigh.

The man jerked, shock rounding his eyes.

Red droplets spurted through the air in the same instant that Totka's bow hit the ground. He raised his shaking hands before him, palms up, empty of revenge. "Blood has been spilt. It is enough."

Chapter 17

The yipping of wolf pups from the adjoining woods lurched Totka from a dream involving a can of nails, a red pole, and a white wampum belt seeping blood. His eyelids flew open to a bowl of stars. Pulse skittering, he jolted into an upright position and groped along his grassy, dew-drenched bed until he located his pouch. At his grasp, the paper within crinkled. He released a pent-up breath and flopped back down.

A feverish chill prickled his skin despite the sultry night. His clothes were damp and irritating. His hair clung to his neck; misery, to his stomach.

Working to govern his fluttering heart, he used his knuckles to buff the fog of sleep from his eyes, then let his gaze rove the Milky Way, that cloudy stretch of spirits bisecting the sky's center from east to west. It brought his beloved to mind front and center.

Was she up there? Traveling that white path to Creator? Her own sweet spirit had been released well over four days ago, the time required for a spirit to reach the gap between the earth's end and the beginning of the stars, but hers was a selfless spirit. It would have stayed behind in the provisionary heaven that hovered above the earth. To encourage and strengthen him, to share in his love a little while longer.

Totka smiled, even though his backbone felt as though it had fused together in the night. Discomfort forced him into a sitting position to stretch out the kinks. He drew and released a cleansing breath that didn't begin to touch the throb behind his eyes.

Wiping a tacky hand over his face, he groaned. There was no time for illness. A certain meadow in Tensaw expected his arrival in four sleeps.

He twisted for a look at what was left of the mulberry month, but the orb had already tucked himself into the horizon. First light was on its way, but the day was far too new to disrupt the lodge with his presence. He would stay here on the bluff and listen to the Coosa cutting through the basin below.

The precipice dropped away several rods from where he'd slept—in the exact spot he'd presented his beloved a peach, basked in her timid gratitude, and felt the first breath of hope that she might forgive him enough to pledge her life to his.

Now, she was gone. With Little Warrior.

A smile trembled on Totka's lips at the thought of them together. It disappeared when he recalled to whom it was they claimed to have gone. The memory of the man's mangled body brought on a fresh wave of nausea.

The previous day, as Minko Yellow Tree had rushed to take Hiloha's weight on his shoulder, Totka had sloughed off Singing Grass' questions and marched from the ceremonial grounds without a backward glance. He'd spent the remainder of the day in the deepest parts of the forest, hiding from inevitable questions. If Tall Bull had been on hand to witness how Totka had caved, he would have laughed Totka straight into a fit of unmasculine rage.

The owls had taken wing before Totka finally admitted to himself what he was truly hiding from: that image burned into his conscience.

It was hard to say which had disturbed him more. Jesus' bloody visage or Hiloha's near collapse when he realized his heart still pumped. Both brought on guilt so dense it clogged Totka's airways. It was easy enough to understand his chagrin at having dragged a good man through such an ordeal, but Totka couldn't fathom how it was he felt to blame for Jesus' suffering. Just the same, it pursued him like a wolf nipping at the heels of a wounded buck.

As did the letter nesting in the pouch he slung over his head. True to form, his little Red Stick had not left This World without a final appeal for him to walk the Jesus way. Her wobbly English script was emblazoned on his eyes.

My quill trembles as I write for fear my death might keep you from knowing Jesus. Seek Him, beloved, while He may be found. His path is beautiful, and His love is perfect, and should you choose to follow Him, we will meet again one day.

In Jesus' Upper World, she'd often told him, that elusive haven for spirits not tarnished by evil. As if that were possible.

His ears picked up a brace of footfalls approaching from behind.

Gray Hawk clamped Totka's shoulder and used it to support his descent, expelling a throaty grunt as his backside settled. He rubbed his knees. "Another winter more, and Nila might be able to use my rickety old joints in place of her turtle shell rattles."

"Father," Totka said by way of greeting, not warming to the mention of the new wife his father had left in Choctaw country. "What brings you?"

"Your noisy stomach dragged me from a perfectly good sleep. Have this." He released a mound of sunflower seeds into Totka's hand.

Uncertain of his stomach, he cracked a seed hull between his front teeth and tested the nutty flavor. "I'll be sure to give Singing Grass my thanks for rousing you to feed me."

Gray Hawk chuckled. "It was White Stone."

Of course. Since Singing Grass was still punishing him. The nuts in his mouth became ash. He muscled the pulp down his throat and spat out a sodden hull.

"White Stone mustn't have caught a single dream," his father continued over top a yawn. "Either that or I have grown immune to her snoring."

"You and Lachlan both."

A period of stillness ensued until Gray Hawk awkwardly cleared his throat. "They will wed soon. Next full moon. She wishes to stay on with Singing Grass but . . ."

But there was no room for another dwelling. The river's tranquil surface ensnared smudges of starlight, like his beloved's spirit suspended between worlds. "White Stone may have my beloved's lodge, along with my blessing." Better it be filled with love, as was intended, than with cobwebs and broken dreams.

"You are a good man, Totka."

"I am the worst of men." So riddled with hate and shame he saw bleak gray wherever he looked. "Half of Kossati will despise me for sparing Hilaho the sting of death. The rest will despise me for delaying the aid offered us last winter, only to back out of my own alternate terms. And the Choctaws"—he snorted—"they will carry home tails of Muscogee cowardice."

"They'll do nothing of the sort. Hilaho passed the afternoon in the square reliving every moment of the Choctaw-Muscogee stickball match. If you'd but been there, you'd have heard him describe your feats. By the time he was through, he'd won Kossati's heart." He bumped arms with Totka and chortled. "There is more than one Muscogee maiden hoping he is among the five brought back to fulfill the treaty."

Totka propped an elbow on a raised knee and allowed himself a smile. "He's a strange bird, but I admit to understanding how you would take a liking to him." How could anyone not approve of a man who faced death so bravely, selflessly?

"I do. In one form or another, he reminds me every day that my son, though somewhat lost, is a jewel among men. Say what you will about yourself, but my chest had never been filled with such pride as it was yesterday. For taking a stand in your mother's honor, then having the wisdom to lower your bow. Near bursting, I was."

"Your praise is unfounded, Father. Taking a stand for Mother was easy, but wisdom?" An abrupt laugh wrenched Totka's torso. "It was your wisdom that saved Hilaho. I'm not sure I would have spared his heart had you not spoken when you did."

Gray Hawk's head snapped toward him so fast his braided hair made a whipping sound. "I never spoke."

"Moments before the arrow flew. You did."

"I did not."

"Your words still roll past my ears," Totka said, a bit put out. He'd not imagined it. Not that.

The pulsing of night insects filled the lengthy void that opened between them. Totka sat immobile, watching as a thin, white band appeared at the horizon where the sun warned of its appearance. His father's studious gaze was hot against his ear.

Finally, Gray Hawk spoke. "At the pole, what did I say? Tell me exactly."

"You said, 'Big Warrior Totka Hadjo, will you not forgive them, as I long to do you?'"

"I said that? Those very same words?"

Totka sighed. "The very same."

Gray Hawk thought a moment more. "When do I ever use your full, titled name?"

"Never!" He swiped a seed hull from his lips and cast it away. "That was what snagged my attention." That and the love with which it had been spoken. Except, clearly, his father had not been the source of either.

If not his father, who had spoken into Totka's mind? A spirit? The one from the vision?

"What have you done that I should forgive?" Gray Hawk asked.

It was Totka's turn to stare at his father. Was the man angling for an apology? Or was he genuinely oblivious? Totka cleared the grit of seeds from his throat. "Of late, I've not been the most respectful son."

"Yes, that." Gray Hawk leaned back on his elbows. "But I understand that, to your way of thinking, I have done little to deserve it."

Gracious of him to say. Emboldened by his father's truce of sorts, Totka extended his own peace feather—vulnerability. "Father, I believe . . . I *know* it was a vision."

"Hmm, a vision. My mind has taken a similar trail. But are you certain it was not the fever plaguing you? Illness has peered from your eyes these two days."

At the mention, a shiver rocked Totka's spine. "It was no delirium-induced imagining. I heard him." And saw him. Not as a medicine maker nor as a teacher, but as an innocent unjustly accused. The parallel between Jesus and Hilaho seemed clearer now, making the vision that much more nerve-tingling.

"Him? Whom did you hear?"

"Jesus."

The name made Gray Hawk sit up straight. "The pale face's spirit-man? Why would he come to a Muscogee?"

"It wasn't immediately obvious to me, but since, I've become certain he wished me to spare Hilaho's life."

"I'll grant you that, but what does Hilaho have to do with this Jesus forgiving you?"

Totka hung his head, massaged the throbbing knot at the base of it. "And that is where I have lost the trail." But it fell in perfect line with the shame he felt every time his memory circled back over that wretched death and the one he'd wished to inflict on Hilaho.

"You had a close connection to the pale faces through the McGirth woman. If you believe her spirits seek you out, you should go on a vision journey. Call on the Jesus spirit, question him. Such a message as his should not be ignored."

"Perhaps I should."

"Your mother had visions. Once, she woke me in the night, flustered and crying. She described a white ghost, dancing in the woods. I went to where she said and found your pawa in his only skin, painted white, and wearing a mask. He was sick with love and dancing a formula the medicine maker had prescribed to make the girl desire him. The man was a vision indeed. One I could have done without." Gray Hawk burst out in uproarious laughter that Totka couldn't help but join.

It soon petered into a melancholy chuckle that ended on a sigh. "Your mother was forever seeing visions, and I loved her for it."

The sadness in Gray Hawk's tone constricted Totka's throat. "You love her still."

"As much as I ever did." His voice turned husky. "Nila gives me new-found joy, but my love for your mother will never die."

Totka examined his father's murky profile and for the first time, understood what drove him, but only in part. Unlike his father, Totka hadn't spent years bound to the woman he worshiped. He'd not lain with her, given her children, loved them alongside her. As fierce as Totka's grief was, his father's must be abundantly more so.

"A man's greatest strength is often his greatest weakness," Gray Hawk said. "Yours, my son, is the same as mine. You love deeply, passionately. Endlessly. It burrows into your marrow and controls your every action."

Yes, that about described Totka.

When fed, it was an empowering passion. When denied, it was maddening. More than once, Totka had considered visiting McGirth, just to feel his beloved near. Even the sight of the Bitter Eyes might bring a measure of comfort. Most definitely a maddening passion . . .

"Do you go to the Choctaws to somehow be close to Mother?" Totka asked, trying to make sense of his father's choices.

"It began that way, yes."

"But they're our rivals for land and game, enemies for as far back as the legends go. How can you show them even the slightest loyalty?"

The deep lines of Gray Hawk's face became clearer as the world gradually shifted from night to day. "Apart from the blood debt I owe them, it was Falling Rain who sent me to Choctaw country."

His shocking mention of a blood debt was forgotten at the mention of Totka's mother who had been long in the grave by the time her husband became attached at the hip bone to the Choctaws. "Mother? How could she—?"

Gray Hawk lifted a silencing hand, then took his time responding. "One of her visions saw the feuding between Choctaws and Muscogees come to an end. After her death, I chose to honor her by honoring her vision. True, on the whole, the Choctaws are our enemy. They were our grandfathers' enemies and that of their grandfathers, but at some point, my son, a man must decide to end the feud. In light of the white tiger stalking our eastern and southern borders, we Natives must strive together for harmony with our pale-face neighbors. This, Yellow Tree understands."

It was a noble vision, but Gray Hawk had always been a dreamer of impossible dreams. From the sounds of it, that was part of what drew Totka's parents to each other—his mother had been a dreamer as well. He thought he'd known his mother, but clearly, he had not. "How was it no one knew Mother's heritage?"

"Before her Choctaw kinsmen could arrive in Coweta to demand the return of their children, your Grandfather Wild Edge took his ill-gotten family and fled. He brought them here, back when Kossati was a peace talwa." A place of refuge for those on the run. In Kossati, Wild Edge would have been protected, untouchable. "Wolf Clan opened their arms and were rewarded with deceit. When questioned about their flight and need for sanctuary, Wild Edge concocted a tale the likes of which is not worth recalling."

Totka absorbed that news with dismay but pressed on. "What of Pawa? Was he born Choctaw as well? And their sister, Tall Bull's mother?"

"Cetto Imala, your pawa, was your mother's blood brother, taken in the same raid. Tall Bull's mother was born of Wild Edge and his wife Singing Voice."

Which spared Tall Bull this drama. Totka harrumphed. Why did it seem the man always emerged on the sunny side of the river? "Pawa never told me a thing."

"Your pawa was ashamed of his heritage. He was young when he and his sister were taken, too small to store memories. Your mother, though . . . Once, she described to me the night she was stolen and how your Grandfather Wild Edge buried a blade in her Choctaw mother's heart. She kept the pain buried beneath her couch and didn't unearth it until she was grown. Even then, she told no one but me for fear news would travel to Choctaw country, and she would wake one night to find her Choctaw pawa reciprocating, standing over your grandmother with a knife. As Wild Edge had done."

Another shiver rippled Totka's back. "In the end, it happened anyway."

Gray Hawk shook his head. "Your mother's death, and that of your grandmother, was a dreadful misfortune. A twist of fate that could not be repeated in a hundred lifetimes.

"Yellow Tree's nephew, Four Bears, was returning from trade in Charleston with a band of fractious youth. Not a prudent man among them. They lodged for a night at the old **tippling house** off the Federal. They'd consumed a cask of tafia the day they stormed Kossati. When confronted, Four Bears had almost no memory of what he'd done."

How could a man destroy half a dozen lives and not even recall the deed? "Was that why he was pardoned? Because strong water filled his belly?" Totka's voice rose with his disgust. "Since when are drunks not held accountable for their actions? Even Strong Deer was punished by the clan mothers every time she laid the cane to Leaping Waters' back." Not that it had ever deterred her from uncorking the tafia.

"If you are to understand, there is more you should know." The audible breath that left Gray Hawk was more a groan than a sigh. "You mother was Reed Clan of the Divided People moiety."

Reed Clan? As in . . . ? The world stilled. Dropped away into dreadful silence. Even the Wind Spirit held his tongue. "Minko Yellow Tree was her clansman?"

Gray Hawk's nod was barely discernible. "Her former pawa." Totka's great uncle. *His* pawa, should fate have taken a different turn. Instead, the Choctaw chief was Totka's . . . What? What would he be to Totka? His mother's maternal uncle but, in an odd twist, not clan.

Air rushed in and out of Totka's open mouth. His stomach began a revolt. "Her own cousin killed her?" He leaned away from his father, fingers digging into the grass.

"Tragically, yes."

And Totka had almost returned the favor. Because if Minko Yellow Tree should have been Totka's clan, then Hilaho should have been also.

Totka punched a fist to his clamping lips, but the flood rose anyway. He scrambled to his feet and reached a cluster of spiky foxtails in time to empty his insides into it. The heaves tormented him until Gray Hawk put a water gourd to his lips and made him drink.

At last, he sat back on his heels and wiped his mouth, anger replenishing the empty places inside him. "Why did you not tell me? You should have told me!" The shout scratched his burning throat.

"I know. I should have." Gray Hawk dropped to one knee beside him. Regret, deep and aching, flowed through his voice and over the slump of his shoulders.

"Why did you not?" Totka snapped, hands shaking. He was becoming Phillip Bailey, losing control.

"Your Grandfather Wild Edge was ashamed of having lived a lie. He made me vow to tell no one. A mistake. You deserved to know. But your pawa, Cetto Imala, reacted poorly to the news and went to his grave in denial. You are so like him, I feared you would do the same and loathe me for it. So even after Wild Edge's death, out of selfishness, I kept the truth from you." He extended the gourd. "Drink, Son. You are ill."

A backhanded swipe sent the gourd tumbling down the ravine. "I almost killed my mother's nephew!"

Gray Hawk shot to his feet and for an instant created the image of a rearing bear, hulking over Totka's crouched position.

Totka floundered to rise. His dizzy-headed sway seemed to arrest Gray Hawk's sympathy, not that Totka cared to have it.

The elder eased his posture back into the semblance of a father. "I wanted to tell you and almost did at the forge. Hilaho was adamant that I mustn't." He stalked to the bluff's edge and, hands clasped behind his back, stared into the purple glow conquering the world's far reaches. "He said that if you knew of your connection, you wouldn't go through with it, and he believed you incapable of letting the blood vengeance go unpaid. The hate was too hot in your eyes, he said."

Was his hatred so obvious that Hilaho had seen it in the few moments he'd spent in Totka's company? Totka's beloved had seen it. She'd been correct in her assessment—he'd become the Bitter Eyes. And it had almost ruined him. It might still if he couldn't contain the anger that propelled his nails into his palms and made his muscles swell. Forgiveness was a feral stallion. He might never capture it, much less tame it.

With deliberate breaths, he unsnarled his fingers, then moved to stand by his father. Like the unrelenting passage of time, the river hastened by as Totka found his composure. A mourning dove alighted somewhere behind them and began its soft, drawn-out call. The perfect lament for everything Totka had lost and everything he'd gained that he never asked for, never wanted.

Cold sweat accumulated in beads on his forehead, his chest, the back of his neck. This illness would not let up until it had its way with him. Maybe it would take his soul as well. But where would it take him? To his beloved? He bit on the thought for a while and found no answer. The not knowing was stinging nettle to his mind, but he unrooted it and thought instead on how delighted she would have been to learn of his Choctaw heritage.

Her image softened Totka's heart and weeded out his temper, giving room for questions to sprout. "How did you learn all this? When?"

"Our pursuit of the murderer led your grandfather and me to Yellow Tree. The minko recognized Wild Edge in an instant. He was the man who'd bested Yellow Tree at knives and stolen his sister's children."

A belittling snort interrupted the story's flow. "You would have thought they were insane the way they snarled and flew at each other. Their hatred for one another ran so deep it nearly killed them both and me with them when I stepped between. It took some doing, but they listened. My recounting of your mother's vision for peace was what finally sheathed their blades and made them sit down like rational men.

"They tallied their losses to learn which of the two owed the greatest debt. Wild Edge had stolen two children, but he'd also lost his own to the Choctaws, albeit to death. Yellow Tree's sister had been killed but so had Wild Edge's wife. And your mother, she'd been slain by her former kin, rendering blood revenge quite pointless.

"Cetto Imala, your pawa, was the one imbalance remaining between them. It was decided Wild Edge would reveal the truth to his adopted son and let him decide what to do with it."

Gray Hawk turned a woeful expression on Totka. "When they were through, their hearts were heavy with regret. They exchanged gifts as a sign of peace between them. Wild Edge received ten chalks of hides and a bolt of calico. He gave Yellow Tree his saddle. I gave him the items Hilaho carried to the slave pole. They'd belonged to Falling Rain, your mother."

It was common practice to bury a person's possessions with him, but Gray Hawk had kept two—her medicine bundle and wampum belt. And they'd been given to Hilaho? Totka looked away, determined not to give rise to the envy pecking his insides.

"If any Choctaw should die by your hand, Hilaho said, it should be him."

Totka's gaze flicked to his father. "I hold no grudge against him. Why should he believe himself the one to die?"

"That, you will have to ask him yourself, and you should without delay. They are your mother's blood. Your own, in a sense. Make it right between you."

A laugh cut from deep within Totka's chest. "As if they would even speak with me."

"You broke no irreparable cord. Try them and see if they are not reasonable men."

The notion churned Totka's rebellious stomach and threatened to send him back to the foxtails. The last thing Hilaho would want was another encounter with his would-be executioner. No, it was the last thing *Totka* wanted, to face the cousin he'd almost killed. To face the young warrior's pawa.

He fisted his roach and groaned, trying to shake the bulky facts into the unwilling crevices of his brain. There was no room in it for the Oaktebbehaw River Choctaws. Yet there they were, in his own talwa. A solid wall of opposition, filled with hate. At least *one* of them was.

Rainmaker might hunt him down for his scalp. Yellow Tree was a mystery; he could go either way. But Hilaho . . .

"How is my young cousin?"

A smile lightened Gray Hawk features. "The leg will mend. It was a clean wound. They intend to stay on a while in Tuskegee. Until he heals enough to travel." He clapped Totka's shoulder. "Grandmother Sun is soon to greet us. Go to water, then sleep. Today, I plan to smoke the duck the Scotsman shot. I'll wake you when it is ready to eat."

Eat? The word alone was enough to make Totka's throat work backwards, but for his father, he would try. He scraped a film of sweat from his forehead and forced a pleasant expression. "Skin on, smoked with applewood?"

Gray Hawk grinned. "You are my pride, my only son. Why would I make it any other way?"

Chapter *18*

As Gray Hawk advised, Totka went to water. When the sun hit the river, transforming it in an instant from gloomy black to vibrant green, he faced it and directed his prayers to Creator.

As he trudged up the bank, others left with him, men and older boys. Most offered either a jovial word or friendly thump on the back. There were a few sour expressions but not the number Totka expected. He left the water lighter than when he'd gone in, wondering how much Hilaho's recounting at the square had to do with this unusually chipper acceptance of Totka's cowardice.

In effect, Hilaho had reminded the town of the man Totka had once been: the renowned stickball player who'd led the way to victory and preserved a vast tract of valuable hunting grounds for his people. The man who'd been granted—who'd *earned*—the privilege to determine the Choctaws' fate using any means he saw fit.

Totka pulled his clothes over his wet body, skimming the area for Choctaws. Blessedly, they were not around, but the women and children could be seen returning from their designated sandy stretch of bank.

Singing Grass guided Speaks Sweetly and Rain Child who held a squirming Black Sky in her skinny arms. White Stone was nowhere to be seen, but Leaping Waters held Tall Bull's son, naked as a newly hatched bird, draped over her shoulder. That tinkling laugh of hers carried easily across the way. Her hair, still free and catching the wind, ferried Totka across the river of pain and loss to a time he barely remembered . . .

A day when she'd been the first and last thing on his mind. When she'd confided her soul to him, promised him her future. Those days had been fleeting. The ones she'd chosen to spend with Tall Bull were irrational and far too lengthy. Sometime over the last moon of sleeps, she'd sent the man on his way yet again, but Totka doubted it would last. A woman as weak as Leaping Waters eventually returned to her destructive habits.

Strong Deer had been fixated on the tafia keg; Leaping Waters, on Tall Bull. It was the same debilitating disease, really.

Totka wrung out his hair, then realizing he had yet to discard yesterday's cane sliver from his broken days, he dug through his pouch. But the bundle he removed could not be his own. Only three slivers remained, and yesterday's still lacked discarding.

"This cannot be right," he mumbled, staring at the all-too-thin bundle, trying to make sense of it.

Had he already removed yesterday's and forgotten? If he had, that wouldn't account for the additional lost day. Four sleeps remained until the new moon. "Four," he said firmly, but the bundle told another story.

He flagged the nearest man. "How many sleeps until the new moon?"

The answer he received sent him racing toward home and Wind Chaser. How could he have broken all but two days and not noticed? Had he been that distraught and unwell? Whatever the case, there was nothing for it now but to fly.

Typically, it was an arduous four-day path to Tensaw. For Little Warrior, he'd done it in three, but every step had been brutal. Reducing it to two would be murderous, but if any animal could do it, Wind Chaser was the one. She had his beloved's pluck and spirit, as well as her drive to head south.

The mare greeted him with an eager whiny. Within moments, she altered to his sense of mission and could scarcely keep from treading his feet as he saddled her. While he tightened the cinch and Lachlan guided the bit between the horse's teeth, White Stone buzzed about them like a meddlesome fly. "You are not going to Tensaw."

"I am going."

She presented a mounting growl. "I thought you had come to your senses! Why go now? You have no chance at all of making it in time."

Totka unhooked her clawed hand from his arm and let the stirrup drop into place. "If I ride through the night, I'll make it." Through both nights.

He went back to the lodge for his bow and quiver, water gourd, and pouch, White Stone railing at him every step of the way. "I cannot allow you ride off in this way, hot with fever and filled with some crazed notion of meeting Copper Woman's spirit in a meadow countless sights from here."

Totka flinched at the sound of his beloved's name but kept going, unwilling to waste breath chiding his sister.

"Mark my warning, Brother, this will not end well! She would not approve."

"Wrong. She is expecting me. A vow is meant to be kept. You know this as well as I." Wind Chaser, ears as straight as sentinels, pranced at the sight of him gusting across the lot toward her. "I told her death alone would keep me away." Totka fisted Wind Chaser's mane and shoved his foot into the stirrup.

Lachlan held the animal steady. "You're lookin' halfway there, but death has yet to claim ya. Be she spirit or be she flesh, best never to keep a woman waitin'."

Leave it to another man to understand. And for once Lachlan's use of English didn't grate like grit between the toes. Wrestling dizziness, Totka flung himself onto Wind Chaser's back, almost tipping over the other side before gaining a proper seating.

While he waited for the earth to stop spinning, White Stone colored the air with a profusion of oaths. "This is no passing illness that plagues you! You will kill this horse along with yourself!" She was screeching now, through tears. "And where in the name of common sense are your moccasins?"

"Fetch them for me. And be quick."

Batting at her dripping nose, she scurried to do as he said.

Lachlan buckled the cheekpiece on Wind Chaser's bridle. "You're leavin' me with a monster, you are."

Totka found a dry smile for the Scotsman and dusted off his English. "My apologize."

"Apologies, lad." Lachlan flashed his perfect teeth before sobering. "You know your sister's right. If you don't stop to rest, you'll kill this fine animal. She's your last true link to Miss McGirth. Remember that, Red Stick, when you're drivin' the lather out of her."

It was nothing Totka didn't already know, but he gave the white man the maddo he expected and took the reins handed up to him.

White Stone returned with his moccasins, rolled blanket, and wooden cup. While Lachlan strapped the bedding behind the saddle cantle, White Stone hooked the cup's toggle into a loop on Totka's belt. "If you come back to me dead, don't think you will be spared a tongue lashing for scorning my counsel." She hurled the moccasins onto his lap and buried her face in Lachlan's shoulder.

"Goodbye, Sister. Tell Singing Grass . . . Tell her when I return, I will be a better brother to her." He laid his heel into Wind Chaser, and soon, her booming hoof beats drowned out his sister's weeping.

Far too slowly, the sights ran one into the other. Every time he reached the landmark that ended one, another loomed ahead, seeming farther away than the last. The sun passed overhead from left to right, scorching his scalp and wicking the abundant sweat from his body. He paused at several creeks to let Wind Chaser quench her thirst and regain her breath.

All through that day, she outdid herself, keeping the torturous pace until nightfall forced them to slow. The last sliver of the old mulberry moon followed their progress from a cloudless sky, mocking Totka with his meager light.

With the first hazy gray of morning, Totka made out the road leading to Fort Claiborne, the halfway point to Tensaw. Such a sense of relief overcame him, he pulled off the path, released an unsaddled

Wind Chaser to do as she pleased, and dropped where he stood, into a patch of flowering life everlasting.

His last memory was that of the aromatic herb invading his nose; his first upon waking, the water drum that beat a merciless tune against his skull. A lumbering cicada killer welcomed him to the new day. Too miserable to swat at the over-grown wasp, he let it whir about him as he crawled to his feet. He squinted painfully into the sky, but the sun would not hold still enough for him to determine whether she had passed her peak or was coming up to it.

Either way, it was well beyond time to get moving. His stiff joints told him he shouldn't have stopped at all.

Not ten paces from where he'd left her, Wind Chaser lay on her side, snoring, legs straight out. At the call of her name, she was up and butting her head against his chest.

The mare accomplished the incredible and stood meekly while he resaddled. He gave her ears a gentle scratch, holding onto her for support. "Glad to see you do not hate me yet. By the time the sun rises again, you might. But for now, put your falcon wings on for me, will you?" Undoubtedly, she wouldn't be able to sustain her previous pace, but he mounted and asked it of her anyway.

The day's heat sapped his waning strength and raised his fever to new heights. It burned within him at prime forging heat, crossing his eyes into a disorienting blur. Pain twisted his gut into hard cordage. It doubled him over Wind Chaser's shoulder and spewed bile into the grass.

Her stumbling trot continued to veer off the trail until he slogged out of a daze to find they were in a pastured dale he didn't recognize. The realization shocked him back to full consciousness. He put the sun to his right and nudged the mare in a southwesterly direction. Wind Chaser had still been slick with froth when he'd come to, so he couldn't have dozed long. The Mobile Road was near. They would run across it soon.

He was certain of it.

In Tensaw's dense, longleaf forest, night fell like a woolen cloak, quick and blinding. The path from the McGirth cabin to the meadow was meager in the best of light, but even in the black of a new moon, Copper Woman could tread it backwards without a stumble.

And little wonder. She'd carved it herself, followed it a thousand times over the last year. That number would be considerably larger if the yellow fever hadn't tied her to her bed for a fortnight. Her full strength still eluded her, but it was returning in increments.

As she wound through the thickets, the lantern swayed before her, flinging its glow left then right and back again, reminiscent of the night Totka's arrow had saved her from a mauling. On that occasion, two years prior, he'd kept to the shadows, working a new trail alongside her. She'd been oblivious to his presence until that first arrow zipped through the dark.

He could be out there now, among the trees, watching her, and she would be none the wiser until he swept her off her feet. She shivered but grinned at the thought, knowing full well he was exactly where he'd said he would be. In their meadow, waiting for her.

She wished she could be as sure of their future as she was the fact he would indeed be waiting for her.

While she'd been flat on her back, Tall Bull had made a surprise appearance. He'd returned the Bible with the message that Totka was dead. The yellow jack had taken his cousin, he'd said, but Totka had left Tensaw in robust health.

A mere seven days later, Tall Bull had arrived claiming Totka had died. Meaning, he'd contracted the disease and died of it in four to five days. Unheard of. But then, Tall Bull was a scoundrel and a liar, and the day she believed a word he said would be the day Little Warrior took up the White Stick and declared himself a medicine maker.

At the thought of the boy, Copper Woman smiled into the dark and lifted her skirt away from the serrated palmetto fronds invading her way. Hopefully, Totka had allowed his nephew to tag along again, but odds were slender. He would want her all to himself with no prying eyes to elude.

Papa was turning a blind eye to Totka tonight, so long as a Christian wedding was performed tomorrow. In her father's estimation, they had gone about this as Indians from the start, with the bride's family requiring nothing more than proof the groom could support her before calling the marriage complete.

On Totka's last visit, he had used Lachlan's word as his bond. Totka had done everything Papa had asked of him. Seeing how he'd been accommodating through the process and enduringly patient besides, he would expect the courtship to end the way it had begun—the Muscogee way.

The simple way.

Copper Woman's way of thinking, however, didn't exactly align with her father's. Totka would come expecting *that*, too. Whatever tonight's outcome, she was finished with Tensaw. She would miss her family dearly, especially Charlie, but her little brother had formed a special bond with Lillian and would continue to thrive even without her.

In contrast, her heart yearned for Singing Grass and the children, for the cooler hills of Kossati, for the unhurried Indian way of life and their firm sense of community. Married or single, she *would* return to Creek country. If she must, she'd take Beaver up on their offer of a place among them. Then she would wait—either for Totka to believe, or for God to release her from her vow.

The meadow opened before her, wide with promise and a star-filled heaven that took her breath away. With its typical cyclical ferocity, the wind caught her skirt. It unbraided hair and drew her in from the perimeter of the forest wall.

She tilted her face skyward and, with a contented sigh, greeted the wisp of a blackberry moon.

The blackberry moon peeked his dark head over the eastern horizon and sent the fiery sun to her couch. He rose clothed in nothing more than a slender outline of what he would become, shedding not a glimmer of frigid light on the unmarked ground that passed beneath Wind Chaser's plodding hooves.

From hips to neck, chills took possession of Totka, cramped the muscles in his back, and rocked his shoulders.

The night was in full swing, and he had yet to encounter the road. Or had he come upon it and crossed right over during one of his foggier, fever-altered moments? Wouldn't Wind Chaser recognize it? She should know to follow it, unless she was as numb in the brain as he.

When the moon reached his crest, panic swelled within Totka. His beloved's spirit would be waiting for him, and he was not there. He was somewhere north of Tensaw, or was he west? The moon was so slender, the night so black, Totka's head so muddied, he struggled to keep the course.

Uncertain of direction now, he resorted to prayer, his parched throat speaking the name of every spirit who might listen. He repeated it until Wind Chaser's rocking gait came to an abrupt halt.

His mind stirred. He sat straighter, focused his eyes.

Wind Chaser had stopped in the center of an expansive meadow hemmed in on all sides by swaying longleaf pines. She had done it. The mare had found her way home.

The relief that overcame him imbued him with enough energy to process a single sweet thought of his beloved. Then, he slipped earthward and landed with a thump not quite jarring enough to rouse him from the vortex of unconsciousness.

White Stone would give him that tongue lashing she'd threatened because Totka had killed himself.

Trapped in the mire of semi-consciousness, he was helpless to stop death's approach. And while life drained out of him, he was watched. Like a man tends pork on a spit, basting and turning, salivating at the aroma, those hideous Shadows, so bold in their mockery, watched and waited.

These could not be mere ghosts lost on the journey. No, they were vile, hissing things, and their cackling bled his ears. He was not theirs yet, but he knew without a shred of doubt his soul was not his own. It never had been.

Like a horn of gunpowder taken on credit for the great winter hunt, his soul had been fitted with a body. But now that body was spent, and Totka had no hides to show for his efforts, no deerskins to trade in and clear the loan. Payment was due, and the Shadows, the essence of all things corrupt, would collect.

Like a hempen noose, terror strangled him, along with the realization that Totka, the Muscogee warrior, the fearless Red Stick, was afraid to die.

Even as his body writhed with pain, his mind strained away from the Shadows, from death's greedy clutches. But in all his experience with these foul beasts, only one thing had ever held them at bay.

A name.

Using the reserves of his strength, he whispered it in his thoughts. The Presence came in like a cool north wind, driving a violent storm before it.

The Shadows retreated, and with them his fear.

Light shed across Totka's spirit. The same light he'd felt last time he'd teetered at death's doorsill. However, this time, its source was no mystery. What was it about that name that gave it such power?

Strengthened, he said it again, feeling a sense of possessiveness. After all, it was the name of a spirit helper who had the power to conquer death as well as the compassion to send Totka a vision that diverted him from a tragic mistake. Yes, Totka would say the Name, and he would claim it, adhere to it as a man did his own skin.

"Totka, *Totka*." His own name came to him from the murk,

delivered in the comforting, tearful tones of a woman. Tones he knew like the beat of his own heart.

As he'd known it would, his beloved's spirit had come to him, met him here. She would accompany him to the spirit land.

His eyelids fought the weight of delirium. For a glimpse of her, for *one* glimpse.

"Yes, very good. Open your eyes." She was moving him, her hand confident, her touch . . . solid? Not the ethereal wisp of a spirit, but firm. Warm. "Please, Totka Hadjo." His name was a plea on her tongue, a prayer.

And at the sound of it, Totka's heart both leapt and crashed. Only one woman spoke his name in such way. To the very end, Leaping Waters would never change.

Not his beloved after all. No, *she* was gone the way of the spirits. A journey he had yet to take. A silent sob wrenched his own spirit.

Leaping Waters settled a hand at the side of his neck. "I know you hear. Come back to me, Totka. It isn't time for you to go. Not now. Not you."

Totka rallied. She might not be his beloved, but she was real. As real as the water that poured over his teeth. It was ice to his fevered lips, and it was sweet life. The trickle was unsteady and insufficient, but he did what he could.

Reassured by the Name and its Presence, as well as Leaping Waters' care, he succumbed to the quiet dark.

Chapter 19

*H*e woke again to the splat of rain and the noisome caw of tree frogs. His lids were broken glass to his eyes, but he forced them back.

Leaping Waters' dimples swept into view. Mist coated her hair and amplified the daylight, giving her a radiant glow. She was a vision, a tear-triggering vision. "Good morning to you, dear one. I always knew you were a champion. Undefeatable." The chipper greeting propelled the moisture overtop his lashes.

His hope that she might mistake his tears for rain was obliterated when she swiped them away with a casual thumb. "At dawn, your fever broke. I suppose I will have to put up with your sour moods a little while longer." The dimples deepened.

He blinked into the branches overhead. Spindly pines towered above him, their tops swaying. "Was I not in a field?" His throat was wooly.

She supported his head and put a cup to his mouth. "I dragged you into the shade. Micco helped."

He was thankful to have no memory of that humiliating experience. "You came after me."

"None of the men would come." There was a shrug in her voice, as if taking a reckless cross-country journey were an everyday affair. "Gray Hawk told them you were on a vision quest and should be left alone. But Creator gave my spirit no peace until I saddled Micco." She put a rolled blanket beneath his head and brushed the hair from his face. "I expected Long Arrow to have figured out where I went and caught up to me by now, but either he's clueless, or I'm a better horsewoman than I believed."

Totka would never believe *that*. But she'd ridden hard to reach him as fast as she had. Then again, there was no telling how long he'd lain in that field before she came upon him. It had been a timeless age to him.

"You left a clear enough trail, if rather circuitous." Her laughter was a bell.

"I was a little . . . disoriented."

"To say the least."

He tried to lift his head to assess his surrounding but was clubbed with pain. "Did I . . . make it to McGirth land?"

Her gaze wandered to some distance point. "I am not familiar with the region, but I know you took the Mobile Road until the Lower Trading Path where you turned east. You rode for several sights before wandering into the brush. I cannot be sure where we are now. Somewhere northeast of Tensaw?"

The Mobile Road was a simple path, an arrow pointing south. And he'd sidetracked? Traveled east and hadn't even noticed? How perfectly incompetent of him. Worse yet, he'd failed his beloved. Broken his vow.

He groaned and covered his face with the crook of his elbow. "I told her unless I was dead, I would be there."

"You almost were dead." She clucked reproachfully. "If Creator hadn't made the way plain to me, you would be."

At her assertion, his arm fell away. "Jesus appears to you as well?"

"In a way." Her head cocked and a lock fell from the knot pinned at the top of her head. "He appears to you?"

"Once. At the slave pole." His voice was reedy, weak; his head, a swirl, but he had to speak of this. "I saw Hilaho transform. For the span of two blinks, he stood there, in Hilaho's place. Later, he spoke. At first, I thought it was my father, but no, it was the medicine maker from the writings."

The Name.

The snarling voices played through his memory. He pulled up, crunching his abdomen, and snatched a fistful of her skirt, clutched it so tight his arm trembled. "He has power, Leaping Waters. Like no other. His name alone makes evil spirit beings tremble. Did you know?"

"So the writings say. Be easy. Lay back." The weight of her hand on his shoulder might as well have been an anvil.

He submitted to her coaxing but kept a hold on her clothes. "He showed himself to me. In his final moments. He was bloody. Arms stretched. Dying." Totka knew he was rambling, but her continual nod told him she was tracking with him.

She stroked the skin that burned over his straining knuckles. "His was a sacrificial death. A blood law substitute. He was an innocent man, perfectly balanced in every way. And while owning all the power of Creator, he hung on a pole and took our death."

And, if Totka remembered the story correctly, he'd done it without fighting back. Without a word in his own defense.

Slowly, Totka's chest relented to a pent-up breath. His fingers unfurled from her skirt. "As Hilaho was willing to do. To bring peace between tribes."

It was a beautiful, flawless parallel. Without equal.

The revelation quickened Totka's heart and soothed him within. Clear to the deep crevices of his soul. In the places the Shadows had never been able to reach. Now, those same corners were filled with the Presence, the Name.

Totka's gaze traveled past Leaping Waters to the sun-drenched meadow that stretched beyond the shelter of the pines. If he gave his imagination feet, it would take him there, to his beloved and her imploring voice.

He closed his eyes and listened to her, then repeated her words. "He loves us with a love that casts out fear of punishment." Perfect love.

Surprise lit Leaping Waters' voice. "Exactly so."

His lips shifted into a smile that confused him. Yesterday, he would not have believed it was possible to experience grief and hope in the same breath. But today, it was reality.

With a burden-lifting sigh, Totka let his sore body relax.

He needed no vision, no otherworldly voice to tell him he'd been granted the peace Leaping Waters described. It resided within him, lightening his spirit, drooping his eyelids, and assuring him he could rest easy.

Even so, from the center of his marrow to the far reaches of his spirit, he ached. Like a lump of soft iron beneath the master's hammer, he'd been heated to near melting and molded into a foreign object he didn't recognize. And in his new form he found himself standing in an odd place, with one foot on the Old Beloved Path and the other on the Jesus Way. Somehow, someway, he would walk them both.

Chapter 20

Even after two days of complete rest, Totka still felt drained. His mood, however, was lighter than it had been since last he'd held his beloved.

Bridle in hand, he swiped again for Wind Chaser's dangling halter rope. She tossed her head, skipped away, and gave a playful whiny that flashed her big yellow teeth. If he didn't know better, he'd say she was laughing at him.

Leaping Waters certainly was from over the blanket she rolled. "She is in high spirits this morning."

"When I finally catch her, she'll wish she'd lowered them a bit."

"Bah. You could never lay a hand to that animal."

She was right, of course.

He approached again, as casually as ever, speaking in soothing tones. "Do you see Micco there, behaving himself? What will he think of you?"

At the sound of his name, Micco lifted his massive head from the grass, hay protruding from his black lips. Disinterested, he went back to grazing.

"See?" Totka said. "The sight of you shames him. Come, you sweet devil. I need your strength. Tensaw awaits, and I cannot face it without you."

Totka felt like a new man in more ways than one. Truthfully, he felt like a child all over again, with an unknown trail to blaze and a world of knowledge to learn. There had been moments since he'd merged his fire with that of the writings' that he'd become overwhelmed by everything he did not know, by the decisions that awaited him.

Leaping Waters assured him he need only take life as Creator doled it out—a day at a time. These many winters, she had balanced her beliefs well enough without becoming an affront to the People and their ways. He would too.

Seek his guidance at every turn, she'd said. *Wait for his answer. Listen for a stirring in your spirit. Listen hard; it will most often be quietly spoken.* The still, small voice that did not come in the wind or the earthquake or the fire.

Today, Totka would go to his beloved's meadow as he'd vowed. He would give her a proper farewell, then he'd turn for home to see what Creator had laid out for him in Kossati.

It seemed a quiver-full of seasons since he'd been at the forge, instead of the five sleeps it was. Lachlan would be glad to see him, and Totka's muscles twitched in anticipation of swinging the sledgehammer.

Wind Chaser pawed the ground, nodding in tall strokes.

"Maybe she has a thistle in her blanket," Leaping Waters called from her shady spot under the trees.

Arm extended, Totka lurched toward Wind Chaser, but she was quicker. Tail high, she galloped to the center of the field. With a guttural bellow, he marched back to their crude camp and threw the blanket onto the ground next to Leaping Waters. "If anyone is tormented by a thistle this morning, it is *me*. A rather large thistle with a fondness for oatgrass and bad behavior."

Chuckling, Leaping Waters whipped open his blanket and smacked its center. "May as well sit. She'll come when she is ready."

"As most women do." He dropped with a gruff exhale and slanted Leaping Waters a smirk. "There are also those who refuse to come at all." He could have been speaking of her refusal to return to the Floridas with her husband, but he wasn't.

The plunge of her gaze said she knew it. She toyed with the end of the soiled yellow ribbon that hung from her upswept hair down across her tattoo. "Totka Hadjo, I—" Her voice cracked.

Instant regret stung Totka's conscience. Why was he dragging them back to those hurtful times?

Two days spent in her pleasant company had built a sturdy bridge between them. It traversed the raging waters that had accumulated since she'd left him standing alone in her grandmother's courtyard. It was a bridge he would be wise to burn at once.

"Leaping Waters, forgive me. I should not have—"

"No. You are right to bring it up." She pointed her gaze at Wind Chaser, who was buried to her ears in pasture. "Once, when I was a girl, my mother told me to toss a jar of cooked beans into the fire. But it was my favorite dish, so I decided to hide the jar under my couch and eat from it later when no one was looking."

"I refuse to believe it. You? Defy your mother?" Grinning, Totka leaned back on his elbows, listening as much to her warm, lilting voice as to the story.

A smile slid up her cheek. "I had my ways. But this time, my way began to stink. It took some time for me to realize what the source was, and by then we were all suffocating with the awful stench." She laughed, but her levity soon dried up. "Our hurts have hidden under my couch for far too many seasons. It's become a stench in my nose, and I want it gone."

It was more than a stench to him. It was a putrid ulcer. He twisted, shifting his weight to one elbow and giving her the back of his shoulder. A cottony dandelion head took the brunt of his dander. "There is no undoing the past. Besides, if you'd bound yourself to me, I might never have known . . . my beloved." He paused to steady himself. "My time with her was brief, but I would not trade it for a dozen winters with any other woman. Yourself included." Totka focused on scalping the dandelion to avoid knowing whether his blunt admission had wounded her. "And without her prompting, I doubt I would've ever had my encounter with Jesus."

"Would you believe me if I told you that was partly why I chose Tall Bull over you?"

Over his shoulder, Totka squinted at her, askance. Leaping Waters could not have known his life would intersect with his beloved's nor that she would urge him to know the great medicine maker.

"Please believe me when I say my decision to bind myself to Tall Bull was not taken lightly." She ran her tongue over her lips, eyes skittish, fingers fidgeting with that ribbon. "I was confused and childlike in my faith, but I knew to ask Jesus for guidance. He gave it, but my heart fought him over it. Hard."

"He told you to leave me? For my cousin?" A man who could not think beyond his own handsome face? "I thought he was said to be a wise and loving pawa."

Movement flickered in the corner of Totka's eye. Wind Chaser, head lowered, plodded toward them.

"He is, which is why he told me to leave you in his care. It made little sense at the time and stung like a mess of nettle. But I—" A jerky sniffle broke her voice, making Totka wonder if she'd loved him even as she'd given him up. At the way she absently caressed the indigo on her throat, he wondered if she loved him still. After a little cough, she continued. "But I see now he has worked in your life far better than I ever could have. You needed a strong woman to drive and challenge you, not one who drained you as I have always done."

She glimpsed Wind Chaser's contrite approach and smiled through her tears. "I felt strongly that he had a noble plan for you that did not include me. My feelings in that regard have not changed. I am blessed beyond measure to have been loved by you, even briefly." Her voice softened to a whisper, forcing Totka to sit up and strain his ear. "Do not lose heart, my dear champion. Be patient. Wait. You will see what beautiful things Creator has in store for you."

Why did it seem as though she was telling him goodbye? Was she planning to return to the Floridas after all? The idea wriggled beneath the pressure of his crushing thumb, refused to die.

Totka pinned her with a reproachful cock of his brow. "As *you* are waiting? For my boar-headed cousin to change his ways?" As if there might ever come a day Tall Bull would relinquish even a tiny fragment of the Old Ways.

"Precisely." She grinned.

Unable to help himself, Totka chuckled. He tossed aside the bald seed head as well as his fear of losing one more person in his life. He would worry about today and nothing more.

Wind Chaser's snuffling breaths grew louder, but Totka ignored her until she rubbed her whiskery nostril against his cheek. He took hold of the dangling rope and let her nuzzle his ear. "Apology accepted."

"See? Even the feistiest creatures can be won through love and patience." Donning a playful smirk, Leaping Waters went to his blanket and began rolling.

"I get the feeling you refer to a certain two-legged Wolf."

"He will change his ways, you know. I am sure of it. Many seasons have seen me lift his name up in prayer. Creator has given me peace that the day will come in which my husband surrenders his willful pride. Until then, you will find me at his side, ever hopeful."

There was no more denying it. Heavy of heart, Totka led the mare into the trees, tethered her to a limb. "When do you leave for the Floridas?"

"We should have left already. The night of the new moon I was to meet him by Old Man Oak." Their old meeting place. Where Totka had loved her without limits.

Her final rejection burned, but he smeared salve on it and squared the shoulders of his heart. It was right that she leave. Healthy. The intersection of their lives had run its course.

Perhaps she was also correct about her husband. If there was any healing song that might knit the wounds in a man's heart, it belonged to the one sung through the writings. Totka was evidence.

He wrapped Wind Chaser's saddle strings around his bedroll while Leaping Waters kicked dirt over the smoldering coals of their fire. "Your husband will be worried about you. I should take you home. My visit to the meadow can wait." A firm yank knotted the last string as a light touch came to his arm.

He turned to find Leaping Waters close, gazing up at him with glistening eyes and trembling chin, confirming his earlier suspicion. She would always love him.

"Maddo," she said. "Forgiveness is a sweet scent."

Without a word, he drew her to him, but ever the faithful wife, she let her arms hang at her sides.

He held her lightly, unmoving, achingly aware that this was a stolen embrace. But he knew like the tears creeping up the back of his lids that this was the only farewell they would be allowed.

At last, he set her away from him, then touched the place where he'd imprinted his love for this woman. "We will forever be bound, you and me. There is no escaping it. But these marks have little to do with it. Our bond is through Creator. It is through him we are bound."

She sniffed and nodded.

"I fear you will never be happy with my cousin," he said.

"Tall Bull was formed from the same clay as I. He is right for me, Totka Hadjo."

A stout exhale left through his nose. It was hard to imagine Tall Bull being right for any woman. "Are you certain? Your journey with him will never be an easy one. Letting you go will come easier for me if you tell me you are not afraid of him or the Floridas."

Her smile was watery and pure and lit from within by a glowing lamp of peace. "Whatever the future holds, I am not afraid."

Totka studied her for the fear that had marked her eyes since a child but sensed not a whiff of it. More than a little awed, he took a step back to better see her. "Then love him, but know this, Leaping Waters—no matter how far you go or the length of seasons you are away, you will always find a home in my heart."

"I know," she whispered. Her fingers tarried at her neck several heartbeats more before she dropped them, a sad smile tightening her mouth. "The sun is getting away from us, and Copper Woman is still waiting."

An iron fist, loneliness compressed Totka's chest. At the bite of tears, he reached for wit. "As Lachlan Gibb has been known to say, spirit or flesh, woman waits for no man."

"If ever a woman were to wait on a man, she would be the one." To the sight of Leaping Waters' sweet smile, he went to retrieve Micco.

The gentle beast came to him without fuss. Totka took him by the halter, offering an appreciative pat on the neck, then turned back and stopped cold.

There, at the forest's bank, like the work of a conjurer, was Tall Bull. He stood erect and still except for the black tresses fluttering at his bare chest. Hate shot from his eyes with rifle precision. The barrel of the musket resting on his forearm was aimed casually at Totka.

Consternation rang through Totka's body, tingling him to the finger ends.

Where had the man come from? And on foot! No, that gray mare of his must be tethered somewhere in the forest, out of sight. He'd sneaked in, like the skulking Indian the Bitter Eyes had once accused him of being.

Wind Chaser's reins led to his hand, and Leaping Waters clung to his sleeve, speaking in urgent tones, but his gaze remained affixed to Totka. It was a bevy of words that gaze, and all of them were black and murderous. They stated that Tall Bull had seen the intimate exchange. Although clearly, he had not heard what was shared between them. If he had, he would know the extent of his wife's faithfulness.

Leaping Waters, her face an indignant mask, spoke hurriedly, intently, convincingly, but her husband granted her not a blink of notice. Bloodshed was in his eyes, and no woman would dissuade him from it.

Thunder Snakes of alarm struck Totka's heart. The scent of his own scorched flesh turned his stomach. This was his fault. He should have known better than to touch her, but in some cobwebbed corner of his mind she still belonged to him. That, undoubtedly, would never change.

This misunderstanding confirmed that her decision to leave was healthy. The sooner the better.

Totka lectured himself on his imprudence while admitting that having camped alone with the woman for two sleeps was probably enough in itself to illicit Tall Bull's fury. A justifiable fury.

Mustering a confident stride, he continued on.

At last, Leaping Waters' pleas could be heard. " . . . would have died if I had not come after him!"

"Wasted effort," Tall Bull said, eyes full on Totka, "for he will die anyway."

She stretched across him, grasping for the musket. "What has gotten into-?"

"I said mount the horse!" He elbowed her and sent her stumbling back into Wind Chaser's breast.

Uttering a cry, she dodged the animal's thumping hooves only to have Tall Bull whip the leather straps toward her, letting them go in the process. "Do it! Unless you want to watch me cut out and roast your lover's heart."

She scrambled to take possession of the reins before Wind Chaser could dash off.

Totka broke into a run. "Enough, Cousin! Will you judge her before you've heard us out?"

"Stop there!" Tall Bull rammed the musket butt against his shoulder. The weapon's steel lock gave off a threatening gleam.

Totka halted, but his pulse raced on. "Here, Leaping Waters." He extended the hand in custody of Micco. "Do as he says and go. But take Micco—"

"Shut your mouth! Your say in my wife's affairs ended six winters past." Tall Bull was in fine form. Finer than Totka had seen in an age. He would not soon be talked down from this rage.

Telling himself to remain calm, Totka lifted a conciliatory hand. "We are innocent of wrong against you, Cousin. Until this morning, I was on my back with a malady. What you saw a moment ago was a farewell between friends." Who'd silently—albeit tenderly—recalled their sweeter moments together.

Tall Bull loosed a scoffing laugh. "Lies have short legs. They make for easy prey. Much the way you find yourself now."

"It is the truth!" Leaping Waters cried. She had yet to climb the horse.

A snarl worthy of the Shadows built in Totka's chest, but he arrested it. If he could not keep his head, he was done for.

Tall Bull was as volatile as the black powder in the horn strung at his side. Any moment now flint would strike his pan.

Was he too far gone to be placated? "Understandably, you are angry, but from the day she bound herself to you, Leaping Waters has been nothing but faithful." Far more than he deserved. "If you would but open your eyes, you would see it!"

"What have you done to her out here?" Did Tall Bull hear nothing but the envy-spawned murmurings in his own head?

"Do not confuse me with yourself, Cousin. I am no violator of women."

Tall Bull slitted the eye peering down the barrel. "One more word, and I will make her ride to Kossati with your corpse slung across her mount."

Leaping Waters gasped, then balled her fists and dressed herself in indignation that fell far short of the power she'd wielded outside the horse pen. "Bite that unruly tongue, Husband! You would never murder your own kin, so point that musket elsewhere before it gets away from you."

"Mount up, woman! Or I will show you how wrong you are." With a sneer for Totka, he sidestepped, backing Leaping Waters toward Wind Chaser's flank. "Your precious Totka Hadjo has several debts to settle. I would prefer you not witness it."

Anger boiled away Totka's hope for a peaceful ending—the man was capable of anything. He clamped his tongue to keep it in check and eyed the bow and quiver on the ground by Leaping Waters' bedding. She stood a few rods from it, but in her state, they were worthless to her.

Her eyes, filling with desperation, darted to Totka, seeking guidance he would not give. She'd chosen this crazed man as her husband. She could look to him for orders, and he'd already given them.

Seeming to catch wind of Totka's sudden neutrality, she firmed her mouth and pitched her chin at an upward angle. She fisted her skirt and, after an unsuccessful first attempt, mounted a springing Wind Chaser.

The animal, eyes rolling, swung her rump wide. Leaping Waters swayed, grappling for a handhold and kicking for the stirrups.

Totka jolted, every instinct telling him to go to her, to get her off that horse.

Stiffening, Tall Bull cocked the hammer, blind to her plight. His shouted curse slicked Wind Chaser's ears.

The animal bolted.

Leaping Waters loosed a scream, barely keeping her seat as the mare lunged into a full gallop that took them along the meadow's perimeter.

Heart thrashing, Totka launched himself onto Micco, shouting the animal into motion before his leg completed its swing of the saddle.

Tall Bull was already in a dead run ahead of him. He threw the musket aside. When it hit the ground, it fired, redirecting Wind Chaser's mad dash.

The animal cut left into the trees and was immediately confronted with a broad trunk. Her abrupt four-footed stop sent her rider sailing over her bowed head.

Leaping Waters' crown broke her flight. Its *crack* resonated through the field as her body crumpled in a heap at the tree's base.

A cry ripped through Totka's body. He kept Micco at top speed the full distance, springing off and hitting the ground at a run. But he knew she was dead before he reached her, before he pulled her limp body into his arms and glimpsed her wide, vacant eyes.

Thirty heartbeats, start to finish—the time it had taken to end

Leaping Waters' life. That, and one man's irrational obsession.

Stuttering for breath, Totka pressed her against his chest. When his hand sank into her softened skull, fury lacerated his throat in a bellow intended to reach her fool husband.

The man reached the scene, heaving convulsively, terror making his eyes wild. Mouth agape, he came to a jagged stop and let grief course unimpeded, shamelessly, down his face.

Pity shot through Totka in an unexpected blast. He loosened his grip, and Leaping Waters rolled onto her back in his unfolded arms, throat arched by her hanging head.

Dead air hung like a burial shroud around them. Not a bird chirped. Even the winds slept. Through the silence, blood pattered onto the stiff, brown leaves covering the ground beneath the live oak that loomed over them.

At length, Tall Bull crashed to his knees, pathetic, almost inaudible moans escaping his tight jaw.

Hadn't Totka always known the man would ruin her?

Now, they would have to make restitution. Her brother would demand a life for a life. That it would also satisfy his cherished hatred would play no small part. Mercy would not be found. From the clan mothers, perhaps, but not from Long Arrow. Not for Tall Bull.

When Tall Bull's gaze finally peeled from his dead wife and sought Totka's, it told a tale of doom. His thoughts followed the same trace Totka's. If he opened his mouth, his death song would emerge.

But Totka, in a more rational state than he, could see the tragedy from a several angles, none of them pretty. One of them ended with the burden of reckoning falling on his own lodge, but he shook off the idea as ridiculous.

"Take her," Totka said, needing him to grieve her a short while, so they could get on with the unpleasant business of carrying her home.

Tall Bull blinked several times slow and did as instructed. He cradled her like a child and rocked with an open-mouthed, voiceless wail that spoke of agony.

Wincing, Totka beat back his own.

He returned to the campsite for Leaping Waters' blanket. Her voice, her faith in Tall Bull, trailed his every step.

He will change his ways. I am sure of it. Creator had given her peace about the man's future. *Until then, you will find me at his side, ever hopeful.*

How true that statement had been. To her last breath, she had remained faithful, hopeful. But Tall Bull's spirit was still propelled by bitterness and rage, unmanned by passion.

And in his thoughtless jealousy, he'd killed the one person who'd ever believed there was good in him worth salvaging.

Not true. He has you.

Bent over, reaching for her blanket, Totka froze.

The Voice had been exactly as she'd described. Soft but unmistakable. There was no way Totka's mind could have constructed such an honorable, selfless thought. It had to have come from a higher source.

He pulled the blanket's scratchy, woolen fibers to his chin and, while staring at the patch of broken grass where she'd lain, he waited for another word from the Spirit, dreaded the nature of the instructions he might receive.

He and his cousin owned an ugly past. What could Totka, of all people, do to redeem the man's life? Did he even want to?

Peering out onto the field, he spied Wind Chaser who'd stopped to forage on the far rim, oblivious to the destruction she'd caused. Her chestnut coat shone in the mid-morning sun, contrasting sharply with her black mane and tail. She was a beautiful creature, once fit for his beloved. Fit now for little more than a musket ball, center forehead.

Under the hand of Long Arrow, Tall Bull would fall next. It was a near certainty. Few, if any, would object to the death of the man who defied the treaty and kept Kossati in the distrustful sights of the Bluecoats.

Would the heartaches never end?

Will you not help him? If not, then whom?

Totka closed his eyes and let the wind eek from his lungs. The sun invaded his lids, but its full brightness could not obliterate the image seared into his mind. The vision of the god-man would follow him the rest of his days, governing his decisions.

Totka rode Micco back to the killing oak. Over the next hand of time, without a sound, he and Tall Bull worked together to round up Wind Chaser, wrap Leaping Waters in the blanket, and gently drape her over Micco's saddle. It was disgraceful and hurried, but Kossati lay three days north, and the days were hot.

By the time they'd begun securing her with cords, Totka had submitted his will and cast his resolve in iron.

He broke the silence. "Does anyone but me know you came after her?"

Tall Bull threaded the cord through the front rigging. "Are you thinking to play the hero? Die in my stead? You were always far nobler than I, but even that is beyond you." He snugged the rope, cringing as he pulled it over the backs of her thighs. "Whatever you may believe me to be, I am no coward," he continued. "I'll return her to her mother. Bury her properly. Then I will bend to whatever payment Beaver demands."

The unsightly grief on Tall Bull's face was a lance to Totka's heart. There had been a day Tall Bull was willing to lay down his life for Totka. He almost had.

Totka took the rope from him, then formed an X over her back and prayed strength from Creator. "This is not about bravery or cowardice but about survival."

"Let me guess. The charitable Totka Hadjo cares little for his own."

Totka allowed himself a glimpse of Tall Bull's hardened eyes, to remind himself what it was like to be led by hatred, to better place himself where Tall Bull stood. "Hers was an unintentional death. Beaver will be merciful. Long Arrow will take payment from me in a form other than blood." Whereas, he would scorn the clan mothers' ruling by slitting Tall Bull's throat, then wish he could do it again. And again.

Tall Bull took Wind Chaser by the throatlatch to steady her so Totka could locate the saddle's rear rigging beneath Leaping Waters' blanket. "What will you give the man? Your chickens? A can of nails?"

Totka's hand stilled beneath the wool. Can of nails? Did Tall Bull have spies in Kossati, or had he been doing his own surveillance?

Tall Bull cocked a corner of his mouth, pleased at Totka's surprise. "You have *nothing* worth giving." He was striking too close to the unsettling truth.

"The horse. He will take Wind Chaser." Totka gently moved aside hair that had escaped the blanket and, gulping bile on the rise, found the iron ring he was after.

"So he can have the pleasure of destroying her?"

"Yes! Why not? Or sell her or ride her until she drops!" Better Wind Chaser's life than that of his sister.

Singing Grass would be the most logical candidate to restore the balance should the clan mothers not be agreeable to Wind Chaser. But they would. For Totka, the man who'd secured five virile warriors for Kossati's maidens, they would.

He yanked the cord through the rigging. "Why are you fighting me over this? We both know you have no chance of walking away from Long Arrow's fierce temper. I do."

"Because he favors you. Because *everyone* favors you."

"This is no time for petty jealousy!" From over top Leaping Waters' body, Totka snatched Tall Bull's arm and his rapt attention. "I want you to get on that gray mare I hate so much and ride for the Floridas. Today. Now. Before you make me so angry I change my mind."

His cousin's eyes widened and watered. "Why do you do this?" The awe softening his face was a momentary slip, scrubbed away by another wave of acid. "It is certainly not due to your benevolent heritage, Totka Hadjo of the Divided People." He *had* been spying.

Totka chose to let the scathing slander go and probed deeper, searching for the heart Leaping Waters claimed was buried beneath all that animosity. "Because your wife swore that more than a scrap of good resided within you. By letting you go, I give you an opportunity to prove she was right."

Tall Bull rounded his eyes and tilted his head, giving his handsome face a childlike curiosity, and in that instant, Totka glimpsed what Leaping Waters had believed was worth preserving.

The bulge of Tall Bull's throat rose and sank quickly. "You tempt me."

Totka let him dwell on his options while working a tight knot into the rope and fighting to loosen the one in his throat. When he was through, he began smoothing the wrinkles in the blanket.

Tall Bull joined him, using long, reverent strokes and attention to detail Totka lacked. "She loved me, Totka. In all my ugliness, she loved me." Whom was he trying to convince?

Totka nodded. "She told me repeatedly."

Tall Bull's brows arched then crashed. "I cannot let you take Long Arrow's heat for me."

Totka adjusted the rope away from its slicing angle across Leaping Waters' neck. "It will not come to violence. Long Arrow has always been a true friend. He will forgive me." He plunged ahead, picking up the prod that would send Tall Bull through the gate. "Besides, the horse belongs to me. Some might say we are equally to blame." Some *would* say it.

Tall Bull's jaw unhinged. In his grief and guilt, he'd missed that unsightly fact.

"Beaver will do well by your son," Totka said. "Go. Do not squander your life. Use it wisely, for in a moment, it can be taken away."

He shared a long, doleful look with Tall Bull, harking back to the days they were more than cousins — the days they tussled on the hot earth, chased birds from the maize, whooped and splashed in the Coosa. But those days were gone, eaten by time and the darkest enmity.

Smiling sadly, Totka led Micco to Wind Chaser, mounted her, pointed their muzzles north.

"Brother," Tall Bull called.

A pang shot through Totka's gut. He halted the mare and looked back in time to snatch an object flying at him.

A leather pokko hit his palm with a heart-warming smack. He spun it, inspecting its worn leather, appreciating its age. Grass stains marred the scored surface, and its seam had been carefully mended in more than one place.

The seasons rolled away and left behind a war party of memories—beautiful, raw, bloody. "I remember it."

It was the the pokko they'd reverently crafted as long-haired braves under Pawa's guiding hand. The same that scored the first goal of their last match together. As far as Totka knew, Tall Bull hadn't played a game since.

"Too long has it filled my pouch and heart with shame," Tall Bull said. "Keep it. You are more worthy of it than I."

"I will. But if your eyes could reach into my heart, they would know I am no more worthy than you." Vying for control of his voice, Totka squeezed the ball. "Come home soon. Wolf needs you. We will swing the sticks again. As we once did." He held the pokko high like a battle trophy, but Tall Bull did not catch his fire.

A remorseful shake of his head brought Totka's arm from its lofty position. "The ball field belongs to the Muscogee Falcon. I think . . . we will not meet again." Tall Bull settled his bloodshot gaze on Micco's burden. "Take care of her for me."

Totka jerked a nod while blinking back an onslaught of moisture. Immobile, he watched his cousin ride at a gallop across the field until the woods devoured the seductive ripple of his hair.

When at last he found his voice, it was but a scratchy whisper. "Blessings on you . . . Brother."

Chapter 21

Long Arrow's indignant voice carried from the courtyard to where Totka slept—the lodge he'd built for his beloved.

To the rattle of split cane, Totka flipped onto his back and rubbed a thumb and forefinger over his scratchy eyes. A rush of cool hit the sweaty arm he'd lain on.

With his next breath, Singing Grass was beside him with a dipper. "Have a drink and go back to sleep. White Stone will take care of him for now."

It was true. His eldest sister parried Long Arrow word for heated word. The man was demanding Totka show himself and account for his negligence with Leaping Waters' care. Negligence? No surprise her brother saw it that way.

Totka sat up and poured sofkee down his throat. "I cannot leave him to her forever." Long Arrow had already been by once—last evening, the same day Totka had left Leaping Water's body with her mother, then stumbled home to crash on his couch.

The journey back had taken a heavy toll on him, heavier than it would have if he'd not been recovering from an ailment. But Leaping Waters had nursed him well those two days. Given him the strength he would need to bring her home.

It seemed fitting that he be the one to do it. He'd been there for her at the beginning. It was right he be there for her at the end. And, as strange as it felt, it was right that Tall Bull be sheltered from this disaster. The peace residing in Totka's center confirmed it.

He passed the dipper back and rose, feeling about how Old

Grandfather looked—bent, stiff, rusty. "Has Leaning Bow come?" The presence of their clan headman would go a long way toward slowing Totka's pulse.

"No, and Lachlan will not leave the courtyard to fetch him. I am glad of it, for Long Arrow looks toward this lodge as a fox does my henhouse, waiting for the dog to turn his head. My brother's life is of little value to him."

The man was behaving more unpredictably than expected and it chafed. Totka swung his feet to the ground, hand going to the bow propped against the wall. Thinking better of it, he let it be. "How are the children?"

If Singing Grass' wringing hands were any indication, her usual fortitude was slipping. "Rain Child cannot stop weeping for fear of what will come of us, and Speaks Sweetly cannot understand why Beaver carried off Journey's End. By now, he will be inconsolable and Ayo will be deep in regret for having forced us apart." Tendons strained over her white knuckles. "She arrived in a storm of tears and latched onto her grandson as though he were Leaping Waters back from the dead."

The news hit Totka with enough force to trip his heart and still the hand that smoothed back his sweaty hair. He let his eyes fill with his sister's beautiful face and knew, like the stench rising from his unwashed body, that Beaver would sue for her life.

He also knew that if the clan mothers consented, he would be powerless to stop the tide that would follow. And here he sat regaining his breath and drinking sofkee. A tremble began inside him as he looked to the foot of the couch where he'd tossed his things the night before. "Where are my clothes?"

Reluctance slowing her moves, Singing Grass retrieved his shirt from the table where it sat perfectly folded. "I washed it for you. Mended the rip in the elbow." The warble in her voice about broke him.

When he'd entered the compound, Singing Grass had been the first to reach him. At her cry of joy, he'd known he was forgiven.

Leaping Waters was right. Forgiveness was a sweet scent.

He let the shirt fall open, inspected the stitching. "Perfect as always."

Her lips were tremulous. "I thought I had lost you, Brother. You've returned to me, but Long Arrow has abandoned his senses. He wants your life."

And make himself a murderer? By the sounds of him, Singing Grass' logic was not completely unfounded, but Totka said, "He has always championed me." He put on a smile but couldn't move it beyond his mouth.

"That was before his sister died. You've not seen him since."

No, but he'd heard. Enough to know that Long Arrow was anticipating not being in agreement with the clan mothers' impending decision on the matter, and that he intended to take things into his own hands if it went any way other than his own.

Totka ran the pad of his thumb over her cheekbone, wanting to pretend this would not go horribly wrong, but respecting her too much to play games. "He can be a reasonable man when he chooses. Given time, his grief will ease. But if worse comes to worst, Lachlan will care for you and the girls." Assuming it wasn't Beaver who'd taken over the role.

She nodded too forcefully to be natural. "Father will provide as well."

With the backs of his fingers, he brushed her damp cheek. "Of course, Father will take you into his care, and do not discount the clan." He had yet to speak with his clan mothers since light had been shed on their Choctaw heritage and their grandparents' deceit, but— humiliation aside—Wolf was sure to be forgiving.

Long Arrow's voice amplified. If Totka did not show himself, the man would rip off the door covering and haul Totka out.

He examined his sister head to toe—her rumpled and patched dress, her nappy hair, the dirt clinging to every pore. Lips twitching downward, he kissed her forehead. "Store your tears for when they are truly needed. The girls should see their mother strong."

Especially if Long Arrow took a swipe at Totka's throat.

Her eyes grew large, but she sniffed, wiped a tear, and nodded solemnly. Then, she arranged her face into a semblance of courage and let down the door covering.

White Stone and Long Arrow faced off beside the cold fire pit— the woman, short and squat but formidable; the man, flushed and bulging with tension. Lachlan was a wall at White Stone's back. Silent, glaring, immovable. The sun sparkled in the hair covering his crossed arms.

Rain Child, clutching onto Speaks Sweetly, huddled in the shadows of the summer lodge. Their terrified faces struck Totka harder than any threat Long Arrow could hurl.

Several strides away, Fierce Raven, sporting his formal plumed headdress, observed the goings on with an expression of unease. His presence and wary demeanor were arrows in Totka's quiver of hope.

At the sight of Totka, Long Arrow ceased his rant. "I knew if I shouted long enough, you would get off your backside." He stalked toward Totka, fists swinging at his sides so forcefully it seemed his next natural move should be to draw the blade affixed to his hip.

Totka lowered his head but not his unblinking gaze. "Your loss is deeply felt, my friend."

"Friend? Does a *friend* allow a man's sister to mount a horse too spirited for her? You knew she was no rider!"

Totka withheld a reply. Out of necessity, he'd kept his account of that horrible day brief and sparse. He would say no more.

Fierce Raven stepped up, features arranged as though a foul taste were on his tongue. "Totka Hadjo, my nephew is unsatisfied with the explanation you provided the clan mothers. Have you anything further to add?"

"Only my condolences and sincere regret. If my horse pleases Long Arrow, he may take her to do with as he pleases."

"The beast that took my sister's life?" Long Arrow spat a wad onto Totka's chest. It dribbled down the front of his freshly laundered shirt.

Inside the summer lodge, Black Sky began to cry. With a barked word, Singing Grass sent Rain Child in after her sister.

"Have Micco, then." Lachlan inserted himself between Long Arrow and Fierce Raven, forcing them to make way for his broad frame. "A finer, more powerful animal you will not find anywhere in Muscogee country. Keep him for Journey's End, or sell him to help provide for the boy as he grows. The animal is yours, if it will bring peace between you and my brother."

Totka's eyes went wide. A thousand blessings on McGirth for forcing Lachlan Gibb on Totka.

Beaver headman hummed approval. "The Scotsman makes a solid offer, Nephew. Take the stallion and let us go. This lodge has its own abundant grief to tend. I'll take a report to the clan mothers to learn if the offer meets blood law to their satisfaction. Collect the animal, so we may put this behind us."

The pounding of hooves rose through Totka's soles before it touched his ears. Their dog took up barking, and White Stone shouted it into tuck-tail submission.

How many horses were coming? Three? Four? They were bearing down fast, from the direction of Kossati's northern limits. Expectantly, he looked to the lane beyond the compound's entrance, but it would be some moments before they passed.

Or arrived. More Beaver, come to demand fulfillment of the law?

"You would compare my sister to a horse?" Long Arrow continued, unconcerned with the party's approach or Fierce Raven's approval of the proposition. "A dozen of the same are not worth the value of her life!"

Totka could not disagree. When his mother's life had been stolen, he'd been equally disgusted at the settlement.

"A life for a life." Long Arrow slid his line of sight to Singing Grass. "I've requested that of your sister and expect the clan mothers to be gracious on account of my nephew."

"Pawa, no!" Rain Child stood in the entry, arms wrapped about a cradleboard almost as tall as she. "Make him go away." Tears wracked her little body. Singing Grass ran to her, ushered her inside, and reappeared at the doorway, looking almost as distraught as her daughter.

Without so much as a pause for respectful consideration, Long Arrow furnished Fierce Raven with a tight-jawed look of expectation.

Despite the flare of his nostrils, the headman jerked his chin down and up again. "It is as Long Arrow says. The request is being weighed this very moment. The babe needs a mother. Singing Grass is the natural choice to fill the gap Leaping Waters left in Beaver."

Naturally.

Totka could hardly be angry. Even so, it swelled within him, ringing in his ears like a piercing bell. It was anger at his own foolish head for not having taken that possibility more seriously. But he'd not thought much beyond simply following the Spirit's leading. Was this the payment he would receive for obedience?

Before he could thaw his frozen tongue, the band of horses exploded into the compound, sending chickens in all directions and bringing on a choking cloud of dust. It cleared to reveal Minko Yellow Tree, war chief to the Divided People. Beside him, Rainmaker and Hilaho and Wolf's own headman, Leaning Bow. They spread out in a semicircle that blocked access to the compound's main exit and drew an abrupt rein.

Totka had forgotten the Choctaw delegates were still in residence, but why would they have come? To witness a—?

The implications of Totka's heritage crashed into him with all the power of a Choctaw defenseman. His mind stuttered, unbelieving.

Each man was completely devoid of ornaments, heavily armed, and wearing the tight-lipped mask of a warrior on the brink of battle cry. Red and black paint could not have better depicted their menace, but it was not directed at him.

Totka's heart flipped in place, then settled back into a gentle, freeing rhythm.

These men were powerful, carrying the weight and fury of the Upper Choctaws. And Yellow Tree had not come to witness the destruction of his sister's household. Of that, Totka was certain.

As certain as the hasty distance Fierce Raven put between himself and Totka.

"My mother's brother is most welcome," Totka said, using his poor Choctaw. "Please consider yourself clan for the extent of your stay." He placed a careful eye on Yellow Tree but found not a hint of approval at his not-so-subtle claim to his heritage.

Countenance empty of emotion, Yellow Tree dipped his chin at Totka as he walked his horse to stand before Fierce Raven. The animal snorted and blew wind heavy enough to bob the man's red plume.

Not deigning to dismount, he peered down at the Beaver headman through that disturbing, squinted eye. "You would dare insult us by negotiating revenge on my sister's household without so much as a messenger to inform me?"

If Totka had not been so close, he might have missed the pallor that came into Fierce Raven's lips. "It was an oversight on our part," the man said. "In our grief, we failed to recall they are your distant relation, that you might care to be informed of the deliberations."

"An oversight that might have cost you dearly should Leaning Bow not have had the wisdom to come to me." Although heavily accented, Yellow Tree's Muskogee lacked no amount of steel. "He tells me you demand my niece's life in exchange for that of your niece's. You would have her become Beaver."

Fierce Raven's gaze bounced from Yellow Tree to Long Arrow and back. "That is so."

Yellow Tree's lips were pursing before Fierce Raven finished speaking. "My heart weeps with yours this day. The woman's death is tragic, but it was not an act of evil. These two winters past have seen more families torn apart than over the last three generations combined. Have you not had your fill?" He lifted a finger to Rainmaker who nudged his horse forward. "For the good of my tribe, I allowed one nephew to lift his neck to the blade of revenge, but you will find my lifeblood wetting this dirt before I allow another sister's son to satisfy the unintended death of one Muscogee woman."

Anger billowed from Long Arrow's bunching muscles like heat waves from a baking stone, but the minko continued, undaunted. "In the name of peace between our tribes, we have carefully weighed your proposal in the scales. It is found to be wanting. Your clan mothers have heard our talk and agree."

Singing Grass' muted cry was brief but poignant and spoke for the hope lightening Totka's head. White Stone, however, looked ready at any moment to trumpet a laugh. Lachlan shot her a look of warning and stationed himself like a sentry beside Totka.

A silent conversation passed between Fierce Raven and Leaning Bow, the latter of whom nodded with the authority of one who could verify the Choctaw's statement.

As Rainmaker passed Long Arrow, he dropped a small duffle bag that slammed to the ground with a profusion of metallic clinks and clanks.

Totka clenched his jaw to keep it from falling open. If something was off in the scales, it was Yellow Tree's confusing behavior. After everything Tokta had put this chief through, there was no call for him to go to such an extent. Reed Clan loyalty hardly seemed a plausible reason since Falling Rain had lived and died Wolf of the Muscogees, but Totka floundered for any other explanation.

"Our settlement is generous." Yellow Tree gestured to the duffle. "As well as our willingness to overlook this lapse in manners."

"Lapse! What lapse?" Long Arrow took no notice of the glittering ornaments spilling from the sack at his feet. "Totka has been one of our own from the day of his birth. You would presume to ride into our talwa and disrupt our custom as though you had any authority here? All for a man who, except for his cowardice, would have killed your kin?"

"Totka Hadjo has proven himself brave and wise. On the ball field, in battle, at the council square. His name is known across your nation and mine. Who are *you*, but the man who foolishly insults Choctaw delegates riding under the feathers of peace?" The sneer that lifted Yellow Tree's voice didn't quite reach his lips, but it lowered Long Arrow's arrogant chin just the same. If only a degree.

Long Arrow redirected the heat of his gaze, landing it on Totka. "It was his negligence that led to my sister's death. Whether the clan mothers agree or not, his blood should pay!"

Totka stared at him, battling horror that his lifelong friend would be so passionate about slicing in half what little remained of his family.

The minko disbanded Long Arrow's argument with a flip of his hand. "Say what you will. The decision has been made. Accept my condolences for the loss of a cherished sister. Take the silver for the child. My niece will remain Wolf, and she will continue to live here with her children, giving suck to Long Arrow's nephew for a count of two Green Corns when he will rejoin Beaver. And Totka Hadjo will keep his horse." There was not the slightest give in Yellow Tree's voice. Considering his tribe and position—and everything that hinged on peace with him—why should he concede anything?

Long Arrow began to speak, but at his headman's quenching hiss, he bit off what was sure to be a witless protest. Not a warrior in the Upper Towns was imbecile enough to incite war with the Choctaws. Except for perhaps, Long Arrow. Crippled as the Muscogees were, it would mean their end.

"The clan mothers have spoken," Fierce Raven said, seeming more relieved than disappointed. "Hvo. It is good." He bid them farewell and led the way through the horses. Silence swarmed the compound while the two, silver in tow, made a protracted, dignified exit.

Singing Grass slumped against the door frame, and White Stone plopped onto the bench by the courtyard fire, but Leaning Bow pulled himself erect and cleared his throat. "Totka Hadjo, the clan mothers have decided to send you away with these men to Choctaw country. Until next summer's Green Corn."

Totka's stomach plunged. Banishment? "Does my presence in Kossati hold so little value?" And to the Choctaws no less!

339

"On the contrary, they are grieved to see you go, but they send their hopes with you. Hopes for extended peace and renewed trade. They wish you to become a liaison between our peoples and to learn the Choctaw tongue, the lay of their land, their customs. I trust you understand that being chosen for this role is a great honor."

Banishment—with orders to play the role of White Stick—an *honor*? He gave an inglorious bend of his head, heart knocking angrily against his ribs.

"In addition," Leaning Bow went on, "Minko Yellow Tree brought to their attention the matter of an unsettled debt. Is it true he spared your life during the war in exchange for payment that has yet to be collected?" One of his wiry brows eased northward.

"What?" White Stone nearly shrieked. "What debt?"

The lift of Totka's hand held her at bay. "Yes, my life was spared, but a debt? I was not aware." Hadn't his father paid it? They'd spoken of it briefly. He'd blown off Totka's concern as though the matter had been settled. What exactly had he said?

Scraps of memory bumbled about uselessly in Totka's head. The sun winked in his eye, causing a squint that matched the challenging one Yellow Tree bore into him.

From behind, a heavy, impatient breath raised Totka's hackles and reminded him of Rainmaker's solid presence at his back.

Against his admonishing, Totka's shoulders went back, his chin went up, and his voice went stiff. "I cannot recall the faces of those present that day. My father tells me Hilaho was among them, but the others . . ." He moistened drying teeth with a swipe of his tongue and shook his head. "Too much happened too quickly."

Yellow Tree's squint became impossibly narrow. "You would doubt the word of the man who buried your woman's mother?" His reply was cold and unyielding. "The price was the value of one white woman's ransom. A sum Gray Hawk agreed would equal two years of a man's life. As hunter, protector, and warrior, should the need arise. You may thank him, Totka Hadjo, for taking responsibility of a portion of it, but a full four seasons remain, and Gray Hawk wishes to invest his time in other matters. His young wife among them. I have freed him to do so. In exchange for you."

Totka stared at the minko, mouth ajar, looking every bit the clueless dimwit he'd been.

Why had his father never said? And then it came back to him, his father's response. *Haven't you more pressing concerns? Such as preparing a lodge for your woman? Get to it.* The stubborn bent to Totka's body gave way to resignation.

Gray Hawk had only ever meant to protect Totka, lessen his burdens, free him to marry his beloved when the time came. How odd the tables were now turned. Gray Hawk had a woman, and Totka did not.

Prickling shame closed his mouth; grief turned it down at the corners. His future was sealed. Inescapable. Humbly was the only way to move forward. "If Minko Yellow Tree claims I am in his debt, then it is so."

"I do. Gather your belongings and provender to last four sleeps." Yellow Tree used the same hard-eyed authority he'd applied to Long Arrow. "I intend for us to be well past the Alabama before sundown."

Totka's eye fell on their fat corn wallets and the bedrolls tied to their saddles. They'd come prepared to ride out.

And they intended to take him with them this very moment. They would not grant a day to gather his things or arrange his sisters' affairs. Was that all they intended to do with him? As usual, Hilaho appeared placid enough, but Yellow Tree's disposition was a mystery, and Rainmaker's gaze was still hot on Totka's throat.

Singing Grass was suddenly beside him, smiling through her tears, whispering encouragement. "Four seasons is not so long, Brother."

It was impossibly long. Four long, brutal seasons in which to mourn, to pace, to worry about his sisters, to wish away the moons until he could return to Tensaw. But Copper Woman, spirit though she was, would wait for him.

"What troubles you, *Cousin?*" Rainmaker grinned wolfishly. "If it's a musket ball in the head you wish, I can—"

Hilaho snapped at him in Choctaw and shortened the reins to still his fidgeting mount.

With a shrug, Rainmaker tugged at his bare earlobe and let his features fall into nonchalance.

Qualm nibbled at Totka's toes, but he stomped it out. The Spirit had not brought him this far only to leave him gutted and hairless on the side of the Choctaw Road.

Totka, son of a Choctaw. An irony-laden laugh rang through his mind alongside the memory of Rainmaker's insult. "A journey of four sleeps. I understand."

At his commanding glance, White Stone scurried to the storehouse, Lachlan to the horse pen. Singing Grass, seeming to remember her role as hostess, jumped to act. She rushed to Minko Yellow Tree, arms extended. "Come. Unburden yourself. Eat. I wish to know my mother's brother."

In the time it took Lachlan to prepare Wind Chaser, Totka assembled his weapons, spare shirt, and winter-weight leggings along with his usual travel items: paint, steel striker with flint, tobacco and pipe, and whetstone. Then he beat Lachlan's broad back in a hug, kissed his sisters and nieces, and left Kossati with his face set in stone, direction west.

Yellow Tree had politely refused Singing Grass' invitation to eat and rest, owing to the need to visit the Great Warrior and thank him for his extended hospitality. Totka was to meet the Choctaws on the Alabama Road where the treetops met in the center.

When Totka came upon them, Hilaho trailed the others by several horse lengths. He rode tall and easy, hair every bit as glossy black and free as Wind Chaser's. The Choctaws rode into the shadow an oak whose crooked arms intertwined with those of its twin residing over the opposite side of the path. Spider webs of moss and vines cluttered the branches and blocked all but the most persistent rays of sunlight.

It would be an awkward meeting for sure, and Totka's fluttering stomach kept up a constant reminder.

That morning, Yellow Tree had come fiercely to his defense, but that did not mean he'd forgiven Totka the trials he'd put them through. Sister's son he might be, but clan he was not. Even clan could live miserably when on the wrong side of his family's pleasure, and Totka was most assuredly on the wrong side of whatever societal position he would be expected to hold.

He urged Wind Chaser into a trot, and at the sound of her tapping hooves, Hilaho's head snapped around. To the merry sound of bells, he alighted from his horse, landing carelessly on his wounded leg. He released the animal with a smack to its hindquarters.

He was unarmed save for the knife strapped to his lower back; the silhouette of its hilt protruded at an angle from his side. Either he was recklessly brave, or he trusted his kinsmen to cover him. It had not been so very long since Totka had aligned his arrow with Hilaho's chest.

Yellow Tree and Rainmaker were late to notice his arrival. Alert now, they turned back to join the younger man in the shade; they were not as eager to part with their mounts.

Could they read humility in Totka's bearing? For good measure, he tucked his chin, propped his elbow on his thigh, and swung the peace bundle in his hand out to the side where they might see it. Ten rods out, he reined Wind Chaser to a walk, then swung down and let her carry his weapons into an adjoining field.

The elder Choctaws responded accordingly, dismounting and flanking Hilaho in a casually protective stance that at once compounded Totka's chagrin and generated a longing he did not have time to ponder.

Totka cursed his lopsided gait and the lawless pounding in his chest. His weakened condition did his confidence no favors.

The barrel of the musket hooked over Rainmaker's shoulder rose from behind him like a second head. Its stock rested squarely in the palm at his hip. Wary scrutiny gouged the space between his eyes, but Yellow Tree's face was as blank as the last page in the sacred writings Tall Bull had left in Tensaw. Brows gently arching, the minko looked at Totka as though he were the quill that would scratch down the final words.

And wasn't he? His next actions had the power to determine the course of his life. The weight of that power settled into each fall of his moccasins. His eagle feathers, resting on a square of spotless white doeskin, lay in the open hand that went before him.

When Totka came within range of a war club blow, Yellow Tree's acute eye bowed Totka's head. The elder said nothing, but waited as stout and motionless as the oak rearing up behind him.

Totka slid his tongue over his teeth as he waited for his pulse to right itself. "Before we can continue, there is a stinking swamp between us that must be drained."

At the chief's slight nod, Totka lifted the peace bundle. "These feathers first belonged to my sister's husband who was taken from This World at the Horse's Flat Foot. This was the only part of him she was able to carry from the battlefield. I have worn them with pride until this day. I give them to you as a sign of peace between us."

He bound his gaze to the man's flat mouth, hoping to see it soften. "For endless winters, Muscogees and Choctaws have found ourselves too eager to raise arms against each other. Not a warrior among us is innocent, and no one warrior is fully to blame. But for my part, I have wronged you. I have wronged your people sorely. For they are also my mother's people."

Eyes stationed at the man's chin, Totka awaited the verdict. "Will you take these and allow me to seek your forgiveness and mercy?"

None came. Not so much as a hum of favor or a shifting of feet. Wind tunneled through the arch of branches, rustled the feathers in Totka's hand, filtered through his clothes, cooled the moisture on his brow. And still, Minko Yellow Tree was silent.

Totka braved a look and was met with the same emotionless eyes he'd arrived to. Would Yellow Tree begrudge him this? He had every right, but Totka was not ready to ride to Choctaw country without the man's blessing.

Setting his jaw, he painstakingly folded the suede over the feathers and tied off the bundle with a length of silk ribbon.

"It is not my forgiveness to give," the elder said at last. "Should you not seek it from Hilaho instead?"

Totka turned to the younger man and found promise in his flawless face.

His blue long-shirt rippled in the wind and brushed the top-most edge of the bandage encasing his bare thigh. Dull red stained the cloth, but he stood legs shoulder-width apart, weight equally distributed. His broad mouth formed a severe line, but his shining eyes crinkled at the edges.

Hilaho's eyes might be a handsome blue instead of Cetto Imala's honey brown, but the expression was the same. If Totka squinted, he would see his pawa standing there. It was an encouraging familiarity, a reminder that their mothers were sisters. These three before him would have been blood, if not for the unpredictable hand of fate.

Totka extended the bundle to Hilaho. "Cousin," he spoke the title with not a hint of mockery. "Accept them, please. Forgive me." His throat closed over the last of his plea, whittling it down to a whisper.

Hilaho's mouth split with a grin that was immediately filled with hair blown about by the wind—an eastern wind, most decidedly eastern. He bypassed the bundle and went straight for a chest-crushing embrace. When he pulled back, the crinkles at the edges of his eyes were deep. "What is this *cousin* nonsense? You are my **elder brother**, and there is nothing to forgive."

Elder brother? A title of high honor, the same given the deer who sustained them with meat and skins, and the Great Father in Washington who ruled the vast stretches of land along the coastal waters.

345

Totka in no way deserved it, but he found, with no small wonder, that he wanted it. Desperately. He pressed the bundle into Hilaho's hand. "Brother, then. With thanks." He dropped a contrite eye to the bandage. "About the leg . . ."

Hilaho shrugged. "You owed me a leg wound, and I owed you my life. Now the scales are balanced." At Totka's brow-pinching confusion, Hilaho elaborated, apprehension slowing his speech. "Beaver Lake. The burning council house."

Totka's head flinched back. He couldn't mean . . . ? "*You* are the foolhardy brave with the poor aim?"

"Poor aim, nothing! That ball was precisely placed." The rope of Hilaho's lips twisted with a gloat that, on his frank features, managed to be charming. "But imagine my horror when I realized I shot the Muscogee Falcon. I'd spent the winter replicating your throws, practicing my leaps, bounding over barrels and logs to fly as you had."

Rainmaker leaned into the conversation with a leer. "He even visited the medicine maker for a formula to transform into a bird."

"Shut up." Releasing a blustery chortle, Hilaho backhanded Rainmaker's arm, then grew suddenly serious. "While you risked your life to save mine, I thought myself a warrior and drove lead into your bone. Singlehandedly grounded the Muscogee Falcon, the best player any man had seen in a dozen winters."

His voice went meek, apologetic. "Later, I was praised for my bravery in the face of the enemy, for defending the minko and the council house. But I could not overcome the fact I ruined the Falcon's life while arranging it so that I owed him my own. My sister's as well." He gave a mournful shake of his head. "No other man was worthier of that pole than I."

Totka stared at him, absorbing the information like sun-scorched grass did the rain. He'd saved his own cousin that day. Extraordinary. Pawa's death suddenly had new meaning, new worth, as did Hilaho's peculiarities. One by one they came into the light.

From the first, his behavior toward Totka had been uncommonly deferential. Totka had attributed it to youthful naivety and glowing childhood memories of the most notable stickball match in their lifetimes. Those surely played a part, but what Totka had actually observed was an odd mixture of indebtedness and remorse.

Both of which Totka was keenly familiar with.

Hilaho's judgment of Totka's character—insisting him to be merciful, an advocate of the weak—no longer seemed insolent but a deduction based on experience. He did know Totka. He knew firsthand the lengths Totka would go to spare the helpless ones.

Consumed by bitterness, Totka had let him down. But *that* man was dead, buried with the pollution that had wreaked havoc on his spirit. He was a new man with a fresh future and a great Hope, and he was not entering it alone. He had a brother.

Careful not to unveil his desperation for clan, Totka moderated his smile and clasped Hilaho's shoulder. "We are truly equals. Brothers. We will put regrets behind us and build a tomorrow we are proud of."

"A pity events have turned out as pleasantly as they have." Rainmaker's blistered scowl deposited Totka back into reality. "I was hoping to scalp the Muscogee witch."

With small success, Totka fended off an answering frown. "Rather petty of you to continue with those hard feelings, is it not?"

Rainmaker maintained his black look a moment more, then burst into a fit of laughter that flushed a pair of doves from their roost. He grabbed Totka's arm in a blood-choking shake that rocked his body and froze his tongue.

"What?" Rainmaker said. "Have you not heard your Choctaw name?"

Hilaho rolled his eyes Totka's direction. "Not everyone calls you that."

"By *not everyone*, you mean *you*," Rainmaker grinned. "Did the medicine maker also give you a formula for infatuation?" Breezy laughter tumbled from the man, remodeling his frightful features into boyish glee.

"No, but he showed me a good tonic for flux of the mouth." With a smirk, Hilaho jabbed the back of his elbow into the base of Rainmaker's throat.

Gagging on his laughter, Rainmaker swung a left hook but missed his nimbler cousin. "Why are you after *me*? He is the one who put that hole in your leg."

"That was for being a braying rooster, and this is for the cicadas." Hilaho doubled over and rammed his shoulder into Rainmaker's middle, making his bells go wild.

Unable to resist, Totka discretely skipped into Rainmaker's backward path, forcing the man to take the brunt of Hilaho's drive. At the whip of Rainmaker's accusatory eye, he held his hands high and pasted on an expression of innocence.

Behind him, Yellow Tree chuckled, and Totka felt the band of apprehension slackening around his nerves.

Rainmaker retaliated, but Hilaho, surprisingly limber for sporting a wound, dodged the swipe, inadvertently putting himself within Yellow Tree's reach.

The minko nabbed him about the neck and locked him against his chest. "If you do not stop pestering Rainmaker about the cicadas," he said over Hilaho's sputtering protests, "I will put a jar-full under your covers myself." He ground his knuckles against Hilaho's scalp and gave his head a good-natured shove, sending him off with another chuckle.

The two kept at it while Yellow Tree looked at Totka from the tops of eyes that twinkled with mischief. "Are you certain you want to be brother to this war party? Understand that you under no obligation to live with us. You are welcome to lodge with another clan."

No obligation? Totka was obliged in the deepest way, and he was not a man to let his accounts go unsettled.

However, remembering Yellow Tree's refusal of the peace bundle, Totka floundered for a confident demeanor and ended up with a smile that even Leaping Waters at her most timid could have outdone. "I will live with you, if . . . you will have me."

Yellow Tree's smile was slow and thoughtful. "You have your mother's eyes." He waved Totka toward him. "Draw closer."

When Totka neared, Yellow Tree gripped him about the neck and pulled him in until their foreheads touched. "You are my sister's son, and I have loved you longer than you know." His voice was low, intense. "Will I have you? The better question is, when the required seasons are passed, will I be able to give you up?"

Chapter 22

"You're a godsend, Phillip."

Lieutenant Phillip Bailey would have preferred to walk beside Zachariah McGirth, but the meager trail through the woodland didn't allow for it. The broader man led the way, cutting through the brush like a plowshare.

"Suits me just fine to give the Almighty the credit." Phillip batted at a string of Spanish moss stuck to his floppy civilian hat. "How long has she been coming out here?"

"Since the new moon."

"What's that, six nights?"

"Eight." There was a wince in McGirth's voice. "I'm about one night short of sleeping across the door."

If McGirth didn't, Phillip would. Adela was as capable as any frontierswoman, but it was dangerous out here at night. Rattlers, panthers, wolves.

Indians. He shuddered.

It was no small irony that he'd come out of the war with an abhorrence for Indians that sculpted his nightmares, while she'd come out of the same with so fierce a love for one that it drove her into the black wilds night after night in the hopes she'd find the savage wasn't dead after all.

Phillip couldn't decide whether to bawl or pull out his hair. A giant wood spider stared him down as he dodged its extensive golden web. "A Red Stick, you say?" He had to hear it again to believe it.

"From Fort Mims, no less."

"You understand how hard that is to believe, right? It's not fitting in my head that Adela could want to marry one of those painted devils."

"Believe it. That painted devil saved my women more than once." McGirth gave a disbelieving huff. "So many times, in fact, I'll be indebted for the rest of my life. Or . . . would have been, if he hadn't met his end so suddenly." He held a vine out of the way until Phillip relieved him of it and ripped the thing from its hold on the branches above him.

"Too bad he's already in the ground. I would rather have put him there myself." A gentleman would strive for a fair tone. He might also give his enemy a chance to explain his actions before stringing him up, but Phillip had left propriety in McGirth's cabin along with his level head.

Blood spiking, he told himself he'd better find both again before he reached Adela.

That being said, from the sounds of it, she might sympathize with the loss of a perfectly good head. She'd always been the judicious one of the sisters, the even-tempered one. It boggled the mind that she'd fallen for a Red Stick—not to speak of this violent, irrational grief she was nursing.

McGirth cocked a brow but kept going. "Careful how you speak of the man, Bailey. I'll defend his honor 'til God calls me home."

"And you should. Appears he earned it, I'll concede." Which added to the blight on the situation.

"Besides, he's dead. Out of the picture. But I'll be honest. It's a crying shame. He was a good sort. I liked his spunk, his fiery Indian courage. And, besides yourself, there wasn't another who'd care for my girl the way he would've. I wasn't keen on him hauling her back to Creek country, times being as they are, but it was a risk I was willing to take. It was either that or wake up one day to find her gone."

Phillip nabbed the expletive on his tongue half a breath before it found release and swiped an unsteady hand down his smooth-shaven throat. He waited to speak until he'd tamed his tone. "Think he would've taken her captive again?"

"Again? Ha!" The humor twisting McGirth's voice wasn't funny. "He might've brought her back and handed her over to me a year ago, but make no mistake, Bailey, she's still enslaved by him. Those chains'll be tough to break, too. But if anyone can . . ." He shoved aside a palmetto frond and broke onto the meadow.

He stepped to the side and halted.

Sunlight hit Phillip full in the eye, and he angled the brim of his hat to block it. In the two years he'd been absent, nothing had changed about the place. The same wind pounded the same sun-browned grass; the same hot, earthy aroma hung about the same ring of trees; the same sense of absolute solitude tingled his spine—despite the woman who occupied the meadow's center.

Under a green fringed parasol that fought for freedom, Lillian McGirth sat tall and prim. Only the top of her could be seen through the knee-high bromegrass. Presumably, she held the shade over Adela, who was invisible from where Phillip stood in the shelter of the forest's outer canopy.

Everything within him said to go to her, but McGirth's far-off gaze and half-open mouth told him there was more he needed to know before he met her.

Sure enough, after a moment, the man spoke. "Lillian's finally starting to show her mettle. That's one good thing that's come out of this." His smile was too sad to appreciate. "Lilly's brought her sister home every time she's come out here. That first morning, she managed it pretty quick, but since then, she just sits and waits Adela out. Lord knows the woman won't come back on her own." His abrupt cough was a sure cover for emotion.

To give him privacy, Phillip looked away, focused on the snatches of blue coming through the swaying weeds near Lillian.

"The fort, the war . . . they changed Adela, Bailey. Made her strong in a way I wouldn't have believed, except I've seen it myself.

At some point early on, she took it in her head to live and to get her mama back to me. Didn't happen." The sniff he drew wasn't disguised quite well enough. "Not the way we all would have wanted, but it was Adela's strength that got them through that year in Creek country. I'm sure of it. She did what she had to and befriended the Indians. Almost can't blame her for falling in love with the one who kept her alive. Even loving him as she did, she made a break for it a few weeks before the treaty was signed. Followed the Wolf Path to Fort Claiborne, then traded for a canoe and rode the Mobile home. Tough as rawhide, that one."

The chuckle that left him was a painful stew of agony and admiration. It lured Phillip's head back around.

McGirth was staring at his daughters, his eyes wrinkling against the sun, his mind a dozen miles away. "Totka once told me she had a warrior's spirit. Called her his little Red Stick."

Totka. The Indian's name.

Phillip let the fingers of his mind roam over it, feel it up and down. It was rough and unwieldy, savage in a way only Indians could be. As much as the admission irked, Phillip had no trouble agreeing with the Red Stick's assessment of her.

Last Phillip had spoken to her, she'd quailed behind a woodpile, heat flushing her cheeks, lips bloodless, eyes wild and frantic. He'd demanded she survive. Screamed it in her face.

By the time he saw her again, some four hours later, she'd become a vision he would never be able to scrub from his head . . .

By a stroke of God's grace, Phillip and Dixon busted out the back of the bastion. Only a few Red Sticks stood between him and the jungle of rushes some twenty yards distant. They fought like men possessed, but Dixon took a ball to his belly. Went down hard and fast.

Then Phillip spotted Adela streaking toward him, and he knew he'd die. He would hold the Indians off, so she could make it to the canebrake. But she wasn't running for cover. The crazy woman was running to *him.* Coming to his rescue, blackened with soot, shrieking his name, war club raised, looking every bit the little Red Stick with the genuine article hot on her trail.

Terror had choked Phillip — much as the memory of it did now.

He would never tell her, but in the distraction she'd caused, she nearly cost him his life. In that moment, his opponent's tomahawk came like a rattler strike at his flank. God alone gave him the swiftness of sword to avoid a gutting.

In a way, she'd also saved him. When he'd crawled through that hole in the picket, he was at the end of himself, spent. But Adela, tearing across that corpse-strewn lot, stoked his fire and kept it going. She never reached him. A blood-soaked warrior caught her first and flung her to the ground.

Her captor, likely. That Totka fellow. The man's face was a blur now. Probably for the best. One less image to fill Phillip's nightmares.

At the time, he'd been grateful to miss what he thought was her death. After witnessing the Red Sticks slice down a hundred-plus women and children, he'd had no reason to believe she would be spared.

So, after Saul darted from the swamp, beat off Phillip's would-be scalper, and dragged him to safety, Phillip didn't go back for her. Not that he would've had the strength to, not with two arrows protruding from his body and a face slitted like a hot cross bun.

McGirth's voice pulled Phillip from that bloody soil. "Her strength's plumb worn out. Beth, her mama, months living as a slave . . . Then the yellow jack. The sickness took her all the way to death's door. Thought we'd lost her for sure, but she licked it. This last blow, though, it did her in." He bowed his head, cleared his throat, cleared it again. "I think she wants to die. Right here on this field."

Die? Not a chance. Not on Phillip's watch. He ground his teeth, aggravated at the despair warbling the older man's voice, etching grooves into his face. "Why don't you carry her back? She's light enough."

"Tried it. Wasn't worth the fuss it caused. We found it's best to let her come home when she's ready." The toe of his boot dug into the forest floor. He overturned loam, laying bare its dark, moist underside. "I hate to put you in this position. It's mighty uncomfortable for both of us."

"I'm not afraid of uncomfortable, Mr. McGirth." At least not where Adela was concerned. "A promise would be a fine thing to make right now, but these days, I'm more careful about how I toss those around." Ever since he'd promised Adela he would take care of her.

"No need for promises. I know you'll do everything you can to bring her back to us."

That he would. But McGirth wasn't necessarily the man he planned to bring her back *to*.

Lillian looked their way and smiled, teeth bright against light olive skin. She closed the parasol and laid it aside, plucked herself off the grass and headed their way.

Phillip walked a solitary path to meet her. McGirth had filled his ears with Adela, but he'd failed to mention how much Lillian had changed. Years back, well before the war, she'd lost her straight girlish figure, but the rounded lines filling out her plain cotton gown were not the ones Phillip had last seen.

Or maybe what accentuated them was the way she came to him. Not running and laughing, locks flying, as she might have done two years ago, but composedly. She came back tall, hips rolling and with as much class and dignity as he'd find in Savannah's most prestigious square.

She glided to a stop, and Phillip half expected her to extend her wrist for a brush of his lips, but she lifted a lace-rimmed kerchief and dabbed perspiration from the delicate bones exposed by a scooped neckline. "Look who the wind blew in." Even her voice was elegant, deeper than he remembered. Smoother. "Lieutenant Phillip Bailey. Back from the dead."

"Miss McGirth." He restrained the bow that her gentility seemed to call for and presented her a smile just broad enough to avoid an uncomfortable tug of his scar. They were old chums, after all. "You're looking lovelier than ever."

Her answering smile was not as simple as his. It was closed and one-sided. And it made her eyes say strange things. "And you've lost none of your charm."

Pure flattery. He was well aware that the scar distorting half his face had done away with his appeal. There was a Red Stick's clumsy scalping knife to thank for that.

Phillip's reply was a disinterested hum; his attention was moving beyond her.

There was a depression in the meadow where Adela lay curled on her side in a protective posture. Her sleeved arm shielded her face from the harsh sun and punishing grasses. Her hair, brilliant in its amber tones, spread across the ground and floated above her like seaweed anchored to a lake bed.

The wind manipulated the blue calico of her gown, flattening it against her and billowing it to expose the whites of her calves and . . . Were those moccasins?

Wild, unbound hair. Moccasins. What else would he find? Paint? A red feather?

Tendrils of fear shot across his ribs. He had no idea who this woman was.

Countless times since he'd learned she was alive he'd dreamed of how their first meeting might unfold. He'd imagined her becoming frightened at the sight of his hideous face; he'd considered she might already be wed to some other man; he'd even prepared himself to find a fragile shell of a woman, warped by the war and all its horrors. But in a thousand years of imagining, he never, *never* would have been able to concoct a story this far-fetched. This stomach-twisting awful.

He fisted his unsteady hands. It was time to write the happy ending this tale deserved. As he began toward Adela, Lillian's touch to his arm arrested him.

"She stayed awake all night this time," she said. "Finally fell asleep a short while ago. I'd rather she sleep in her bed, naturally, but after depriving herself for so many nights, I'll let her take it wherever she wants." The look she doled out was pleading. "Give her another minute more?" At his hesitation, she continued. "I heard you joined the Regulars. Have you resigned your commission? I expected to find you wearing a dashing uniform, not buckskins."

He fingered the ruffled neckline of his hunting shirt, half wishing she would go away, half grateful to delay the difficult moments ahead. "No one wants a reminder of the war. Thought it best I walk in looking like my old self."

"How very prudent of you. I, for one, appreciate it. Whatever took you so long to get back?"

A shrug jerked his shoulder. "Didn't think there was anything left for me here but bones and burned-out cabins."

She made a clicking sound in her cheek. "Sure you weren't running?"

The question hauled his eyes to hers. How had she hit on it so quickly, so accurately? And far too bluntly. Anger sent prickles down his neck, but he kept a cool tongue. "I don't run from anything, Lillian McGirth." Only memories. "Not then. Not now." He tore at the grass batting at his knees, crumbled dried seed heads between his fingers.

She had the good sense to turn her lips down in remorse. Then she stretched up her toes and tenderly kissed him full on his scar. "Thank you," she said, with a wistful smile. "For fighting and surviving. For coming home." She wrapped her arms around his neck and embraced him so tightly he felt every mound and dip of her body.

A drum call to retreat sounded between his ears. After a brisk pat on her back, he set her away. He was experienced enough with women to know this one's father should be concerned—whether she understood the impact of her behavior or not.

She showed no upset at his stiff response, only hooked a dark strand of hair behind her ear and directed a sweet, wide-eyed smile up at him. After a moment, tension formed in little creases at the corners of her mouth. "But take it from me. It isn't easy being back. Adela had planned to leave. Since she's staying now, I'll be leaving for . . ." She gave a nonchalant flip of her hand. "Well, I don't mind where I go. So long as it's not here. The farther I can get from the savages, the better I'll feel." A little shiver wiggled her shoulders.

He understood that shiver intimately, enough not to press her.

Searchingly, she looked in the direction of Mobile as though expecting a schooner to break through the forest wall and, sails billowing, carry her to civilization. A European court would suit her.

Phillip's gaze went a mere fifteen yards to where his future lay.

"But you" — she poked his chest — "are going nowhere. You have a job to do. Mine. And I'm more than happy to give it up."

"What job is that?"

"She was going to marry an *Indian*, Phillip. A heathen Red Stick." Her chest jolted with a huff, and color seeped into her cheeks. "Doing what's best for those we love isn't always easy, for them or us. but I've been strong, stronger than I thought myself capable. I've done what I could to save her because I knew you'd come. Sooner or later, you'd come for her."

He nodded, eyes returning to the where Adela slept. "As soon as I got leave."

"Her heart is sick, and sometimes I think her head is too. But you're here. You'll make her well." Lillian took his hand and squeezed it with a desperation stunning enough to snap his attention from Adela.

Fear swam in her eyes, trembled her chin, and transferred to him, quickening his pulse.

"Is it so bad?"

As she stared at him with those massive brown eyes, her lips drew inward and went white beneath the pressure of her teeth.

His heart thundered. "What are you not telling me?" The severity of the situation or . . . something else?

Head shaking, she unclamped herself from him. "Just fix it,

Phillip. Please. Pick up where you left off."

He considered the unlikelihood of that and tasted the vinegar of hatred. On paper, Phillip's army had won the war, but at night, the Red Sticks still battled inside his mind. They seemed an indomitable enemy. Even their ghosts—one in particular—had the power to ruin his life.

With a finger, he wiped a bead of sweat teetering on his eyebrow and flung it away. "Easier said than done. If she's as rigidly loyal as before, she won't give up the Indian's memory any time soon. This won't be the easy fix you're hoping for."

"You're exactly right. She *is* loyal. A stickler for abiding by her word, which is why she'll honor your betrothal."

Lillian had a point, and it was just sharp enough to prick the darkening clouds and allow a thin ray of hope to shine through. "Maybe you're right."

"I am." Her confidence empowered him, put a dowel in his spine. "For now, get her out of this meadow. Keep her out. Marry her. Next month, next week. Tomorrow, if possible. Give her children, Phillip. Quickly. Wring this Red Stick from her head. Make her move on." After *marry her*, the rapid-fire commands had become surplus.

He used the crook of his sleeve to mop perspiration from his brow, adjusted his hat, and attached his gaze to the blue fabric being swallowed by a field of ugly brown. Putting aside apprehension, he set out toward the woman he'd loved through the ease of childhood, the fires of Fort Mims, and now, through the anguish of loss.

Marry her? Give her children? Slay a Red Stick ghost?

Absolutely.

Chapter 23

Beaver Lake Town, Choctaw Country
Little Spring Month (March) 1816, Nine months later

Totka's shoulder slammed the ground, knocking both ball sticks from his hands. His body flew over his head and landed with a spine-cracking *thwack* that rendered him senseless. A beautiful, cloudy blue sky arrested his attention until the booming of feet kicked his brain back into play.

That stampede was coming for the pokko, for him. Moments ago, it had been lodged between the cups of his sticks. Now it was . . . under him?

The size and suppleness of the bulge digging into his back could be none other.

Totka shoved to his knees, nabbing the pokko between them as he did. He flung himself several rods to the right in a belly flop that sloughed skin off his chest and put a ball stick back in his hand.

A glimpse of the field told him half the opposing team—and a good number of his own teammates—were bearing down from both flanks and from dead ahead. From behind, Rainmaker was recovering his wind and scrambling to rise. Totka could hear the frantic scratch of his cousin's bare toes against the dirt, could practically feel the heat of the big man's breath on the back of his neck.

The score was nineteen to thirteen in the Divided People's favor. This close to their goal, the game could be over with one more strategic set of shots, and the players for the Beloved People were in a panic, which was exactly where Totka wanted them.

In one swift move, he scooped the pokko from his knees and flipped to his backside. Thunder vibrated through his tailbone and up his back. Rainmaker was hunched and charging. Mere breaths remained for Totka to rid himself of the ball, but where to send it? To whom?

His ear homed in on faint bell-song coming from behind Rainmaker's looming bulk. He reeled the stick back but froze as Rainmaker launched himself over top of him. The thud and smack of colliding bone and flesh confirmed his cousin had driven at least one opponent back.

Praying it was enough of a margin, Totka hurled the pokko, sending it on a sharp climb that arched toward those obnoxious bells. "Hilaho!"

The name was still ripping his throat when the herd reached him. He rolled like a pill bug until the main body of players trampled past and over him. Shaking off a stinging kick to the ribs, he extricated himself from their dust and strained to get a bead on the pokko's position.

Before he could mentally untangle the melee, the ball witch's victory shout rent the air. It fomented the crowd into a roiling cheer that surely carried clear to Kossati.

It was the Divided People's fifth straight scrimmage win, and Totka wasn't humble enough to deny that his town-appointed role as trainer had everything to do with it. Reed men, especially, had become a force to reckon with. Their seamless teamwork and unparalleled aim were fast becoming the pride of Beaver Lake Town.

The Beloved People would eat crow for yet another moon, but they would do so knowing that next time they went up against a true foe, they would not lose.

Totka loosed a trilling shriek, then chortled at the sight of Hilaho, legs awry, being lifted over the heads of the townsmen, Beloved People included.

"Finally letting others partake in the glory?" Gray Hawk strode across the emptying field. His leggings and moccasins wore the dulling smut of three dozen leagues, but his face was brilliant with undiluted affection.

"Father!" Totka trotted over and met Gray Hawk in a full-body embrace. When he slapped his father's back, his arm fumbled over a handsome rifle. Its finely woven sash crosscut Gray Hawk's chest and spoke of advancement in the tribe. "How long have you been in town?"

"Long enough to see you are putting Cetto Imala's favorite plays to good use."

Totka's smile felt that of a boy snaring his first rabbit. "There are still a few we have yet to master, but my kinsmen are eager to learn and easy to train."

Less than a moon after his arrival, Reed had voted unanimously to adopt him into the clan. Wolf of the Muscogees, always. Now, Reed of the Choctaws, as well. A good thing, all in all.

"Hilaho works well at your side. Better than Tall Bull ever did."

Totka wiped a tacky layer of dirt from his chest. "Hilaho shares the pokko. He seeks the team's betterment." Instead of his own.

"As is his nature. What of the others? They seem eager enough to follow their chief."

"To the man, they are exceptional. Walks Long is a bit slow to remember the formations, but his aim rivals Hilaho's, and he practices tirelessly. Puts the rest of Reed to shame. Sun Eagle sprints like a buck. Leaps nearly as high. Rainmaker, well, he is the simplest of the lot. Give him a target to tackle, set him loose, then run for shelter." Totka laughed, and it felt good.

"You have the scar to prove it." Gray Hawk applied his knuckles in a feather-light blow to Totka's chin, his eyes pensive. "Your pawa would be proud of what you have done here."

Totka wasn't so sure. He looked skyward to use the blinding sun as a cover for his dimming smile.

There were plenty of days he felt like a traitor to his pawa, to

Kossati, to everything he'd been brought up to believe. But the Choctaws had unreservedly opened their hearts to him. Totka figured his esteemed lineage and contributions to the town made his unlovely past easier to forgive, but even so, he often got the sense the Choctaws had been more accepting of him than his own pawa would have been at the harmony Totka had found with them.

"I would like to think Pawa would be proud of me," he said, picking at the leather thongs on the cup of his stick, "but the truth is, where I am and what I'm doing is good and right, regardless what others think." Apart from his broken vow to his beloved . . .

After receiving soul-warming agreement from his father, Totka went to collect his other stick from where it had fallen in his tumble.

Overall, the ten moons Totka had spent with his new clansmen had been happy ones, filled with many lazy days at the council square, swapping stories, becoming acquainted. Choctaw came easy to him; laughter did not.

But he was learning that happiness and laughter were not the same thing, and one did not necessarily produce the other. The contentment Totka had experienced in Choctaw country didn't originate with his clan's acceptance of him or with his success on the ball field or even with the reconciliation he enjoyed with his father. No, it came from deeper within, from a river flowing with Living Water that nourished and refreshed, even in the driest seasons.

And there had been plenty of those. Whenever he lay on his pallet in Yellow Tree's storehouse loft, he felt dry and barren, stripped of the children's sighing and White Stone's snoring. Most of all, deprived of the touch of a woman he'd never fully known. Looking back, it was best he hadn't.

In those times, when his ache was most powerful, the Spirit was most present.

As he always had, Totka often sensed the Spirit in the elements He'd created. In the kiss of wind, the tap of rain, the warmth of Mother Earth. But those things couldn't hold the greatness of him. Not even the sun could contain such a Spirit. A Spirit who spoke in the night, in whispers so gentle and loving they defied reason.

Yes, Totka had been content in Choctaw country, but he'd always been a man of action, a man impatient with idleness. Most others, when not on the hunt or the warpath, were pleased to while away the days lounging at the square, recounting myths, gambling, embellishing exploits. Such indolence had served its purpose in Beaver Lake Town—he'd done as the clan mothers requested, filled his head with knowledge, and earned a respectable position among them.

But now, he was restless for something more, something bigger than himself, as though the Spirit, like a mother eagle, were nudging him toward the edge of a cliff-top nest, urging him to spread his wings and let himself be carried to greater heights.

Or battle. He'd promised his bow to the White Warrior, Major McIntosh. The Floridas had become a heaping mound of biting ants that was growing higher by the moon, and Totka had an insane urge to poke a stick at it. That should quench his thirst for action.

He picked up his errant stick and began back toward his father. From out of nowhere a pokko smacked his already lacerated chest. Before it hit the ground, he snatched it up, and turned mock disgust on Wandering Elk.

Grinning, the defensemen of the Beloved People strutted toward him like a cock on a ridgepole. Dried blood caked his eyebrow and swollen lip; it crusted over his elbow and dripped from his calf. "Only six goals today, witch? Shocking. That one good leg of yours must be letting you down."

"If anything is shocking, it's that with two good legs, you scored none. A little advice from the Falcon—you will run faster if you tuck your skirt up between those pretty legs of yours." With a tight, lateral flick of his wrist, Totka sent the pokko between Wandering Elk's knees, forcing the man to stomp a tiny dance.

They laughed, and Wandering Elk jogged backwards to retrieve the pokko. "Speaking of pretty legs," he said, "my sister wants to show you hers. How long will you play the stabled gelding?"

Quite possibly forever, if the bottomless hollow in his chest was an accurate measuring tool. "Longer than your sister intends to wait, I am sure."

Wandering Elk's screwing lips and shaking head could be interpreted as confusion or disdain. Neither mattered. If ever the day came the man had the other half of his soul ripped from him, he would understand.

As Gray Hawk did.

Totka rubbed the circular, red sting on his chest and scanned the field's crowded sidelines. Nila should be nearby.

She was. Mingling with Reed clanswomen, but her face, sweetened by a smile, was pointed his direction. A painted cradleboard rode on her back. Its sturdy frame rose above her shoulders, trimming her pretty face in vibrant blue. She lifted a hand in greeting, and Totka returned it.

He reached his father and led the way to the bench that held his water gourd. "How is my baby brother? That little fist of his ready for a pokko yet?"

Gray Hawk's stomach, rounder since he'd wed, bounced with laughter. "Not quite, but I think he has your strong swing." He pointed to a speck of red on his cheekbone, ribs puffing as though the miniscule cut were a hard-won battle scar. "I forgot how sharp a baby's nails can be."

"Working on his panther claws, is he?"

"The women won't have a prayer of getting away."

"Not if he takes after his father. That's no broken-down nag you caught."

"Indeed, no. She is not." Gray Hawk's eye traveled to his wife. The heat that charged into his tone might make Nila blush if she came near enough to witness.

The woman was sweetness and light, and compared to Gray Hawk, she was young. Younger perhaps than Totka. But she was meek and even-tempered, and she adored her husband. It was written in every crinkle of her smile. Totka had decided right away that he liked her.

"She has done well, my Nila. Motherhood suits her."

"You suit her."

"So it seems. Astoundingly." Theirs had been an arranged marriage. Being bound to the niece of a minko secured an outsider his position in the tribe. But according to Hilaho, their pretty cousin had been easy to persuade.

Gray Hawk, Totka had swiftly learned, was preeminent among the Oaktebbehaw River Choctaws, lauded for his cunning on the battlefield as well as his command of diplomacy. It was widely believed he was a perfectly balanced man—equal parts white and red.

An unusual occurrence to say the least.

Stranger yet was the rumor that Totka's combination of astute maneuvering and brute force used during the little brother of war was proof he'd inherited his father's gift. If the argument were put to him, Totka would refute it, but he would admit he had more white in him than he'd always allowed.

Furthermore, every moon, his white tendencies seemed brighter, more prominent. Wouldn't Old Grandfather be pleased to know Totka was coming into harmony with his white side? Melancholy settled over Totka as his thoughts shifted toward Kossati. How he longed to press the ancient beloved man to his heart.

Turning his back to a hovering gaggle of ardent-eyed maidens, he bent for the water gourd resting in the shade of the bench. He uncorked the gourd and held it out to his father. "And my sisters? The children? Are they well?"

"Perfectly well." Gray Hawk waved off the gourd, so Totka put it to his own mouth.

He swished the warm water and spat, wondering about the way his father's eyes flicked to Totka then quickly away again. Something was on his mind, and Totka doubted it had to do with his sisters, despite his father continuing to speak about them.

"Their life continues much as it did before. Except for your absence, of course. Lachlan and I see to the property and keep them in meat. Wolf has been as gracious as ever. Your household lacks for nothing."

"Good to hear. Good indeed." Though he missed them terribly. Them, the comforting familiarity of the lodge, the Coosa's clear water, even the forge's clangor. "I would ask you to bring them for a visit, but I don't plan to be here but another sleep more."

Gray Hawk's head drew back. "Where are you going?"

When Totka halted the gourd at his lips, water splashed over his chin. "The Floridas, by way of Coweta. To join the White Warrior." The Coweta chief had put out the red club, seeking volunteers to knock out a wasps' nest of renegades who sullied the treaty with the whites. "When he came through, he asked for my bow. I leave tomorrow."

If Long Arrow knew, he would be pleased Totka was joining the war party. He would likely pray for some Seminole hatchet to find its way into Totka's chest.

"Ah yes, the fort on the Apalachicola." Gray Hawk chewed his lower lip, gaze unsettled. "Last I heard, the Floridas were still a short ways beyond the bounds of Choctaw country."

Totka lifted a smug cheek. "Yellow Tree declared the debt paid. Due to my work with Reed on the ball field." He soaked in the applause written in his father's eyes while pouring water over the back of his bent neck. It coursed in streams down the front of him, driving dirt before it. "The White Warrior was eager to take the warpath again."

"Much like yourself? I imagine you weary of stickball and are anxious for true battle."

Giving rise to a laugh, Totka hooked the gourd's strap over his head and rested it on his hip. "Weary of stickball? Has fever melted your brains? I will never tire of the game." Totka collected his shirt from the bench, balled it, and began scrubbing at the grimy scratches raking his breast. "My only concern is Tall Bull."

"Oh? What of him?"

"Some time back, he mentioned joining an army of blacks who were on the rise against the whites. I suspect I'll encounter him. Given a choice, I would never stand against him in battle." He hadn't spared his cousin the blade of revenge just to pursue him through the swamps of Florida. "That might present a problem."

"Tall Bull is with that mongrel Francis." A scoff surfaced to Gray Hawk's puckering mouth. "And at last report, they'd fled Negro Fort for the protection of the Spanish at San Marcos de Apalachee. Desperation at its most vulgar. As if the Spaniards hold any sway in this land."

"You are certain?" He dropped the shirt and reached for his pouch.

"Quite."

His head dipped to receive the pouch strap he flipped over it, then jerked toward to the rifle on Gray Hawk's back. "You look battle-ready. Are you going, Father?"

"The Floridas are playing grounds for younger men. This" — he lifted the sash over his head — "is for you. From Lachlan. The old mule misses you."

"For me? Surely not." Totka took the weapon anyway, for a look.

The barrel was warm in his palm; the oaken stock, stained a robust chestnut hue. He tested the cock and frizzen, admiring their fluid mechanisms. This was no smoothbore Indian trade gun, and it was far too valuable a gift for a man who disdained firearms.

"Lachlan knows I prefer the bow. He cannot have meant for me to have it." He tried to give it back, but his father lifted a refusing hand.

"You preferred the bow. After squeezing that trigger, I swear on my gray hairs, you will change your mind. Besides, are those not the symbols of your name there?"

Totka looked again. There *were* symbols etched into the copper butt plate, but they were not his.

A dull pain clamped his throat. He traced the beautifully rendered C and each of the following letters in turn. Lachlan's hand had created them, but it was his beloved's — white, small, and covered in ash — that Totka saw.

He dispatched the burn in his eyes and cleared his throat, not having the strength to correct his father. "It is too fine a gift," he said, while doubting there was a man who could pry it from his manacling fingers.

"It is quite fine. As is this, or so White Stone tells me." He withdrew a small leather-bound book from his pouch.

Losing the battle to contain his emotion, Totka drew a shaky inhale. He absorbed the writings' five gold-embossed letters as he might the contents of a sofkee gourd after an exhausting stickball match. He set the rifle butt between his feet and took the Sacred Writings between his hands, cradling it. "White Stone sent this?"

"She must have processed a keg of hickory nut oil for it. The trader was a wily sort and demanded five chalks of hides in addition. He said she could search for a year of seasons and not find another like it in all of Muscogee country."

A row of hasty blinks cleared Totka's blurring vision. "He was right, but I wager White Stone knows its value far exceeds what she paid."

"If you say so." Gray Hawk's mouth perked into a dubious smirk. At Totka's confident smile, it fell away. In its place was a trail of undisguised apprehension.

While setting the writings on the bench, Totka studied his father and waited for him to confide his concerns. When Gray Hawk said nothing, he lifted the rifle, pointed it at the top of the goal post, and aligned the sights. "What worries you, Father?" He squeezed the trigger and, at the solid fall of the hammer, hummed approval.

"You."

Totka slung the weapon over his shoulder and conducted a mock examination of his chest. "Have I broken out in a pox?" He chuckled and cupped an affectionate hand about his father's arm. "I am well. Perfectly content here."

"That is precisely what worries me. I would do nothing to spoil the healing you've found. But . . . it is right that you know what is being said, even if the rumor proves false."

Foreboding settled like sludge in Totka's middle. "What rumor?"

Gray Hawk passed a nervous tongue over his lips. "A trader from New Orleans came through Kossati. He spoke to Lachlan of a ghost. Thought to be the spirit of a woman. She . . ." He flicked a sideways glance at Nila who looked over her shoulder at that precise moment. She formed a supportive smile to which Gray Hawk seemed to affix himself.

A woman's ghost? There was only one reason his father would be telling him this. "She what?" He snatched his father's arm in a biting grip. "What of this spirit, Father?"

At last, Gray Hawk sharpened his focus, aimed it straight into Totka's eyes. "She haunts a field in Tensaw."

Totka flinched, despite having already surmised those details.

"It is said the grasses glow each night at moonrise, and if one listens carefully, the woman can be heard weeping."

A sharp inhale swelled Totka's chest. "Copper Woman." Although it was but a whisper, the name ripped him as it came out.

"Nila and I thought the same, but truly, it could be any number of spirits from Mims' place. So many perished, lay unburied for—"

"It can be no other!" He hadn't meant to bark, but there was an unstoppable tide rising within him. No, a tidal wave. Of-of . . . What was it? His fingers, claw-like, dug into his hair as a growl vibrated his throat.

It was anger, pure and hot. At himself for having broken his vow and abandoned her to that place. Ten interminable moons of betrayal.

"Easy, Son. Sit. Breathe. You will topple and break your neck. Then how will you go to her?" His attempt at levity was strained and ineffective.

The tide ebbed into the sting of urgency. Go to her? Yes, he must. Rumor or fact, he must go at once.

When his backside reached the bench, he brushed off his father's nudging touch and leapt to his feet and gathered his things. "Maddo, Father. But I-I need to go." With guilt in pursuit, he began a jog across the field, blood nailing his temples.

A glance at the sky told him Grandmother Sun was well past her peak. There would be no arriving in Tensaw this night. Tomorrow. Yes, tomorrow's moon would see him there.

"There is more," Gray Hawk called after him.

Totka's feet came to a slow, shuffling stop. More? He could take no more. He looked back, torso undulating with the rhythm of his accelerated breath.

His father came to him, stood behind, and placed a hand high on his shoulder, fingers pressing gently into the rapid pulse on his neck. "Lachlan said there are those who disagree with the report." He spoke in a hesitating hush. "Those same swear she is no ghost at all."

At that, Totka spun to face him. "What are you saying?"

Gray Hawk thumbed his earbob. "Only what I've heard. That there is a chance—a slight chance, mind—that you will not find a spirit, but a flesh and bone woman."

"Not a ghost, but a . . . ?" Totka's knees unlocked, threatened to quit.

A chance, flesh and bone, a woman, woman, woman . . . The words billowed and circled and dipped through his head in a dizzying frenzy. White stars flashed in his periphery. He flung himself over and propped on his unsteady knees. The momentum slapped the rifle to the ground.

"A woman. In Tensaw." The place was but a speck on the countryside, and it held so few inhabitants they could fit into his lodge with room to spare for the dog.

Her voice came to him, transported him to another time. *Ghosts? Here?* She'd sat before him, feet tucked. Her soot-bathed face angled up, eyes blinking guilelessly. *But I do not believe in them.* Even so, he did. The palms of his hands rested on the evidence—rows of scars on his legs. A spirit, he could most definitely believe. But a woman? His Copper Woman. Not dead?

The effort to breathe took second place to the scramble for answers. "How could that be possible? That would mean . . . Tall

Bull, he-he swore. He said the sister—" Heat flashed in waves from

Chapter 24

*É*very jounce and thump, every rock and rut of the road between Choctaw country and Tensaw had imprinted on Totka's bones. They rattled inside him, longing for solid, unmoving ground.

Soon, soon. The moment he proved the rumors true and filled his eyes with his beloved's face.

Totka leaned back over Wind Chaser's haunches as, to the meager light of an infant little spring moon, she plunged down an embankment leading to the Alabama. They entered the river at a trot, kicking up sprays that speckled Totka clear to his scalp. It brought on a sigh of relief and prompted a tumble from her back. He was happy to latch onto the saddle and let her pull him along, and to let the water's cool embrace kiss away the aches and tacky grit that clung to every part of him.

They emerged refreshed and dripping, Totka peeling away his sopping shirt and Wind Chaser nickering to be off. For the last two days, she'd fed from his urgency. The stony shore clattered beneath her hooves as Totka simultaneously mounted and grunted a command that lurched them into motion.

A little farther.

The brisk wind they created licked them dry before they'd reached the turnoff to Mims' burial ground. When caustic memories tried to infiltrate his senses, he galloped past, not allowing them access, quickly putting the place where it belonged — behind him.

Greater things lay ahead. Specifically — should the Master of

Breath be so kind — his little Red Stick.

Overshadowed by moss-hung trees, the trail thinned, as did the air in Totka's constricting lungs. Breath had been elusive of late, sucked away by every fear-driven thought that he would find only a ghost. That he'd crafted a dream world in which Copper Woman was still alive. It was a beautiful dream, and the happiest ending would be one that included Totka claiming her, body and soul, beneath this very moon.

But if any moon stood witness to their joining, it would be the blackberry. He would wed her first. Before that, his obligation to the White Warrior. Totka was due at Coweta's council square in three days.

Another satisfying ending would involve the Bitter Eyes groveling for forgiveness. What other explanation could there be but that she'd deceived them both? Achingly obvious was the fact she hadn't acted alone.

A knot burned in the muscle of Totka's jaw. He unclenched his teeth and redirected his furious energy into the fingers gripping Wind Chaser's mane and the heels digging into her sides.

Tall Bull was cunning, like a panther, danger unseen. Until his teeth were in your neck. He and the Bitter Eyes were two thorns from the same thistle. She spoke his language and would have no trouble tricking him. Of that, Totka was sure.

Whether Tall Bull had been an innocent party or not, if Totka hurt the sister, he hurt his beloved. She would forgive the Bitter Eyes anything. He must remember that. However, as a falcon cannot molt in a night, so Totka could not soon change who he was. Forgiveness would come hard, if at all.

All this, assuming Copper Woman was more than an intangible spirit.

Like soil from a wound, he scrubbed the doubt from his head. She *was* flesh and bone. He sensed her presence here, faithful and strong. Smelled her sweet breath on the wind and felt her tears in the moisture clinging to the air.

"She lives, she lives." To the *drub-drub-drub* of a hurried canter, the words moved his tongue in a continuous stream until they reached his head, then soothed his spirit.

Shadows consumed him as he plunged into a forest so thick Grandfather Moon was kept at bay by the dense foliage whispering overhead. His greeting on the other side of the copse was pale and went almost unnoticed. There was no competing with the pinprick of what appeared to be firelight on the far edge of the meadow.

Their meadow.

He drew Wind Chaser to a head-tossing stand and stared straight into what could be a stationary, unwinking firefly. Except the creatures had yet to hatch. He stood in the stirrups and blinked to clear haze from his eyes, to make certain.

Yes, a fire. A glow. The one that spawned the rumors, but it was no otherworldly aurora. It was a lantern, a single candle. Small, feeble.

Powerful enough to change the course of a man's life and ignite an inferno in his gut.

"Copper Woman." Her name left him on a groan, but the ache that carried the name was a far cry from the variety that, over the seasons, had turned every mouthful of food into tasteless paste and dulled every desire but one. This was a mildly pleasant discomfort, of the sort the body leaned into. And lean he did, over Wind Chaser's neck as he spurred her onward with a shout.

She stretched herself long in the effort to please him, increasing her speed until her flapping mane stung Totka's cheeks. When the lantern grew to a bold orange beacon, he arched her neck with the force of his halting yank on the reins.

In the next heartbeat, his feet connected with earth. They moved toward the flame, lured in like the half-dozen insects that fluttered clumsily through its light.

The lantern sat on a bed of trodden grass. Alone.

He, the moths, and the yellow beams thrown about in a wavering circle were the only signs of life.

Cold hands of danger crept up his spine, and even as his heart screamed for him to call her name, the warrior in him clamped his lips, sent his hand to his knife, and halted him well beyond the reach of light, within the deep, black night. Before he could free the blade, a silhouette rose from the grasses before him. It was short yet rigid and bearing the unmistakable outline of a woman.

He didn't need the dull glint of her long gun pointed at his chest to know she was not Copper Woman. Anger heated his eyes; his fingers twitched as they stroked the antler handle of his blade.

"Far enough, Indian. State your business and be quick," she said in English, confirming her identity.

The sister. The Bitter Eyes herself. Rooted, weapon held high with proper form, unwavering, voice flinty. Nothing like the sniveling child he'd returned to McGirth.

A strange situation, this. And bitterly disappointing.

She was here though, his beloved. The air was thick with her nearness, his throat thicker yet.

The clicks from the musket's mechanism locking into place spurred Totka's response. "You know my business, Bitter Eyes," he replied in Muskogee, stalking toward her, ire blinding him to her threat.

With her sharp inhale the iron barrel plunged earthward.

"I come to trade. A lie for the truth." He withdrew the worn letter from his pouch and threw it at her like a disc. Its white surface flashed against her chest and skittered down her front. "Would a snake such as yourself even know what that is?"

"You, you—I'd assumed you long dead!" She scrambled backward, managed to keep just out of his reach.

"Unfortunately for you, I am *not*." Three stride more and he twisted the weapon from her grasp.

"Where have you been?" A wise woman would back down, shrink from him, but she stopped her retreat and directed her voice straight into his face. "Couldn't be bothered before now to visit her grave? If you truly loved her, you'd have come right off!" It was a tall accusation, but weak in the shadow of his towering frame.

"You would dare continue the charade? I have played the fool at your hand long enough!" He shook in the effort to keep from striking her. "Woman, you are vile."

"Say what you will, I acted out of love. Which is more than I can say for you, Red Stick. Seems I was right to—"

He snatched her by the forearm and gave her such a shake her head jerked. "Where is she?" At her silence, he tried again, his voice a low, gravely threat. "Where is she?"

"Lillian? What are you doing out there? Are you all right?"

He dropped the musket—Bitter Eyes forgotten—and whipped about at the sound of his beloved's voice. It sounded as it often did in the first moments of a newborn day—groggy, roughened by sleep. But no less beautiful or mesmerizing.

Totka's brain, legs, lungs, they refused to function.

"I . . . I'm fine, Adela." The sister's voice went meek. "It was for your good that I did it. Please . . . remember that." The tramp of Bitter Eyes' scurrying footfalls dissolved behind him.

"Did what? You sound frightened." She rushed from the murk that lay beyond the lantern and placed herself under its influence. It coated her in a flickering caress, sinking her eyes into ebony pools and setting her hair aflame.

Her hair . . . It was gone. *Gone.* Cropped to the chin.

Sorrow, deep and rugged, rumbled in his throat. She'd grieved him thoroughly with the passion of a Muscogee.

She spun at the sound, sheared hair catching on her lips. "Who's there? Lillian, who are you with?"

He felt his heart ripping within him, torn by the unnecessary pain she'd suffered, but he hastily stitched it together. She was alive. Very much so and within reach. No mistaking. No dream world. No ghost.

"It is me, beloved." He lifted his voice and began toward her.

Her face was pointed his direction, but she squinted. "Who?" The question, given in Muskogee, was tremulous, cautiously hopeful. Her feet, however, brought her toward him with unerring confidence. She swooped up the lantern on her way, holding it before her. "Give me your name!"

Voice locked in his tight throat, he charged through thick, uncharted grasses, entered the reaches of her light, and slowed. Allowed her a head-to-moccasin rake of the eye.

A cry flew from her. The lantern slipped from her fingers, plunging them into darkness and wiping her from his sight. "Totka? Totka!"

His eyes went wide to battle the sudden black, but his stride was unperturbed. "Here," he rasped. "I am here."

In the next breath, she found him. Not a tentative reach nor a fumbling grasp, but a full-body, entwining embrace that put her breath at his ear, her hands in his hair, and her soft neck within reach of his mouth.

The cincture about his throat refused him words, so he let his kisses speak for him, laid them in fervent patches anywhere, everywhere, whenever she stilled her own long enough to allow him the pleasure.

Their bodies quaked with sobs. Where hers ended, his began. His were unmanly tears but heard only by his beloved and Grandfather Moon, neither of whom would hold it against him. So he let them free.

"Totka," she uttered his name on a croak, chest rising and crashing. "Where have you—? Why did you not return to me?" She gulped air, taking up a violent tremble. "Why, why, why?"

"Shah, shah." He stroked her blunted hair and held her more firmly. "Later. For now, let me love you."

The hunt for her mouth was swift; his quarry eager to be ensnared.

Like a moonflower to the night, she opened to him, seduced him with her fragrance. He was hungry, ravenous, but he moved at a moderate pace, giving more than taking, happy for this moment to simply listen to her little squeaks and sighs.

Without warning, she withdrew and became increasingly

inflexible.

"What is it?" he asked.

Her breath came more jagged, then stopped altogether before bursting from her on a wail. "She did this. She-she said as much herself. Oh God, why?" She was speaking English, but the pain that seared her voice was the same in any tongue. "How could she? My own sister!" She gripped him about the ribs, poured tears onto his chest until they slicked his skin and cooled his belly.

All the while, he held her, struggling to keep a handhold on this latest wave of rage. Unpleasant though it was, he refrained his tongue until she'd simmered to a whimper and he'd found a purpose for it all. "It was needful I lose you, dear one, before I could find Him, your Jesus." The rest would have to wait.

The breath blowing against him slowed. After a time, her fingers began to explore the parallel ridges crisscrossing his breast. "My Jesus?" she whispered.

"Hmm." He inhaled, drawing in her scent, that of grass and . . . Yes, there it was. Honey. "And mine."

The last of her tension melted away, making her limp against him. Had she always been this warm? "Then it was worth it. All of it," she said through a stuttered hiccup that rocked her too-frail body.

Worth it? Yes, but she'd suffered. Severed her beautiful hair. Become ill or simply been unable to eat. Who knew what other disturbing truths the dawn would reveal.

Because of the Bitter Eyes, who'd slithered away like the vermin she was.

"Even so, if she did this . . ." Her voice pinched with emotion. "She will pay, but not by our hand. Swear to me you will not harm her."

Ah, but didn't he know his beloved well? As well as she knew him and the yearning he had to punish her sister. "I swear it." He answered promptly, intending to put her mind at ease.

Instead, she began shaking her head in broad, uneven strokes as though to unhook a thought from it. She pressed the heels of her hands into her eyes and jerked with the beginnings of fresh tears.

No. She would not waste one more drop on that girl.

"Shh, beloved. I am here. With you." A gentle tug stationed her hand at his heart. He cradled her jaw and peered into the shadowy contours of her face. The pulse in her neck tapped an agitated tempo against his fingertips. "For this night, all that matters is that we are alive. Together."

She sniffed through a nod and, over the course of a dozen quieting beats of her heart, matched the flow of her chest with his. After a kiss to his palm, she snuggled her cheek into it. "On the chance I've been unclear, I intend to love you forever."

She'd already proved it, for she'd remained true beyond his grave.

Ten moons beyond and through countless vigils. For the love of him.

"And I am yours. Forever," she whispered, rising on her toes and settling her salty-sweet mouth against his, bathing him in her warmth and goodness. "With all my soul, Totka Hadjo, I am yours."

"Mine." Every trill of her heart.

And trill it did. Gone was its careful regularity. In its place, a lawless drum to match his own.

Imprisoning her searching mouth, he answered the call. As great as her love was, he was quite certain it would vanish in the depths of his own. It overwhelmed him, straining at his ribs, so he poured it into her, coupling it with the fire in his Red Stick bones.

As was its pattern, her flame brightened and merged with his in a cadence so beautiful it swamped his eyes.

Nearly drained of restraint, he broke off, panting as though he'd sprinted a battlefield. "Best you plead mercy, or you'll not reach our marriage blankets as whole as at present."

The pad of her finger traced his lower lip. "A little late for mercy. I am already half consumed."

His chuckle resounded from deep within his chest and was thick with suggestion. "You have yet to know the meaning of *consumed,* but your efforts are bold. Fearless. More than worthy."

"Worthy of what?"

"Of the wife of a Red Stick warrior."

"I thought I *was* a Red Stick."

This time, his laugh emerged free and light. "Ah, yes. My little Red Stick. But you are more, so much more."

He might bear the element's name, but this pale wisp of a woman was his spark, his kindling, his equal. The other half of his fiery soul. More than all that, she was his.

He tucked her head beneath his chin and wondered whether it would be possible to let her go long enough to mount Wind Chaser tomorrow. Anything could happen to either of them while he was away. The war path was a tenuous one.

Then again, this very meadow had held dangers all its own. At the catch of apprehension in his chest, he honed in on the night, on the grazing mare, and the doe picking casually at the shrubs along the forest's edge.

He and Copper Woman were alone. Safe.

The blustery meadow carried the summery scents of sweet hay and blossoming clover. An eastern wind reeled about them, entwining his hair with hers, binding them with a blessing only the Master of Breath could give.

Laying his cheek against her crown, he emptied himself of breath and took the next on faith. He would return.

To a welcoming embrace beneath the glow of a blackberry moon.

Thank you for reading!
If you enjoyed Totka's journey to Christ and Copper Woman,
please consider leaving a review at an online venue.

Turn the page to learn more about *The Sacred Writings*
and to see what's ahead for these characters and others in
The Ebony Cloak...

Beneath
the
BLACKBERRY
MOON

PART 3
The *Ebony Cloak*

APRIL W GARDNER
Creek Country Saga

The Ebony Cloak
Beneath the Blackberry Moon, Book 3

In the wilds of 1816 Florida, a beautiful slave is free game for depraved men. But for an honorable man, she is a military objective, an asset to be protected, a love that should never be pursued.

Milly's pale skin provides her with special privileges, but every luxury comes with a command. And Milly is done yielding. On the run, she can pass for white only as long as no one demands she lower her hood. But there's hope. It lies in the Floridas in a refuge commanded by an army of runaways. Negro Fort. The first sweet taste of freedom convinces Milly that surrender is not an option. But the U.S. Army is keen on the fort's conquest, and when it accomplishes the unthinkable, Milly must decide whether life is worth fighting for.

Major Phillip Bailey has orders to subdue the uprising and return the runaways to their masters, all the while being forced to fight alongside Creek warriors—the same who etched the scars into his mind and flesh. The same who, in a storm of flame and blood, ripped out Phillip's heart and took her for himself.

And then came Milly...

While musket balls fly, a war of another sort rages inside Phillip—perpetuate a crumbling dream or pursue the forbidden; follow orders or follow his heart.

AVAILABLE NOW

To stay informed, visit **www.aprilgardner.com** and
subscribe to April's newsletter.

April W Gardner

writes Christian historical romance with a focus on our Southeastern Native Tribes. She is a copyeditor, military wife, and mother of two who lives in South Texas. In no particular order, April dreams of owning a horse, learning a third language, and visiting all the national parks.

Enjoy these other books by April

HISTORICAL ROMANCE

Beneath the Blackberry Moon:
The Red Feather
The Sacred Writings
The Ebony Cloak
The Untold Stories (supplemental reading, e-book only)

Drawn by the Frost Moon:
Bitter Eyes No More
Love the War Woman (2017)
Seeking Pretty Wolf (2018)

CO-AUTHORED
Better than Fiction

Facebook: AprilGardnerBooks
Twitter: @AprilWGardner
Website: AprilGardner.com
Email: aprilgardnerwrites@gmail.com

Author's Notes

If you're a warm-blooded female, you might have been grumpy at me for keeping you hanging with Totka and Adela's love story. Trust me. I understand. No one likes to be strung along!

But Totka Hadjo is who he is because of how this story has evolved over the thirteen years since I first typed his name, and I wouldn't change a thing about him. Would you believe he started out as a minor character with little bearing on the plot? Amazing how a character can take over a novel and transform it in unpredictable ways! If you've been with me from the start of my writing career, you've likely read the first version of this series and can agree that putting their romance on hold to tell Totka's story was a much-needed improvement.

Historical novels are generally categorized as Historical Romance and Historical Fiction. My goal as a writer is to create a pleasing blend of those two. *The Red Feather* (book 1) is my hearty tribute to romance. Isn't Totka dreamy? *The Sacred Writings* (book 2), while giving a respectable nod to romance, delves into the cultural aspect that history buffs yearn for. *The Ebony Cloak* (book 3) is a lovely blend of both. It introduces new characters, while following the old, and it explores a tragic event you most likely have never heard of before.

Thank you for your patience and dedication to the characters and landscape that have swept my heart away. That Happily Ever After you've been waiting for is right around the next bend . . .

This is typically the portion of the back matter in which I elaborate on the story's historical plot points — those that are accurate to history and those that are my invention. Interestingly enough, this is the first novel I've written that is not structured around a historical event. I'd often wondered whether I could actually write an engaging plot without the backbone of a historical timeline. Did I succeed? I'm happy with the results and hope you are too!

And that glossary? Oh my word. A girl shouldn't have so much fun compiling definitions for little-known words. If you found it half as helpful as I found enjoyable to create, it was worth the effort.

The one event in the story that is based on history is the stickball match. While researching the sport, I came across a tiny paragraph that described a 1700s stickball game between Muscogees and Choctaws. The result would determine which tribe would have full rights to hunting grounds and a body of water called Beaver Lake. Tempers flared during the match and a fierce battle broke out. Sadly, the winner was not recorded, but we'll pretend it was Totka—er, I mean, the Muscogees. When I read that bit of history, I'd already plotted the game in the book, but I was stoked to learn it actually happened. Beaver Lake Town in *The Sacred Writings* is my salute to those unknown warriors who got in a tangle over a lake and made it into Wikipedia.

The novel itself is a memorial to the tribes who for centuries dominated our Southeastern United States. If you live in Alabama or Georgia, pause for a moment, touch that gorgeous red earth beneath your feet, and remember that this land was not always ours. It first belonged to the Muscogees.

April W Gardner

Please note that while I enjoy using and following history as closely as possible, I made the characters—even the historical figures—as I wanted them to be. I try not to misrepresent history, but I always put the fiction first.

Glossary

Acadians: descendents of 17th-century French colonists who were exiled from Canada by the British. Those who settled in Louisiana become known as Cajuns.

Alabama: Roll Tide! (Couldn't help myself.)

Alabama Town: a town of my creation based off a tribe that still exists, the Alabamas. Ancient Alabamas lived in seven towns near the location of my fictional Kossati. Alabama Indians were *not* Muscogee but a separate tribe of the Muskogean linguistic group and part of the confederacy. They were closely related to the Koasatis (see Kossati) and more distantly to the Choctaws.

Blood Vengeance: among the topmost legal principle of Southeastern Indians of the time. If a person was killed, it was the responsibility of his male clansmen, under guidance of the clan mothers, to retaliate in equal manner. The purpose being to restore balance in the clans.

Bluecoat: soldiers in the United States Army. So named because of their blue wool coatees. For this era, my creation.

Breechcloth: a long rectangular piece of animal hide or cloth that was brought up between the legs and under a belt at the waist. The ends hung like a flap over the belt in front and behind. Worn as outerwear by men and sometimes as underwear by women.

Broken Days: counting sticks bundled together to keep track of the passage of time. They were distributed to towns to mark the approach of special events such as battle or ceremony.

Chokofa: circular townhouse found in the ceremonial centers of some towns. Used in cold or inclement weather in a manner similar to the town square.

Chunkey: a variety of hoop and pole game in which a stone was rolled and sticks were thrown to the location the player believed the stone will land.

Clan: a category of people who believed themselves to be blood relatives, even if untraceable. Clan permission, authority, and protection were often called upon. The blood law fell on clan shoulders. Clan structure and responsibilities extended across the confederacy so that a member of Deer Clan would expect to be received as a family in any Deer Clan home in any town. Clans were associated with particular animals and natural phenomenon, the care of which they were often responsible. Deer Clan elders, for example, would monitor proper hunting in proper season.

Cock Fletch: the fletch of an arrow that varies in color from the other two. Often points down when nocked on the bowstring.
Couch: used for sitting and sleeping. Couches were arranged along the wall, raised two-three feet off the ground, made of saplings and cane, and covered with split-cane mats and animal skins.

Creek Confederacy: formed by survivors of the devastation wrought by 16th-century Spanish expeditions. The Muscogee were the strongest tribe at the time, and over the course of one hundred plus years, accepted refugee tribes under the umbrella of their protection. At its peak, it was so mighty George Washington treated the confederacy on a level of respect equal to that of France and Britain. The Creek War of 1813-14 began its decline.

Creek countrymen: sons of European traders and Creek women who grew up in Creek country yet lived slightly apart in a blended lifestyle.

Darkening Land: the spirit world; where a soul goes after death; located in the west. Also called Spirit Land, or the Haven of Souls.

Earth Spirit: female; one of the four law-giving elements. Takes forms such as soil, rock, and Corn Woman who is the embodiment of the spirit and from whose body corn originated. Also called Mother Earth.

East, Sacred: one of four sacred cardinal directions; associated with the Sun Spirit, the sacred fire, life, and success.

Elder Brother: 1. a title of honor. Elder brothers were supposed to be kind and protective to toward their younger brothers. **2.** A woman's brother was her closest blood relative, and in some ways closer to her than her husband. Their relationship carried over to her children. In place of their father, an elder brother taught her sons much of what they needed to know to be men. In the absence of an elder brother, a younger brother filled the role.

Federal Road: a U.S. postal route bisecting Creek country. It linked trading establishments and became a route for pioneers passing through to lands in the west. The road became a point of disturbance between Creeks and Americans.

Five Civilized Tribes: consisted of Creeks, Seminoles, Chickasaws, Choctaws, and Cherokees. So named by George Washington in his "plan for civilization."

Fire Spirit: male; assistant to the Sun Spirit.

Flageolet: a simple wind instrument made of cane.

Four, Sacred: a "magic" number that is expressive of the Creek belief system. Their *four* can be understood in a rough comparison to the Christian *three* for the Holy Trinity.

Four-day Journey: the number of days it was believed to take for a soul to journey to the Darkening Land.

Go to Water: ritualistic bathing done all year at dawn to overcome pollution and increase longevity.

Grand Council, 1811: the annual Creek grand council in which Shawnee-Creek Tecumseh arrived from the north with a plea for all tribes to join forces against the whites. There is debate on whether he preached peace or violence, but regardless, it was the spark the eventually enflamed the Creeks to civil war.

Great Warrior: the warrior selected led the town in war. He arranged ball games with Great Warriors from other towns and carried out the will of the micco.

Healing Song: a formula chanted or sung over a patient with the intent of engaging his spirit, restoring the correct flow of energy, and returning him to full health.

Herbal Warriors: the spiritual role of herbs as they work to heal a person's body.

Hunting Dreams: instead of saying "good night," the Creeks said, "I go to hunt a dream."

Ibofanga: neither male nor female; was above all and was the unifying principle of the spirit world. Ibofanga was the impersonal Creative Force. It created and set in motion laws that govern the universe. Every element of nature had a part of Ibofanga residing inside it. Its counterpart was the Chaotic Force, represented by such beings as the tie-snake.

Knower: an individual with spiritual and psychological wisdom who also possessed second sight. A knower could foretell death and interpret dreams, among other things. A knower diagnosed but did not cure illness. Not to be confused with medicine maker.

Kossati: a town of my creation based off of a Muskogean tribe that still exists, the Koasatis. Ancient Koasatis lived in two towns very near the location of my fictional Kossati both bearing the name Wetumpka. Big Wetumpka was situated on the site of present-day Wetumpka, Alabama. Koasati Indians were *not* Muscogee but a tribe of the Muskogean linguistic group and part of the confederacy. They were closely related to the Alabama.

Lineage: a Creek's closest blood relatives, specifically those who lived together in the same family settlement. The Creek social system was organized as follows: individual, lineage, clan, town. The Creeks were a matrilineal society, meaning their blood (and clan) was traced through the women. Although a man was involved in his children's lives, he was not their blood relative nor was he ultimately responsible for their upbringing.

Little Brother of War: stickball. Defined as such because of its violent nature and its use as a substitute for war.

Long Guns: Indian term for white settlers. My creation.

Long Hairs: extinct Muskogee term for Choctaws. The Choctaws originally wore their hair long and unshaven. By the historic period (the story's setting), warriors had begun to shave their heads in a manner similar to the Creeks, but I revived the term to add flavor.

Long Snake: a term I borrowed from the Cherokee's river deity.

Lower Towns: all Muskogean towns established along the Chattahoochee and Flint Rivers and their tributaries. Being geographically closer to Georgia colonists, the Lower Towns had easier access to trade goods. Because of that, they became dependent on the whites and were supportive of keeping peace with whites and assimilating their cultures. Many Lower Towns allied with the Americans during the Creek War. See Upper Towns.

Lunar Retreat: the time during menstruation when a woman was to stay separate in a designated moon lodge. Her latent power during that time would weaken a man. To break a lunar retreat rule was to commit a crime similar in nature to adultery or even murder.

Maddo: thank you (Muskogee language).

Master of Breath: see Wind Spirit.

Medicine: Creeks' equivalent to our terms "magic" or "power." Bad medicine was used by witches. Examples of good medicine were herbal warriors or healing songs. Medicine could also be neither good nor bad. A woman's medicine during menstruation was powerful but not bad, so long as it was properly handled.

Medicine Bundle: small items wrapped in a package and worn by warriors for spiritual protection. Items varied from individual to individual but each held special significance to that warrior.

Medicine Maker: men who were trained in the nature of diseases and healing herbs. Valued for their knowledge, not for any innate power they might have.

Micco, talwa: town chief. There were many levels of micco in both civil and military roles. This particular title was political.

Milledgeville: capital of Georgia from 1804-1868.

Minko: chief. Choctaw language.

Mississippi Territory: an organized incorporated territory of the United States that existed from 1798-1817 and was comprised of present-day Alabama and Mississippi.

Moon Lodge: a place set apart for women.

Muscogees: an indigenous people who once dominated the Southeast. They occupied land from the Atlantic coast to central Alabama and were the founders of the Creek Confederacy. Also known as the Creeks.

Muskogee: language spoken by the Creeks and Seminoles.

Muskogean: indigenous languages originating in Southeastern United States. They consist of many dialects which are divided into two regions. East—Creek and Seminole (Muskogee), plus four others. West—Chickasaw and Choctaw.

North, Sacred: one of four sacred cardinal directions; associated with cold, trouble, and defeat.

Old Beloved Men: old war leaders retired from battle but venerated in council.

Old Beloved Path: tribal traditions handed down by elders generation after generation.

Order of Things: natural law that encompasses ecological principles. A way of doing things to promote harmony, show reverence for law-giving elements, and to avoid their displeasure.

Owl: an ill-omen, a witch on the wing.

Pawa: maternal uncle. A pawa oversaw the discipline and training of his sisters' sons. See elder brother. (Muskogee language.)

Peace Town: a sanctuary where no violence could take place. Places of refuge for runaway slaves, the homeless, bands in conflict, and lawbreakers. The peace was enforced by Red Sticks.

People of the Point: Muskogee term for Seminole Indians. So called because of the peninsula (Florida) they lived on.

Red Sticks: 1. one of two social labels available to Creek men (Red Sticks/White Sticks). Red Sticks were known for courage, strength, alertness, physical skills. They held leadership roles in warfare, security, and law enforcement. So called because of the red war club, the symbol of war. **2.** During the Creek War, the term "Red Stick" took on new meaning for the white settlers. For the duration of the war, a Red Stick was a Creek warrior who opposed the Americans; however, many warriors of the White persuasion shared their views and fought alongside them.

Red War Club: symbol of war. Before the musket, it was the preferred hand-to-hand combat weapon. To call men to battle, a red war club was raised in the square.

Regular Army: soldiers under the direction and pay of the federal government. Contrast with militiamen, who were volunteers organized by state.

Roach: a stiff crest of hair running down the middle of the head. Also called a Mohawk.

Sacred Fire: the principle symbol of purity. Sun's representative on earth. Believed to report evil to the Sun who would dispense punishment. Found in each town's square and chokofa.

Scratching: a practice used to train for hardiness, to purify, to seek spiritual knowing, and to invoke the spirit of the individual's totem animal. A sharp, four-pointed instrument was raked across the chest, back, arms, legs. Depending on gender, age, and purpose, scratches varied from simply breaking the skin to creating wounds that bled and left scars.

Shadows: ghosts, evil spirits. The term is my invention, although the Muskogees did believe that ghosts of bodies improperly buried or those of ancestors whose deaths were not avenged could haunt a man. The Muskogees before Christian influence did not have a "good great spirit" or an evil counterpart such as Satan. Their concept of "evil" was one of chaos.

Sight, a: as far as one could see. Rough equivalent to our mile.

Single-pole Ball Game: played by men and women together around a pole up to fifty feet tall. A player who succeeded in hitting an object on the pole with a ball earned points. Men used stickball sticks; women used hands.

Slave Pole: a pole stationed in the town square to which slaves and captives were tied and often tortured. By the historic period (the story's setting), slave poles were no longer in use. I brought them back into use to serve the story's purpose. However, during the

Creek War, soldiers *did* come across Red Stick towns (see Red Sticks definition 2) that featured red poles adorned with scalps.

Sleeps: the marking of days or the passage of time. One sleep equals one day.

Sofkee: a thin gruel made of cornmeal or rice. Cooked with wood-ash lye and often eaten after being left to sour.

South, Sacred: one of four sacred cardinal directions; associated with warmth, peace, and happiness

Standing Militia: the most reliable units of militia (volunteer soldiers). They were well-equipped (at their own expense), organized, and met annually to train.

Stickball: a violent team sport resembling lacrosse in which a set of cupped sticks were used to lob a ball against a pole or between two poles that formed a goal. Used as training for battle and sometimes used as a substitute for war. Also called the little brother of war.

Stomp Dance: intertribal celebrations or social events. As with most every Creek event, stomp dances were religious in nature and, through ritual, blended the four law-giving elements in a reverential way.

Sun Spirit: female; one of the four law-giving elements. Source of all light and life. Also known as Grandmother Sun.

Tafia: a cheap trade rum, the primary liquor consumed by the Southeastern Indians of the 18th and 19th centuries.

Talwa: a Creek community. Muskogee language.

Tippling House: an establishment in which liquors are sold in small quantities.

The Floridas: the combination name given the two regions of Florida (West Florida and East Florida) which existed during the setting of this book. In 1813, both were owned by Spain. Also called Las Floridas.

This World: the middle world of the Indian three-world cosmos. The place Indians lived.

Tie-snake: believed to be powerful snakes that crawled up on land to drag victims under water.

Under World: the lowest of the Indian three-world cosmos. Existed below the earth and water. Epitomized chaos.

Upper Towns: all Muskogean towns established along the Alabama River, its branches (the Coosa and Tallapoosa), and their tributaries. Being sheltered from the Georgia colonists by
geographic distance, the Upper Towns were more staunchly traditional. Because of that, they resisted assimilation and fought to retain their way of life. Many Upper Towns put out the red war club against the Americans and their allies during the Creek War. See Lower Towns.

Upper World: the highest of the Indian three-world cosmos. Existed above the sky. Epitomized order.

Warriors' House: the communal lodge where warriors met for council, purification, and to plot warfare.

Water Spirit: female; one of the four law-giving elements. Takes the form of rivers, lakes, rain, mist, streams, and the ocean.

West, Sacred: one of four sacred cardinal directions; associated with the Moon Spirit, souls of the dead, and death.

White Sticks: 1. one of two social labels available to Creek men. White Sticks were known for reasonability, patience, mediation skills, scientific knowledge. Their roles included medicine maker, civil duties, diplomacy, ensuring of peace. **2.** During the Creek War, the term "White Stick" took on new meaning. For the duration of the war a White Stick was a Creek warrior who allied with the Americans; however, many warriors of the Red persuasion shared their views and fought alongside them.

White Drink: an herbal tea brewed for ceremonial purposes. It was consumed in large quantities in the council square and had a stimulating effect similar to excessive quantities of coffee. It often caused vomiting, which was done outside the square and was said to empty the body of impurities (alcohol) and ensure a clear mind. Called black drink by the Anglos.

Widow: required to mourn four years. During that time she was to crop her hair (representing a severing of accumulated memories) and not care for it. She was to dress unattractively and sleep over her husband's grave.

Wind Clan: the most prestigious clan. Specialized in predicting weather.

Wind Spirit: male; one of the four law-giving elements. Also called Master of Breath.

Winters: the span of a year. My creation. The Creek year began in late summer at the Green Corn Festival.

Witch: any person who is heartlessly evil as to be beyond forgiveness. A witch sought the demise of others to add the deceased person's life to the span of his own.

Yatika: speaker, orator (Muskogee language). Every talwa had a yatika who was well-versed in the nuances of the many Muskogean dialects. Typically, a micco did not make public speeches. This job fell to the yatika who knew the micco's mind and used his oratory talents to convey the micco's (and the council's) wishes.

CPSIA information can be obtained
at www.ICGtesting.com
Printed in the USA
LVHW111314160120
643856LV00001B/158